If he'd meant to m⟨...⟩ really afraid—he'd succeeded. She was suddenly anxious to escape him, but he was standing between her and the adobe. "I-I have to go," she said, her voice trembling. "My father and I— We have a lot of work to do to get the paper out on Saturday." She choked on a sob. "Good night."

She started past him toward the door. Three more steps and she'd be out of his reach.

One.

Two.

She felt him snag her arm and move around behind her. "Ginny, wait. I— God! I can't let you go like this," he said, his voice strained. His breath stirred the hair at the back of her neck. She didn't struggle, didn't make a move to get away. She couldn't. Her feet were frozen to the ground.

Disaster. Hate. Loathing. Fool. Savage. The words echoed in her mind even as she lifted her hand up and reached behind her to touch his face. "Bonner." She opened her mouth to say his name but she wasn't sure any sound came out. She couldn't hear above the pounding of her heart.

"I want to kiss you, Ginny. Just one kiss."

Embrace the Wind

Chelley Kitzmiller

A TOPAZ BOOK

TOPAZ
Published by the Penguin Group
Penguin Putnam Inc., 375 Hudson Street,
New York, New York 10014, U.S.A.
Penguin Books Ltd, 27 Wrights Lane,
London W8 5TZ, England
Penguin Books Australia Ltd, Ringwood,
Victoria, Australia
Penguin Books Canada Ltd, 10 Alcorn Avenue,
Toronto, Ontario, Canada M4V 3B2
Penguin Books (N.Z.) Ltd, 182–190 Wairau Road,
Auckland 10, New Zealand

Penguin Books Ltd, Registered Offices:
Harmondsworth, Middlesex, England

First published by Topaz, an imprint of Dutton Signet,
a member of Penguin Putnam Inc.

First Printing, October, 1997
10 9 8 7 6 5 4 3 2 1

 REGISTERED TRADEMARK—MARCA REGISTRADA

Printed in the United States of America

This one is for my brother,
Gerald (Gary) Clarke,
the finest writer I have ever known.

And for my new friend
and fellow writer,
Jack Palance,
with great appreciation.

Chelley Kitzmiller has written a romance novel that threatens to set a pattern for all future novels of this genre. A tender and passionate love story between a beautiful white woman, Ginny Sinclair, and an equally attractive half-breed, Bonner Kincade, whose goal in life is to save the Apache Nation from extinction. Kincade knows that if the Apaches are to survive, it can only be done with the full cooperation of the white people. This means the Apaches must surrender and become virtual prisoners of war. With the help of Ginny Sinclair, Kincade works to achieve that end without surrendering Apache pride and honor. How this is achieved is a glorious accomplishment by the author. The novel is a warm and wonderful explosion of love and human sensitivities. Ms. Kitzmiller has given us a story of love—a romance between Bonner and Ginny that burns through the pages of this book and helps restore the dignity of an entire Apache Nation. Ms. Kitzmiller is a writer who deserves our attention.

—Jack Palance

The Quest

The time had come. He knew it, felt it deep within him. For months he had been at odds with everyone including himself. He had lost his sense of purpose and no longer believed he could live up to his own ideals. Worst of all, he had begun to doubt the reason for his existence. He *had* to go. Now. Before it was too late.

He left on foot with only his instincts to guide him. Those instincts were strong—thanks to his grandfather, Gianatah, who had taught him to trust in himself. It was Gianatah who told him the story of Wind Cave—a cave inhabited by the wind spirit. Of all the Mountain Spirits, Wind was the most elusive—hiding itself from those who sought its power.

He carried only the essentials, a bow and a quiver of arrows, a knife and flint. He would have no need of food until he returned. In spite of the threat of rain, he dressed simply in the breeches his mother had made for him and a muslin shirt he'd bought in a Tucson mercantile. His clothing, like himself, was of two worlds—the Apache and the *pinda lickoye,* the White Eyes.

He walked throughout the day, never stopping, never slowing his pace. Late afternoon found him on the jagged shoulder of a mountaintop where the earth ended and the sky began. From this vantage point, he could look down into the heart of Arivaipa Canyon, where Wind Cave lay hidden among the rocky walls.

His gaze found a stream that meandered along the canyon floor like liquid silver, alternately narrow then wide, swift then slow.

Just before sunset, he made his descent, then headed upstream, moving deeper and deeper into the canyon. Near midnight, at the moment the moon reached its zenith, a coyote howled and a chill wind touched him with icy fingers, then sped past him into the night. He paused and glanced behind him as if to watch it go.

And he knew.

Wind Cave was near.

He continued on and after rounding a sharp bend, the canyon walls yawned wide open and the stream spilled into a placid, grass-fringed pool. Without warning, a blast of wind hit him—pushing him against the wall and pounding him with tornadolike force. The wind burnt his face and battered his body. He didn't try to fight it for he knew this was no ordinary wind, but an emissary of the wind spirit. And it was testing him.

The wind subsided slowly, as if reluctant to be done with him, then gathered itself into a whirl and danced away.

He peeled himself away from the canyon wall and stumbled toward the water's edge, then plunged head-first into the pool to wet his parched mouth and soothe his wind-burned face. Feeling refreshed, he walked onto the shore and shook himself off.

Then he saw it, a large, gaping hole in the canyon wall.

Wind Cave, his grandfather called it, for Wind did live here.

Remembering his grandfather's instructions, he set about gathering firewood, then prepared himself for a long vigil. Toward dawn, his eyes grew heavy and the rain that had threatened the day before began to fall. He stripped off his clothes and laid them over the pile of wood in hopes of keeping the bottom pieces dry. Naked except for his moccasins, he sat facing the cave.

Watching.

Waiting.

Praying.

By nightfall when the wind spirit still had not come, he began to have doubts. Maybe the stories of Wind Cave were just that—stories. Like the ones his little sister read. Never before had he doubted the Apache legends of the Mountain Spirits. Just as he had never doubted the existence of Ussen, the almighty Giver of Life. But as the night grew longer, his doubts grew stronger.

When at last the rain stopped, he built a fire and warmed himself. Suddenly an explosion of firebrands flew into the air and flames rose up in front of him like fiery snakes preparing to strike. He leaped to his feet, then saw a whirl of wind—like a desert dust devil—moving toward him. Even as he watched, it grew into a tall, sleek-looking funnel. Then there came a sound—a fierce roar that echoed off the canyon walls.

"S . . . e . . . e . . . k . . . e . . . r!"

The man lifted his chin and straightened his shoulders. "I am here."

From inside the top of the funnel, the head of an old man squeezed out like a butterfly emerging from its cocoon. His wizened face was unmistakably Apache and his long gray hair flowed back into the wind that swirled about him. "Why are you here?"

"I seek knowledge and power," he answered without hesitation.

"Many seek knowledge and power. Why should I give it to you?"

"So that I may help my people."

Wind roared with mirth. "You have no people, half-breed."

He gritted his teeth and held back the anger that

always came when someone called him half-breed. "You're wrong, Wind. I have two peoples and they are at war with each other."

Wind reared back as if affronted. "The Apache and the white man have much to learn. Peace without price will teach them nothing."

He paused, took a deep breath, knowing it might be his last if he angered the spirit. "Already, too many have paid the price with their lives."

When Wind looked away, the man turned and reached for his clothes.

"You turn your back on me, Seeker?"

"Because you turn your face from me, Wind," he said over his shoulder.

"I look at you n . . . o . . . w."

With his clothes in hand, he turned and faced the ominous vortex.

"You must learn patience, half-breed. And tolerance," Wind said.

As he opened his mouth to reply, the wind pushed against his face and dove down his throat.

The half-breed awoke to a cloudless, blue sky, feeling nothing except a terrible thirst and hunger pains. Had he dreamed his encounter with the wind spirit? Or did he now possess the power of the wind? How would he know?

Confused, he gathered his things and started for home, stopping briefly at the place where the earth ended and the sky began. A sudden wind rose up from the canyon floor and eddied around his feet—warm and familiar.

Then it was gone as quickly as it had come, but now, on the outsides of his moccasins were small white tracks—wind tracks, to make him fast and light like the wind.

Wind had given him the greatest power of all, Enemies-against, the war power.

Our duty is to keep the universe thoroughly posted concerning murders and street fights, and balls, and theaters, and pack-trains, and churches, and lectures, and school-houses, and city military affairs, and highway robberies, and Bible societies, and haywagons, and a thousand other things which it is in the province of local reporters to keep track of and magnify into undue importance for the instruction of the readers of this great daily newspaper.

—Mark Twain,
Territorial Enterprise

Chapter 1

The question of paramount importance since the acquisition of the Territory, has been and is now, the hostility of the Apache Indians. The history of these Indians is written in blood. They have caused the bones of our people to lie bleaching along every highway and in every settlement of the Territory; their tortures, murders and robberies, hang like the dark pall of night over every enterprise.

—*Arizona Citizen*

Tucson, Arizona Territory
Sunday, January 15, 1871

Ginny Sinclair read the first few lines of the governor's speech with skepticism. Its melodramatic tone reminded her of the dime novels that had become so popular since the end of the war. Shaking her head, she set the paper aside and was once more faced with the impossible task of how to make the tiny, adobe-walled sitting room look warm and inviting.

Ginny reached into her trunk for the bundle of lace-edged tablecloths and doilies she'd made that last year of the war while waiting for her fiancé to come home. She hated to use them on such old and ugly furniture, but the room was badly in need of brightening up, and at the moment, so was Ginny.

Tucson wasn't anything like the way she'd imagined it. It was worse. How it could even be classified as a town was beyond her. Having arrived yesterday by the afternoon stage, she had yet to explore the area, but what she'd seen so far was anything but heartening. It was a dreary place with its mud adobe buildings and its wide, rubbish-strewn streets that sported potholes so big they could swallow a man or an animal whole . . . and did, according to the stage driver.

Ginny was trying hard to hold on to her optimism, but it dimmed every time she opened the door.

Looking into the trunk, Ginny saw her favorite length of Brussels lace. Carefully, she removed it and held it up to the sunlight coming in through the window. Besides making lace, she collected bits and pieces of vintage needlework. She'd been saving this piece to sew into her wedding dress. But now that dress would never be made.

The war had ended her wedding plans and her dreams of marriage. Losing Tom, her first and only love, had been a crushing blow, made even worse because there was no body to bury and mourn. The official letter explained that he and several others had been caught in a volley of enemy cannon fire and buried near the site.

Ginny spread her fingers behind the lacy treasure and admired the strength and fineness of the linen threads. "So fragile and yet so strong," she whispered aloud, viewing it from different angles.

"Confound it, Ginette, where are those back issues of the *Citizen*?"

Ginny turned to the sound of her father's voice. "Did you look under the worktable? I distinctly remember you putting them there last night."

Sam Sinclair scowled. Though only forty-five, excessive drinking had caused his once-handsome face to become blotched and deeply etched with lines. "I've looked everywhere and can't find them."

Ginny rolled her eyes. Like most men, her father's idea of *looking everywhere* was to give the room a cursory glance. "Pop, how can I get us settled when you interrupt me every five minutes wanting to know where something is?"

"This is the last time. I promise." He peered at her over the top of his steel-rimmed spectacles.

"I'll be right there." Ginny waved her father away. A smile spread across her face as she watched him leave. It had been a long time since she'd seen him so enthusiastic about work. After being fired from the *Alta California*—his sixth editorial position in the five years since her mother had died—he'd said he would never work for a newspaper again. And now, six months later, here he was, about to breathe life into a weekly newspaper of his own. Now, too, here she was, albeit reluctantly, helping him.

When her father had first presented the idea, nothing and no one could have convinced Ginny that buying the *Tucson Sun* sight unseen was a sane thing to do. It was a newspaper whose owner had become critically ill before producing even one issue. A newspaper that for all intents and purposes was nothing more than a rented office, a hulking, old Washington Hand Press and a half-dozen fonts of worn-out type.

Had Ginny been older and even more set in her ways, the bill of sale, shown to her on Christmas Day, would have given her an apoplectic fit. But being twenty-five and used to her father's irresponsible behavior these past five years, the news did little more than render her speechless with anger.

The print office was connected to the sitting room by a short hall. Just as Ginny entered the room, her father stood up, a stack of newspapers in his arms. "I, uh . . . found them," he announced sheepishly.

Ginny clucked her tongue and shook her head. "So I see. Were they where you put them last night?"

Sam chuckled. "Yep, but I swear I looked there and didn't see them."

"Pop!"

"All right. All right. I admit it. I didn't look there. Your mother used to give me the devil for calling her away from her chores to help me find something that was right in front of my nose."

Ginny smiled, her mind going back to a particularly

fond moment when her father couldn't find his red flannel long johns. After *looking everywhere* for them, Ginny had found them under the bed, where he'd kicked them the night before. Before her reminiscences got the better of her, she walked across the room and planted a kiss on his cheek just above his beard. "Mama wouldn't have had it any other way. And neither would I. I like you just the way you are . . . with one exception." She purposely changed her tone so there could be no mistaking her seriousness.

"Confound it, Ginette," he said, his frustration evident. "I promised that I would try. That's all I can do. You've got to have some faith in me."

"You have to give me a reason to have faith in you, Pop. I hesitate to remind you that you've made that promise before. Several times. *This* time I want you to swear to me that you won't take so much as even *one* drink." Ginny didn't like the role his drinking problem forced her to play. She felt it made her sound like a shrew, or at the very least a nag.

He set the stack of papers on the worktable, then turned and pulled her into his arms. "I swear, honey. I won't let you down. Not this time."

Ginny rubbed her cheek against his woolen shirt. "I hope not, because there's no place to go from here. This is the end of the road."

Sam tucked his daughter's head beneath his chin and exhaled a long sigh. "I know. But everything will be different now. You'll see."

"Our savings are almost gone," she reminded him, determined to make him understand how desperate their financial situation was.

"We'll be fine," he said, patting her on the back as if she were still a little girl. "I'm a damn good newspaperman, you know. There isn't anything about this business that I don't understand and nothing that I won't try to gain advertising and subscribers."

Ginny leaned back and looked up at him, thinking this might be a good time to tell him that in addition to the duties she'd agreed to handle—office clerk, bookkeeper, and compositor—she wanted to write for the paper as well. Not only did she want to cover the local amusements, dances, and town meetings, she wanted to write news articles and maybe even editorials. Like her father, she had a burning desire to inform and educate people. She *wanted* her writing to help make the world—or at least Tucson—a better place.

"I'm glad you see things that way because there's something I've been meaning to talk to you—"

A woman's scream stopped Ginny midsentence. Ginny and Sam gave each other questioning looks, then ran to the door, flung it open, and hurried outside. Another scream, followed by a man's booming curse, turned their gazes west.

Shading her eyes against the sun, Ginny saw two high-sided freight wagons lumber up the street, each drawn by four pairs of mules. The heavy pounding of the mules' hooves ricocheted between the mud adobe buildings. All along the rutted roadway, doors and windows opened. People streamed out of shops and homes to join those already on the street. The mutterings of anger and fear grew into a roar.

Ginny sidled up close to her father. "What is it? What's wrong?" she asked, straining to see the source of the commotion.

"My God. Look at that." He removed his spectacles and stared at the approaching wagons.

"Look at what?" Ginny asked, studying the trooper driving the first freight wagon. She didn't see anything out of the ordinary.

"Looks like they used the freight wagons for target practice."

"Who did?" The question was no sooner out of her mouth than she saw what her father had seen. Arrows—several dozen of them—protruded from the wagons' sides like porcupine quills. "Apaches," Ginny whispered. A shiver of fear chased itself down her spine.

Out of the corner of her eye she saw the baker's wife run into the street and up to the lead wagon. "Is this the Fish and Company freight train?" she demanded, her voice high with hysteria.

The driver, a tired-looking private, looked down at her from his lofty seat. "What's left of it, ma'am," he answered, nodding solemnly.

The woman grabbed at the wagon seat. "My boy— Johnny! Johnny O'Rourke. He was driving one of the wagons and—"

"Sorry, ma'am. The only one we found alive is old Amos here," the soldier cut her short and gestured to his right where a man was slumped down on the seat beside him.

Breathless, the woman asked, "And the others?"

"Back in the wagon bed, ma'am."

Ginny's heart broke for the woman as she saw her slowly back away from the freight wagon and stare at it as it rolled past. As the second wagon approached, a man in a white apron joined the woman and took her into his arms.

"Where will you take the bodies?" he called out to the trooper driving the wagon.

"Up the street to the Fish and Company Mercantile," was the reply.

Ginny's throat knotted. She choked back a sob. She was thankful she couldn't see over the wagons' sides. If the bodies looked anything like the wagons—with all those arrows. . . . She intercepted her own thought, forbidding herself to draw that mental picture.

Creaking leather and jingling harness accompanied the detachment of soldiers who rode several yards behind the wagons. To Ginny, they appeared to be seasoned troopers, riding in a loose column, two by two. They looked weary, their faces drawn, their backs hunched over. She saw evidence of dried blood on their uniforms.

Suddenly, from between buildings, a horseman galloped into the street and caught up to the end of the column. Ginny couldn't see his face for his head was turned away from her, but something about the man held her attention. Clearly, he wasn't a soldier. His hair was too long and his clothing in no way resembled a uniform. Instead it was a strange mixture of this and that, the likes of which Ginny had never seen in San Francisco or back east.

Curious, she noted every detail and committed them to memory, thinking she might need the information later for an article. The man wore a blue checked, long-sleeved shirt, untucked but cinched by two ominous-looking cartridge belts, which were missing more than half their load. The lower belt was decorated with red paint and supported a holster holding a bone-handled revolver. He wore it down around his hips like the pictures of the gunmen she'd seen. His right hand lightly rode the top of his thigh, as if at any given moment he might need to draw his revolver and shoot. Just looking at him Ginny knew that this was a man in whose hands any weapon would be deadly.

Her gaze moved to the rawhide thong cross-stitches that ran the outside length of his dun-colored trousers. She glimpsed traces of flesh where the leather strips pulled apart along his muscular thigh and at the bend of his knee. His trouser leg disappeared into a boot-length moccasin that was bound above his calf.

In contrast to the troopers' posture, the man sat his horse tall and straight, his broad shoulders squared. Everything about him emanated pride . . . and, if she wasn't mistaken, arrogance.

Beneath him, equally prideful, his big, high-headed buckskin danced and pranced as if impatient with the slow pace.

They're two of a kind, she thought, openly staring

at the man and his horse. There was something about them that sparked her writer's imagination.

In some distant part of her mind, she knew she needed to go into the office and get paper and pencil, then head over to the mercantile where the driver said the wagons would be unloaded. There was definitely a story here, questions to be asked, information and names to be gathered—if only she could tear herself away.

"I wonder who *he* is," her father said, speaking over her shoulder. "Must be one of those Indian scouts I read the army was going to hire."

Ginny nodded, her gaze unwavering. The man had captured her father's attention too.

"Get me some paper and a pencil," he told her, urgency in his voice. "We need to get over there to the mercantile and get their story."

Whatever spell had been holding Ginny in thrall broke at her father's request and she went running to the office. But by the time she reached the worktable with its piles of foolscap, boxes of type-sticks, pencils, and inks, she'd forgotten what she'd come for.

She stared at the clutter, but in her mind's eye all she could see was his hand resting on his thigh . . . ready, waiting.

"Ginny!" Her father's voice dashed the vision and gave her back her memory.

"Coming," she called back as she grabbed some pencils and a few pieces of paper. On her way out the door she plucked her shawl off the coat rack.

"What took you so long?"

"I—I couldn't find any paper," she told him, hoping she would be forgiven the little lie. Better to lie than tell him she'd been musing about a man—a man whose face she had yet to see.

"If we hurry we might beat Wasson to an interview."

Half walking, half running, Ginny fell in next to

him. They reached the mercantile just as the soldiers gathered to unload the bodies. A large gathering of townsfolk stood watching and waiting.

Nothing Ginny could have imagined was even close to what she saw. Clutching her pencils and paper, she bowed her head and squeezed her eyes shut, afraid that if she continued to look, she would be sick right there in front of half the town.

"Easy now, Ginette," her father whispered. He put an arm around her shoulders and gave her a gentle squeeze. "I need you to take down information."

"I'm all right," she assured him. "Just give me a moment." Opening her eyes, she stared at the ground, determined to get a grip on herself. An avid reader, she'd read hundreds of newspaper accounts of battles—Vicksburg, Bull Run, Little Round Top—and of Indian attacks and tortures. She'd seen illustrations too—awful scenes of death and destruction—but reading about the terrible carnage and seeing illustrations was far different from witnessing it.

As the first body was handed out, Ginny heard the sounds of grief, despair, and anger. Her throat knotted painfully under the strain of emotion.

"Write this down," her father said, leaning close.

Taking a deep breath, Ginny readied her pencil.

"The freight train of E. N. Fish and Company was attacked by Apaches. More than a hundred people gathered in front of the Fish and Company Mercantile to watch the bodies of the teamsters being unloaded."

When one of the troopers passed close to Ginny and her father, Sam reached out and grabbed his arm.

"Corporal. If you could give me a moment of your time. I'm Sam Sinclair and this is my daughter, Ginny. I'm the new owner of the *Tucson Sun*. I'd appreciate it if you could tell me exactly what happened."

The soldier turned a world-weary face to Sam. "Ask somebody else. I'm headin' for the saloon."

Ginny stepped directly in front of him. "Please,"

she said, clutching her paper in front of her like a Bible. "We've just arrived here from San Francisco. We know very little about the Indian situation, and we want to report on it accurately. Since you're obviously the one in charge, your name should appear as the informant." Ginny hoped her father wouldn't think she was overstepping her bounds, but she wanted to be a help to him.

"Why, I—" He broke off and cleared his throat. "Sure. I guess I've got a moment or two. What do you want to know?"

Sam moved up next to Ginny. "Where were the wagons attacked and when?"

"Fifteen miles out, maybe more. On the overland mail route. Kincade says they was attacked at sunrise, so you can pretty much figure that's when it happened."

"Kincade?"

"Yeah, the half-breed who rode in with us. Big fellah. Rides a buckskin."

"Was it Apaches who attacked the wagons?" Sam queried.

"Who else?"

"Any idea what prompted the attack?"

The corporal laughed. " 'Paches don't need no promptin', mister. Killin' and stealin' is just what they *do*. Keeps us hoppin', I'll tell you. I can hardly wait till my enlistment is up so I can hightail it on home to Ohio."

Ginny took down the corporal's every word along with the way he expressed himself. By the time her father finished asking questions, the freighters' bodies—nine in all—had been unloaded and carried to the side of the mercantile where they were laid out for relatives and friends to claim.

Sam thanked the corporal and shook his hand. "Since you're headquartered at Camp Lowell, I expect we'll be seeing you around town."

"Expect so," he said, looking directly at Ginny and smiling.

Ginny smiled back, hoping he wouldn't take it as anything more than a warm, friendly smile and not an encouragement. The last thing she wanted to do was involve herself with another military man.

When the corporal headed across the street, Ginny looked over her notes, dotting *i*'s and crossing *t*'s. She felt her father looking over her shoulder.

"Did I leave something out?" she asked.

Sam shook his head. "Not as far as I can tell."

Ginny breathed a sigh of relief. "I was wondering—"

"So was I," he broke in. "What made you think that the corporal was in charge?"

"Well, wasn't he?" she asked, pretending innocence. She wasn't about to admit to using a little feminine ingenuity to seduce the corporal into talking with them.

"No, but you certainly flattered him by assuming that he was."

Folding her paper in half, Ginny looked up to meet her father's eyes. "I'll have to be more careful in the future. With so many soldiers about, I wouldn't want to make the mistake again."

A wide, knowing smile smoothed the lines of dissipation on Sam's face, reminding Ginny of the handsome man he had been before her mother's death. If only she could keep him smiling like that, make him forget his sorrows. But she could no more make him forget than she could bring those nine teamsters back from the dead.

A small group of businessmen, led by John Wasson, the editor of the *Arizona Citizen,* moved through the onlookers toward the mercantile. Wasson was younger than Ginny's father by ten years or more, with deep-set eyes and a morose expression. He'd been on hand to greet Ginny and her father at the stage stop. It had both pleased and surprised Ginny that he'd been so friendly, considering they would be competitors. Later, Ginny learned that her father had known Wasson when he worked as editor of the *Oakland Daily News*.

It was then that Ginny noticed Kincade, the half-breed who had ridden in with the cavalry detachment. He stood in front of the mercantile, his arms crossed in front of him, negligently leaning against a support post. A forbiddingly handsome face, with high cheekbones bespoke his Indian heritage. He wore his blue-black hair pulled straight back and tied with a strip of red cloth. He made no attempt to hide the fact that he was staring at her. His black eyes were narrowed in open scrutiny. They reminded her of polished onyx, cold and hard.

Ginny's breath caught in her throat. No one had ever looked at her the way Kincade was looking at her now, as if he was examining her. She gathered the edges of her shawl together across her bodice and turned her gaze to Wasson.

"Who was in charge of this detachment?" Wasson asked the young soldier standing on Kincade's left.

The murmurings of the people gathered in front of the mercantile silenced.

"Major Garrity," the soldier replied.

"And where is the major now?"

"He rode ahead to Camp Lowell to make his report."

Ginny thought the newspaperman looked annoyed at the news of the major's whereabouts, though she couldn't imagine why unless it was because he had hoped to interview him. "Was the attack Cochise's doing?" he asked.

The soldier shrugged indifferently. "Ask Kincade. He's the Indian expert."

Wasson looked to the right. Kincade was leaning against a post. "Well? Was it Cochise's band?"

Ginny felt her father's nudge—a silent signal that

he wanted her to take notes. She touched her pencil to the tip of her tongue, then repositioned it over the folded paper. Even though she didn't know who Cochise was, she sensed that Kincade's answer was vitally important.

Dark brows lifted over inscrutable black eyes. "No, they weren't Cochise's braves." His voice spoke with quiet authority.

Wasson pulled a frown of impatience. "All right, then who were they?"

"Lahte's band."

"You're sure?"

Kincade flashed Wasson a look of disdain. "I'm sure," he affirmed shortly.

Ginny felt an almost tangible buildup of discord between the two men. She felt a buildup of a different kind within herself as she listened to Kincade's rich, resonate voice. Low and rumbling, it made her think of distant thunder.

Wasson rubbed his bearded chin. "Any idea which way they were headed?"

Kincade shook his head. "Your guess is as good as mine."

"I would think yours would be better, seeing as how you're one of them."

A sudden hush came over the onlookers. Ginny tensed as she looked back and forth between the two men. Something told her that they had crossed swords before, but that this time Wasson had gone too far. She poked the end of her pencil between her teeth.

Kincade pushed himself away from the post and started walking across the street.

Ginny's eyes widened with alarm when she realized that he was walking directly toward her. She heard a crunching sound as her teeth bit down on the pencil. He stopped less than an arm's length away and glared down at her. The fire in his eyes was so intense that she feared she wouldn't survive the heat.

"Name's Bonner Kincade," he told her. "Spelled: K-I-N-C-A-D-E."

Say something! her brain commanded her. But she had no idea what to say, and even if she could think of something, she wouldn't be able to get it past the melon-sized lump in her throat. So she just stared at him.

Without warning, he reached up and pulled the pencil out from between her teeth.

"Welcome to Tucson, Miss Sinclair."

Chapter 2

The Apache Indians have never manifested the least disposition to live on terms of peace, until after they had been thoroughly subjugated by military power, and any attempt to compromise before they are reduced to this condition, is accepted by them as an acknowledgment of weakness and cowardice.
—*Arizona Citizen*

Ginny's lips parted in stunned surprise. She stood facing Bonner Kincade, her eyes wide with disbelief and anger, and his narrowed and searching. Her brain scrambled for a proper retort, but the words died on her tongue when she saw a muscle in his jaw spasm and his dark, fathomless gaze move up and down her body.

His facial expressions openly reflected loathing, doubt, and curiosity. Then, for just a moment, she thought she saw the corner of his mouth lift in a salacious smile, but before she could be sure, he handed her the pencil and walked away.

Ginny stared after him, her heart drumming a wild beat against her breast, a rhythm that felt oddly more like excitement than anger.

He walked like he rode, tall and straight, his stride loose-jointed and arrogant. He headed across the street to his big buckskin, mounted up, and rode down the street.

Only after he turned the corner did Ginny release the breath she didn't know she'd been holding. But her relief was short-lived, for as soon as she turned around, she realized that while she'd been watching Bonner Kincade, the good citizens of Tucson had been watching her.

Ginny felt her face flame with embarrassment,

though why she should be embarrassed, she didn't know. She hadn't done anything wrong. But apparently the citizenry thought so. Ginny knew disapproval and censure when she saw it. They must have misinterpreted her surprised response for flirtation.

This was all Bonner Kincade's fault, she thought. If he hadn't singled her out . . . But he had. And there was nothing she could do about it.

Thinking quickly, she realized she *had* to say or do something to vindicate herself. If she didn't—if she just turned her back and walked away—people would see it as an admission of guilt.

She couldn't take that risk. There was too much at stake. She and her father had come too far, sacrificed too much to lose everything over some misunderstanding.

Ginny sensed that the best way to exonerate herself and repair the situation was to bitterly complain that Bonner Kincade's behavior had been rude, insulting, and humiliating. But complain to whom? Her gaze lit on her father's chief competitor, John Wasson, and she knew that he would be the one to speak to. He'd already shown himself to be friendly, but more than that, he seemed to be a man of some influence in town. If she convinced him of her injury, chances were everyone else would be convinced too.

Squaring her shoulders and lifting her chin, she started toward him but stopped short when she saw him coming toward her, a thoughtful smile softening his otherwise stern mouth.

"You mustn't pay Bonner Kincade any attention, Miss Sinclair. He has an aversion to journalists—actually anybody and everybody even remotely connected with a newspaper—but dislikes me in particular. He says I exaggerate the Territory's Apache problem."

Ginny didn't know whether John Wasson exaggerated the Apache problem or not, but she did know that his editorials favored Apache extermination. And she knew that there were others who agreed with him, but she wasn't one of them. In her opinion, nothing could justify the extermination of an entire people.

She'd geared herself up to complain about Bonner Kincade's behavior, but suddenly, inexplicably, she lost the will to accuse him. "I have no idea what I did to make Mr. Kincade so angry," she said instead, looking down and wondering what had caused her change of heart.

"I'm sure you didn't do anything, Miss Sinclair. That's just the way he is."

Ginny breathed a sigh of relief. John Wasson seemed to be in complete sympathy with her situation, which was just what she'd hoped for.

"It was all so unexpected. I didn't know what to think," she added for good measure.

"Of course you didn't," he said, putting his hand on her arm. "You're new in town, so let me give you a little friendly advice. When you see Bonner Kincade coming toward you, you turn around and go the other way. He's nothing but trouble. Folks are real wary of him and you should be too."

Ginny looked up to find him studying her. Was he really giving her friendly advice or was he reproving her? Either way, his words grated. She wasn't some boarding school miss, after all. She was a grown woman well beyond her majority. An independent woman. If anyone was to decide whom she should and shouldn't be wary of, it would be herself.

Ginny drew a deep, steadying breath and reminded herself what was at stake. "Thank you," she said, pretending a sincerity she didn't feel. "I appreciate your advice."

He studied her a moment longer, then smiled approvingly. "You're welcome."

Ginny smiled back but only because it would have been blatantly rude not to. She hoped her facial expressions hadn't given her true feelings away. She saw her father coming from the direction of the mercantile and motioned him to join her.

"Pop, where have you been?" She knew she probably sounded as if she'd been worried, but the truth was she hadn't even noticed he'd been gone until she saw him coming toward her.

"Talking to one of the victim's families. Why?"

Wasson spoke first. "Your daughter here just had the unpleasant experience of meeting one of the army's civilian guides, Bonner Kincade."

"Oh?" Sam looked at Ginny with concern.

Ginny waved her hand dismissively. "It was nothing really. He was just a little rude."

Sam glanced toward the crowd. "Where is he? Maybe I should remind him of his manners."

Guffawing, Wasson lightly slapped Sam on the back. "Believe me, my friend, you don't want to have words with Bonner Kincade. Not if you value your life and that of your daughter's. He may be only half Apache, but he's one hundred percent savage." With that Wasson left them and made his way to the mercantile.

Feeling a sudden chill, Ginny wrapped her shawl more tightly about her shoulders. She glanced at the freight wagons, at the arrows protruding from their sides. Fearful images of arrow-shooting Apaches built inside her mind. Fifty or more, galloping across the desert after a small train of freight wagons. Bonner Kincade was leading the pack of murderous savages, his face striped with vermilion and white war paint.

"Ginette?"

Hearing her name, Ginny blinked the image away. "What?"

"You haven't heard a word I've said, have you?"

"I— No," she admitted, still trying to free herself of the disturbing vision.

"I asked what this Kincade person did that was so rude."

Ginny was saved from having to explain when John

Wasson's stentorian voice addressed the crowd, drawing her father's attention away from her.

"I've only been here a few months," Wasson began, "but I know that no people in the Territories have suffered more or met with greater loss of life and property than you have."

His words seemed all too familiar to Ginny. Then she remembered. They were the words she'd read this morning in the *Citizen*. John Wasson was parroting the governor's speech.

"Over and over you've asked the government to send more troops. And *still* they refuse." He reminded Ginny of a preacher sermonizing to his congregation, putting dramatic emphasis on certain words in each sentence. "I don't mean to discredit the force we have, but it's entirely *inadequate* as today's incident and other incidents have proved *again and again*." He paused, looking from person to person. "We lost nine brave men today," he said with quiet anger, wrenching Ginny's heart—and everyone else's if tight faces and strangled sobs were any indication. Then he lifted his hand and made a fist. "How many more will die before *you*—the people of Tucson—*take action*?"

Irate grumblings and expressions of exasperation rolled through the gathering like a small earthquake.

A man standing near Ginny spoke out. "You don't think we've tried, Wasson? I reckon half the men here have tried. But soon as we take out after one band of savages, they send another 'round to burn our houses and chase off our stock."

Wasson looked the man square in the eyes. "Yes, I know. Believe me, I know. But you've been going about things the wrong way."

Another man called out, "Wrong way? You don't know what you're talkin' 'bout Wasson. I s'pose you think the army's been goin' 'bout things the wrong way too?"

"As a matter of fact, yes! How many of those troopers at Camp Lowell and Camp Grant have homes and families in the Arizona Territory? How many will be making their homes here once their enlistments are up? How many joined the army to fight? How many have suffered the loss of loved ones or property to the Apaches? I'll tell you how many. Damn few!"

The more he talked, the more Ginny began to see his point. Of all the troops in the Territory, only a handful had anything at stake. The majority were merely putting in their time, collecting their pay, and waiting for the end of their enlistment so they could go home to someplace considerably more civilized than Arizona.

The people talked quietly among themselves, but no one made to answer.

Wasson gripped the support post next to him and leaned forward. "Governor Safford and I agree that what you need—what *we* need," he corrected himself, "is to raise volunteers from our own people—men who are inured to the climate, acquainted with the habits of the Indians and the country, and want to protect their homes and firesides."

Low conversation buzzed like swarming bees.

"I ain't no Injun fighter," a grizzled old miner, well past the age to fight anybody, blurted out. "But I'd go after them red devils if'n there was a bunch of us." He raised his old flintlock in the air and let out a squeal.

"It doesn't have to be a large company of men," Wasson clarified, "but they need to *know* Apaches and have something at stake. All I want you to do for now is think about it."

"The only good Indian is a dead Indian!" someone shouted, his loud voice overriding Wasson's.

"Bullets is too good for them," added another.

Like a fast-growing cancer, the hatred spread through the crowd until they all seemed to be of one mind and one voice.

A grandmotherly looking woman in a cornflower-blue dress stepped up next to Wasson. Clenched in her outstretched hand was a tattered Bible. "The Good book says, 'An eye for an eye.'" She raised the Bible heavenward as if to call upon God Himself for verification.

"Thank you, Mavis," Wasson said, his tone patronizing. "We appreciate you reminding us what the Good Book says." He helped her down the step to a younger woman's care.

Whatever was coming next—more of Wasson's speech-making, more testimonials, or more religious fanaticism—Ginny had heard and seen enough for one day. Pleading a headache, which she did indeed feel coming on, she handed her father her pencil and paper and excused herself.

In spite of her eagerness to leave, Ginny was in no hurry to go home. There was nothing there. No loving memories. No sense of place. Nothing but dingy rooms and a cluttered office. Not an ideal place to sort out her thoughts—troubled thoughts, born a little more than an hour ago. Prior to that, her only major concerns were money, and her father keeping his promise. Now she found herself worrying about Indian attacks, wondering whether or not her good name was still intact, and trying to figure out her unexplained change of heart toward Bonner Kincade.

Walking south from the mercantile, she longed for a grassy park and a large willow tree to sit under and think things out. The kind they had in San Francisco and in New York. But there was no grass in Tucson that she could see. Only dirt.

A walk, she thought. A walk would give her time to think. Instead of continuing south on Main Street, she turned left onto Congress Street and stopped for a moment at the corner to look at the display of sturdy women's shoes outside on a table in front of Lord &

Williams. Poking her foot out from under her skirt, she glanced down at her own somewhat dainty shoes and knew they wouldn't hold up long on Tucson's streets.

Ginny moved on, glad for the short diversion. Across the street she saw a half-dozen horses tied to hitching posts outside the Congress Hall Saloon. One of the horses was the high-headed buckskin. Ginny's heart skipped a beat. Warily glancing around, she made certain that the animal's owner was nowhere about. The last person she wanted to run into was Bonner Kincade.

Hurrying her step, Ginny was almost clear of the saloon when she heard a dog yelp. She turned to see a man push open the bat-wing doors and viciously kick a scruffy-looking dog out into the street.

"I tol' ya to git outta here," the man slurred his words. "I don' wantcha no more. Ya eat too damn much."

He was drunk. Very drunk. But he had no call to kick the dog.

The man staggered outside waving his arms. "G'won. Git!" he shouted, heading toward the dog that lay whining in the dirt. "Ya mangy cur, I'm gonna kick the holy hell outta ya."

Ginny shook with anger. She couldn't stand by and let the drunk kill the dog. "No," she cried out and ran toward him, skirts flying. She had thought only to intercept him, instead she barreled directly into him, sending him reeling into the hitching post.

He came away from it looking dazed. "Jesus Pete!"

Ginny glared at the man. Confident that the only injury he had sustained was to his ego, she hurried to where the dog lay on its side. Bending down she moved her hands over its furry body, checking for broken bones. She didn't feel any breaks but she did determine that the poor animal was starving and that it had a number of sores on its body.

"Come on. Get up," she coaxed, anxious to see if the dog could walk. "Up, now. Up!" But the dog didn't even lift his head. He was either badly hurt or he'd lost his will. "I'm not leaving you here," she said, stroking the animal's head and looking into his liquid brown eyes. Such sad eyes, Ginny thought, her heart breaking for the pitiful creature. "All right, I'll carry you," she said at last, then gently worked her arms beneath the bony body. Even as sickly thin as the dog was, he still weighed a good fifty pounds, a little less than half what Ginny weighed.

"Getch yer hands offa' my dog."

In her struggle to lift the dog, Ginny had forgotten about the drunk. Glancing up, she saw him weave his way toward her, a mean look in his eyes and a revolver in his hand.

Ginny tried to think. Even if she could manage to lift the dog, she wouldn't be able to run away from a bullet. Could the man be reasoned with? Probably no more than her father when he was drunk. Which was not at all. Shamed, maybe? Highly unlikely. Drunks had no shame. Perhaps a bargain of some sort?

"I'll buy the dog from you," she blurted. "Five dollars."

He sniggered. "Dog ain't fer sale."

"Dog? That's his name?"

"Simple, ain't it?"

"Twenty dollars."

He waved the revolver. "Ya don' hear too good, do ya, missy? He ain't fer sale."

"But you don't want him. Why not let me buy him from you?"

He extended his arm and cocked the trigger. "I'm gonna count to three, then I'm gonna put a bullet right through his ugly head."

Think, Ginny. Think, she told herself. *You have to do something—* She plopped down on the ground behind the dog and held him to her. "If you shoot this dog, you're going to shoot me too." She hoped the consequences of shooting a human being—and a woman at that—would be enough to deter him. Her courage faltered when she saw him take aim. She closed her eyes and prayed.

An instant later the revolver went off.

Ginny's body jerked convulsively. She tucked her head into her chest and waited for the awful pain. But the pain never came. She nearly cried out with relief.

"Dog?" The animal whimpered pitifully and Ginny assumed the worst. A quick all-over inspection of his body told her that he hadn't been shot either. It didn't seem possible but it was true. She nuzzled her chin against the animal's head and thanked God.

"You murderous, half-breed bastard!" the drunk wailed. "You shot me, damn you."

From somewhere close by Ginny heard Bonner Kincade's low, ominous voice.

"Unless you want me to take a matching chunk out of your other thumb, I suggest you get the hell out of here, Mulligan."

The cold, unemotional warning chilled Ginny to the bone. She turned to see Bonner standing off to the side of the bat-wing doors, a smoking six-shooter in his hand.

Mulligan made a sharp, wheezing noise that sounded like startled disbelief. "Jesus Pete, Kincade! I was only gonna kill the dog!"

Ginny dared a sideways glanced at Mulligan. He was cradling his right hand in his left. Blood dripped between his fingers and down his arms, splattering his boots and the ground. A few feet in front of his right boot lay his revolver, blessedly cold with disuse.

"I'm going to count to three, Mulligan, then I'm going to put a bullet through *your* ugly head." Ginny turned her gaze back to Kincade in time to see him raise the barrel of his revolver. "One—" He was taunting him, using the same words Mulligan had used.

Ginny stared into his dark, glittering eyes and knew that he wouldn't hesitate to kill Mulligan. Somehow she knew, too, that Mulligan wouldn't be the first man he'd killed or the last.

"Folks is right 'bout you, half-breed," Mulligan hissed between tobacco-stained teeth. "You ain't no different than the rest of them cold-blooded savages. Could be yer even worse 'cause you make out to be a white man."

Ginny didn't miss the look of raw anger that flashed across Kincade's face. Even in his drunken stupor, Mulligan seemed to know that his barb had poked too deep. He held up his good hand like a white flag.

"Two—"

Kincade pulled back the hammer. It made a hollow click as it rotated the cylinder to the next full chamber.

"I'm goin'!" Mulligan shouted. "Jes lemme git my gun." He stooped to reach for it. A series of closely spaced shots sent it frog-hopping into the street.

Ginny covered her ears in a useless effort to muffle the explosive sound. Gun smoke swirled on the breeze, stinging her eyes and nostrils. Too stunned to move, she sat with her back to the water trough.

Mulligan stumbled over where the revolver had been, then picked himself up and ran like a frightened jackrabbit.

A dark shadow fell across her body. Glancing up through watery eyes, she saw Bonner Kincade standing in front of her, his long legs like twin oaks. Her stomach clenched in fear as she stared at the rawhide thongs that bound his moccasins just above his calves. *One hundred percent savage.*

Without moving her head, she lifted her gaze. He was so tall. His legs seemed to go forever. On his left leg at midthigh, she saw another rawhide thong, this one holding his holster in place. Shifting her gaze front

and center put her in line with that part of his body
that she had no business looking at. Realizing her mistake, she lowered her head.

*Folks hereabouts are wary of him. You should be
too.*

She was. Now more than ever.

Without warning, he squatted down in front of her
and pulled her hands away from her ears. "Are you
all right?"

Ginny gave a start, a momentary panic as her mind
jumped ahead of itself. "What?" She hadn't been able
to hear him above the noise reverberating inside her
ears.

"Can you hear me?"

"Barely," she said in answer to his question.

He nodded, then sat back on his haunches, evidently
prepared to wait until her hearing returned.

This close, little more than a type-stick away, Ginny
found it as awkward to avoid his gaze as to meet it.
What was he thinking? His eyes gave nothing away.
Neither did his expression, which remained closed,
aloof. She envied him that. Many were the times when
she'd wanted to keep her thoughts to herself, but her
eyes, her facial expression, or both always gave her
away. Making it difficult to tell a lie and practically
impossible for her to keep a secret.

Was he thinking that she'd been a fool to intercede
on behalf of the dog? Her father would have thought
so, but then he always thought she went too far.

Did Kincade know by looking at her that she feared
him? If he could see her fear, then he might also have
seen her fascination.

Under his steady perusal, she became increasingly
uncomfortable. At length, her ears popped and her
hearing returned. Bonner must have seen her look of
relief. He leaned forward.

"Better now?"

She nodded.

He reached out and stroked the dog's head. "Now that you've got him what do you plan to do with him?" His voice had lost its cold, unemotional edge.

Ginny looked down at the dog cradled in her arms and shrugged. "I don't know. Take him home with me, I suppose," she said, running her hand along the dog's fur. "What else can I do?"

"He looks to be in bad shape. Why don't you let me put him out of his misery."

Ginny's head shot up. "No! How could you even suggest such a thing? For all you know a little food and care might bring him around." She glared at Bonner, challenging him with her eyes.

Bonner emitted a sibilant sound that indicated his frustration. "Whatever you say, lady."

Ginny's hackles rose at his sarcasm. "You may not think it's worth the effort to try to save him, but I'm not you," she reminded him, looking him straight in the eyes. "*I* don't give up so easily."

"No, you're definitely not me." His gaze stayed with her as he rose to his feet.

Ginny started to get up, then realized she was helpless under the dog's weight. She struggled to reposition him and only succeeded in straightening her right leg. It was asleep.

"Want some help?"

She did and she didn't. She stared up at Kincade, trying to decide which was worse—sitting in front of the saloon all afternoon with a half-dead dog in her lap, or accepting Kincade's offer of help. For the dog's sake, she would let him help her, but before she could voice her acceptance, Kincade bent down and slid his hands between the dog's body and hers, the back of one hand pushing past her breast, the other across her thigh.

Ginny stiffened at the unexpected intimacy and pulled a startled breath. Instead of drawing back, as a gentleman would have done, he proceeded to get his grip on the dog.

It was the dog's pained whimpering that took her mind off his hands. "Easy, boy. Easy, now," she crooned, keeping her arms under the animal, supporting his limp body as Bonner made the transfer.

"I've got him," Bonner said, lifting the dog easily.

Getting to her knees, Ginny grabbed on to the edge of the water trough behind her and pulled herself up. Her right leg tingled from toe to thigh. She didn't dare put any weight on it just yet, or she'd end up back on the ground.

Out of the corner of her eye, she saw two gaudily dressed Mexican girls standing in front of the bat-wing doors. The snickering smiles pasted on their brightly rouged faces told Ginny they'd witnessed her embarrassing exchange with Bonner. She gritted her teeth, hating their knowing expressions as she walked off the numbness in her leg. She tried to tell herself it didn't matter, and that if they were the only people in Tucson who had seen what happened, she was lucky.

Slowly turning her head, Ginny prepared herself for the curious gazes she was certain to encounter, but no one else was about. The street was virtually empty, except for the horses tied to the hitching posts. The only thing she could figure was that most everyone was still over at the mercantile. Either that or gunshots were so common an event in Tucson that nobody paid them any attention.

Whatever the reason, she was thankful. Blowing out a sigh of relief, she stomped her foot a couple of times to get rid of the tingling that remained.

"You ready yet?" Bonner asked, impatience in his voice.

He waited by the hitching post, Dog's limp body draped over his arms. She started toward him, eager to go home.

"Get my horse? The big buckskin on the end."

Ginny didn't need to be told which horse was his. She'd admired the buckskin the first time she'd laid eyes on him. He was a pale canvas color, but his tail, shins, and hooves were almost black. "What's his name?" she asked while untying his reins.

"He doesn't have one."

"He doesn't have a name?" she asked, thinking she must not have heard him right.

"No. He doesn't have a name," he repeated coldly.

"I see." First a dog named Dog. Now a horse with no name at all. What next? she wondered. "Come on, boy," she said, reaching for the reins and finding them already untied. She glanced at Bonner, only to find him watching her.

Chapter 3

It would be economy to the government and humanity to both whites and Indians to prosecute the war with relentless vigor until they [the Apaches] are completely humbled and subjugated.

—*Arizona Citizen*

Ginny walked the buckskin several paces behind Kincade, her thoughts running amuck with suspicion and worry. In light of what John Wasson had said about Kincade's virulent dislike for anyone connected with a newspaper, the man's heroic behavior aroused her suspicions. Since she couldn't be sure what was motivating him to help her, she thought it best to keep as much distance between them as she could.

Another worry was what her father would say when she brought Bonner Kincade home. He'd be angry. Not because of who Kincade was, but because he'd been rude. Sam Sinclair, being a gentleman, would likely demand an apology.

And Bonner Kincade, a man of an entirely different persuasion, would likely refuse.

Ginny envisioned a quarrel in which her father would use his command of words to make his points and take Kincade to task. If the quarrel turned into a confrontation, he wouldn't stand a chance against Kincade, whose six-shooter spoke a distinctly different language.

She shook her head, chastising herself for letting her imagination run away with her—again.

At least one thing was going her way. The street was still empty. It irritated her that she had to worry about being seen with Kincade. Ordinarily, she wouldn't care a fig for what people thought. She had never been one to conform to social conventions. But now there was the business to think of. In a frontier town like Tucson, a newspaper was often the most civilizing influence the people had. It stood to reason that people would not only want the publishers to be sensitive to their needs and wishes, but that they should also be above reproach in all things.

Instead of continuing down the street, Kincade cut in behind the saloon and led her through a narrow alley littered with sour-smelling whiskey barrels and broken tables and chairs. At the end of the alley, he stopped and turned around.

"Leave my horse here," he told her. Ginny looked around for a place to tie him up. "Just drop his reins," he said, seeming to read her mind.

"But—won't he run away?"

"Not unless he wants to."

"What if he wants to?"

"Then I'll have to get another horse."

Ginny reluctantly dropped the reins and walked away. She hurried into the street to catch up with Kincade and was startled to see that they were within yards of the *Sun*'s office. How did he know where she lived?

Ginny rushed ahead to the door. "Pop?" She held it open for Kincade, then closed it behind him after he'd stepped inside.

"Who's Pop? Sam Sinclair?"

"Yes, my—" Ginny stopped midsentence. The way news traveled around here, it was a wonder there was anything left for a newspaper to report.

He looked around the office. "Where do you want him?"

"Through there," she said, pointing to the short hall that led to the sitting room. She followed him into the room, again calling for her father. Still no answer. He must have stayed behind to conduct more interviews and ferret out information about the attack. In that event, he could be gone for hours, which meant she had only Bonner to deal with.

Only Bonner? Good grief, she'd rather deal with a dozen angry, overprotective fathers than *one* Bonner Kincade.

Ginny was struck speechless by how incongruous Kincade looked standing in the middle of her sitting room, among her linen tablecloths and lace doilies. She found herself studying him. His Indian-dark eyes and black, shoulder-length hair handsomely accented his angular features. Several days out on a scout had produced a shadowy beard that gave him a sinister and slightly disreputable look. His face was lean and hard, his expression as before—inscrutable. So unlike any other man she'd known.

"Let's see now," she said, trying to marshal her thoughts about what to do with the dog. "How about putting him over there next to the—" She shook her head. "No, Pop would step on him there." She combed her fingers through an errant curl that fell across her right ear. "I know. Under the window." He moved toward the window and bent over to lay the dog down. "Wait!" He glared up at her, cocking one eyebrow. "Let me make him a bed." He straightened. Ignoring his frown of impatience, she opened the trunk in which she stored her vintage laces and pulled out an old patchwork quilt. Walking around him to the window, she knelt down and spread the quilt out on the floor. "There. That should do it." She sat back on her heels, smiling at her handiwork.

"You're sure?" he asked, a glint of amusement in his eyes.

Ginny stiffened. "Of course, I'm sure." She didn't like the way he was looking at her, like she was some muddle-brained female who couldn't make up her mind. Admittedly, she wasn't acting like herself, but it was because of a bad case of nerves.

He bent down again and laid the dog on the blanket. "Get me some water and a couple of clean rags."

Ginny leaned forward to pet the dog's head. His eyes were open and he seemed to be looking directly at her. "It's kind of you to offer to bathe him," she said, turning her head toward Kincade, "but he's my responsibility now." She started to stand up. "I want you to know how grateful I am. You saved both our lives." She hoped her anxiety to get him to leave didn't tell in her voice or in her expression. If he didn't leave soon, there was no telling what other blunders she would make.

"Come here," he said, grabbing her hand and pulling her back down. "Here's the problem." Hunkering down, he reached his hand to the back of the dog's neck, pulled up a loose fold of skin, then let it go. "You see how slowly his skin falls back into place? He's dehydrated. And he's too weak to drink on his own. I need a wet rag to squeeze some water into his mouth."

Ginny flushed with embarrassment. "Oh," she intoned woodenly. "I thought you wanted to bathe him and—" She cleared her throat. "Excuse me, I'll just go get—" She jumped to her feet and hurried off to the kitchen. Once she closed the door behind her, she blew out a breath, then crossed her arms over her chest and hugged herself. She'd always considered herself to be a levelheaded woman, not one given to tumultuous emotions or fantasizing. Until today. Today, she had experienced more disturbing emotions in a few hours than in the whole of last year!

It was maddening, disconcerting, and entirely out of her control. "I can't go back in there!" she whispered to herself. She glanced at the back door. Maybe she could just slip outside and—run? She'd never run from anything in her life.

On safe ground for the moment, she rubbed her

hands against her arms and resolved to get hold of herself. She was being absolutely ridiculous.

"I need some whiskey too," Kincade called out, interrupting her reprieve.

Ginny's eyebrows raised in question. Then it struck her that he wanted to clean the dog's sores. She choked a short laugh. Thank God she hadn't asked if he wanted a glass.

"There must be a bottle here somewhere," she called back, as if she doubted there was liquor in the house. It was a game she played in front of strangers.

She found one almost immediately. That it was half-empty gave her a sinking feeling, but she fought her way out of it, confident in her father's promise. Pop knew how much was at stake. She hurried to fill a deep bowl with water and get some clean rags.

Kincade was still crouched down in front of the dog. She set her supplies on the floor and knelt down beside him.

"Show me what to do."

He dipped one of the rags into the bowl of water. "Open his mouth for me," he told her. The dog didn't so much as stir when she pulled his jaws apart. Nor did he make any kind of protest when Kincade pressed the wet rag against the dog's teeth and gums. "Good, boy," he said when the dog swallowed the water dribbling into his mouth. Kincade patiently repeated the process, squeezing water into the dog's mouth, then rewarding him with words of praise.

Caught off guard by the compassion she heard in Kincade's voice, Ginny studied him from beneath her lashes, thinking she would see emotion in the hard, ruthless set of his masculine features. Instead, she saw a man who wore a thin veneer of civility. An army guide when he had to be. A savage half-breed when he chose to be. A man who was feared as much as he was respected.

"You'll have to do this every couple of hours until

morning. He'll need food too. Beef. Liver if you've got it. Grind it up real small and put it in his mouth. Hold his muzzle if you have to. Not too much at one time."

Ginny nodded. "I have some beef left over from last night's supper that I can give him right away. I'll go to the butcher's once Pop gets back."

Her knees hurting, Ginny leaned sideways to sit down. When her foot tangled in her skirt, she started to lose her balance. Without thinking, she grabbed Bonner's knee but it was already too late. Her bottom hit the floor with a resounding thump that rattled the oil lamp sitting on the table near the window.

"Sorry," she mumbled, snatching her hand away the instant she righted herself. She bit down on the inside of her lip and moved up closer to the dog. "Besides being dehydrated and half-starved, do you think he has any other injuries?"

"No broken bones," he answered flatly. "I don't know about his insides. Mulligan kicked him pretty hard, and I doubt it was the first time. If he doesn't look better in a day or two, you might want to think about putting him down."

"All right." She couldn't bear to see any animal suffer unnecessarily.

Kincade made quick work of cleaning the dog's open sores, suggesting a horse salve to speed the healing. Though he'd been crouched down for more than a half hour, he got to his feet with smooth agility and backed away from the dog.

"You've got your work cut out for you." He proffered his hand to help her up.

She accepted. "I'm not afraid of work. And if I succeed in making him well, then I'll have myself a lifelong companion."

He released her hand and gave her a long, hard look. "Maybe. Maybe not. Chances are he'll run off with the first bitch who comes along. What you *need* is a man to look after you."

Ginny bristled at his high-handedness. "I have a man, thank you. My father. And we look after each other."

Kincade scoffed at her anger. He deliberately stepped in front of her, his height forcing her to tilt her head back to look at him. "A woman like you can stir up a lot of trouble in a town like Tucson."

"A woman like me?" She was so angry she could hardly breathe. "Don't presume to think you know me," she said, poking her index finger into the middle of his chest. "You don't know anything at all about me."

He grabbed her hand. "Don't be so sure, Miss Sinclair. You'd be surprised at what I know." Tightening his grip on her hand, he effortlessly brought her toward him. His gaze traveled over her face, then settled on her lips.

Too late, Ginny realized she'd failed to keep her distance from him. If she'd been careful, she wouldn't be standing this close to him, so close she could feel the heat from his body. Her stomach tightened into a wary knot, and a prickly sensation crawled up the back of her neck. His last statement was full of disturbing implications, one being that he knew full well the effect he was having on her. She swallowed and took a deep breath. If by some chance she escaped him without incident, she promised herself that in the future she would stay far away from Bonner Kincade. He was more man than she was used to dealing with. More man than she could handle.

But Ginny wouldn't let him have the last word. "If indeed you know me, Mr. Kincade, then you know I'm not some naive schoolgirl who can be easily intimidated." She jerked her hand out of his grasp and stepped back, glaring at him. The confrontation was interrupted by someone singing loudly and off-key outside.

"Weep no more, my lady. Oh, weep no more today . . ." The office door opened and closed. *"We will sing one song for the old Kentucky home . . ."*

Sounds of shoes shuffling across the wooden floor came to Ginny's ears. "It's Pop," she said, her gaze veering from Kincade's toward the hall door. A pang clutched her heart as her father staggered into the sitting room.

"For the old Kentucky home, far away." His voice trailed off when he caught sight of her. "So there you are," he said, peering at her over the tops of his spectacles. "Where'd you go?"

"Pop—" Ginny tried to stop him from making a fool of himself.

He came farther into the room, weaving left, then right. "I looked all over town for—" His bloodshot eyes shifted to Kincade. "Who the hell are—" He blinked, then, "You!"

Ginny moved around Kincade, her arm brushing his as she passed. She stood in front of her father, her anguish at his condition threatening to shatter what little control she had left.

"Oh, Pop. You promised you wouldn't—" Her voice gave out, as if something inside her had broken.

Sam Sinclair waved his hand dismissively. "Outta m'way, Ginette," he slurred, ineffectively trying to push her aside. "I wanna speak to the guide here. He owes you an apology for being rude."

"He already apologized, Pop," she lied, hoping to pacify her father's anger.

It didn't. He grabbed her by the shoulders.

Kincade was suddenly between them, pushing her behind him out of harm's way.

The two men stood toe to toe, Kincade towering over her father.

"Everybody in town's talking about what you did to my girl in front of the mercantile."

This was the quarrel Ginny had envisioned.

Kincade appeared unmoved by her father's anger, but Ginny knew from watching him with Mulligan that his face revealed nothing of his emotions—if, indeed, he had any. Her gaze dropped to his gun hand making sure it wasn't too near his holster.

"Pop! Please. Just let it—" Her plea became a cry of shock when suddenly her father threw a right punch at Kincade's jaw. To her relief, he missed. Then, in the next instant, he fell forward into an unconscious slump.

Kincade caught him, holding on to the drunken man as easily as he'd held the dog. He looked at Ginny. "Where do you want him?"

Horrified, Ginny pointed behind her to the bedrooms. "In there," was all she could say. Kincade hefted her father over his shoulder like a sack of flour and carried him across the sitting room. He was inside her bedroom before Ginny realized his mistake. By the time she got to the door, Kincade had already turned around and was coming toward her, still carrying her father over his shoulder. She stepped back out of his way and reached behind her to open the opposite bedroom door.

"In there," she said weakly.

"You're sure?" he asked, cocking a brow.

She started to say of course she was sure, then thought better of it, realizing she wasn't really sure of anything anymore. Leaving her father to Kincade, she retreated to the kitchen where she threw herself into the task of chopping up last night's roast beef. She had to do something to keep from falling apart.

She'd fooled herself into believing her father would keep his promise. It wasn't the first time she'd put her trust in him and he'd failed her. It was just a different circumstance. Circumstance number one thousand and twenty or was it one thousand and thirty?

Lost in her thoughts, she continued chopping. When Kincade appeared in the doorway moments later, she didn't look up.

"How is he?" she asked.

"Sleeping."

Using the knife blade, she scraped the beef into a neat mound, then started chopping again. "Thanks for not hurting him."

"He was no threat."

Ginny gave a humorless laugh. "Not with his fists, that's for sure. But he's deadly with his pen."

Without warning, Kincade covered her hand with his and carefully took away the knife. "You're going to pulverize that meat."

Ginny looked down at the mess she'd made. "I guess I got carried away." She lifted her gaze to his. "It's just that he promised he wouldn't . . ."

Kincade set the knife down. "Try me."

Ginny watched his hand, so strong, so capable. She couldn't help but wonder how many men he'd killed. It was the same hand that held the gun on Mulligan, that pulled the trigger and saved her life. The same hand that had touched the dog with such tenderness. Touched her . . .

At odds with herself as to what to do, she finally pulled her gaze away and stepped back. "Excuse me, I have things to do."

Kincade stared down at her. A slight smile touched the dangerous curve of his mouth. "Another time," he said, and was gone.

Ginny spent the rest of her afternoon sitting with the dog, coaxing him to eat and take water. "I'm going to have to think up a name for you," she told him, rubbing her hand down his side. He was so thin. She could feel every rib and there was a deep hollow by his hipbone. When he could eat or drink no more, she left him alone to sleep.

Ignoring her father's wall-rattling snores, she ventured into the newspaper office and tackled the desktop clutter that she'd been working on earlier that morning. By tonight, when she went to bed, she wanted the office to be in perfect order so that tomorrow morning she could start learning every facet of the newspaper business.

Sitting with the dog had given her time to do some serious thinking, and when thoughts of Bonner Kincade entered her head, she forced them back out. A man like that had to be contemplated in a rational manner, without emotion.

Because she realized that her father couldn't be counted on, she decided to take a more active role in the business than originally planned. She'd have to do it discreetly. He wouldn't appreciate her meddling in affairs he deemed to be his responsibility.

Ginny finished clearing the desktop and began putting things to rights on the worktable. Her father had broken his promise, but it wasn't the end of the world. When he was sober, which was most of the time, he was an incredibly capable man. Organized. Enthusiastic. Ambitious. Horace Greeley had once called him the most talented field correspondent he'd ever known. He hadn't been fired from his editorial positions because of lack of writing skill, Ginny knew, but because he didn't show up for work on time, missed deadlines, and forgot appointments—things that she could take care of.

Earlier this morning she'd been on the verge of talking to him about her journalistic aspirations. She'd been prepared for him to say that there was no place for a woman in a newspaper office other than clerking, bookkeeping, and typesetting. The latter only because a great deal of dexterity was needed to pick the tiny lead characters out of the type-case. She'd also been prepared with a counter, which was simply that they couldn't afford to hire any help right now, and since she *had* experience, having written serial romances for *Godey's Lady's Book* and for the *Alta California,* she was perfectly capable of helping out in that area.

All he could say was no.

And there were ways around that.

Chapter 4

They [Apaches] do not base their desire for peace upon the condition that it is wrong to murder a white man or woman or steal property.

—*Arizona Citizen*

Outside the *Sun*'s office, Bonner hauled in a deep breath. Facing the alley where he'd left his horse, he gave a loud whistle, then turned away and started walking south down Main Street. An answering whinny behind him was followed by the sound of trotting hooves. Snorting and blowing, the buckskin quickly caught up with him. Bonner felt the horse's nose nudge his back. He ignored it. Then came a second nudge, much harder than the first.

"Damn horse." He reached around and took hold of the reins. "You need to learn some manners," he said, half-serious.

The horse shook his mane as if in protest.

Turning his head to the side, Bonner eyed the buckskin narrowly. The gelding was too smart for his own good. Bonner had first seen the horse as a wild stallion leading a herd of mares and foals deep into the Valley of Thunder. He went after him, never expecting the horse to outmaneuver him at every turn. It was a chase he'd never forget, taking him close to a week and ending only because a landslide trapped the herd in a box canyon.

He gave the mares and foals to his old friend, Toriano, whose camp was nestled deep within the valley, and kept the buckskin for himself, working with him day after day from dawn to dusk, trying to get the animal's trust. Just thinking about the first time he rode him brought back painful memories—a fractured collarbone, a broken nose, and a multitude of bruises. But it had been worth it.

Once gelded, the buckskin was as fine a mount as Bonner had ever known. He possessed a keen intelligence that made him quick to catch on to even the most complex commands. He was responsive and intuitive, qualities that gave Bonner an extra advantage over his quarry. And he was fast—fast as the devil winds that whirled across the desert floor.

But what Bonner admired and appreciated more than all those things was the horse's wild spirit. Bonner believed that spirit was to the horse what *diyi*, power, was to the Apache. Out of respect, he refused to name him or tie him up.

Ginny Sinclair would never understand. It would've been a waste of time to try to explain it to her. She was a city woman, bound up tighter than her corset with all kinds of strict notions. In her world, things had to be tamed and named.

Bonner rubbed his hand over his face, his thoughts drifting back to this morning when he'd ridden in with the troopers. Ginny and her father were standing in front of the *Sun*'s office watching the procession. It hadn't taken great brain power to figure out who they were. For several weeks, the town had known about the sale of the newspaper and had been speculating on the new owners, a father and his daughter.

He purposely hadn't paid her much attention. Being half Apache and half white made things hard enough. He didn't need to make more trouble for himself by publicly taking notice of a *niña blanca*. From a distance, she'd looked like a schoolmarm with her wavy, brown hair pulled back from her face and her blue, high-necked dress. But no schoolmarm ever looked at a man the way she looked at him. Her direct gaze had made him feel more than a little conspicuous.

Later, in front of the mercantile, he'd seen her again and done some hard looking of his own, which had made *her* noticeably uncomfortable. He would've enjoyed his revenge a little longer if Wasson hadn't come on the scene. Bonner didn't think much of Wasson—the man, his politics, or his newspaper.

It was Wasson who had put him in such a surly mood. Bonner had grown used to people making snide comments about his mixed blood. Most of the time, he just ignored it. But not this time. This time was different.

The situation had gone from bad to worse when he saw Ginny Sinclair jotting something down on paper. His first thought was that something he'd said or done was going to end up printed in the *Sun*. Yanking the pencil out of her mouth had been a damn fool thing to do, but he wanted to let her know that he wasn't fodder for an article.

His one and only consolation in approaching her had been in satisfying his curiosity about whether she was as pretty up close as she was from a distance.

Prettier.

Her features were delicate like the English bone china he'd seen in the Boston storefront windows. And she had a mouth that made him think of his ma's roses when they were still in bud. But it was her eyes that fascinated him. Blue and clear as a mountain stream, they gave away her every emotion—fascination, embarrassment, and fear being three she probably wouldn't have appreciated him seeing.

Bonner grudgingly admitted to feeling that same fascination toward her, but he would keep it to himself. The last time he showed interest in a town girl, the girl's father threatened to kill him if he ever went near her again. That had been twelve years ago, when he was seventeen. It had taken an entire jug of *tulapai* to get him over his hurt and humiliation. The experience left an indelible imprint on his mind and a bitter taste in his mouth where white women were concerned.

Bonner put his thoughts behind him when he reached Jim and Indy Garrity's whitewashed adobe. He had a standing supper invitation for whenever he came to town and he almost always took advantage of it. After all, a man could only eat so many beans and so much jerked beef.

"Come on, boy. Let's get you settled," he said to the horse, leading him around the back to the remuda. He made quick work of removing the horse's saddle and headgear, then brushing him down. Hay, grain, and fresh water had already been portioned out.

Finished with the horse, he took the next few minutes to clean himself up with water, soap, and a razor provided by his thoughtful hostess. After changing into clean clothes from his saddlebags and running a comb through his hair, he was ready for supper.

Bonner entertained only a few friendships. He'd known Jim Garrity since before the war. When Jim went east to join up with the Union forces, Bonner chose to stay in the Territory and serve the Union as a civilian, securing safe passage for Union troops through Apache lands. A mission Jim was on went awry and he'd been wrongly accused of murdering four men. Just hours before his execution, he escaped and made his way west, where for six years he'd lived with Toriano's clan in the Valley of Thunder, learning Apache ways.

Last year, Camp Bowie's newly appointed commanding officer, Colonel Taylor, made a bargain with Jim, which resulted in Jim being granted a full pardon and having his rank reinstated. He'd elected to stay on with the army because he felt it was the only way he could be effective in helping the Apache people.

In that effort, Bonner and Jim shared a common goal. Both of them recognized that the Apaches, in spite of their resourcefulness and cunning, could not win the war against the White Eyes. The Apache numbers were too small and their weapons too outdated and limited. Yet they couldn't seem to grasp the futility of it all and continued to make war, continued to fight and die.

Bonner respected Jim for having made a difficult decision. After living with a Chiricahua group for all those years, it couldn't have been easy for him to train soldiers in the art of Apache warfare for the sole purpose of hunting down the very people who had befriended him. The hope was that once they realized their enemies could find them in their own strongholds and best them at their own war tactics, they would see the inevitability of their fight and surrender to reservation life.

Bonner shared a similar hope. The sooner the Apaches succumbed, as disheartening as that thought seemed, the more lives—Apache and white—would be spared.

Six months ago Bonner had offered his services to the army as an interpreter. Officially called a civilian guide, he was assigned to whoever required his services.

Bonner pushed his job to the back of his thoughts as he knocked on the heavy plank door and waited until he heard Indy's voice invite him inside. The moment he opened the door, he sniffed the air. Fresh bread. Roast beef. And apple pie.

"Bonner!" A beautiful, brown-haired woman flew across the room to greet him. "You're late. I've been so worried."

"We ran into trouble on the main wagon road," he said, dropping his dirty towel into the basket beside the door, then unbuckling his gunbelt.

She took it from him and hung it up. "Where's Jim?" she asked, her hazel eyes alight with fear.

Bonner chided himself for his stupidity. His thoughtless comment had led her to draw the wrong conclusion. "He rode ahead of the column to make his report. He should be here any moment."

Relief flooded her eyes and relaxed her expression. "What kind of trouble?"

"Lahte and his band attacked Fish's freight wagons. Jim will tell you about it."

She pointed him to the chair closest to the hearth, then sat down across from him and folded her hands over her stomach. Though Bonner had only known Indy a short while, he knew that she was special. Toriano had said it best when he called her such-a-woman. She was that all right. And more.

"I'm not a fragile flower, you know," she said and Bonner smiled.

Maybe not a flower, but at four months pregnant, Indy Garrity *was* fragile and even more beautiful than when he'd first met her. If he were the type to settle down, he would want someone just like Indy. Someone who would love him for all he was and for all he wasn't. But such-a-woman was one of a kind.

"You can tell me what happened," she continued. "I'm not going to faint."

Still Bonner stared at her, saying nothing.

Independence was her given name—a name she lived up to in everything she did. Bonner didn't know how Jim managed her, but then Jim Garrity was the Territory's recognized master of tactics. He'd accomplished the impossible when he'd taken a group of misfit soldiers and trained them to fight and survive as well as any Apache brave.

"You're as bad as Jim," Indy charged, working herself into a huff. "Just because I'm going to have a baby doesn't mean you can't tell me what's—"

"Oh, yes it does!" Jim Garrity's sudden appearance at the door startled Indy so that she jumped out of her chair. Dropping his dirty clothes in the basket, he removed his campaign hat and hung it next to Bonner's gunbelt. Like Bonner, Jim was tall and of a similar build. Both had dark hair and dark eyes, but that's where the resemblance ended.

"I knew that sooner or later I'd catch you trying to pry military secrets out of Bonner." Jim turned to Bonner and winked.

"You scared me half to death," Indy said, blushing prettily as she moved across the room and into her husband's arms.

"That's not all I'm going to do to you if you don't stop sticking your pretty nose into places it doesn't belong," he teased, then bent to kiss her.

Feeling like an intruder, Bonner got up and walked over to the shelves he helped Jim build last month in anticipation of the arrival of Indy's books. After her father's death last year, Indy had sold her home in St. Louis and had her personal items brought to Tucson by way of the transcontinental railroad into Sacramento, then by freight wagon to Tucson. A few of the titles Bonner had in his own library at the ranch, but there were a couple dozen he'd never even heard of that looked intriguing.

Bonner had always been interested in books and education. In the early days, long before the war, his father had gone to a great deal of expense to bring in a tutor all the way from Boston to work with Bonner and his younger brother, Logan. When Logan went east to college, Bonner stayed on at the ranch to help his father. But he continued to educate himself by reading everything he could get his hands on.

"You're welcome to borrow anything you like," Indy offered.

"See anything interesting?" Jim asked, seating himself in the chair Bonner had vacated.

Bonner nodded, then pulled a book off the shelf. "This one, *Frankenstein.* Have you read it?" He flipped through the pages, pausing occasionally to read a few lines.

"Not me, but Indy has. Gave her terrible nightmares."

"It did indeed," Indy concurred. "It's about a doctor who creates a living being out of parts of dead bodies."

Bonner cocked an eyebrow as he read a particularly descriptive scene. "I hope Logan hasn't read it. He's got enough peculiar ideas about doctoring as it is."

"Shame on you, Bonner Kincade, talking about your brother like that," Indy said, jabbing her index finger into his chest. "Why I'd give anything to have him here to deliver my baby. I don't have a lot of faith in Dr. Wilbur. There's just something about him that disturbs me."

Jim reached up and caught his wife's hand, then pulled her onto his lap. "Just because a man takes a drink now and then doesn't make him a drunk," he said in the doctor's defense. "He's a good surgeon, Indy. I've seen him at work."

"Me too," Bonner seconded.

Indy sighed with resignation. "All right. I'm over-reacting. Forget I said anything. By the way, Bonner, have you heard from Logan recently?"

Bonner shook his head. "He's not much of a letter writer."

"How are King and Ruey?" she inquired.

"Pa took a bad fall off that old mule of his. Laid him up for a couple of days. But last time I was home, he was doing better. Ma's been busy tanning hides to make a dress for Martine's puberty ceremony."

"She'll be twelve in June, won't she?"

"June 1," Bonner answered.

"I always wanted a little sister," Indy said with a wistful smile. "Especially when my brother was being mean to me. Which was most of the time."

"I'll give you Martine," Bonner offered.

Indy laughed. "Thanks all the same, but I've met your sister, remember? Not that she isn't cute and very, very sweet. But she's—"

"A pest!" Bonner finished for her. "Follows me around like a puppy."

"And you love every moment of it," she returned, a knowing smile on her face.

It was true. He did. But there were times . . .

Indy got up from her husband's lap and started for the kitchen. "Supper will be on the table in five minutes."

Bonner snapped the book shut and reached for another one, his mind wandering back to earlier in the day when Ginny Sinclair jabbed her finger into his chest.

Just like Indy had done a few moments ago. He rubbed his chin thoughtfully as his gaze followed Indy into the kitchen.

Supper conversation centered around Governor Safford's speech, which had been printed in the *Citizen* and simultaneously delivered Saturday afternoon to the joint convention of the sixth legislature. The assembly had met across town at a warehouse that served as the territorial capitol.

Since Bonner and Jim had been on assignment when the speech was delivered, Indy read parts of it to them aloud, then stopped to take a breather and a few bites of food.

Jim drummed his fingertips against the tabletop. "It's hard to tell whether Safford's advocating the Peace Commission's reservation plan or denouncing it."

Indy looked up from beneath her lashes. "If you think that's confusing wait until you hear this. He says he believes the Coyoteros and the Apache-Mojaves earnestly desire peace. In June, when he visited their reservation, he found they were very poor, with no seed for planting except what little had been furnished by the military authorities. He admits that the Indians had no choice but to leave the reservation to hunt game."

"In other words," Bonner injected, "if they hadn't left the reservation to hunt, they would've starved."

"That's what it sounds like," Jim agreed, setting his fork down with a clatter. "I'd like to see a few selected government officials try living on the Apache's food allotments for a while." Jim ran his fingers through his hair in obvious frustration.

"Shall I go on?" Indy looked from one to the other.

Bonner nodded. "I think I know where this is leading, but tell me anyway," he said, leaning his elbows on the table.

"He says, 'Much dissatisfaction and ill feeling exist on the part of the settlers on account of the general belief that portions of this tribe join with marauding bands against them, and as soon as their nefarious work is done, return to their reservation for safety.' "

Bonner made a scornful sound, then leaned back against his chair and stared at the ceiling.

"Let me read this last part," Indy said, looking for her place. " 'Another source of uneasiness to settlers adjoining the reservation has arisen in consequence of the lines of the old reservation having been extended by survey under authority of the government, so as to include many valuable farms belonging to the settlers who made their locations in good faith outside of the reservation.' " She looked up from her reading, a sadness in her eyes. "There's more but it's sort of pointless to read it."

"There's no satisfying the White Eyes," Bonner bit out, his tone bitter. It was at times like this when he was in danger of losing his sense of purpose, when he questioned the role he'd chosen for himself. An interpreter—someone the Apaches could trust to translate not only their words but the meanings behind them. He could translate until he was blue in the face for all the good it would end up doing the Apaches. In the end, the White Eyes would get exactly what they wanted in the first place—extermination of the Apache people.

The only thing that kept Bonner from abandoning

his ideals was the lesson he'd learned from the wind
spirit. *Peace without price will teach the people nothing.*
Wind had cautioned him to learn patience and tolerance, and given him a strong *diyi*—enemies-against
power—the real war power to use to help the
Apaches.

"Safford's smart. I'll give him that. He's doing his
best to appeal to both sides," Jim said. "On one hand,
he speaks to the Eastern do-gooders who want the
military to lure the Apaches onto the reservations. On
the other, he speaks to the people of the Territory
who say reservations are nothing more than supply
depots and refuges where Apaches can regain their
strength before going back out to commit more
atrocities."

Indy turned her wide, troubled gaze to her husband.
"There's got to be a middle ground—something between the two."

"Crook," Bonner said with a suddenness that
seemed to take his host and hostess by surprise.

Jim gave him a level look. "You think General
Crook is the middle ground?"

Bonner nodded. "Crook doesn't play to an audience. He believes like us that the longer the Apaches
are at war with the White Eyes, the more people will
be killed."

"There *is* talk of a proposal to bring him here," Jim
confessed. "But so far it's only talk. He says he's tired
of the Indian wars, that it only entails hard work without corresponding benefits. Besides which, he doesn't
like the climate." Jim put his fork down. "Meanwhile,
we have Stoneman. He's a good man, if a bit naive."

Indy glanced down at the newspaper and shook
her head.

"What's wrong?" Jim asked.

She looked up at him, scowling. "I can't believe that
Governor Safford is actually recommending a citizens'

militia. Isn't that a little like taking the law into your own hands?"

Bonner crossed his arms over his chest. "White man's law doesn't apply to Apaches, Indy."

"I thought we'd seen the worst of it," she said, folding her hands across her stomach and rubbing it lightly. The gesture was oddly protective, and Bonner's insides clenched. "But it just seems to be getting worse and worse. Will it never end?"

"Eventually," Jim said, pushing his plate toward the center of the table. "Meanwhile, I know of one Apache problem that can be fixed right now." He reached across the table, pulled the newspaper out from under Indy's arm, wadded it up, and tossed it into the fireplace. "That's about all it's good for."

"Maybe the *Sun*'s new editor will take a less prejudiced approach," Bonner said, offering a new topic for conversation. "That is, unless he's already been bought by the local merchants or politicians."

Indy looked up in surprise. "He's here? You met him?"

"I still say, Tucson needs a third newspaper like a dog needs fleas," Jim said, chuckling. "As it is, it's only a matter of time before the *Arizonan* packs up its press."

"So, who bought the *Sun*?" Indy persisted, looking to Bonner for the answer.

"Sam Sinclair. He came in on Saturday afternoon's stage. They say he's been in the newspaper business a long time as a field correspondent and an editor."

"Sounds like he might be competent, anyway," Jim observed. "Still, he'll have to work some to compete with Wasson."

Indy got up and started to stack the dishes. "Does he have a wife?"

"It looks to be just him and his daughter, Ginny." The moment the words were out of his mouth Indy started with more questions. Bonner hated being questioned, but because it was Indy asking, he didn't complain. By the time she was finished, she knew everything he knew about Sam and Ginny Sinclair.

Maybe not everything, he silently amended. His thoughts wandered back to the scene in front of the Congress Hall Saloon, when he'd taken the dog from her, and later, when she'd grabbed onto him to get her balance.

"I think I'll pay a call on Miss Sinclair and welcome her to town," Indy said, regaining his attention. "Is she pretty?"

Bonner slid his gaze to Jim and found him trying to hide his laughter. He turned back to Indy. "I guess you'd call her pretty," he said, shrugging.

Ordinarily, he was a man of few words, but Indy had a way of turning those few into many. He was just about all talked out and if it wasn't for the apple pie that he'd smelled when he walked in, he would've made an excuse and headed on over to the Congress Hall Saloon to finish that drink he'd been nursing when he heard Ginny begging Mulligan to give her the dog.

He made a mental note to go by her place tomorrow and see how the dog was doing. In spite of her efforts, she might need his help putting the dog down.

"A piece of pie for your thoughts." Indy's voice pulled him back.

"They aren't worth it, believe me."

"I'll bet they're about Ginny Sinclair," she ventured. "Tell me more. What's she like?" Indy cut her husband a generous slice of pie, put it on a plate, and set it in front of him. Then she looked at Bonner, but made no move to slice him a piece.

Bonner recognized a bribe when he saw it, and he knew that Indy was well aware that he would do just about anything for a piece of her apple pie. He thought a moment. "She's a lot like you."

"Really? How's that?"

She sectioned off a large slice of pie.

Bonner's mouth watered.

"She wants to tame the frontier and everyone in it."

Indy changed the position of the knife and cut a piece significantly smaller than the one she'd given her husband. "I see."

Her comment was brief and succinct. Like his slice of pie. She set the sliver in front of him, then picked up the pie pan and took it back into the kitchen.

Bonner looked down at his plate. "Women!"

"You've got a lot to learn where women are concerned, my friend," Jim said, acting the sage advisor.

"I've got a lot to learn?" Bonner laughed. "I haven't made half the mistakes you did." Seeing Indy walk back to the table with a coffeepot in her hands reminded him of one such mistake that Jim had told him about. One very big mistake.

"Coffee?" Indy asked, the pot poised over Bonner's cup.

"Please," Bonner choked, leaning back away from the table while Indy poured. He cast a sideways look at Jim, keeping a wary eye on the coffeepot.

Jim gave Bonner an assessing look. "I wouldn't say anything if I were you."

Bonner quirked an eyebrow. "I've only heard your side of the story. Maybe I could gain some insight if I heard the other side," he teased, enjoying Jim's obvious discomfort. "Women are strange creatures. A man can use all the help he can get."

Indy finished filling Bonner's cup, then walked around behind him to where Jim sat. "I seem to have missed something here. What women are strange creatures?"

Jim drew his chin toward his chest, avoiding his wife's questioning gaze.

Indy looked at one, then the other. "Jim? What are you two talking about?" Suspicion edged her question.

"Nothing, Indy. Just pour the coffee before you spill it on me like you did—"

Indy gasped sharply.

"Jim Garrity! You swore you'd never bring that up again." She glanced at Bonner who couldn't help but smile. This was, in fact, the moment he'd been waiting for, encouraged. "You told Bonner, didn't you?" She set the pot on the table with such force that hot coffee jumped out of the spout.

"It was a long day. He needed a laugh," Jim admitted, throwing Bonner an evil look.

Indy rolled her eyes. Even as Jim shook his head, she turned to Bonner. "I don't know what he told you, but you need to know that none of it would have happened if he'd been forthright and told me he wasn't an Apache. He was dressed like a warrior. My father invited him to our quarters to bargain with him. I wanted to make him feel comfortable, so I offered him a chair. When he didn't take it, I assumed it was because he didn't understand English and—"

"She pointed her finger at me," Jim interrupted, "and said, '*You.*'" Jim got up and stood next to his chair, a wide grin now on his face. "Then she did this." He patted the air just above the seat. "And said, '*Sit.*' Like I was a dog!"

Indy was aghast. "Jim Garrity!"

"And then," Jim continued, retaking his seat, "she brought out a pot of coffee. Just like that one," he said, pointing to the blue-speckled pot. "By the time she got to filling my cup, her hands were shaking so bad she spilled it all over the table, me, everything."

"I did indeed," she said, her voice dripping with sarcasm. "Because you chose to speak to me *in perfect English* just as I started to pour. If someone would have had the courtesy to tell me that you weren't Apache— But no! You had to let me say and do all those *things*! Oh," she groaned. "I get embarrassed just thinking about it."

Bonner couldn't help but laugh out loud when Indy proved her point by blushing bright red.

Jim slanted a look at Bonner and said something in Apache that made Bonner grimace.

Bonner stood up. "I think I'd better say good night."

Chapter 5

The voice of truth and reason.
                                    —Motto of the *Tucson Sun*

With the *Frankenstein* novel under his arm, Bonner said his *thank you*'s to Jim and Indy and stepped out into the night. The temperature had dropped drastically in only a few hours. It felt almost cold enough to snow.

He cursed the cold, knowing that Gianatah's small band had made their winter camp along Arivaipa Creek, and that they were in short supply of winter blankets and robes. Constant conflicts between the bluecoats and Cochise's much larger band had kept his grandfather's people on the move throughout the summer and fall to avoid trouble. Consequently, there had been little time for hunting and even less for tanning hides.

On his last trip into Arivaipa Canyon, Bonner had taken two pack mules loaded down with woolen blankets. But the old man had refused them, saying they were tainted with the smell of the White Eyes.

Bonner walked around the adobe to the remuda and saddled his horse. He took his buckskin coat out of his saddlebags, then replaced it with the book. He didn't have far to ride, just a couple of miles up the Santa Cruz River to a stand of cottonwoods he'd staked out a few months back. Once there, he'd build a fire and settle in for the night.

As he rode through town, a three-quarter moon illuminated the street, which was deserted except for a couple of shavetail lieutenants, a pair of stray dogs, and a wild burro, which was eating hay off the back of a forage wagon.

The street erupted in chaos when the hapless strays wandered too close to the hay wagon. Bucking and braying, the little burro took out after them, its long ears flat against its head.

Farther up the street, Bonner noticed light in the windows of the *Tucson Sun*'s office. As he got closer, he saw Ginny Sinclair sitting at the desk, her head in profile. As he watched, she put her pen down, sat up straight in the chair, and twisted her head from left to right, as if trying to work out the stiffness.

Bonner sawed back on the reins when he saw her reach up behind her and pull a hairpin out of her hair. The horse halted. Bonner sat forward in the saddle, one hand on the top of his thigh, the other on the saddle horn. He fixed his gaze on her profile, watching her pluck out hairpins one by one from their confining knot.

He cleared his throat. His whole being seemed to be filled with waiting for her hair to fall, while *she* seemed to be in no particular hurry to complete the task. The patience and self-control he'd learned at his grandfather's knee failed him now.

Time seemed to stand still. Main Street and all its moon-washed adobe buildings narrowed down to one thing.

The window.

A wisp of hair fell over her ear.

Bonner swallowed.

She bent her head forward, holding the twisted mass with one hand and searching for hidden pins with the other.

His fingers dug into the muscle of his thigh.

At long last, she let it go. Its shining length tumbled down her back like water rushing downstream. Apache warriors were trained to be observant of everyone and everything, yet until a few minutes ago, he hadn't noticed her hair. He wondered how that was possible,

how he could not have noticed the rich brown color—
or that it was wavy all over.

He shook his head to clear his thoughts. This fascination he felt for her was distracting. Ever since he'd
left her this afternoon, he'd been thinking about her.
And now here he was, sitting on his horse in the middle of Main Street watching her through her window
like a randy youth.

Disgusted with himself, Bonner started to rein his
horse away. He abruptly halted when Ginny stood up.
Hands on hips, she threw her head back, arched her
spine, and stretched. His gaze dropped from her hair
to her arms to her jutting breasts.

His mouth went dry.

He'd been willingly seduced by a number of women,
some of them experts in the art of seduction. But what
Ginny Sinclair was doing unknowingly was more entic-
ing than the techniques those experts had spent their
lives perfecting.

Ginny closed her eyes, rolled her shoulders, and rotated her head, cringing at the sound of creaking and
cracking bones. She'd been sitting at the desk too
long, trying to come up with an appropriate motto for
the paper. It had taken her more than an hour, but
she'd finally come up with one she thought Pop might
like and approve. *The voice of truth and reason.*

Following that, she'd spent the rest of her time
going over every issue of the *Citizen* since its inception
last fall, making copious notes about content and format, as well as the paper's weaknesses and strengths.
Later she'd look at some back issues of the *Arizonan,*
which her father said wouldn't survive the year because of the editor's politics.

It was late and she was tired. It had been a long,
tension-filled day. She reached across the desk and put
out the lamp.

For the last hour or more she'd been fighting to

keep herself from becoming melancholy, but now, in the dark and the quiet of the night, she gave up the fight and let the mood envelope her.

Unexpected memories of Tom came to mind. She tried to push them away but they persisted until she was forced to acknowledge them. Tom asking her to marry him. His excitement at her acceptance. Their bodies coming together in celebration and joy. It had been the first time for both of them, and it had been funny and sweet and wonderful.

That happened over six years ago. Ginny had thought she was over the terrible pain of his death, that she'd come to terms with living the rest of her life without him. But now . . .

She closed her eyes, crossed her arms, and hugged herself. The moment she did it, she knew the reason for her mood wasn't because she still loved Tom or because she missed him, but because she longed to be kissed and touched—because her body ached to once again experience the glorious passion he had awakened in her all those years ago.

She drew in a long, difficult breath and tucked her chin into her shoulder. She imagined she could feel strong hands caressing her arms, moving down across her rib cage to her waist. She shivered in reaction, not realizing until a moment later that it wasn't her imagination—that it was her own hands that had brought her pleasure.

Shame and guilt overwhelmed her. She balled her hands into fists and held her arms stiffly at her sides. She wished she were a man. When a man longed to alleviate his need for passion, he simply visited a bordello. But a woman—a respectable woman and even a modern-thinking woman like herself—had no such option.

The sound of galloping hooves drew her gaze out the window. Peering through the glass, she saw a horseman race down the street.

Bonner Kincade.

Her body stiffened in shock. She hadn't heard any-one outside. Did he just happen to be riding past, or had he been watching her? "Oh, God," she said, her mind going over every move she'd made in the last few minutes. The pulse in her throat pounded errati-cally at the thought of how she'd stretched and arched her back. But a worse thought than that was the way she'd hugged herself. Touched herself. She groaned in exasperation. Why did he of all people have to witness her one and only moment of longing?

Embarrassed, and feeling more than a little sorry for herself, she hurried out of the office and went into the sitting room. She sat down on the floor and spent the next few minutes lavishing her attentions on the dog, trying her best not to think about what Bonner Kincade had or had not seen.

"Maybe what you need is a name," she said, inter-rupting her own thoughts. Head cocked to the side, she concentrated all her attention on the dog, desper-ately looking for something—anything—in his coloring or his features that would help her come up with something appropriate. She scratched him behind his ears and looked into his eyes. "Such sad eyes. Such a sad face." Whatever she ended up calling him, she wanted it to be a name that had some sort of meaning behind it. "I'll sleep on it," she told him, patting his head one last time, then she went to her bedroom.

Until she crawled into bed, Ginny hadn't considered sleep as a way of escaping her troubled thoughts. But in sleep she would be released from the custody of her memories . . . and from thoughts of Bonner Kincade.

She closed her eyes and prayed that sleep—dreamless sleep—would come quickly.

Monday morning Ginny woke with a start to the sound of loud barking. The dog! Her heart pounding, she grabbed her wrapper off the end of the bed and ran for the door, flung it open, and stopped short on the threshold. There, standing in the middle of the sitting room, was her father, and across from him, sitting up with teeth bared, was the dog.

She quickly assessed the situation as being a case of mutual surprise and fear. Pop had walked out of his bedroom into the sitting room and frightened the dog, who'd barked and frightened Pop.

Having hardened her heart toward her father after last night's drunken scene, Ginny decided that of the two, it was the dog who needed her reassurance and comforting. Belting her wrapper around her waist, she walked past her father as if he weren't there.

The dog's ears perked and his tail thumped against the floor when he saw her. "You're looking better this morning," she said, bending down in front of him until they were eye to eye. His overnight recovery seemed like a miracle. A moment later, when he whined and laid back down, she realized he wasn't doing as well as she thought.

Behind her, Pop cleared his throat. "Ginette? What is that animal doing in our sitting room?"

Ginny stood up and twisted around to look at him. She hated these morning-after confrontations. That he never seemed the least bit remorseful always made her angry, but this time it infuriated her. She glared at him. The way he appeared now—all freshly scrubbed, his hair still wet and slicked back, and his beard neatly trimmed—no one would ever guess that he was the same man who'd staggered into the sitting room last night and made a complete fool of himself.

He looked at her over his steel-rimmed spectacles, his expression devoid of any wrongdoing.

"He's recuperating," she said coldly, shooting him a reproving look.

"Recuperating from what?"

"Starvation, neglect, and abuse," she spat out, unable to stop herself.

"Where did you find him?" he asked, ever patient.

"In front of the Congress Hall Saloon." An image of Bonner Kincade, holding a smoking pistol, flashed through her mind. "I rescued him from a *drunk* who was going to shoot him because he eats too much." She watched her father to see what effect her barb would have on him. He didn't even flinch.

"Eats too much? Why, he's skin and bones," he said, appearing to study the dog. "What do you plan to do with him?" He switched his gaze to her.

In the blink of an eye, his expression went from questioning to knowing. "As if I can't guess." He slanted her a crooked smile, then he started to chuckle.

Ginny swallowed and took a deep breath. All she had to do was smile back and last night would be behind them—a memory. It would be so easy to pretend that she'd forgiven him, which was what she'd always done. But this time she couldn't do it. Wouldn't do it. This time she felt strongly that she needed to let him know that she was angry and upset that he'd broken his promise and that last night's behavior was unacceptable.

"I'm keeping him, of course, if that's what you mean," she said with easy defiance.

The animation left her father's face. "He's a big dog, Ginny. He'll eat us out of house and home. Not to mention that he needs a place where he can run. He belongs on a ranch."

"He *belongs* with someone who'll take care of him and love him."

"All right." He rolled his eyes. "I know how you are when you set your mind on something, and you've obviously set it on keeping that dog. But don't expect me to feed him or take him for walks."

Ginny crossed her arms. "I won't. He's entirely my responsibility."

He studied the dog carefully. "He's a homely animal. But you know, there's something about him that reminds me of someone, only I can't think who it is."

Ginny saw this as another ploy to get her over her anger and forget about last night, but she wasn't about to surrender.

"It's his expression," he said, narrowing his eyes to look at the dog more closely. "Or maybe it's his whiskers. They sort of wreathe his face. Yes. It's the whiskers. They're like Horace Greeley's."

"Pop! What a terrible thing to say."

"No, no. I don't mean it in a derogatory way. Horace and I— Well, you know. We go way back. I would never speak ill of him. But come on now, Ginny. Use your imagination when you look at those whiskers and tell me that dog doesn't remind you of Greeley."

Ginny was determined not to cooperate with him on using her imagination or anything else. Ignoring him, she moved about the room, straightening things that didn't need straightening just for something to do.

He pulled a deep breath and exhaled noisily, as if he recognized his defeat. "I guess I'd better get to work. I have a newspaper to get out."

Ginny glanced at him while she smoothed a lace doily. "Yes, you do."

He nodded, then turned and walked away.

Ginny waited until she heard the office door close after him before letting out the breath she'd been holding. There had been a moment when she'd wanted to laugh with him, but she'd been stern and held her ground.

She blamed herself for letting his drinking get out of control. She should have done something about the problem a long time ago when she first saw what was happening. Trouble was, she hadn't recognized it as a problem then. She'd thought of the whiskey in a medicinal sense—as a tonic that helped him get through the pain of her mother's death. Ginny understood that kind of pain, having lost Tom only the year before.

Retreating to the kitchen, she got the stove going and put a pot of coffee on to boil. Next, she fixed something for the dog to eat, then took it into him and fed him while she waited for her coffee. That he'd sat up and barked at her father was encouraging.

She was even more encouraged when he drank water on his own and ate everything she put in front of him. "Good, boy," she congratulated. "As soon as it warms up, I'll take you outside," she told him, even as she told herself that he probably didn't understand a word she was saying. However, she enjoyed talking to him and pretending he did.

"You know, Pop was right about your whiskers. They do remind me of Mr. Greeley's," she said quietly so her father wouldn't hear her. "Maybe that's what I should name you—Greeley!" Ginny laughed behind her hand. "Greeley," she repeated, studying him. "It fits."

Saying the name over and over just to hear how it sounded, she got up and went back into the kitchen. It was a good name. And a meaningful one, if only to her father. Every time he said it, he'd be reminded of the man who'd called him the most talented field correspondent he'd ever known. Maybe the dog's name would help him remember what he'd been and what he could still be.

Ginny sat in the kitchen and savored her first cup of coffee. The second one she took with her into her bedroom and sipped while she performed her ablutions and got dressed. It was barely eight o'clock when she finished and went into the office.

Her father was sitting at the desk, studying her notes. He looked up when she came in. "These notes of yours, Ginny, they're really quite remarkable. I never realized you knew so much about the newspaper business."

Any other time the compliment would have given

her a great deal of satisfaction. Now, it merely made her suspicious. "Everything I know, I learned from watching and listening to you," she said without emotion.

In spite of her lack of emotion, he seemed startled by her statement. Flushing, he looked down at her notes. "You've done an excellent job here of analyzing the *Citizen*'s strengths and weaknesses," he hurried to speak. "For all his eloquent talk, Wasson's articles do indeed lack a certain literary something, although I can't exactly put my finger on it. The majority of the articles seem politically inspired. And you're right that there's hardly anything of interest to women. A smattering of social news, next to nothing on temperance or women's suffrage, and no serial fiction, like the kind you write."

He hesitated a moment, then looked up. "I know I shouldn't ask you this because you've agreed to take on so many other jobs. But do you think you might be able to find time to write a weekly column? One geared specifically to women, with articles on suffrage, temperance, fashion, social news, whatever you think is important."

Excitement bubbled up inside Ginny, but she forced herself not to show it because she was afraid it was just another of his ploys aimed at getting himself back in her good graces. Torn between her resolve to teach him a lesson and her burning desire to write, she could only stare at him.

A dozen different expressions played upon his face, all of them seeming to be very sincere. It was his sincerity that helped her let go of her fear. "Please. Ask me anyway."

He got up from the desk and walked over to her. "I'm not only asking you, honey, I'm begging you. The *Tucson Sun* needs a women's column and you're the only one who can do it."

"I accept," she said, tears welling in her eyes.

"I thought we could also reprint some of your serial fiction, especially the Joaquin Murietta story that you wrote for the *Alta California*. What with our limited space, we'd have to run it over a period of about eight weeks to get it all in, but I think it's something both men and women would enjoy."

"Oh, Pop." She grabbed his hand. "I was going to ask you yesterday if you'd consider letting me write for the paper, but then we were interrupted."

"Yes, we were." He looked down, then up again, his gaze imploring her to listen. "I need to say something . . . to explain."

"There's nothing you can say that will excuse the fact that you broke your promise to me. No matter what, I can't forgive you for that."

He rubbed his chin. "I don't blame you, but please know that I didn't do it intentionally. Wasson asked me to join him in the saloon for a drink. I couldn't turn him down, Ginny. I told you before that I knew him when he worked in Oakland. He said he wanted to give me some practical advice."

Ginny had grown accustomed to her father's ever-growing list of explanations. As first he blamed his drinking on losing his wife, then on losing his job, and lastly on where they lived. There had always been a logical and valid reason for his drinking. In spite of knowing this time would be no different than all the others, she prepared herself to listen.

"Exactly what kind of advice did he give you?" she heard herself say.

"He said that if I was smart, I'd pack up the *Sun*'s press and all the equipment and move it to another town where there isn't so much competition."

"And you said . . . ?"

"I said I wasn't afraid of competition and that I had no intention of packing up and going to another town."

Ginny breathed a sigh of relief. "What did he say to that?"

"Nothing. He bought me another drink and we toasted to competition. Then he left."

"But you didn't. You stayed and had a third drink. And a fourth."

"I was worried."

"Liquor doesn't solve problems, Pop. It creates them."

"I got to thinking about how much was at stake and—" he cut himself off, then began again, "what would become of us if I failed."

"You won't fail. You said yourself that you're a damn good newspaperman. And you are. You have to believe in yourself."

"I'm sorry if I was difficult."

Ginny dropped her arms to her sides. "Difficult? You call what you did *difficult*?"

"I know I must get a little unreasonable when I've had a drink or two."

"Pop!" She stared at him. "You don't remember what you did, do you?" she asked, incredulous.

"Yes, of course. I broke my promise."

"Oh, Pop. Believe me you did a lot more than break your promise." It had never occurred to her that he didn't remember what he'd done. But that explained why his expression never showed any wrongdoing, why he never displayed any remorse. She considered whether or not she should tell him just how really difficult he'd been, what a fool he'd made of himself, how rude he'd been, how unreasonable, how he'd taken a swing at Bonner Kincade, then passed out. But she decided against it. He probably wouldn't believe her anyway.

"I don't know whether that's good or bad," he returned.

"Some things are better left unsaid. Now, why don't

we discuss our prospectus? After that, you can help me take Greeley outside."

"Greeley?"

"The dog," Ginny prompted.

Her father raised his eyebrows. "You named the dog Greeley?" At her nod, he burst out laughing.

Chapter 6

PROSPECTUS

We offer to the people of the Arizona Territory this first publication of the Tucson Sun, to be published every Saturday. In addition to covering matters specific to Tucson in Spanish as well as English, we will provide news of the world at large, a financial and commercial column, stock market reports, amusements, mining and land notices, issues of importance to women, and serial fiction. We will endeavor to verify all new sources and we guarantee political neutrality.

—*Tucson Sun*

Dawn had barely broken when Bonner rode onto the Camp Lowell reservation. Last night, he'd made the decision to leave Tucson for a while, and now he needed to let Colonel Dunn know he'd be unavailable for the next couple of weeks.

It was time he went home to check on things there, to see how his father was doing and to make sure Martine was staying out of trouble.

Besides, as the events of yesterday proved, it wasn't a good idea to hang around Tucson with nothing to do. It was too hard to avoid trouble. Because he was a half-breed, folks just naturally took offense to his presence, no matter where he was or what he was doing. Inevitably there was someone who forced his hand.

For good or bad, no one had ever drawn on him more than once, a fact that was becoming a little too well known for his liking. He owed much of his skill to his .44-caliber Remington, which he'd had custommade the last time he'd visited Logan. He'd have to be more lenient on his challengers from here on out, like he'd been with Mulligan. He sure as hell didn't want to get a reputation for being a quick draw. He'd have every gunman in the Territory after him, wanting to kill him.

The thought of dying didn't frighten Bonner. What did frighten him was that he wouldn't be around long enough to keep his promise to The People.

He slowed his horse to a walk. Camp Lowell sat in the northwest corner of a three hundred sixty-seven acre reservation. It was well situated on a gravelly mesa, clear of mesquite and sagebrush, less than a mile east of Tucson. A distance considered sufficiently far away from the Santa Cruz riverbed to be free of malarial fevers.

About a hundred men were garrisoned there now, one company each of infantry and cavalry. They provided escort troops for civilian travelers and wagon trains moving on the overland road directly south of the post and held the eleven-man picket posts at Cienega de las Pimas and Tres Alamos. They also served as a depot to the surrounding camps for rations and supplies, most of which were purchased locally in Tucson on the open market or by contract.

Bonner rode past the adobe guardhouse, the only actual structure in camp. South of the parade ground were two perfectly straight rows of enlisted men's A tents. He had to laugh at the way they were lined up side by side, like bottles on a fence.

It was this kind of conformance to order, to conventions, and to battle plans and tactics devised long ago for a different kind of enemy that helped make the frontier army so ineffective against the Apaches.

The Apaches' very lack of structure, their flexibility and unpredictability, contributed to their success at evading the bluecoats. But trying to convince the U.S. Army that they needed to do things differently was like trying to convince a temperance crusader that whiskey had its uses.

Bonner left his horse in a stand of cottonwoods. The officers' tents were sheltered by tall jacals. He announced himself to the private standing guard outside Colonel Dunn's quarters.

"Come in. Come in," Dunn called out over the private's voice. Bonner pushed back the tent flaps and entered. Despite the early hour, Dunn looked to have been up for some time. He was sitting at his desk, his uniform cleaned and brushed, the buttons polished so that they gleamed like gold nuggets. Without looking up from his paperwork, he motioned Bonner to a three-legged stool in front of his desk. "I'll be right with you," he said, obviously intent on finishing whatever he had been working on.

Bonner gave the interior of the tent a long look. Called a wall tent, it was considerably larger than the enlisted men's tents, but fitted up nearly the same, with a narrow bunk raised two feet off the ground, a small camp table, and a foot locker. The bedding had been rolled up to the head of the bunk to prevent any unwanted creatures from crawling in. Bonner compared the tent to an Apache wickiup and decided that the wickiup, crude as it was, was by far more comfortable and quieter. For one thing, it didn't snap and flap in the wind like a tent did.

The only advantage the tent had was the stove that sat in the middle of the wooden floor. In spite of its small size, it radiated a circle of warmth that felt especially good this morning. It also kept the coffeepot hot.

Bonner gave some thought to buying several of the small stoves and taking them out to his grandfather's rancheria for use in the wickiups, then thought better of it, realizing that Gianatah would react to the stoves the same way he'd reacted to the blankets.

His grandfather's hostility toward the White Eyes—though not without justification—was typical, especially among many of the older warriors and shamans.

Their hate and mistrust blinded them to the reality that the days of the Apaches living like nomads were over. They could no longer move about like the wind.

At length, the colonel organized his papers into a neat stack and weighted it down with a rock. "I'm glad you're here. I have something I want to discuss with you. But first, what brings you here at this early hour?" Dunn was a thin man with sharp, angular features that made him look unhappy even when he wasn't. At their first meeting several months ago, Dunn had impressed Bonner as being an army regulation officer, but now, after having accompanied him on several scouts, Bonner knew differently.

"I'm leaving Tucson for a couple of weeks. I have some personal things I need to take care of."

"Do any of those *things* have to do with tracking down Lahte?" he asked, looking at Bonner inquiringly.

The man was reading his mind. "They might," Bonner half confirmed.

"Is there something you want to tell me about Saturday's freight train attack?"

Bonner sat forward. Now that the subject had come up, he'd see what Dunn thought. "It strikes me as odd that Lahte would risk coming this far south with Cochise out to kill him."

"Yes, I agree. Anything else?" the colonel prompted.

"Of the ten teamsters, five were new hires. All of them young, inexperienced. Their first time hauling into Apache country."

The colonel raised an eyebrow. "I wasn't aware of that. They wouldn't be much help in fending off a raiding party, would they?" It was a question that required no answer. Dunn paused a moment. "What else?"

"On the whole, the shipment was of little value— bags of rice, potatoes, hominy, flour barrels, some bolts of muslin and calico . . . and twenty-four Sharps carbines and ammunition. They were army surplus, special ordered by a group of Santa Rita miners."

The colonel took a deep breath. "It could be it's all a coincidence."

"Could be, but something tells me it isn't."

"You know that General Stoneman has implied that certain merchants actually induce Indian hostilities to keep the troops in the Territory?"

"More troops. More contractor sales to the army. Bigger profits," Bonner said. "I haven't put all the pieces together. I'm not even sure they'll fit, but I think Lahte might have some answers—if I can find him."

"You could be right, but I pray to God you aren't. In any case, I'd like to ask you to postpone your plans." The colonel looked him straight in the eye as he picked Saturday's copy of the *Citizen* off his desk. He held it up for Bonner to see and pointed to a paragraph he'd circled. "Have you read the governor's speech?"

"I'm familiar with what he said," Bonner told him.

"Good. Then you know he recommended that the citizens of Tucson form a volunteer militia to protect themselves?"

"That's not the first time it's been brought up."

A frown drawing his arrow-thin eyebrows together, Dunn stood up. "True. But it is the first time the governor openly and officially endorsed it. I don't know about you, but I'd say the chances are pretty good that they'll do it this time." He looked past Bonner to some distant point. "I don't fault them for wanting to protect their homes and families, but you and I both know there are zealots among them who will convince the others that the only way to protect themselves is to kill every Apache they can find."

Bonner crossed his arms and stretched his legs out in front of him.

Clasping his hands behind his back, Colonel Dunn turned sideways and moved out from behind his desk. "We've talked before, you and I," he continued. "You know my views on the Apache situation and I know yours. Neither of us wants to see the Apache people exterminated, but we both know that things can't proceed as they are. The people of the Territory will prevail and eventually the situation will be resolved. Though I doubt it will be a satisfactory resolution for the Apaches."

Bonner shared the colonel's opinion. A couple of years ago it might have defeated him, but not now. The wind spirit had given him the gift of knowing his purpose—his reason for being, which was to help the Apaches accept the changes that were coming and to teach them a new way of life.

"I know what your official position is with the army, Kincade," Dunn said. "You're a civilian guide, an interpreter. I have no right to ask for your help in this, but—"

"What is it you want me to do?" Bonner interrupted, hoping to steer him toward his point. The man could outtalk Martine and that required some doing.

Dunn spread his hands over the warm air rising from the stove. He looked sideways and met Bonner's questioning gaze. "I need you to be my eyes and ears around town for a while. I want to know how people are reacting to the idea of getting together and forming a militia. I want to know who, if anyone, is doing the most talking. I realize there's nothing the army can do to stop them from organizing, but I don't want to be taken by surprise. And I *don't* want them getting in the army's way."

Bonner thought it over. An image of Ginny Sinclair standing at the window, wrapped in her own embrace, flitted through his mind and tempted him even now in the light of day.

Staying in Tucson was the one thing he didn't want to do, for more reasons than he cared to own up to. But he owed Dunn a favor for agreeing to keep army patrols away from Gianatah's rancheria. He had no choice.

"A week," Bonner said at last. "I'll stay one week, but that's all I can give you."

"Good enough," Dunn said, extending his hand that Bonner accepted and shook.

Bonner left the tent and rode toward town, thinking that his first stop would be the Shoo Fly Restaurant, the name based on the principle that *the flies wouldn't shoo worth a cent.* Since flies weren't a problem this time of year, he looked forward to sitting down to a breakfast of Mrs. Wallen's bacon and beans. The Shoo Fly was as good a place as any to hear what people were saying, and Mrs. Wallen was a reliable information source as well as being one of the few friends he had in town.

There were one or two others, he supposed. A couple of San Pedro River valley ranchers who came in for supplies now and then, the banker who handled his pa's money affairs, Doc Wilbur. The senoritas at the Congress Hall Saloon were especially friendly, and there was one, Mercedes, who'd offered her friendliness for free on more than one occasion. And Jim and Indy. He enjoyed their friendship the most.

When he came to the end of his mental list, he considered one more person. Ginny Sinclair. Ginny could never be his friend. A man didn't think about a friend the way Bonner had been thinking about Ginny. Yesterday afternoon he'd thought about stopping to see how the dog was doing, but after last night, he'd rejected the idea. And now, here the thought was back again, fighting him for priority over the Shoo Fly and Mrs. Wallen's bacon and beans.

*   *   *

As the morning wore on, Ginny's confidence in her father's business abilities soared. Until now, she'd had no idea he was so well prepared to begin operations.

He pulled out a stack of general interest and humor articles he'd written before they left San Francisco and said they could be used as needed to fill space. He showed her several prepared metal advertising plates and contracts from patent-medicine companies. The plates had been made in New York and were ready to go into the type form without any additional setting of type. He had a letter of intent from a legal advertiser out of San Francisco and one from Sacramento. He'd also arranged to exchange the *Sun* with several Eastern papers from which he would extract government and foreign news.

"I can't believe you accomplished all this without me knowing," she said, looking at him in awe.

"It didn't take all that much time," he replied dismissively. Sam Sinclair was a humble man. Accepting compliments or praise had never been easy for him. "I thought we'd go with the same five-column, four-page sheet as the *Citizen*," he said, confidence in his voice. "We'll cover all the standard topics: Indian affairs, law and order, education, churches, and town concerns. The most important thing is the tone and temper of the paper. People need balance. For every theft, shooting, or Indian attack, we have to find something good and positive to report."

Ginny had an idea. "How about an article campaign to push the town fathers into repairing and maintaining the streets on a regular basis? I read a letter to the editor in one of the past issues of the *Citizen* that the streets haven't been worked on in months. When it rains, some of those potholes will look like lakes."

"Consider that your first assignment," her father said, surprising her.

"Are you sure?"

"Sure I'm sure. You should know all about campaigns and crusades." He was, Ginny realized, referring to her drum beating for the suffrage movement in San Francisco. "The premier issue will go out next Saturday," he said, sliding into another topic as easily as butter slid across a frying pan. "Tomorrow we begin canvassing the businesses for advertising, so wear something pretty." He lifted his eyebrows, a mischievous look in his eye.

"Pop! I don't think—"

He reached out and put his fingers to her lips, silencing her. "We're going to need all the help we can get, Ginette. A pretty young woman in a pretty dress will be a welcome sight to some of those crusty old merchants."

Ginny grabbed his finger and was about to tell him he was just as crusty as some of those merchants when the office door opened.

A woman, appearing close to Ginny's own age, walked in. Ginny's first thought was that she didn't look like the other women in town. Not only was she exceptionally pretty and fashionably dressed, but there was a sophisticated air about her that marked her as having come from a large Eastern city. On her arm she carried a beautifully woven Indian basket.

"May I help you?" Ginny met her at the front desk.

The woman smiled. "Good morning, or is it afternoon? I'm afraid I've lost track of time."

"It's nearly noon," Ginny supplied. The woman set her basket on the desktop and took a deep breath. Where her woolen cloak parted in the front, Ginny saw that she was pregnant. "Would you like to sit down?"

She shook her head. "You must be Ginny."

"Yes."

"I'm Independence Garrity. Please call me Indy. My husband and I have a house near the edge of town. It was just last night that I was told you had arrived.

I baked you an apple pie to welcome you to Tucson."
She took the pie out of her basket and pulled off its
red and white calico covering. Fragrant steam spiraled
up from the vents in the crust.

Ginny sniffed the air and groaned. Her mother used
to bake apple pies. They never lasted more than a
day. "I— Thank you. It smells delicious."

"Did I hear somebody say apple pie?" Sam Sinclair
came from the back of the room to stand next to
Ginny.

"Pop. This is Indy Garrity. Indy, my father, Sam
Sinclair."

"Might you be Major Garrity's wife?" Sam asked.

"You know my husband?"

"No, but I heard his name mentioned yesterday as
the officer in charge of the troopers who brought the
freight wagons in. If memory serves me, there was an
article on him a few months back in the daily *Alta
California*. Something about him being court-martialed
for murder, then he was proven innocent."

Ginny remembered the article as well, but what
stuck in *her* mind was that the major had escaped
hanging and lived with the Apaches for a number of
years.

"I didn't realize that the news went beyond the territorial papers," Indy admitted.

"Indeed it did," Sam informed her. "I was still
working at the *Alta California* and I took the news
off the telegraph from the San Diego paper to use in
my Pacific Coast column. It was a terrific story."

Indy Garrity's face paled as she looked at him.
"You'll have to excuse me, but it's all still a little too
recent for me to think of as a terrific story. Maybe
someday I'll look at it like that, but not right now."

"I'm sorry. I didn't mean—" Sam threw his hands
wide. "Forgive me. I'm a newspaperman. I was thinking in terms of the story and how it was put together,
the who, what, when, where, and why."

"I understand," Indy returned graciously. But Ginny doubted that she did. Only another journalist could understand what her father meant.

Ginny turned to her father. "You can spare me a moment, can't you, Pop?" At his nod, she squeezed his arm reassuringly, then smiled at Indy. "Would you care for something to drink? I brought a tin of Chinese tea with me from San Francisco."

Indy brightened. "That sounds wonderful."

Taking the pie off the desktop, Ginny led the way through the hall into the sitting room.

The moment Indy saw Greeley she went over to him and bent down. "Oh, poor thing. Isn't this Mulligan's dog?"

"He's mine now," Ginny stated. "I named him Greeley, after Horace Greeley, the editor of the *New York Tribune*." Ginny offered Indy a seat, then excused herself to take the pie into the kitchen and fix them their tea. When she returned, she was surprised to see Indy sitting on the floor next to Greeley.

Indy looked up when Ginny came into the room. "I hope you don't mind me sitting here next to Greeley. I was never allowed to have any pets as a child," she confided, "which, I suppose, is why I adopt every animal that comes to my door—even a few who won't. For the last two weeks I've been trying to make friends with this little wild burro who comes into town now and then." She petted Greeley and smiled down at him. "Tell me, how did you get him away from that no-account, drunk Mulligan?"

Ginny told Indy the story without going into any of the embarrassing details. At the end of it, Indy broke into a wide, open smile.

"I have to admit," Indy said, getting up off the floor, then sitting down on the horsehair sofa next to Ginny, "Bonner Kincade is part of the reason I'm here. Bonner and my husband, Jim, work together and they're also friends. Last night we had Bonner to supper and he mentioned that he met you. When I pressed him for more information, he stubbornly avoided all my questions, which, of course, made me very suspicious. Bonner isn't much of a talker, but I'm usually able to get him to speak to me, although I do have to wheedle him a bit and occasionally I have to resort to out and out bribery. He loves my apple pie. But last night not even my pie could get him talking about you."

Ginny was momentarily speechless that Indy was acquainted with Bonner. But more startling was an image of Bonner Kincade sitting at a cloth-covered table set with china and silver, eating apple pie. She couldn't imagine that someone as worldly and sophisticated as Indy Garrity obviously was would have a man like Bonner to supper. In the myriad visions she'd had of Bonner over the last twenty-four hours, she'd seen him as the half-naked, breech-clouted Apache warrior so vividly illustrated in *Harper's Weekly*, imagined him hunkered down in front of a roaring campfire, galloping on his buckskin horse across the desert, even dancing a war dance.

Ginny saw Indy's eyes widen and knew her prolonged silence was causing suspicion. "I'm not surprised," she blurted at last. "From the moment we met, we seemed to be at odds with one another. I was told it might have something to do with his dislike for newspaper people."

Indy straightened as if to relieve an ache in her back. "I suppose that could be the reason," she said, not sounding or looking very convinced. "It's true that he dislikes journalists. And, frankly, I don't blame him. Territorial newspapers have always exaggerated the Apache problems, but more so recently, especially in the *Citizen*. It's no secret that John Wasson wants to see the Apache people exterminated, as does most of Tucson. As does most of the Territory."

Ginny sipped her tea thoughtfully. "It's such a sad state of affairs. I suppose there is no easy solution."

Indy smiled indulgently. "One day next week, I'll have you and your father to supper. You might be interested in knowing what my husband is doing toward a peaceful end." She set her teacup on the table next to the sofa.

Ginny nodded. "We'd like that."

"Good. And if Bonner's still in town, I'll invite him too."

Chapter 7

Thursday, January 19, 1871

Ginny and her father spent Tuesday and Wednesday calling on Tucson businesses, showing potential advertisers a printed poster of the *Sun*'s prospectus and layout.

Ginny acted the dutiful daughter and helper, careful not to let on as to the extensiveness of her duties. Clerk, bookkeeper, and compositor were acceptable jobs for women in newspaper offices, but editorial and journalism positions were not. It was a mystery to Ginny why the hand that rocked the cradle wasn't considered competent in those fields, but that was the way of it, for now anyway. Maybe one day, when the *Sun* was holding its own, she could make some changes.

Ginny knew she'd have to be particularly careful to keep her writing a secret. If anyone found her out, she and her father would be the object of ridicule and contempt. Only her serial romantic fiction could bear her name. It wouldn't be exempt from criticism, but it would be criticism of a different sort.

They made the rounds, going from business to business. Sam did most of the talking. Ginny was impressed with his salesmanship, especially his ability to convince merchants who were already advertising with the other two newspapers to give the *Sun* a try. He guaranteed that they would see a dramatic difference, not only in the look of their ad but in the results. By late Wednesday afternoon, he told Ginny he had all the advertising he needed for the premier issue.

Now, with the Friday deadline only a day away, Ginny and her father had been working in the office since before dawn. They had developed a comfortable routine—Ginny picked the tiny lead letters out of the type-case, gave them to her father, who marshaled them onto a composing stick, then put them into a galley.

It wasn't yet noon when they finished the last of the ads. Ginny stretched and rubbed the stiffness out of her fingers. "I need to take Greeley outside and get a drink of water," she told her father, then left the office, Greeley right behind her.

The dog was doing extremely well, but he still had a long way to go before she could consider him recuperated. He was eating and drinking entirely on his own now and could get up and walk about, although slowly and only for several minutes at a time. His care had taken precious hours of her time, but Ginny didn't regret a moment of it.

Ginny grabbed her shawl off the back of a chair, opened the kitchen door, and went outside with Greeley following close on her heels. There was the smell of rain in the air, but only a few dark clouds dotted the sky.

Watching Greeley, Ginny found herself wishing Bonner would stop by so she could show him how well the dog was doing. Conversely, she hoped he wouldn't. She didn't want to have to explain to her father how Bonner knew about Greeley. So far, Pop still didn't remember anything about that night and she would just as soon it stayed that way.

Another reason to hope Bonner stayed away was her acute fascination with him. It was unlike anything she'd ever known—a physical response so strong that it made her feverish with desire. Not even Tom had aroused her to such a level of wanting. It was frightening to be so out of control with her own body and her emotions. Even seeing Bonner in her mind—his dark-eyed gaze, his arrogant, loose-hipped stride, his large, imposing body—raised her temperature and twisted her stomach into knots.

It had caused her no small amount of worry. She wanted desperately to overcome it but she didn't know how.

Adding to that was her inability to understand her defense of him—first with John Wasson, then with her father. She should have figured it out by now. There had been opportunity enough—all those quiet times while feeding and tending to Greeley. A logical answer would be that she'd been trying to avoid trouble, but she knew it wasn't that, though exactly what it was, she couldn't say.

Ginny groaned in frustration. This wasn't like her. Not like her at all. She hardly knew herself anymore—and all because of *him*, of the way he made her feel—like a wanton.

A wanton.

The thought froze in her brain, and suddenly she knew what had happened Sunday night, the real reason behind her melancholy mood, the longing, the wanting.

Bonner Kincade.

She stared at the ground, the pulse at the base of her throat throbbing so wildly she could almost hear it. Had she subconsciously known that he was outside her window? No, what a ridiculous thought. Or was it?

She pushed herself away from the wall. "Come on,

Greeley! Hurry up and do whatever you have to do. It's cold out here."

Greeley sniffed yet another weed that had sprung up next to the adobe wall. Apparently this one was more to his liking. He hiked his leg and gave it a sprinkle, then the one next to it. Too bad Greeley's sprinkles didn't kill them, Ginny thought absently. It would save her from having to pull them later. She shook her head, amazed at the things she could find to think about when she was trying to get her thoughts off Bonner.

"Greeley!" she shouted impatiently. He walked toward her, his head hanging. Ginny took a deep breath and stooped to his level, ashamed of herself for her impatience. "I'm sorry I yelled at you." Feeling like an ogre, she tried to make up by throwing her arms around him and hugging him. When it didn't work, she took him into the kitchen and tried a bribe. "How about a nice piece of chicken?" she asked, hoping his favorite food would perk him up. It did and he was himself again.

She got herself a drink of water and went back into the office, wishing that leftover chicken could do for her what it had done for Greeley.

Ginny was alone in the newspaper office, her father having left a short time ago to track down a report of a theft. Holding her pencil between her teeth, she read over her first in a series of articles campaigning for the improvement of Tucson streets. The light and humorous tone pleased her. Writing from her father's point of view, Ginny used real street conditions in a comical situation that she hoped would get the attention of the town council.

Being new in town, I asked for directions to Bostick's Shaving Saloon and was told to head up Main Street and turn right at the second manure pile, which was

Congress Street, then to keep to the left past the dead burro and I'd be there.

Then, she took on the sizes and the shapes of the potholes.

Of particular note is a pothole on Congress Street that is as deep as the Grand Canyon. Mrs. Ben Thompson reports that Monday last, her buggy horse strayed a few feet from where she left it and fell into the hole. The horse and buggy have not been seen since.

Thanks to her father asking every advertising client he talked to their opinion on the condition of the streets, Ginny had a number of colorful comments to select from for her article. After exercising a little editorial license to reword statements for clarity and decency, she used as many statements and names as she could fit in. The more people acknowledged the better, according to her father. He said people liked to see their names in print. It gave them the feeling that they were being heard.

The good-luck bells over the door jingled announcing a customer. Seeing that it was Indy Garrity, Ginny put her work aside and weighed it down with a heavy glass inkstand. She was tired of the wind blowing her papers all over the office every time the door opened.

Indy had promised to come by today with the names of Tucson's most prominent women as well as a list of women's organizations. Almost every town had a relief society and a few even had a suffrage club. At the very least, Ginny hoped there would be a women's literary society. Indy had admitted to being an avid reader with a shelf full of books just arrived from back east.

"Brrrr. It's cold out there," Indy said as she closed the door behind her.

"It's that devilish wind." Ginny came from behind

her desk to take Indy's fringed, woolen shawl. "Go stand by the stove and warm yourself."

"I'm afraid you're going to be disappointed with my news," Indy said a moment later, rubbing her hands together above the stove. "There isn't one women's organization in all of Tucson."

Ginny stopped and turned around midway to the door to hang the shawl on the hook. "No literary society?" She felt her hopes tumble down around her.

Indy shook her head.

"No relief society either?"

Indy lifted one shoulder in a small shrug. "No. Nothing. But my news gets worse than that," she paused and sighed. "Probably the reason there aren't any women's organizations is that there are so few white women living in Tucson."

Ginny swung around. "How many?"

"Thirty-one."

Ginny's face paled. "Thirty-one?" she whispered.

"A few of them are officers' wives like me, but most are wives of merchants and other business owners. Of course I didn't include the good Sisters of St. Joseph's in that figure or the two laundresses out at Camp Lowell."

"I—I don't understand. Pop told me that last year's federal census set Tucson's population at thirty-two hundred. There's got to be more than thirty-one women!"

"Thirty-one *white* women," Indy repeated with emphasis. "The rest are Mexican and Indian. Very few of them speak English let alone read it. I guess I've been so busy setting up house and learning to be a wife that I didn't notice. It's too bad too, because I was looking forward to visiting and teas and all those things I used to do back home."

Ginny slowly walked back to her desk and sat down. "I can't believe it. This is awful." She leaned forward, resting her arms on the desktop.

"I know it's disappointing, but just because there aren't any organizations now doesn't mean we can't start one. I'd be willing to help you start up a literary society. We only need four or five women to begin with. Then, as the town grows . . ."

Ginny shook her head. "No, you don't understand. It isn't just that—it's my articles on women's issues and my serial fiction and—" Ginny cut herself off, realizing what she was saying.

"What are you talking about—your articles and your serial fiction?"

Ginny worried her lower lip. If her expressions didn't give her away, she could always count on her mouth. "Oh, it's nothing really. I do a little writing now and then," she confessed. "But reading is my real love," she added, hoping to turn the direction of the conversation. "You're right, there isn't anything to stop us from starting a literary society."

Indy regarded her assessingly. "Ginny Sinclair. I'm surprised at you. I thought we were going to be friends and confidantes."

"You did?"

"Of course I did. And do," she said. "But how can we be confidantes when one of us isn't being completely honest? I've always admired writers, especially people who write fiction. I'm in awe of their imaginations and their ability to create something from nothing."

"But what would you think of a woman who did that?" Ginny asked warily.

"I'd think she was very brave—a very special woman. A woman I'd be honored to know." Indy grabbed a chair, pulled it up to the desk, and sat down. "Are you going to tell me on your own or do I pry it out of you word by word?"

Ginny rolled her eyes, then laughed. "Everyone will know that I write serial fiction because it will have my name on it, but if people find out that I write articles for the *Sun*—we're ruined."

Indy put her right hand over her heart. "I won't tell a soul. Not even my husband. I promise."

Ginny gave the woman across from her a long look. "All right," she agreed, then little by little revealed her real duties at the *Sun*.

Fifteen minutes later, the good-luck bells punctuated the end of their conversation.

Indy stood up. "I really need to be going. You've got customers," she said, turning to look at the boy who had walked into the office. "But before I go, I want to ask if you and your father would like to have supper with Jim and me this evening? About six o'clock. I know it's short notice but Jim just told me this morning that he has a two-day leave."

"We'd love it," Ginny answered without a second's hesitation.

"Good. I was counting on it so I drew up a map," she said, handing it to Ginny. "See you tonight."

"Yes, tonight," Ginny repeated. Even before Indy grabbed her shawl off the hook, Ginny motioned the boy over to her desk. "What can I do for you, young man?" He was a boy of about fourteen or fifteen. Instead of answering her question, he simply walked up to the desk and handed her a scrap of paper that was as rumpled as the clothes he was wearing.

"Thank you," she said, accepting the paper. Almost as soon as Ginny had opened the office for business last Monday, people started bringing news items in, everything from obituaries to reports of Indian depredations to vicious gossip. Much of what they brought to her was unreadable because of sloppy handwriting or unusable because it was unverified gossip.

Ginny laid the note on the desktop and tried smoothing out the wrinkles with her fingers. The handwriting was scrawled but legible. "Who wrote this?" she asked, poising her pencil to write down the name.

"My pa," the boy answered. "He says he wants ya t'put it in yer newspaper."

Ginny smiled indulgently. "What's your pa's name?"

"Rupert Stinnett."

As Ginny wrote down the name, the good-luck bells rang again.

This time it was Bonner Kincade who came through the door along with a snap of wind. The moment their eyes met, Ginny felt a shock run through her. He closed the door and nodded his head toward the corner, indicating he'd wait until she was finished.

He leaned against the wall, his arms locked in front of him, his right leg crossed over his left at the ankle. The indolent pose was in sharp contrast to the six-shooter strapped around his lean hips. He looked all things he was—arrogant, confident, and dangerous. She would have found his presence disconcerting even if she hadn't realized that he was the cause of all her emotional upset last Sunday night.

His onyx eyes stared at her, a knowing light burning in their depths.

A jolt of alarm paralyzed her. He *had* been watching her outside her window. She hadn't known for sure, but she knew now. He wasn't making any attempt to hide it. She felt her face and neck grow hot but was powerless to stop it.

"Hey, lady," a voice said, bringing her back to the business at hand. She switched her gaze to the boy and wiped a hand across her forehead, not at all surprised to find it damp with perspiration. She reread the note and struggled to remember what it was that she'd meant to say.

"This is a little confusing," she said at length. "It says that Apaches stole two horses from your corral while everyone was sleeping."

"That's right," the boy confirmed.

"If everyone was sleeping, how does your father know it was Apaches who stole the horses?"

"He just knows, that's all. They steal from us all the time."

"I'm afraid that's not enough information for me to put it in the paper. There needs to be a witness or some kind of proof."

"Mr. Wasson—he didn't say nothing about needin' no witness or proof."

"That's the *Arizona Citizen*. This is the *Tucson Sun*." Ginny handed him back the piece of paper. "Two different newspapers. Two different printing policies. I'm sorry but without better information, I can't print it."

"My pa ain't gonna take kindly t'you refusin' t'print his news. He says folks gotta know what them savages is up to so's they can protect what's theirs."

Ginny forced a polite smile. "Tell your pa to stop by and see me the next time he's in town and I'll be happy to explain our printing policy. Now if you'll excuse me, I have another customer waiting." She stood up and glanced over the boy's head at Bonner. "Mr. Kincade?"

The boy whipped around and stomped out of the office, leaving the door open behind him. Ginny silently thanked him. The cold air that he'd let in felt good on her face.

Bonner closed the door, then stood in front of it. "I came by to ask how the dog is doing."

"He's doing fine. Would you like to see him?"

"If it's no trouble."

Ginny moved from behind her desk into the work area. "Greeley?" She looked behind the printing press, his favorite place to sleep but he wasn't there. "Greeley, where are you, boy?"

"You named the dog Greeley?"

Ginny gave a start and twisted around. She hadn't

realized that Bonner was right behind her. Her eyes were level with the third button down from the collar of his coat. "I— Yes," she said breathlessly. "After Horace—"

"I know. The famed journalist. It's just a strange name for a dog."

Ginny stiffened. "Not as strange as Dog or no name at all," she quipped.

He gave a short, derisive laugh.

Behind her, Ginny heard Greeley shaking himself and was glad for the excuse to turn around. "There you are. You must have been hiding." She walked over to him and petted his head.

Bonner's casual reference to Horace Greeley had surprised her. She wouldn't have thought him to possess knowledge of journalists, famed or otherwise. She had the same difficulty imagining Bonner reading Horace Greeley's articles as she did imagining him sitting down to supper and eating apple pie with Indy Garrity and her husband.

"He still has a long way to go before he's completely recuperated but—" Her observation not seeming to interest him, Ginny cut herself off.

Bonner hunkered down, his thigh muscles stretching the rawhide cross stitches that ran the outside lengths of his trousers. "Come here, boy," he said, slapping his knee. Greeley took a tentative step forward, then another.

Stepping back so she wouldn't be in the way, Ginny tried to keep her eyes on Greeley and off the bronzed flesh revealed by the gaping side seams.

"Be careful. He may bite," she warned when she saw Bonner hold out his hand for Greeley to sniff. She didn't know how Greeley would respond to him. He didn't like her father and growled at him every time he saw him, then when he realized that Sam wasn't interested in touching him, he backed off and behaved himself. Bonner turned his hand palm up and started talking to him.

Ginny couldn't be sure what effect Bonner's deep, resonant voice was having on Greeley, but it was certainly having an effect on her, arousing feelings that she didn't want to have, especially not now. He continued to speak to the dog, switching to a language she could only assume was Apache. It seemed a complicated language, full of glottal stops and nasalized vowels, but the way Bonner spoke it made each word sound romantic.

The words stirred her, heightened her awareness of him until she could feel his presence surrounding her, then enveloping her as surely as if he'd put his arms around her. Ginny mentally pulled back, frightened by his power over her.

Greeley, Ginny noticed, had his eyes closed and was letting Bonner rub the sensitive area behind his ears. Then, to Ginny's utter amazement, the dog laid down and stretched out, giving Bonner full access to his stomach.

Bonner smiled and Ginny thought he looked inordinately pleased with himself. She hadn't seen him smile with genuine pleasure before, only sarcasm. She found herself envying Greeley's ability to please him like that. Bonner gave Greeley a final, all-over rub, then stood up, the smile slipping from his face as he turned to face Ginny.

"You've done well," he said quietly, simply. "I didn't think he'd make it."

The compliment caught her off guard and she was a long time in responding. "I—I've enjoyed taking care of him," she said, stumbling over her words like a schoolgirl instead of a twenty-five-year-old woman. Why did just listening to his voice and seeing him smile arouse her?

"You were right not to let me put him down."

There had been a time when she would have

gloated at such an admission, but not now. "I couldn't just give up on him without trying."

"I see that now. I imagine you don't give up on anything or anyone unless you're forced to."

Ginny didn't know what to say. He was right, but she felt uneasy that he seemed to know so much about her when she hardly knew anything about him. Her father was always saying that she fought too hard, often for things that were of little consequence, and that she didn't know when to surrender. But the fact was, she didn't know any other way to live and wouldn't want to. "I would prefer that you don't try to analyze me, Mr. Kincade," she said coldly. She started to turn away, but he caught her arm.

"Don't turn away from me. I wasn't analyzing you, Ginny." He pulled her around to face him.

The low, rich way he'd spoken her name settled over her. Instead of pushing him away like she knew she should, Ginny lifted her gaze to his. "What do you want from me?" she snapped.

"I want you to stop being afraid of me."

"Don't be ridiculous. Why should I be afraid of you?"

"I think you know why, Ginny."

Ginny breathed in sharply, denial springing to her lips, but whatever she might have said got lost somewhere in the fathomless, black depths of his eyes. She felt herself drawn into them, past their mirrored surface that reflected her own frightened image, to a mysterious place, full of secrets and ancient wisdoms.

The good-luck bells pealed out a warning and stopped Bonner from saying anything more. Ginny bolted away from him like a frightened doe and stumbled toward her desk. Her heart was pounding so hard she thought it would pop out of her chest. She heard men's voices through the crack in the door. From their conversation she knew she had a moment or two to compose herself before they came in.

Heaving a sigh, Ginny sat down and willed herself to breathe normally and to ignore the fact that Bonner Kincade stood just a few feet away, knowing her most intimate secrets. Ginny groaned in silence as her stomach clenched. If she didn't get herself together quickly, Bonner wouldn't be the only one who knew exactly what she was thinking and feeling.

The door opened all the way and two men came inside. They were strangers to Ginny. Their hats were pulled low over their foreheads and their coat collars were up around their necks to ward off the freezing wind.

"Good afternoon, gentlemen. How may I help you?" In spite of the fact that her face felt flushed, her heart was pounding double time, and the neck of her blouse felt so tight she couldn't catch her breath, she thought she sounded reasonably calm.

Taking off his hat, the older of the two men stepped forward. Ginny thought she remembered seeing him last Sunday in front of the mercantile but didn't know his name.

"I'm Edward Fish," the man said, as if she should have known. She purposely gave him a blank look. He frowned and Ginny hid a smile. "I'm a merchant here in town. I want to speak to Sam Sinclair, the publisher. It's a matter of some importance." The man's sharp tone was the slap in the face Ginny needed to regain her composure.

"He isn't in right now, Mr. Fish." An appropriate name, she thought, looking at his cold, flat eyes. They brought to mind a wagon load of fresh-caught tuna she'd seen at a San Francisco wharf. "Is there something *I* can do for you, Mr. Fish? I'm Ginny Sinclair. Sam is my father." There had been two other instances that had tested Ginny's professionalism. She had the feeling that Mr. Fish was going to be number three.

As if sensing something awry, the other man came forward and shouldered his friend out of the way. "Let me take care of this, Ed." Mr. Fish reluctantly retreated into the background. "I apologize for my friend here," the younger man drawled, a strong note of Dixie permeating his voice. "My name is Clay Foster. I own Foster's Emporium." He removed his hat and held it against his coat front. "It is indeed a pleasure to meet you, Miss Sinclair, though I have to admit, I have already heard a great deal about you. And if I do say so, what I heard didn't come anywhere near doing you justice."

Clay Foster was a charming rogue, far too handsome for his own good, with a wealth of blond hair that fell over his forehead, long, thick eyelashes any woman would envy, and whiskey-brown eyes. Ginny was immune to his flattery, but it was nice to hear it all the same. It had been a long time since a man had told her she was pretty.

"What can I do for you, Mr. Foster?" she asked, her head tilted to one side.

He flashed her a devastating smile and leaned toward her slightly as he handed her an official-looking document. "We'd be so very grateful if you'd give this to your daddy as soon as he returns."

Ginny perused the notice. More than a dozen signatures of prominent citizens were emblazoned across the bottom of the page.

"This meeting—it's about forming a citizens' militia, isn't it?"

"I don't think that militia is the right word, Miss Sinclair. We're choosing to call ourselves the Tucson Committee of Public Safety. In actuality we're nothing but a group of concerned citizens."

"I see. But considering your intentions, Mr. Foster, I really do think militia is the more correct word."

"Do call me, Clay."

A noise somewhere behind her desk attracted Clay Foster's attention. Bonner! Oh, God! Somehow she had completely forgotten that he was still in the office.

Hanging on to her composure by a thread, she twisted around to see Bonner bent in concentration over the worktable, writing. Greeley was lying close to his feet.

"Ah, Kincade," Clay Foster said to Bonner's broad back. "The last place I would expect to see you is in a newspaper office, but then you do get around, don't you?"

Bonner glanced over his shoulder and gave Clay Foster a perfunctory nod, then went back to his writing.

"I haven't seen King or Ruey in the store for a month of Sundays. That big spread of theirs must be keeping them busy."

Bonner didn't turn around or speak. A moment later he picked up his piece of paper and strode toward Ginny's desk, his expression giving away nothing of his thoughts. "Pa took a fall a couple of weeks back and has been laid up," he answered tersely, not even giving Foster a glance.

"Why, I declare. I am truly grieved to hear that. You tell him that his new boots will be in early next week. I'll send them out if he likes."

"That won't be necessary. I'll pick them up." Bonner set his paper on the desk. To Ginny he said, "I'd like you to run this ad in the next four issues. Bill it to King Kincade, Firehorse Ranch. I'll be in next week to pay for it . . . when I pick up my pa's boots." The look in his eyes told Ginny that he had unfinished business.

Ginny looked down and read what appeared to be an advertisement. *Stud Service available. Firehorse Ranch. Contact Bonner or King Kincade.*

Ginny choked on her own saliva. She put her hand in front of her mouth and coughed. "Next week will be fine," she said with difficulty, her voice scratchy. "I'll have your bill ready."

"Good."

Without another word, Bonner left the office, the

opening door giving access to another cold blast of wind. A godsend as far as Ginny was concerned.

"Begging your pardon, Miss Sinclair. I don't want to tell you what to do, but if I may be so bold as to suggest that you should try not to be here when Mr. Kincade comes back to pay his bill." Clay Foster gave her a long, meaningful look. "He is not the kind of man a proper young woman like yourself should be seen with."

Ginny's mood veered sharply to anger. "You are indeed bold to make such a suggestion, Mr. Foster, and I hope you'll understand why I can't take your advice, well meaning as it may be. But you see my father and I have a business arrangement—he's the editor and publisher and I'm the clerk and book-keeper. It's my job to prepare bills and collect payments." She spread her hands in a gesture of helplessness.

"I see," he said icily.

"You best listen to Clay, missy," Mr. Fish said from near the door. "Bonner Kincade is as wild as that no-name horse of his and twice as dangerous. Business arrangement or no, you're taking a big risk being anywhere around him. And not just with your reputation! If we hadn't walked in when we did, he might have—"

"Mr. Fish!" Ginny interrupted. "That's quite enough! I'll thank you to keep your opinions to yourself. I refuse to listen to your slanderous remarks."

Edward Fish's face contorted with rage. "I'm gonna take into account that you're new in town and don't know our ways. So I'm gonna say this as plain as I can. A white woman what consorts with a half-blood ain't no better than a whore."

Ginny jumped to her feet. "And I'm going to take into account, Mr. Fish, that you have obviously forgotten that you're speaking to a lady." Switching her gaze to Clay Foster, she added, "I'll thank the two of you to remember that this is a newspaper office, a place of business. Not a gossip hall."

"Humph!" Ed Fish jammed his hat back on his head and walked out, leaving the door open behind him.

Clay Foster shook his head. "I beg your humblest pardon, Miss Sinclair. He hasn't been himself since Sunday when the cavalry brought his freight wagons in with all those bodies. On his behalf, I apologize. I hope you won't think too unkindly of him or me."

Ginny lifted her chin, meeting his gaze straight on. "Why I won't think of him or you at all, Mr. Foster. Now, do you wish to pay for your meeting notice in advance, or do you want me to bill you?"

Chapter 8

OUR CAMP GRANT LETTER

Our correspondent must be indulgent. Having published the main portion of his account of Col. Bernard's Indian clean-up, last week, a brief summary of the remainder of the letter (date Jan. 6th) must suffice. . . . He justly compliments the officers and men—Col. B. for fully sustaining his known reputation as an Indian fighter, and Lieuts. Robertson and Kyle for coolness and bravery.

—*Arizona Citizen*

Bonner Kincade led his horse down the jagged scar of a road that some fool had named Main Street. He could tell by the way people veered around him that his angry scowl was warning them to stay out of his way.

He was in a particularly foul mood. It had come upon him the moment Clay Foster had walked into the office of the *Tucson Sun* and interrupted his conversation with Ginny. The smoldering dislike he felt for the Georgia-born merchant went back to Bonner's youth when Foster called him a bastard because the law said his ma and pa weren't really married.

Bonner had made it his business to find out what law Foster was talking about. He discovered a territorial law—intended to keep the white race pure—that prohibited whites from marrying Indians, Negroes, mulattoes, and Mongolians. But since his parents were married before Arizona became a territory, the law didn't apply to them. And the word bastard didn't apply to Bonner, his brother, or his sister.

The truth hadn't stopped Foster from calling Bonner's family names.

But Bonner's fist had.

Over the years, Bonner had developed a sort of cold detachment from Foster and people like him, and he prided himself on his ability to ignore them. But today, something had snapped inside him when the man had turned on his charm and started flattering Ginny in that sappy Southern drawl of his. It was Ginny's reaction or rather the lack of it that had held him back from rearranging Foster's vocal cords. Most women would have tittered and preened at his compliments. But Ginny had ignored them.

It surprised him. And now that he thought about it, everything about Ginny Sinclair surprised him. The iron will, the vulnerability, the bewilderment and nervousness she displayed whenever he came near her.

His instincts told him she was afraid of him but not because of his Apache blood, or the dangerous image people said he projected, but because of the things he made her feel—wants and needs she didn't want to acknowledge to herself or to him.

He'd been making an honest effort to convince her that he had no intention of taking advantage of her, but when her eyes—fever-bright with longing—had looked into his, he'd changed his mind.

If the bells over the door hadn't interrupted them, he wouldn't have been able to stop himself from grabbing her and kissing her. A damn fine thing that would have been if they'd gotten caught—a white woman and a half-breed Apache. It was as much of a taboo as a white woman and a Negro man. Ginny's reputation would have been ruined, and he would have been hanged from the nearest tree.

Needing to clear his thoughts, he vaulted onto his horse and rode over to Camp Lowell. He delivered the news to Colonel Dunn that the citizens' militia meeting was scheduled for Monday night and that official notice of it would be in Saturday's newspapers.

Having completed his assignment, he told Dunn he was going home and that he'd be back sometime next week. His business had only taken an hour, but when he left the tent and went outside it was already dark. He started to mount up when he heard his name called.

"Kincade! Hold up a second." Bonner twisted around to see Jim Garrity riding up on a red roan. The major reined in beside Bonner's horse. "I'm glad I caught you. Where are you heading?"

"Home to check on my pa." He mounted up and eased into the saddle.

Jim leaned forward in his saddle. "I've got something I'd like to talk to you about."

"Can it wait? I've got a long ride ahead of me. If I don't leave soon, I might as well not leave at all."

"All I need is a half hour. I've received a personal communication from Stoneman," he said, as if that explained everything. "You won't be going out of your way if you ride home with me. Come on, we can talk as we ride."

Because Bonner knew better than to take Jim Garrity lightly, he agreed. Keeping their horses to a slow walk, they left Camp Lowell.

Wasting no time on preliminaries, Jim told Bonner his news. "Next Saturday, General Stoneman's report to Washington will be made public. He's making a recommendation to dispense operations at all but eight posts and to break up all the quartermasters' depots except Yuma. Camp Lowell and the quartermaster's depot in Tucson are on his list to be closed down."

Bonner contemplated the information a moment before giving Jim a sideways look. "You know that's going to cause one hell of an uproar? The citizens will scream that the army's abandoning them, and the merchants and contractors will complain the army's taking away their chief source of income." Bonner could tell by Jim's expression that he wasn't pleased with Stoneman's decision. But then, neither was he.

They followed a well-worn track that led them back to Tucson. Instead of going through the center of town, they kept to the outside fringes.

Jim hauled in a deep breath and let it out with a groan. "I tried to warn Stoneman what he would be up against if he goes ahead with his plans. I also told him I thought he'd be sealing his own coffin career-wise, but he didn't care. He was adamant. He's of the mind that the posts he's recommending to close have outlived their usefulness and are nothing but an unnecessary expense to the government." Jim met Bonner's gaze. "It's true. A concentration of troops would save money and improve military effectiveness."

"I agree," Bonner concurred, "but with tempers all riled up the way they are, he's a fool to recommend so many closures at once."

Jim nodded. "Cost cutting and troop efficiency aren't the only things prompting his recommendations. He claims that there's a Tucson Ring—a group of corrupt contractors, merchants, Indians agents, and politicians who are not only swindling the government out of huge amounts of money but are inducing the Indian hostilities to keep the troops in the Territory."

Bonner stared off into the night. "He's been alluding to that ever since he took command."

"He thought he could scare them into stopping by making his suspicions known, but it didn't work."

"Does he name names?"

"They won't be in his report, but in his letter he mentioned several including Clay Foster."

"Foster?"

"According to Stoneman, your old friend is averaging between five to ten thousand dollars' worth of business each week from government contracts. He'd be in for a world of hurt if the army up and left."

"Five to ten thousand a week?" Bonner stared at

Jim in disbelief, his mind racing. After a long moment he said, "Then my hunch was right."

"What hunch?"

"Those freight wagons of Fish's we brought in—I've been wondering if some enterprising merchant didn't arrange to have Lahte attack it in exchange for the Sharps and the ammunition the wagons were carrying." He raked his fingers through his hair, his mind going forward. "The whole thing—it just seemed a little too coincidental and convenient—the attack, the governor's speech charging the army with not providing adequate protection, followed by his endorsement of a volunteer citizens' militia." Thinking while he talked, he said, "I know that the newspapers would have been handed that speech ahead of time so they could print it to coincide with the governor delivering it. But what if Foster had gotten hold of it in advance?"

Jim sat up stiffly in his saddle. "Christ, Bonner, do you know what you're implying here?"

Bonner nodded. "The more I think about it, the more convinced I am that Foster planned the whole thing."

"I have to admit," Jim said with disgust, "it's just the ammunition the Tucson Ring needs to make the army see the necessity of keeping the troops in the Territory. It might even convince them to bring in a few more companies." He shook his head. "But wait a minute. I can see where Foster might arrange to have his own wagons attacked, but those were E. N. Fish and Company wagons."

"But half of the goods belonged to Foster, including those Sharps and the ammunition."

"How do you know that?"

Bonner grinned smugly. "There's this little senorita I visit now and then who checks in his stock."

"Figures," Jim said with a chuckle, then his voice turned serious again. "Except for the weapons, the load itself wasn't worth much. But the nine men who were killed—now that would be worth plenty to the right people. Fuel for Governor Safford's fire, so to speak."

"Interesting we should see things the same way," Bonner said.

"I gotta tell you, Bonner. I don't see Fish doing something like this. I know he's argumentative and outspoken but he's a regular churchgoer and a family man."

"I don't think Fish had anything to do with it. I think Foster used him. What I can't figure though is why Foster would help lead the movement to organize a citizens' militia. Seems to me a militia would make things more difficult for him." Bonner paused a moment to sort out his thoughts. "Unless he thinks the army will view them as troublemakers—in which case it could be another reason to keep the troops around."

"You have a point there," Jim said. "Or maybe he thinks they'll be all talk and no do. That's what I think. When it comes right down to going out and fighting Apaches, every one of them will have a good excuse why they can't go."

Minutes later they pulled up in front of Jim's adobe. "Come on in for a while and we'll try to figure things out."

Bonner shook his head. "I can't. I have to go. But I'll be back late Monday afternoon. I don't want to miss the meeting. I want to see who does the most talking about Saturday's attack."

Jim got down off his roan. "It should prove interesting, that's for sure. Indy and I will plan on being there too."

The front door of the adobe opened and Indy Garrity stepped outside looking exceptionally pretty in a light green dress with a lace-edged bodice. "Jim Garrity. You're late!"

"Bonner and I had something to discuss."

"Well, you can finish discussing it over supper. I have a baked ham, honeyed yams, green beans, and biscuits."

Jim glanced up at Bonner, then turned to his wife. "He can't stay. He has to go home for a few days."

"Oh, fiddle faddle!" She waved her right hand dismissively. "He can leave after he has some supper." She raised up on tiptoes to give her husband a kiss, then walked around in front of the horses.

"You can't refuse me, Bonner Kincade. I made *two* apple pies. And to show you that I've forgiven you for helping my husband embarrass me the other night, I'll cut you as large a slice as you like." She stood near the buckskin's head, her hands on her hips. Bonner got a glimpse of what Jim meant when he spoke of Indy's determination.

His stomach picked that particular moment to growl, and he knew by the way Indy's eyebrows shot up that she'd heard it.

"I'll go set you a place at the table." She smiled up at him, then turned to go back into the adobe.

"Fascinating, isn't it?" Jim asked.

"What?" Bonner dismounted.

"How a certain kind of woman can talk you into doing things you really don't want to do."

Thinking quickly Bonner said, "She's pregnant. I didn't want to upset her."

"Uh-huh." Without another word, Jim led his horse around to the remuda.

Bonner stood still a moment, considering what Jim had said. It was fascinating all right. What kind of woman was she that she could do that? He called out to Jim to wait up. If there really was a *certain kind*—he damn well wanted to be able to recognize it when he saw it.

*   *   *

Ginny was perusing Indy's bookshelves, touching the leather spines with her index finger as she read the titles. Some of her favorite novels were there: *Vanity Fair, Jane Eyre, The Scarlet Letter,* and a dozen more. Ginny attributed her love of reading as the thing that had inspired her to try her hand at writing serial fiction. With the exception of her Joaquin Murietta story, all the others had been pure fiction, romantic stories of lonely young women and handsome men. Writing them gave her a great deal of satisfaction, but knowing that people enjoyed reading them was even more rewarding.

"Please feel free to borrow anything you like," Indy offered a moment after coming back inside. She was prettily flushed. Whether from the cold or from seeing her husband, Ginny didn't know.

"I appreciate the offer. I had to sell all my books along with the furniture my father and I acquired while we lived in San Francisco because we couldn't afford to freight them here."

"What a shame." Indy sounded saddened. "I would have been terribly upset if I couldn't have had my books sent to me. They're the only thing I wanted from my father's estate." Indy pulled a copy of Louisa May Alcott's *Little Women* off the shelf and held it in her hands. The book opened to the center where there was a lock of baby hair. She laughed lightly. "I remember how upset I was when my mother cut this. She told me she'd keep it safe for me here on page one hundred eighty." She touched the softly curled lock with the tip of her finger. "Someday, I'll tell you my family's whole sordid story. It would make a good plot for one of your stories." She put on a brave face, then ran her hand along the bookshelf. "I've read most everything here at least once. If you tell me what kind of book you enjoy, I might be able to recommend some titles."

"My tastes are so varied. I like a little bit of everything," Ginny replied, shrugging.

"Well, you think about it, then let me know." Indy glanced down at the book in her hands and turned the page. Almost absently she said, "I'll have to ask Bonner if he's enjoying the book he borrowed the other night. I didn't think *Frankenstein* would appeal to him but he wanted to read it. It gave me nightmares, but I doubt it'll have the same effect on him. Bonner Kincade doesn't strike me as the kind of man who's afraid of anything." Indy started to laugh, then stopped abruptly and said, "Oh, speaking of Bonner—I almost forgot. I didn't get a chance earlier today to invite him to supper because I couldn't find him in town, but luckily he rode home with Jim and he's going to join us. Isn't that wonderful?"

Ginny stared at the books, momentarily speechless with surprise. "Y-yes, won-derful." Her voice broke.

Indy appeared repentant. "Oh, Ginny. I'm so sorry. I just assumed you wouldn't mind. Bonner, well, he's sort of a family friend and I—"

Ginny laid her hand on Indy's arm. "I don't mind. Really. It's just that he—I mean—whenever I'm around him—he makes me so nervous."

Indy's eyes widened. "Oh, I see."

Just then the door opened. Indy lingered a moment longer, a twinkle in her eyes as she gazed at Ginny. She handed Ginny the book she'd been holding, patted her arm reassuringly, then excused herself and hurried toward her husband. Ginny stared down at the book. No one had to tell her at what point Bonner Kincade walked in and saw her. She felt it. She glanced up from the book, drawn to a pair of eyes that were as dark as a moonless night.

Only a few hours ago she'd lost herself in those eyes. And if she wasn't careful it would happen again, right there in front of everybody.

It was Bonner who pulled his gaze away first. "You

didn't tell me you had guests," he said, looking down at Indy. "I'm intruding." He turned toward the door.

Indy grabbed his forearm and pulled him back. "You're not intruding, Bonner Kincade. I had intended to invite you all along, but I couldn't find you in town. Now hush up and let me introduce everybody." She moved across the room to stand beside Sam Sinclair. "Sam, I'd like you to meet my husband, Major James Garrity. And of course, you've already met Bonner Kincade. Jim, Bonner, this is Sam Sinclair, the new owner of the *Tucson Sun.*"

Sam smiled and extended his hand to Jim. "Good to meet you, Major Garrity. I've heard a great deal about you." They shook hands.

Jim chuckled. "I hope you don't believe everything you hear, Mr. Sinclair."

Sam's smile faded the moment he turned toward Bonner and their eyes met. He stood there a moment, looking as if there was something he was trying to remember.

Ginny closed the book and clutched it in her hands. She wished now that she'd told her father about his drunken behavior in front of Bonner. If coming face-to-face with Bonner reminded him of their confrontation, he'd either be terribly embarrassed or terribly angry.

"I remember you," Sam Sinclair said at last. Ginny's heart sank. "You're the army's civilian post guide," Sam continued a moment later. "You rode in Sunday with the detachment. I told Ginny I thought you were a scout, but someone"—he touched the fingers of his left hand to his temple—"I can't remember who, Wasson maybe, corrected me." He stared at him a moment longer, then shook his hand.

Ginny breathed a sigh of relief. Her father still didn't remember. She hoped Bonner had the good sense not to bring it up.

Indy stepped forward. "I'm so sorry. I thought you two had been formally introduced."

"I'm glad to make your acquaintance, sir," Bonner said, glancing at Ginny as he returned the handshake. "The Territory can use a responsible journalist like yourself."

"You're familiar with my writing, Mr. Kincade?"

"Not your more recent writings, but during the war when you were a field correspondent."

"Well, I'll be," Sam said in wonder. "I didn't think anyone remembered my glory days but Ginny and me. Oh—" He let go of Bonner's hand and turned around toward Ginny. "Please forgive my bad manners, gentlemen. I'd like you both to meet my daughter and my helper, Ginny."

Jim inclined his head. "How do you do, Miss Sinclair. My wife has told me a great deal about you."

"I'm glad to finally meet you, Major," she replied with all the social grace her mother had drummed into her. She stiffened in preparation for her formal introduction to Bonner, as if they really needed one.

"Miss Sinclair," Bonner said. She realized he was leaving it up to her to decide whether or not to say they'd met before.

Knowing how utterly impossible it was for her to keep secrets and make pretenses, she decided that it would be best to tell the truth, or at least a portion of it. "It's a pleasure to see you again, Mr. Kincade."

"You know each other? Where was I when you two met?" Sam asked, looking at Ginny.

Ginny put her finger to her chin to show she was thinking. "Well, let's see now, the first time you were interviewing victims of the Indian attack. The second time—well, it was today. Mr. Kincade came into the office to place an ad for—" She broke off, unable to continue. To cover her embarrassment, she shrugged expansively, as if the nature of the ad had escaped her.

Amusement flickered in Bonner's eyes. "My father

and I breed horses," he explained. "I placed an ad offering our stud services."

"Stud services?" Sam repeated.

"That's right," Ginny said quickly. "I—I forgot what it was called." She swallowed and turned toward Indy, her eyes begging for help.

"Oh, dear!" Indy said suddenly, lifting her chin to sniff the air. "I smell my biscuits. Ginny, would you mind helping me bring out supper?"

"Of course, I'd love to." Thankful for the reprieve, Ginny followed Indy into the tiny adobe kitchen. "Thanks. You're a true friend."

Indy turned around to face her foursquare. "Yes, I am. But you have to get hold of yourself. There's enough sparks between you and Bonner to set Tucson ablaze."

Ginny glanced away, unsure as to what to say. "I don't know what it is about him," she confessed, "but he's like a fire in my blood. I can't stop thinking about him. I've known him less than a week and I—" She couldn't bring herself to say what she was thinking— that she wanted him, more than she'd ever wanted anything in her whole life. "I have to stop this nonsense. It makes absolutely no sense whatsoever."

A secretive smile curved Indy's lips. "I felt that way about Jim the *first* time I laid eyes on him," she confided. "Time has nothing to do with it. Sometimes it happens so quickly you aren't prepared. It might happen in a moment, a day, a week . . . And there's absolutely no explaining it. But"—her gaze lowered as did her voice—"there are some things you need to know before this goes any further."

"What kind of things?"

Indy put her hand on Ginny's arm. "We'll talk about it after supper, in private. Meanwhile, every time you find yourself getting flustered like you did a few minutes ago, or you don't know what to say, look over at me."

"Look at you? How will that help?"

"I can't explain. I just know that it will. Trust me."

"All right. But you don't know the effect he has on me. I'll be looking at you all evening."

When Indy and Ginny brought supper in, the three men came over to the table. It was a small round table that would have been crowded with six but was cozy with five. Ginny sat down between Jim and Bonner while Indy seated herself between Bonner and Sam.

The smell of baked ham made Ginny's mouth water. She was the first one to admit that she wasn't much of a cook. She didn't have the inherent talent for adding a dash of this and a pinch of that that had made her mother such a good cook.

In spite of her talk with Indy, Ginny's nerves were in such a state that she didn't know how much she could eat. But she didn't want it to look like she didn't like the food, so she took a small helping of everything.

"Everything looks wonderful, Mrs. Garrity," Sam said. "I haven't had a home-cooked meal like this since my wife passed away." The moment he finished speaking he grimaced, evidently realizing that his compliment to Indy was also an insult to Ginny. "Don't misunderstand me," he amended hurriedly. "My Ginette is a good cook. It's just that she has never had much time to—"

"It's all right, Pop!" Ginny cut him off. "You didn't hurt my feelings. I don't pretend to be a good cook."

"I wouldn't cook either if I didn't have to," Indy chimed in. "I'd much rather do what you're doing, Ginny. Of course, I don't have any talent for writing. I can't even write a good letter."

Ginny gulped down a green bean. So much for Indy's promise not to tell a soul about her writing. In one fell swoop she'd managed to tell her husband and Bonner at the same time. Ginny was certain Indy hadn't done it on purpose but that didn't remedy the problem.

Ginny thought quickly. "The kind of writing I do is just fiction," she clarified, staring pointedly at Indy whose face went suddenly pale.

"What kind of fiction, Miss Sinclair?" Jim inquired.

Major James Garrity was a man who would capture any woman's attention. His hair was black, his eyes dark brown. Ginny didn't miss the rakish slant to his mouth or the lively sparkle in his eyes. "I write serial fiction. The kind that comes out in weekly installments in newspapers and some women's magazines."

"You know now that I think of it," Indy interjected, "didn't I see one of your stories in *Godey's Lady's Book*? I'm sure I did."

"I've sold them several," Ginny admitted. "And now we're going to reprint them in the *Tucson Sun.* Aren't we, Pop?"

"We are indeed," Sam stated, a proud smile warming his heavily lined face. "We want the *Sun* to be significantly different in format and tone than the other papers in the Territory."

"Have you been in the newspaper business a long time?" Jim asked.

"This is the first time I've owned my own newspaper, but I started out when I was a young man—as an apprentice's devil, learning to hand-spike type on a New York paper." He shook his head and laughed. "Those were the days."

A look of concern etched Jim's brow. "Then, you're not worried that there are already two other papers in town?"

Sam pointed his fork at Jim. "The *Arizonan* isn't going to last. I've talked to Dooner. He knows he's losing ground and he's only keeping things going until he finds something else to do. He blames the majority of his problems on his political involvement." Sam looked down at his plate and cut several bites of ham.

"Come spring there will be only two newspapers in Tucson and they'll be as different as night and day."

Bonner leaned forward and spoke out for the first time. "I assume you've read the back issues of the *Citizen*?" At Sam's nod, Bonner went on. "Then you know where Wasson stands on the Indian situation."

Sam picked up his napkin and touched it to his mouth. "Indeed I do." He paused a moment, looking first at Jim, then at Bonner. "I want you two gentlemen to know that regardless of how I feel about the Indian situation, you won't find my personal opinions in the body of my articles. I firmly believe that the news is the news—who, what, when, where, and why. The opinion of the editor should be confined strictly to editorials."

"That'll be a refreshing change," Bonner said, nodding to Jim.

So far, Ginny had successfully managed to ignore Bonner by focusing her attention on Jim and her father, but now, perhaps because he'd leaned forward, she was once again acutely aware of his presence. She sat up straight, her spine flat against the back of the chair and her hands folded in her lap. The longer he sat there like that, the more nervous she became. She turned her gaze toward Indy, whose raised eyebrow and set mouth cautioned her to compose herself.

"I knew John Wasson when he worked on a newspaper in Oakland," Sam said. "He's a good newspaperman, but he's too opinionated and he likes to dip his pen in acid. If he decides to challenge me or the *Sun* in the *Citizen,* he'll be in for a surprise, because I refuse to exchange invectives with him, nor will I engage in editorial combat. It's not my style."

"Seconds, anyone?" Indy picked up the green beans and biscuits and started them back around the table.

Bonner had been watching Ginny with the intensity of a cat. In a perverse sort of way he enjoyed her nervousness because he knew he was the cause of it.

He thought her determination to hide her emotions admirable but a complete waste of time and effort because it wasn't working.

People often said that he didn't have any emotions—that he was nerveless and cold as ice. They wouldn't say that if they knew what hell he was going through tonight. Every time Ginny leaned forward, the low-cut neckline of her dress allowed him a peek at the soft, rounded fullness of her breasts. The high-necked blouses he'd seen her in before hadn't given him any indication of how well endowed she was.

Tonight, she wore her hair brushed straight up from her nape and piled on top of her head in loose curls that bounced when she moved. Her face was curiously arresting with its high cheekbones, arched eyebrows, and alabaster skin so perfectly smooth he longed to touch it just to verify that it was real.

Although certain she didn't know it, she was seductive beyond description, and he was a damn fool to let himself be tempted. It could only cause him trouble.

A growing tightness in his groin made leaning forward uncomfortable. He sat back, damning a certain part of his body for having a mind of its own. His right leg accidentally hit against Ginny's left leg and he heard her gasp. "Sorry," he said, frowning. But he wasn't sorry at all. In fact, he had half a mind to do it again—on purpose this time—just because he enjoyed her reaction.

"It's all right," she said, but her disconcerted look contradicted her words. She glanced away hastily, turning her gaze to Indy. Bonner watched Ginny a moment longer, then swung his head to his left and caught Indy in the act of mouthing something to Ginny.

He knew it! They were in cahoots, talking about him when he wasn't looking. He gave Indy a smile calculated to intimidate her and said, "Could you repeat that? I didn't get it all."

Indy snapped her mouth shut and glared at him. "I hope you have room for dessert," she said, her voice as sweetly piercing as a honey-tipped arrow.

Something told him he'd just made a tactical error. He grinned his most winning smile. "You *did* say you made two apple pies, didn't you?"

She ignored him and stood up. "Coffee? Tea?" After getting everyone's orders, she headed for the kitchen.

"Major," Sam said as he took another slice of ham from the platter in the center of the table. "There are some things I'd like to ask you. I know very little of the Indian situation in the Territory and I need to be able to understand certain things in order to write with confidence and competence."

Jim finished what he was eating before speaking. "Sure, what do you want to know?"

"Everything you can tell me, but for the moment, I'll settle for asking if you feel the situation between the whites and the Apaches can be resolved."

"Eventually. But it isn't going to come easily as long as neither side is willing to make concessions. What do you say, Bonner?"

Jim was the conversationalist, not him. And this was a topic he didn't like discussing because there was no easy answer and that's what most whites wanted—easy answers. He replied reluctantly. "Peace between the whites and the Apaches is a long way off. When it does come, it won't be because of a mutual agreement or a treaty, it'll be because the Apaches have no choice but to surrender and live on the white man's reservations, under the white man's laws."

Ginny reached for her water glass and brushed her arm lightly against him. Her scent washed over him. "The way you say that, I get the impression you don't approve of the reservation plan," she said, looking at him out of the corner of her eye. "I only know what

I've read about President Grant's Peace Policy, but it seems like a workable idea—you don't think so?"

He turned toward her. "I did at first, when Grant set up the Office of Indian Affairs. But he shifted all the responsibility of making the plan work to others and didn't keep it going the way he'd originally proposed."

"So, how far off is a peace?" Ginny asked, raising the water glass to her lips. If he wasn't mistaken, her lips were trembling.

Bonner hesitated, momentarily unable to think let alone speak. "Ten or fifteen years."

Having sipped her water, she put her glass back on the table, then turned to meet his gaze. "At the rate Indians are killing whites and whites are killing Indians, I don't know whether there will be anyone left to worry about peace ten or fifteen years from now. Why can't they make a treaty of some kind now and get it over with?"

He would have laughed but for the seriousness of her expression. "I hate to disillusion you, Miss Sinclair, but government treaties aren't worth the paper they're written on."

"With so much conflict between the whites and the Apaches, it must be very difficult for you being—"

"A half-breed?" he finished for her, pretending an indifference to the two-word term that he didn't feel, at least not where she was concerned. "There are moments when it's more difficult than others. The hard part is deciding who's right and who's wrong." He looked down at the table. "I admit that there are times when it's impossible for me to know *because* I am who I am."

Ginny stared at him, her eyes luminous in the lamplight.

"Major Garrity," Sam said. "Your wife told Ginny that you were doing some things toward a peaceful end. What might they be?"

Jim looked across the table at Indy. "Bonner and I have tried to be realistic in our thinking. We know that the longer the Indian wars go on, the more people will be hurt and killed. We're convinced that speeding up the Apaches' defeat will help save lives."

"I'm afraid I don't understand, Major," Ginny said.

Bonner appreciated the fact that she seemed genuinely interested and wasn't just trying to make conversation. The list of the things he liked about her was growing and he wished it wasn't.

"One thing I'm doing to speed up the defeat is to train white men in the art of Apache warfare," Jim said. "You see, the fact is that the regular troops are no match for the Apaches. So by training some select troopers to think and fight like the Apaches do, we can confront them in their own strongholds instead of running from them on the desert."

"You said the *art* of Apache warfare?"

"Yes, ma'am. An Apache warrior is the greatest guerrilla fighter there is. He's quick and cunning. He knows how to disguise himself so thoroughly that you'd step on him before you'd see him. He can find food on every hillside and he always knows where to find water. Bonner can tell you. He was raised to be a warrior."

Bonner stiffened and glared at Jim. God, he hated it when Jim used him as an example. Out of the corner of his eye he saw Ginny grow very still and very pale.

In the moment of silence, Jim took the conversation back from Bonner. "There are good things and bad things about both peoples," he explained. "One of the bad things about the Apaches is that they're insistent upon doing things the way they've always done them. They aren't receptive to change, to improvement or progress."

Sam sat forward. "But they must see how things are changing around them—how the white man has progressed."

Jim shook his head. "They see only that the white men are coming in greater numbers and that their weapons can do more damage than before."

Bonner was glad to let the conversation continue on without him. He sensed that Ginny was too. Her face was a changing patchwork and for the briefest of moments he saw something in her expression akin to understanding.

Chapter 9

THE INDIAN QUESTION
CALL FOR A PUBLIC MEETING

Whereas, the hostile Indians of Arizona are enlarging rather than decreasing the area of their ravages as well as the number of their depredations. We've learned the military authorities intend to abandon Camps Crittenden, Lowell, and Whipple, and reduce the force at Camps Bowie, Grant, and McDowell, all of which need to be retained and strengthened for the reasonable protection of the people. We deem it highly expedient to meet and make such just and true representations to those having authority in the premises as may lead to better instead of less security to life and property. We will assemble in Tucson's Court House at 7 ½ P.M. Monday, January 23, 1871. Signed: E. N. Fish, P. R. Tully, Samuel Hughes, D. A. Bennett, and a large number of prominent citizens.

—*Tucson Sun*

Indy and Ginny cleared the food and the dishes away from the table, then brought out the apple pies. Ginny sat down while Indy served. She noticed that Indy cut Bonner an extra large piece.

"Big enough?" Indy asked, nudging Bonner's shoulder as she set the plate down in front of him.

"Better than last time," he said, a smile playing about the corners of his mouth. He speared a piece of apple with his fork and chewed it appreciatively. "Mmmm." He looked up at her. "This is the best."

Ginny was envious of the fact that Bonner loved Indy's cooking so much. Maybe the way to a man's heart really was through his stomach. She smiled to herself. It was almost enough to make her want to learn how to cook. When he finished, he pushed himself back from the table. "That was good. Really good." He wiped his mouth with his napkin, then got up and stood behind his chair. "I hope you'll excuse me, but it's getting late."

"I'm glad you stayed," Jim said.

"Would you like some pie to take with you?" Indy asked. "You've got a long ride ahead of you."

Bonner smiled and shook his head. "What? One man to fatten up isn't enough for you?"

Indy tilted her head to the side. "I just don't want you to get hungry."

Bonner extended his hand to Ginny's father. "Sam, I'll be looking forward to reading your first issue."

Sam stood up and shook Bonner's hand. "I look forward to a chance to talk again."

"As do I."

"Have a good trip."

"Thank you, sir." Bonner turned to Jim. "Unless something comes up, I'll be back for the citizens' meeting."

"If you get back to town in time, come for supper," Indy said as she began clearing the few remaining dishes from the table.

Bonner nodded, then his dark gaze swung to Ginny. "Good night, Miss Sinclair." There was a flicker of profound emotion in his eyes that made Ginny catch her breath, made her reach beneath the table and push the flat of her hand against her stomach to stop the waves of longing.

It was the look in his eyes. The same one he'd given her earlier today when he'd left the office—the look that said they had unfinished business.

"It was nice to see you again, Mr. Kincade," she heard herself say.

Ginny ate the rest of her pie in silence while her father and Jim continued talking. She tried to make herself concentrate. But a part of her refused to pay any attention at all because it was locked in Bonner

Kincade's powerful arms, sitting astride his big buck-skin, riding off into the night.

Indy clapped her hands right in front of Ginny's face, startling her. "Bugs! I'm so tired of bugs I could scream!" Indy stood in front of her chair, leaning across the table, intent on catching the flying insect. "I've ordered some spring chicks from a Mexican farmer I know," she told Ginny as she grabbed at the air. "In March, Jim is going to build me a chicken coop." She followed the circling insect with her eyes and when it landed on the table, she smashed it with the palm of her hand. "Got it!" she announced proudly.

Ginny was completely baffled. "If you don't mind my asking, what do bugs and chickens have to do with each other?"

"Why, chickens eat bugs—all kinds, crawling ones, flying ones, big ones, little ones," she explained. "What with the baby coming, I've been doing a lot of reading. One of the things that concerns me is malaria. We're so close to the river and there's a serious mosquito problem during the summer. It was suggested that a small flock of chickens would help keep the mosquitoes under control around the house and give me fresh eggs at the same time. Who knows? Maybe I'll start a new fashion," she said smugly.

Ginny slowly nodded her head. "I see." At least, she thought she did, but she wasn't sure. At the moment, nothing seemed to make a great deal of sense, including Indy, whose volatile moods were forever catching Ginny by surprise.

"Why don't we get our shawls and go outside for a bit?" Indy suggested. "I want you to meet my little friend." As Ginny moved toward the door, Indy ducked into the kitchen and returned a moment later with a bunch of carrots under her arm. She stopped beside her husband's chair and said, "We're going outside for a few minutes."

Jim looked up at her and smiled. "Give Paco a scratch for me."

She bent over his shoulder to give him a quick kiss. "I will," she said, then motioned for Ginny to follow her to the front door.

A pumpkin-colored moon rode along the jagged edge of a distant mountain. Storm clouds coming in from the northwest were slowly stealing the moonlight and darkening the sky. The wintery air was redolent with animal smells, spicy foods, and burning mesquite. A couple of adobes away a baby cried and a pair of dogs barked. Ginny settled herself in front of the hitching post and listened to the tinny music and raucous laughter coming from a nearby saloon. A feminine squeal punctuated the din making Ginny think of the two Mexican girls who had witnessed her encounter with Bonner outside the Congress Hall Saloon when she rescued Greeley.

"Do things ever quiet down around here?" she asked.

Indy walked out to the middle of the street and looked around. "Not until the saloons close down around one or so," she said.

"What are you doing?" Ginny asked.

Indy turned around and came back. "Looking for Paco, but I don't see him," she said with obvious disappointment. "Sometimes he doesn't come until later."

"Who?"

"Paco. The wild burro I told you about."

"Oh."

"I'll give him a few minutes." A sudden wind caused Indy to wrap her shawl tighter around her shoulders. She leaned against the hitching post beside Ginny. After a moment she began rubbing her stomach.

For the longest time neither of them said a word.

Ginny gave Indy a sideways glance. One minute she was out to murder every bug in Tucson and the next she was rubbing her stomach, soothing her unborn child. Ginny decided that the mood changes must go along with being pregnant.

"Ginny, I—" Indy began, turning to face Ginny, her expression having turned somber. "Earlier, in the kitchen I told you that there were things you needed to know before your relationship with Bonner goes any further. But before I explain, I want you to know that I already consider you a friend and I think—I hope—you feel the same way about me."

Ginny smiled. "Of course I do. The minute you came into the office and introduced yourself, I liked you and knew we were going to be friends. Good friends." She took Indy's hand within her own as if to prove her words.

"Then please try to understand that what I'm going to say, I'm saying because I care for you and don't want to see you hurt." Indy nodded and squeezed Ginny's hand. "There's nothing that would please me more than to see you and Bonner together, as a couple. Next to my husband, Bonner Kincade is the bravest, finest man I've ever known. I respect and admire him greatly."

"I feel the same way and I've only known him a few days."

Indy pulled her hand away from Ginny and smoothed her hair back into its knot. "Bonner has had to make some very difficult decisions in his life. He could have chosen an easier path for himself, one where he wasn't hated and ostracized. He could have walked the white man's path. His father's wealth and influence would have allowed him to do anything he wanted to do. Instead, he chose to be true to his Indian heritage and stay in Arizona and work to bring peace to the Territory." Lowering her voice to a whisper she said, "Ginny, you're new in town, but you already know how the people here feel about Apaches." Ginny nodded. "Well, half-breeds are hated even more. If word gets around that something is going on between you and Bonner, your reputation will be ruined. People will say terrible, cruel things about you, right to your face. They'll call you a whore, a white squaw . . ." Indy sighed and shook her head. "They'll heckle and harass you everywhere you go. I wouldn't be saying this if I hadn't seen it happen before. I don't want to see it happen to you."

Ginny's blood ran cold. She knew what Indy said was true. Through no fault of her own, she'd already experienced two examples of the town's censure. She backed away, needing to gather her thoughts. "I admit Bonner fascinates me," she said after a long pause. "Like I told you in the kitchen, I don't know what it is about him that intrigues me so." She struggled for a better way to describe her feelings, but there simply were no words. "I don't want you to think I'm not grateful for your warning," Ginny said. "I appreciate your concern more than you can possibly know. But please don't worry. Whatever it is that I feel for Bonner—it'll pass. I'm sure of it. I've been feeling a little melancholy lately and . . . well . . . as I said, it will pass." She waved her hand dismissively.

Indy's eyes brimmed with gentle understanding. "I saw how you acted with Bonner, Ginny. I don't think what you feel for him is something that will pass when you're over your melancholy. I think it goes a lot deeper than that."

Ginny waved a hand. "You don't understand." She hesitated to confide her past in Indy, but it seemed the only way to make her see. "Six years ago I was engaged. My fiancé, Tom, had been trained as an engineer at West Point and neither of us thought he'd be called to battle. Then he got his orders and we— I guess you could say we got carried away. The night before he was to leave, we made love." She was surprised that her confession held no embarrassment. "A while later a letter came informing me of his death." She took a deep breath and stared up at the night sky. "When I'm near Bonner, I feel things—the same kind of things I felt that night with Tom, but even stronger," she said, praying Indy would get her meaning without a more detailed explanation.

Indy smiled and touched Ginny's arm. "It's called desire, Ginny, and I do understand. It happened to me too."

Ginny looked at Indy.

Indy nodded. "I felt—still feel—those things for Jim. Sometimes it's so overpowering that I—we—lose control."

"But Tom and I—we'd known each other a long time. For years. I was in love with him." To her dismay, her voice broke.

Indy looked Ginny square in the eyes. "Desire and love don't always go hand in hand. Love is what you feel in here," she said, placing her hand over her heart. "Desire . . . well, desire is a sort of deep longing, a craving that—"

Whatever Indy said was lost when a noise unlike anything Ginny had ever heard rent the air. Ginny peered into the darkness looking for the source.

"It's Paco. He hears us." Indy laughed and put her arm around Ginny's shoulder. "I've said enough for one night. I just wanted you to be aware of the problems." She looked toward the sound of trotting hooves. "Here he comes."

Paco brayed again. The sound was a cross between a foghorn and a screeching train whistle. A little gray burro came into view. Ginny had seen whole pack trains of burros pass by the office window, sad-looking little creatures carrying unwieldy loads of wood or mining supplies. Paco was anything but sad-looking.

Indy moved toward him, laughing with delight. "It's about time you got here." He stopped in front of her and pushed his muzzle into her hand. She rubbed his mane, which stood up stiffly, like the bristles of a brush. "Ginny, come say hello," Indy coaxed. Forcing a smile, Ginny joined them and scratched Paco behind one ear while Indy fed him carrots. "I think he escaped from one of those pack trains," she added.

"Um-hmm," Ginny mumbled, but she wasn't thinking about Paco, she was thinking about Tom. Her eyes misted and she clenched her fists as she tried to remember what it was about him that had made her fall in love. She tried to picture his face, but the image she thought she'd carry with her until the day she died was blurred and indistinguishable. She tried to remember his voice, but all she could think of was Bonner's voice . . . like distant thunder.

"Ginny."

For a moment she thought she'd imagined Bonner speaking her name, then she heard it again behind her, low, resonant, unmistakable.

Indy grabbed Ginny's arm. "Bonner Kincade, you scared the death out of me, sneaking up on us like an Indian."

"I am an Indian, remember?"

"Half Indian," Indy corrected.

"Half Indian," he agreed, his voice strangely tight.

"Did you forget something?" Indy asked.

He nodded, his gaze sliding to Ginny. "More or less."

Ginny's pulse pounded at the sight of him. If she didn't know better, she'd swear that there was magic afoot and that her thinking had brought him back to her. Anticipation coursed through her, playing with her mind as well as her body. Her mouth went dry and she was incapable of speech.

Indy looked from one to the other. "We were just about to go back inside. Would you care to join us? Maybe have another piece of apple pie?"

"No thanks."

"Ginny and I—we were just discussing you." Indy gave Paco a brisk rub along his mane. "I was trying to tell her how things would be if you and she . . . I hope you don't think I'm interfering, Bonner. But I don't want to see either of you hurt."

The lights in his eyes flickered with emotion. "No. I don't mind, Indy. That's partly why I came back. To explain."

Indy bit down on her lip and nodded. "Whatever you two decide, Jim and I will be behind you all the way." She started back toward the house, then stopped and turned. "If anybody asks inside, and I doubt they will, I'll tell them Ginny is getting acquainted with Paco." When Indy opened the door, Ginny heard her father and Jim still involved in discussion.

A sudden gust of wind caught Bonner's hair and whipped it about his chiseled features, giving him a slightly feral look. His black eyes pinned Ginny where she stood. "We need to talk."

Talk. Ginny almost laughed. She'd spent the entire evening fighting her desire for him and here he was, here they were, together, alone. The last thing in the world she wanted to do was talk in spite of Indy's dire warnings. On a shaky breath, she asked, "What do you want to talk about?" Her voice came out in a hoarse whisper.

Bonner gave Paco a tap on the rump and sent him trotting off down the street. He turned back to Ginny. "I think you know." He leaned against the hitching post, looking so sure of himself—and of her. It was as if he knew every secret thought she'd ever had about him.

He reached out his hand, catching the edge of her shawl. "Come here," he said, giving it a tug. Compelled to do as he asked, she took a step toward him but nearly jumped back when he put his hand on her shoulder. "Easy, Ginny. We're just going to talk. Nothing more."

There was that word again. *Talk.* Her breath caught in her throat when she felt him curl his thumb around the lace that edged her squared neckline. His thumb burned her skin as he slid his hand slowly downward, to where the neckline made a right angle across the tops of her breasts. For long seconds he gazed at her heaving chest, silent, unsmiling, then he dropped his hand to his side and stuffed it into his coat pocket. "You're a beautiful woman, Ginny Sinclair, and I'll admit that there's nothing I'd like more than to put you on my horse, take you into the hills, and make love to you the whole night long." Ginny swallowed. A short while ago she'd dreamed of him doing exactly that. "But I know it would end in disaster," he added unexpectedly. "And I think you do too."

Emboldened by her desire, Ginny fingered the edge of his buckskin coat. It was soft. Pliable. "I'm a grown woman, Bonner. I can make my own decisions. I'm sure there would be some who would condemn a relationship between us, but Tucson is full of civilized, intelligent people. I can't believe all of them would."

Bonner's lips thinned and his eyes narrowed dangerously. "Those civilized, intelligent people would make our lives a living hell," he said, his voice lashing out like a whip.

Ginny shook her head. "Oh, Bonner, I think you're making too much—"

Bonner took her by the arms and held her so tightly she gasped. "Wake up, Ginny! The people of Tucson aren't nicey-nice Eastern do-gooders who want to do the right and humane thing by the poor mistreated Indians. They want blood. Apache blood. And on top of that, they want the blood of anyone they think sympathizes with the Apaches. If you don't see that, you're a fool!"

"You're judging all of the people of Tucson like you say they're judging all Indians!"

Bonner shook her. "Dammit, Ginny! Listen to me!"

"Bonner." A sob tore from Ginny's throat. "Let me go, you're hurting me." His fingers pressed to the bone.

He abruptly released her, then stood glowering at her as she rubbed her arms. "How can I make you understand? I admire your spirit, your never-give-in attitude, but the hate between the Apaches and the people of this Territory is something you can't mend or change or fight, no matter how hard you try."

She lifted her chin, eyes flashing. "You're right, Mr. Kincade. I am a fool. I misjudged you. You're afraid of prejudice. You're afraid to stand up against them. You aren't the man I thought you were."

Cold, dark fury moved across his face like a storm cloud. "You're right. I am not the man you thought I was. I'm not a white man," he said between his teeth. "My blood may be only half Apache, but I am *all* Apache here," he said, pounding his fist against his heart. "The Mountain Spirits talk to me. The beliefs of my people are strong within me. These clothes I wear, this revolver and gunbelt, they're all of me that is white." He pulled his knife out of the leather sheath at his waist. "*This* is the kind of man I am, Ginny," he said. He began to circle her. She felt his hand brush her hair but didn't realize what he'd done until he opened his fingers. "I'm a warrior. A savage."

She stared at a lock of her own hair.

"You read the newspapers, Ginny. They say things like, '*Apache—the very name strikes terror in the hearts of brave men. Knife-wielding, breech-clouted savages.*' What makes you think I'm any different?"

If he'd meant to make her afraid of him—really afraid—he'd succeeded. Admirably. Completely. She was suddenly anxious to escape him but he was standing between her and the adobe. "I—I have to go," she said, her voice trembling. "My father and I—we have a lot of work to do to get the paper out on Saturday." She choked on a sob but tried to make it sound like a laugh. "Good night."

She started past him toward the door. Three more steps and she'd be out of his reach.

One.

Two.

She felt him snag her arm and move around behind her. "Ginny, wait. I— God! I can't let you go like this," he said, his voice strained. His breath stirred the hair at the back of her neck. She didn't struggle, didn't make a move to get away. She couldn't. Her feet were frozen to the ground.

Disaster. Hate. Loathing. Fool. Savage. The words echoed in her mind even as she lifted her hand up and reached behind her to his face. Her fingertips wandered from his temple to his jaw, savoring the texture of his skin. She closed her eyes when he captured her hand and pressed it to his lips.

"Bonner." She opened her mouth to say his name but she wasn't sure any sound came out. She couldn't hear above the pounding of her heart.

"I know I should ask you— But I want to kiss you, Ginny. Just one kiss."

It had been so long since she'd been held and kissed. Six years. All that time her body had lain in wait . . .

He put his hand on her cheek and turned her face toward him. He looked at her in silence, then tilted her chin up to his mouth and kissed her, deeply, possessively.

He tasted of apples and spice and sugar. His scent was pure male and it seemed to fill her entire being. His kiss took her to a place she'd never been before. It was all new to her, exciting and more than a little frightening. Wave after wave of sensation rioted through her body as his mouth worked its magic on her. She made a move to turn around so she could kiss him back, but he held her still, denying her freedom. A moment later she knew why.

Just one kiss.

"Good night, Ginny."

Chapter 10

CAMP THOMAS—Officers and men are bending all their energies to complete the Post. . . . From all accounts it will be soon finished and one of the most complete and comfortable in the great interior. Indians furnish wood at $4.00 per cord and hay at $30.00 per ton.
—*Arizona Citizen*

Ginny stood back as her father proudly lifted the front page of the newspaper off the Washington Hand Press and held it up in front of him.

"Ladies and, uh, gentlemen," Sam said, looking first at Ginny, then at Greeley. "I give you the first issue of the *Tucson Sun!*"

Ginny clapped her hands and Greeley barked.

After the ink dried, Sam and Ginny examined it carefully and found it to be absolutely flawless.

"Now that's a newspaper," Sam declared. Ginny knew he was particularly pleased with the layout, which was different enough to call attention to itself— not a single ad on the front page. Only news. The ads were inside and on the back, placed between the articles so that each one stood out on its own. He'd developed the layout while working at the daily *Alta California,* but had never succeeded in talking the editor into giving it a try.

Side by side, Ginny and her father worked throughout the night toward their goal of three hundred copies. Near dawn on Saturday, they put together the last of the papers, stacked and bundled them, then set the bundles beside the door. Sam pushed the two-wheel cart he'd purchased from the wheelwright over to the door and started loading it up.

Ginny knew how anxious he was to get the papers delivered. He wanted Tucson to be able to wake up to the *Sun* and read it before the other two papers became available. "Just give me a minute so I can wash some of this ink off my hands," Ginny said, starting for the door into the hall.

"Ginette. Wait. Before you go—I need to speak to you a moment."

She turned around. "Is something wrong?"

He bent his head slightly downward. "No. Nothing's wrong," he assured her. "I just want to talk to you a moment, that's all."

Ginny's brow creased with worry. "About what?" Thinking the worst, she immediately suspected that his memory had come back, or that he knew how she felt about Bonner.

Sam's expression was somber as he walked across the room to stand in front of her. "Your mother— God bless her—used to complain that I was always so busy I didn't take the time to tell her I loved her and . . . well . . . she was right."

Ginny was relieved that her suspicions were incorrect; however, the mention of her mother was puzzling. In the five years since her mother's death, the only time Pop ever mentioned her was when he was drunk. It was as if the liquor gave him special permission to remember and talk about her.

"She knew you loved her. She didn't need to hear you say it."

Sam bent his head forward. "I should have taken more time with her, told her how much she meant to me . . . and I should have said the words," he insisted. "Now, it's too late." He lifted his gaze to hers. For the first time Ginny noticed how lost he looked, how alone. She realized in that moment that even though she'd lost Tom and would never have Bonner, her loneliness was nothing compared to her father's. "I don't want to make the same mistake with you," he said. "I'd like to think I learned a lesson—a hard lesson, but a lesson all the same." He put his hands on her arms as if to make sure he had her full attention. "I want you to know how much I love you and how proud I am to have you working beside me."

Tears filled Ginny's eyes. After all they'd been through in the last five years, the drinking, the multitude of lost jobs, three major moves, it felt good to know he loved and was proud of her. "Oh, Pop." She leaned forward on the balls of her feet and rested her brow against his chin. "I love you too."

He chuckled softly, then kissed the top of her head. "Thanks, honey. Now go wash off that ink so we can get these newspapers out on the streets."

They returned an hour later. Ginny put the CLOSED sign in the office window and locked the door. Her father went straight to bed and Ginny went straight to the kitchen to heat water for a bath. Once she removed her clothes, she saw that she'd managed to get ink in places that hadn't even seen the light of day.

After her bath, she went to bed thinking she'd fall asleep as soon as her head hit the pillow. Instead, she lay awake and watched the sun climb the sky over the baker's building across the street.

Since leaving Indy's house Thursday night, Ginny had worked almost around the clock writing, editing, proofreading, and typesetting. She'd driven herself mercilessly, not only to help her father but to keep herself so busy that she wouldn't have time to think about Bonner and the way they'd left things between them. But now, with the first issue of the *Tucson Sun* out of her hands, the time had come.

Tears sprang unbidden to her eyes, then slid down onto the pillow. "Stop it, Ginny. Just stop it," she chastised herself, wiping at her eyes with the sleeve of her nightgown. She wished to God she'd never laid eyes on Bonner Kincade. From the moment she'd seen him ride in with the troopers, his dark presence had filled her thoughts and dreams.

Her throat constricted as she visualized him standing in front of Indy's house, the powerful perfection of his body etched against the big orange moon. She'd been trying to send him one message while he'd been trying to send her another. Hers was that she desired him and was willing to take the risk. His was all about what would happen to them, that she couldn't change people's prejudices no matter how hard she tried, and that she fancied she knew all about him, when in truth, she didn't know anything about him at all.

He'd called himself a savage and had shown her a side of him that had scared the death out of her. And then not more than a minute later, he'd asked to kiss her and displayed another side. A gentle and tender Bonner.

Excitement. Fear. Passion. They were a heady combination of emotions that had robbed Ginny of her reason, overpowered her self-control, and left her raw with need and desperate wanting.

She had wanted him. She still wanted him. More now than ever.

Ginny rolled onto her side and drew her knees up tight. She'd never felt so empty.

"Yee-haw, ya cock-eyed sons of a bang-tailed, knock-kneed jackass. Git on with ya now or I'm gonna sell the lot of ya to the butcher man!"

Ginny came awake with a start. The booming voice seemed right outside her window. She raised up on her elbow and looked out through the curtains. A block-long span of mules pulling a high-sided freight wagon and four wagons in tandem lumbered past, harness jingling like Christmas bells. The mule skinner, a giant of a man with a flowing white beard that melded with his hair, was perched on a seat as high as the flat roofs of the buildings he passed.

Ginny threw the covers aside and reached for her wrapper at the end of the bed. She stood up and stretched, wondering how much of the day she'd slept away and why she didn't feel any more rested now than when she'd crawled into bed.

She walked across the room and caught her reflection in the mirror above the dressing table. She was shocked at what she saw. Puffy eyes. Blotched cheeks. And a red nose.

She sat down and continued to stare at herself. Not only did she look awful but she realized that the person looking back at her wasn't the logical, sensible Ginny Sinclair she'd always known. Something had happened to that Ginny. This new Ginny was a lonely, impulsive woman ruled by her emotions and passions.

Displeased with herself, she got up, dressed warmly, then took Greeley out through the office door.

Main Street virtually hummed with activity. She hadn't been outside long when she realized there were more people and animals on the street than usual. A group of Mexican housewives, their faces concealed by dark *rebozos,* hurried by, water splashing from their ollas. Their chatter reminded Ginny of a tree full of angry blue jays. In front of the bakery, two fashionably dressed matrons stood talking. Thinking they might be the social type, she decided to walk across the street, introduce herself, and ask them if they might be interested in joining a literary society. She checked on Greeley first and saw that he was busy sniffing anything and everything, then started across the street only to be stopped short by a military detachment led by Major Jim Garrity. Ginny waved and Jim touched the brim of his hat in acknowledgment.

No sooner had they passed than Greeley started barking. He sounded irritated, even a little frantic. Ginny hurried to see what was causing it.

He was rooting around in the wood pile beneath her father's bedroom window, sniffing, blowing, pawing at the wood.

"Greeley!" Her father wouldn't appreciate being

awakened by a dog. He completely ignored her and started barking again.

"Greeley, for heaven's sake, what's the matter with you?" Then it occurred to her that there was something in the wood pile that was causing him to bark. Thinking he might have sniffed out a mouse, Ginny approached with trepidation. She hated mice. "What's in there, boy?" With her hands clasped behind her back, she cautiously leaned forward to examine the wood pile. She wasn't about to go poking around with her hands until she knew what was in there, but nothing seemed to be moving. "I don't see—" She cut herself off when she saw something shiny. Whatever it was, it was buried beneath a couple of pieces of mesquite. She looked at it from various angles before deciding it wasn't going to jump out and bite her, then moved the wood away and reached in for it.

"Oh, no," she whispered as she pulled a whiskey bottle from the wood pile. The bottle was half-full, Pop's favorite brand. She glanced up at the window. A coincidence? Or had he taken to hiding his bottles so she wouldn't see them?

She examined the label that was curled at one edge, and decided it looked old, or at least weathered. It must have been in the wood pile for some time, which meant it couldn't be her father's. She felt elated by her conclusion as well as relieved. She was considering what to do with it when Greeley started to growl.

Ginny looked down at him, confused. "What now?" He was staring at the bottle, his ears lying flat against his head. "Is it this?" she asked, lowering the bottle to his level. Whining pitifully, Greeley shrank away, his tail between his legs. Ginny tucked the bottle into her skirt pocket and bent down to pet him. "It's all right, boy," she said in soothing tones. "Come on." She stood up and beckoned him to follow her. After a moment he came, walking slowly, head down. He looked as if he were going to his own funeral.

Once Greeley was back inside, he perked up. Ginny fed him and got him settled down in his bed, which consumed one corner of the sitting room. She settled herself down on the sofa across from him and studied him. She wasn't sure what to think about what had just happened. Was it possible that Greeley had associated the whiskey bottle with the beatings he'd received from Mulligan? She leaned her elbow on the table beside her and rested her chin against her hand as she continued to stare at the dog.

Dreary, Desolate. Ugly. Ginny didn't know which of those words best described Tucson. Even the three of them combined didn't do it justice. Everywhere she looked, she saw long, narrow adobe buildings, some plastered with mud, a few whitewashed.

She spent the rest of the afternoon familiarizing herself with the various mercantiles and dry goods stores and shopping for groceries. Tucson had no shortage of goods from which to choose. But the prices were considerably higher than in San Francisco, more than likely due to the high cost of freighting, which averaged about twelve cents per pound if freighted from San Francisco. Eggs were $1.25 a dozen, coffee $4.00 per pound, and bacon $.75 cents per pound.

Everywhere she went, people were talking about the coming meeting. Ginny realized she'd underestimated how important the meeting was to the town.

A large group of men were gathered outside Mansfeld's Pioneer News Depot and Bookstore, many of them with newspapers under their arms or sticking out of their pockets. Ginny recognized a few of the men as business owners she and her father had solicited for ads.

"Good afternoon, gentlemen," she said when several of them looked her way. An avalanche of snow could not have had a more chilling effect on their conversation than her presence. She heard a mumbled chorus of salutations that were accompanied by doffed hats and half smiles. She felt them watching her as she walked inside the store.

Ginny picked up one copy each of the *Arizona Citizen* and the *Weekly Arizonan,* but she didn't see any copies of the *Sun.*

"Sold out!" declared Jacob Mansfeld, the round-faced business owner, when Ginny inquired as to what had become of twenty copies she and her father had delivered earlier that morning. "Ve could've sold a dozen more if ve'd had them," he said, his German accent permeating his nearly perfect English. "I told anyone who vanted one zat zhey could get zem directly from you and your fazer, right?"

Caught by surprise, Ginny nodded quickly. "Yes, of course," she answered automatically. They *had* kept some extras, hadn't they? She couldn't remember.

"Vord of mouth travels fast around here about anyzing new."

"And what is the *word* about the *Sun* if I may ask?"

"Folks seem to like ze layout and zey got a good laugh out of ze repair ze streets article," he offered.

Ginny hadn't realized how anxious she'd been until now. She breathed a sigh of relief. "My father will be pleased to hear that. Anything else? What about the news of the citizens' meeting?"

He stroked his long, dark whiskers and rolled his eyes. "Vell, now zat's ze big news. Lots of talk about ze meeting. Lots of excitement. Of course, you know ze *Sun* vasn't ze only paper to report on it."

"Yes, I know. But what I didn't know until just a little while ago was how people would react to the news of the meeting. I've never seen such excitement."

"The formation of the citizens' militia is ze first ray of hope a lot of zese people have had in a long time. Lord knows ze army hasn't done anyzing. If ze troops here in Tucson would devote a little less time to fan-

dangos and billiards and a little more time to pro-
tecting our citizens, zere vouldn't be any need for a
volunteer force."

"No, I suppose not." Ginny paid for her purchases.
"Thank you, Mr. Mansfeld."

Eager to see if John Wasson had printed the Stinnett boy's unverified report in the *Citizen,* Ginny
started searching the columns the moment she turned
away. She found a small article on the second page.
It was no more than two hundred and fifty words and
stuck near the bottom. The information was highly
embellished from what had been written on the note
and what the boy had told her. Anyone reading it
here would never guess there hadn't been any wit-
nesses and that the entire incident was speculation.

Deep in concentration, Ginny walked out of the
news depot and into a pair of strong arms. "Oooh!
Excuse me. I—" The man grasped her tightly around
her shoulders. With a wall of newspaper between
them, she couldn't see who it was. She tore down the
wall. "Why, Mr. Foster. I'm so sorry. I didn't see you."

"It's no wonder what with a newspaper in front of
your face," he said. There was a gleam in his eyes
that made Ginny nervous.

She stepped back, glad to be free of him. "Yes,
well . . . you're absolutely right. I was comparing notes
so to speak and not paying attention to where I was
walking." She neatly folded her newspaper and
stashed it into her carpetbag. "Nice seeing you again,
Mr. Foster." She started to move away but was
stopped by his hand on her elbow.

"Please don't hurry off, Miss Sinclair. I'd like to
speak to you a moment—about the *Sun.*" She half
turned and met his gaze. Seeing that he had her attention, he continued, "I have to admit I've doubted the
logic in bringing a third newspaper into town. But now
that I've seen the *Sun* . . . well, I feel I owe it to you
to tell you that I no longer have any doubts."

Ginny eyed him with a quizzical gaze. "I didn't know you felt this way in the first place, Mr. Foster, why do you feel it necessary to tell me about your change of heart?"

He hesitated. "Because I like you, Miss Sinclair. I admire your loyalty to your father, your intelligence, your industry, even your pluck. And I wanted to clear my conscience and tell you that you and your father have my good wishes and my support."

Ginny eyed him uncertainly. "Thank you, Mr. Foster. I'll be sure to tell my father."

"I do wish you would call me Clay. It's so much friendlier."

"That's true, Mr. Foster, however, we aren't friends, but merely acquaintances," she said with all earnestness and saw his jaw go rigid.

"Yes, well, that would be easily remedied if you would give me permission to call on you."

Ginny had no wish for Clay Foster to call upon her. In spite of his good looks, there was something about him that didn't ring true. "I'm flattered, Mr. Foster, but I really can't be away from the business until we're on some sort of schedule." Ginny lowered her eyes. "I'm sure you understand, being a business owner yourself."

"Foster," a voice boomed somewhere behind Ginny. Ginny turned to see a hugely fat man with a bulldog face and a barrel chest coming toward them.

"Rolfe!" Clay Foster declared, clasping the man's outstretched hand. "I didn't know you were back in town. May I present Miss Ginny Sinclair. Her father owns the new newspaper, the *Tucson Sun.*"

"*Miss* Sinclair, is it?" The man smiled, eyebrows raised. "I'm Rolfe Brown."

"It's a pleasure to meet you, Mr. Brown." He seemed a friendly man.

"I read the *Sun* first thing this morning. Impressive. Very impressive. Particularly liked the coverage of last week's attack on the Fish wagons. Very dramatic. Sensitive. Just the kind of thing that makes the folks back east cry." His mouth quirked in a small smile. "I should know, since I was recently one of those folks who looked forward to reading the Western presses with great enthusiasm. Why, if it wasn't for Clay here, talking me into coming to Tucson and opening a bank to put all his money into, I'd still be reading about it rather than living it." The man burst into laughter and slapped Foster on the back. "I don't know whether to thank him or hate him."

Clay Foster didn't look amused. His mouth tight, he nodded briefly. "Will we see you at the meeting Monday night?" Foster queried.

"Of course. Me *and* the missus. She's determined to have a part in everything going on in *her* town. And you know Emma." He shook his head and rolled his eyes.

Ginny smiled. She liked Rolfe Brown. He seemed utterly genuine in spite of his association with Clay Foster. "Mr. Brown, I'm considering starting a women's literary society in town. Could you ask your wife if she'd be interested in joining us?"

He raised one eyebrow. "Well, I— Of course. I think she'd like that. Lord knows we have enough books that she could probably start her own library."

"I'd appreciate it. The *Sun*'s office is on Main Street, across from the bakery. Maybe you could ask her to stop by."

"I will. Now, I have to be going but it was good to meet you, Miss Sinclair. And I'll see you later, Foster."

"Land sakes! A literary society no less," Foster said, grinning. "Before you know it, Tucson will be a thriving metropolis."

It was the tone of Clay Foster's voice that made Ginny think he was mocking her. She looked him right in the eye, jutted out her chin, and smiled. "I was also

considering starting up a suffrage club," she said, just
to be contrary.

"A suffrage club! My goodness! I don't think that's
a good idea, Miss Sinclair."

Ginny stiffened. "Why, Mr. Foster, don't tell me
you're one of those men who opposes a woman's right
to the ballot."

"Why, I—I don't oppose or support the woman's
suffrage movement, Miss Sinclair."

"Perhaps you don't understand it?"

"I understand it perfectly well."

"From the male perspective, of course."

"Well, I can hardly understand it from the female
perspective, now can I, Miss Sinclair?"

Ginny struggled to keep her voice light and even.
"It just so happens I'm writing a special article for my
father on an upcoming women's rights convention in
San Francisco. It'll be in next week's issue. I think
you'll find it quite enlightening." She raised her chin
and said, "In fact, I'd better get back to it. Good day,
Mr. Foster." She turned on her heels and walked off.

Congratulating herself on the way she'd handled
Clay Foster, Ginny headed up the street. She hadn't
gone far when she saw her father.

"Pop," she called, immediately gaining his attention.
He came over to her and she squeezed his forearm.
"I think the *Sun* is a success," she said in a low tone
so no one but her father would hear her. "Mr. Brown,
the banker, was very complimentary just now. And
Mr. Mansfeld, the owner of the news depot, said folks
liked the format. He's already sold all the copies we
delivered to him this morning. I couldn't remember,
but did we keep any extras? He told people who
didn't get one to come by and get them from us."

"I set aside twenty-five, but half of them are gone.
People came to the door asking for them."

"Oh, Pop! This is your dream come true!"

"Indeed it is, Ginny. Indeed it is," he said, patting

her arm affectionately. He turned toward the group
of men Ginny had passed on her way into the news
depot. "What's all that about?"

Ginny shook her head. "I don't know. They were
there when I went into the news depot."

"Do you have your pencil and notepaper with
you?"

"Of course. Would I be your daughter if I didn't?"

Sam laughed. "Let's move a little closer so we can
hear what they're talking about."

"Pop, that's eavesdropping!"

"No it isn't, honey. Not where journalists are
concerned."

"Oh, Pop," she said, grinning.

"It's high time somebody took the situation in
hand!" one man's voice rose above the others.

"I want justice for my boy!" Ginny recognized the
baker, whose son had been killed driving one of the
E. N. Fish wagons last week.

"Don't be gettin' your hopes up too much," the
liveryman interjected. "It ain't like this is the first time
the town has put a militia together. They did it back
in '65. Didn't last a year 'cause there weren't no
money to support it. The men near starved to death."

Rolfe Brown spoke out, his voice as big as his girth.
"Things are different now, gentlemen. Tucson has
grown. We've got some strong leaders like Foster,
Fish, and Hughes. Men of courage and decisiveness.
They'll see that things are done properly."

Ginny grimaced at the mention of Clay Foster's
name as a strong leader.

"I'll believe it when I see it," the liveryman grumbled. "Until then, I ain't even gonna bother dusting
off my old Henry."

Ginny scribbled notes as fast as she could, hoping
she didn't miss anything. A few minutes later the
group disbanded.

"The saloons are going to be lively tonight," Sam

said, looking wistfully after a trio of men heading down the street.

Ginny knew where his thoughts were. "I have to finish getting my groceries. Would you like to come with me?"

Sam smiled. "Sure. Let's go."

Ginny spent Sunday afternoon writing the article she'd mentioned to Clay Foster.

THE WOMEN'S RIGHTS CONVENTION

Beginning May 17th, San Franciscans will host a convention dealing with all aspects of women's rights. Women from all over the country and from all walks of life are invited to attend and share their experiences and expertise with their sisters.

One of the greatest obstacles to the growth and progress of the women's suffrage movement springs from the inherited and generally accepted idea that women are by divine arrangement far below men in intellectual power, reason, judgment, and foresight. It is believed that they are incapable of self-support and self-control, and consequently are unable to properly appreciate the complicated duties of citizenship.

In spite of this, women do not wish to denounce men as tyrants or usurpers. In fact, they have confidence in men's sense of justice. However, the most respectable and popular male leaders, whose opinions carry great weight, stand aloof from this movement. By doing so, they virtually declare to the public that women are not entitled to the ballot.

Ginny could only hope that Clay Foster would see himself in the article as one of those respectable and popular leaders who by not committing stood in the way of women getting the vote. She'd met the man only twice but she already had a clear sense of the kind of man he was, and she wanted nothing to do with him.

She continued on with the article, deprecating the

law that gives a man the power of using his wife's income immediately after marriage for his own purposes. She pointed out that women in several other countries retain the rights to their property even after marriage and show great aptitude for business.

It was late afternoon when Ginny finished and put down her pen. She walked over to her father's desk and stood behind him, looking over his shoulder. "What are you doing?"

"Comparing our coverage of the news to Wasson's and Dooner's." His spectacles had slipped all the way down to the end of his nose.

"And how *do* we compare?" she asked, eager to hear his evaluation.

"Our articles tend to be shorter than theirs. We have more quotes. More facts. No personal opinions. No speculation. And we're not as wordy."

"Is that good or bad in your opinion?"

"My opinion is of no importance. It's the public's opinion that matters. There were a lot of positive comments today, but we have to remember that the news of the town meeting sold a lot of papers. It will be weeks yet before we know where we stand against our competitors."

Ginny moved back, laced her fingers together, and stretched. "I'm going in to start supper. How long do you think you'll be?"

"I'm nearly done. I'll be there in a few minutes."

Ginny went back into the kitchen and started gathering ingredients for supper. She'd been thinking about tonight's meeting all day long. She realized now how important it was to the townspeople, and knew what was important to them was important to the newspaper.

She dropped an egg and watched it splatter on her shoe. A few minutes later she dropped the teakettle.

"Crimeny!"

She opened the kitchen door to get a breath of fresh

air. She'd tried to tell herself that she was nervous about tonight's meeting—because she wanted to take good notes. But she knew it wasn't the meeting that had her nerves frazzled.

It was the knowledge that Bonner Kincade would be there.

Chapter 11

"The Indian is a peculiar institution. And still, he is a human being. A good many persons seem anxious to forget that fact."

—General George Crook,
Tucson Sun

Bonner rode by rote down out of the foothills of the Santa Catalina Mountains. Tucson lay straight ahead, its lights glittering like a handful of rough-cut diamonds against a blue velvet sky.

By day, Tucson looked more like a dirt clod—brown, and shapeless. With each rain, some of it washed away, back into the earth from which it had come, only to return as soon as the sun came back out.

Bonner hated the long, barren stretch of miles that lay between the foothills and the northern edge of town. It always made him think of the vast gulf of misunderstanding that existed between the Apache and the white man. He wondered if there was anything or anyone who could bridge that gap and bring the two peoples together in peace.

He pushed the buckskin into a ground-eating run, anxious to put the last few miles behind him. He was too late for that pre-meeting supper Indy had invited him to last Thursday. He would have to take his chances that the Shoo Fly would stay open for those who wanted to gather for pie and coffee after the meeting. But the big money would be made on whiskey at the saloons, where the majority of the meeting-goers would gather to rehash everything that had gone on.

His visit with his mother and father had been a short one—too short as always, but in this instance he was especially glad he'd taken the time to go.

His father's leg didn't seem to be healing as quickly as Bonner thought it should. The swelling had gone down but the bruises remained. A sturdy walking stick enabled him to get around without too much difficulty, but it was obvious that he couldn't put his full weight on the leg yet. Of course, he denied being in pain but Bonner knew better. There were some things a man couldn't hide.

Bonner had tried to talk his father into coming to town with him to see Doc Wilbur but he'd stubbornly refused. "It's healing," King had said. "Getting better every day. Just ask Ruey. She'll tell you."

He *had* asked his mother, and she'd backed her husband up as Bonner knew she would. She was Apache, brought up to obey her husband in all things. She would not go against his wishes, even when he was wrong.

Bonner decided that tomorrow he would stop by Doc Wilbur's office, describe his father's condition, and ask the doctor what he thought. Regardless of what he said, Bonner thought he'd draft a telegraph message to Logan and ask him for his opinion as well. He would send it with the next stage to the telegraph office in San Diego. They'd relay it to San Francisco, then it would go east. Logan would probably get it by the end of the week.

It had been four years since his brother had been home. Logan and their father didn't get along too well, but he wouldn't stay away if he thought his father needed him. And it just might be that King did. Bonner wasn't going to exaggerate his father's condition, but he thought it might not hurt to make Logan feel a little guilty that he'd been gone so long.

Martine had been away when Bonner arrived at the ranch. According his mother, his little sister spent more time in the mountains with her grandfather, learning the ways of The People, than she did at home.

Seventeen years ago, when Bonner had been her age, he, too, had spent a great deal of time with Gianatah's band, playing games with other boys his age and learning the ways of a warrior. Two years later, Logan had followed in his footsteps.

But things had been different then. There hadn't been the danger there was now with whole companies of soldiers patrolling the mountains and searching out their old strongholds. In spite of Colonel Dunn's promise to keep his troopers away from Gianatah's band, there was still the chance that the two groups would meet and there would be trouble.

Bonner had talked at length with his parents about Martine's future and her education. They'd decided that Bonner would inquire about the curriculum at St. Joseph's Academy for Young Ladies in Tucson. The school had opened last year and the sisters took boarders and day scholars.

Bonner hadn't mentioned it to his parents, but he didn't think St. Joseph's would be the best choice for Martine. He knew they wanted to try to keep her as close to them as possible, but he remembered an ad in the newspaper about the academy that said they paid *particular attention* to plain and ornamental needlework. Music, drawing, painting, and flower making were also on the list. But there was no mention at all of the academic subjects.

Bonner couldn't see Martine sitting down for any length of time doing needlework or flower making. She liked sewing hides together to make clothes and knife sheaths and such, but he doubted she'd ever made a sampler or a doily.

He thought he might check the newspapers for tutors, someone who would come live at the ranch for a few years. Someone who could teach Martine not only history, geography, and mathematics, but some social skills as well. And how to dress and act like a lady. God knows, it would take an extraordinary person to get Martine out of buckskin breeches and into a dress, let alone make her sit down and do her studies. Obviously, she would need a female tutor. A spinster or maybe a widow.

If a suitable tutor couldn't be found, Martine would have to be sent east to school, which might be the best choice after all. She wouldn't find the stigma attached to half-breeds or Indians there that she was certain to encounter in the West.

He doubted Martine would like anything they were proposing, but Bonner wanted to see her grow up with every available opportunity.

Suddenly he had a thought. While he was drafting the telegraph message to Logan, he would mention that their father was looking for a female tutor for Martine and state what qualifications she would need. Maybe Logan would know of just such a paragon of academia, virtue, and courage.

Finally, he would tell Logan that Martine's puberty ceremony was coming up and remind him that he'd promised their little sister he would come home for the occasion.

Once he's sent off the message, he'd pick up his father's boots from Foster's and stop by the *Sun* to pay his advertising bill.

Ginny had been on his mind almost constantly since he'd left her standing there alone last Thursday night. He knew now he'd made a mistake going back. His intentions had been good. He'd built up a full head of steam to tell her all the reasons why they had to ignore their feelings for each other.

But Indy threw him off guard by stating before he got there the things he'd meant to say. It had surprised him at first. He didn't think their attraction to each other had been that obvious, but then, Indy was an astute woman. She'd been thoughtful to warn Ginny, but Bonner realized Ginny hadn't taken her as seriously as she should have.

Ginny hadn't taken *him* as seriously as she should have either, which was why he'd resorted to scare tactics—to make her genuinely afraid of him—of the savage Apache side of him that she refused to acknowledge. He'd succeeded, but instead of feeling victorious, he'd felt like a rat. It was one thing to scare a man with his knife-wielding tricks, but another to scare a defenseless woman.

Guilt had hampered his judgment. He should have left well enough alone. It would have been better for her. Better for him too. Instead, he'd tried to make amends and the next thing he knew he was kissing her.

Now, there would always be that memory between them.

"Injun meetin' at the Court House. Time for action." The drummer beat the alarm drum as people traveled through the streets.

In spite of the cold, a large noisy crowd had gathered outside the Court House waiting for the doors to open. Ginny and her father had arrived early so they could meet people and hear what they were saying.

"You can pick up better information by listening to idle conversation than from all the prepared speeches and interviews the politicians give you," Sam whispered to Ginny in an aside.

Ginny saw several people she knew by name. John Wasson was shaking hands and welcoming people to the meeting as if he had sent each of them a personal invitation.

"Sam. Miss Sinclair. Congratulations! Terrific first issue," he said in his stentorian voice.

"That's kind of you to say, John, considering that we're competitors," Sam replied in his usual even tone.

It looked to Ginny like John Wasson was amused by her father's reaction.

"Well, there's nothing like competition to keep a man on his toes. I'm going to have to go some to keep up with you, but then, I expected as much. You always were a brilliant newspaperman." Wasson turned to Ginny. "And before I forget, Miss Sinclair, I really enjoyed your Joaquin Murietta story. I had occasion to meet Joaquin some years back in a California mining camp, and he was just as you've described him, *handsome, dashing, and utterly dangerous.*"

Ginny felt her cheeks flush as Wasson quoted her own words. "That's very generous of you, Mr. Wasson."

"Not at all, Miss Sinclair. I simply like to commend talent when I see it. I've always aspired to write fiction but I don't seem to have the imagination for it," he said, smiling.

Having read his articles and editorials from the last six months, Ginny would have disagreed with him, but she thought better of saying anything.

"Anyway," he continued, "I think the people of Tucson will enjoy having some short, well-written fiction to read. It will be a welcome respite from the problems that are plaguing our Territory. Will you be writing articles and editorials as well?"

Ginny glanced at her father. "No. My contributions are going to be limited to serial fiction and an occasional article pertaining to women, such as suffrage, temperance, fashion, and social activities. I'll leave the editorials and the local, national, and foreign news to my father. He knows about such things," Ginny replied, hoping she was convincing.

"A wise decision, Miss Sinclair. Now, if you'll both excuse me, I must get to saying my hellos."

Ginny wound her arm around her father's. "How'd I do?"

"You were brilliant."

She breathed a sigh of relief.

Edward Fish arrived with two other men. His lips

thinned disapprovingly when he spied Ginny. The only thing the man could possibly have against her was that she hadn't let him intimidate her.

Clay Foster rode up to the hitching post on a flashy palomino. He acknowledged her gaze with a nod, then joined Fish's group, standing near the doors to the Court House.

"I'm freezing," Ginny complained. "I wish they'd hurry up and let us inside."

Sam checked his pocket watch. "Only about a minute to go." When he looked up from putting the watch back in his vest pocket, he nudged Ginny. "Here come your friends."

Ginny glanced up to see Indy Garrity walking toward the Court House between two unusually tall, formidable-looking men, Major Jim Garrity and Bonner Kincade.

Bonner. Shivers of longing coursed through her. She'd known this moment would come, and though she'd mentally tried to prepare herself for it, she was unable to control the excitement that sparked inside her. She couldn't help but wonder if he felt it too.

She turned away, determined to put her feelings for him where they belonged—in the past. Because there couldn't be any future. Her hands, hidden beneath her heavy woolen shawl, twisted nervously.

"Oh, Ginny," Indy said, rushing forward. "The *Sun* is wonderful and I *loved* your Joaquin Murietta story. I had no idea you were so talented. I can hardly wait to read the next chapter."

Indy's enthusiastic response brought a short, pigeon-breasted woman over to them. "Excuse me. I couldn't help but eavesdrop. I'm Mrs. Rolfe Brown." She looked at Ginny. "You must be Miss Sinclair. I, too, loved your story and am so looking forward to more. My husband said he spoke with you and that you're going to start a literary society."

Ginny glanced at Indy and they smiled at each

other. "Mrs. Rolfe Brown, this is my friend, Mrs. Jim Garrity. *We*—Indy and I—are going to start a literary society," Ginny corrected the woman. "And we'd be delighted to have you join us and anyone else you know who would be interested."

Out of the corner of her eye Ginny saw that Jim and Bonner had joined her father. A moment later she saw Mr. Brown approach the group accompanied by several other businessmen who seemed generous with their praise of Sam, smiling and patting him on the back.

It looked to Ginny that her father was actually blushing from all the accolades. She pressed her lips together to stop herself from getting emotional, but her eyes misted anyway.

Behind her, the Court House doors finally opened and people hurried to get inside out of the cold. Mrs. Brown bid Ginny and Indy good-bye and promised to drop by the *Sun*'s office later in the week to set up a first meeting.

Indy took Ginny's arm and walked into the meeting room ahead of the men. "Where do you want to sit?"

"Pop?" Ginny asked, turning slightly.

"Near the middle of the room but at the end of the row. That way we can see and hear everybody."

Jim moved around the two women and led the way. He stopped at a center row, then took Indy's hand and pulled her along between the wooden benches. Ginny followed Indy and was relieved to see her father right behind her. An entire evening sitting next to Bonner Kincade would have been impossible to bear.

They were about to take their seats when Ginny noticed that Bonner wasn't with them. "Where's Bonner?" she asked, looking around the room.

"He doesn't like to be cooped up," Jim said. "Makes him uneasy."

Ginny nodded. More than likely Bonner had gone his own way to stay as far away from her as he could.

She sat down and smoothed her skirt over her knees, then readied her pencil and writing tablet.

About eighty people attended the meeting. Vast majority—merchants, freighters, saloon and hotel owners, lawyers, supply contractors, and some ranchers.

J. E. McCaffry, Esq. walked up to the podium, introduced himself, and presided over the election of a chairman, secretary, and the appointment of a ways and means committee. On motion, Judge John Anderson, judge of the Territorial Probate Court, was elected chairman. William J. Osborne—secretary. Messrs Rowell, Fish, and Alsop—ways and means.

Judge Anderson took the podium and quickly dispensed with the meeting formalities, then opened the discussion with a prepared message. "The purpose of this meeting is to allow each and every one of you to bring forth your grievances about the Indian situation and the army. Afterward, we will undertake to decide on a proper course of action based on what we've heard." He paused a moment, his keenly observant eyes assessing the crowded room. He cleared his throat. "Every man and woman here knows that the present condition of the Arizona Territory is deplorable in the extreme, by reason of the continued successful raids of hostile Indians."

Grumbles filtered through the room, and somewhere a muffled sob.

Ginny's mind replayed the frightening scene when a knife-wielding Bonner Kincade sliced off a lock of her hair.

Judge Anderson continued, his expression a little softer. "Hardly a one of us hasn't suffered the loss of a loved one, a friend, valuable stock, or the destruction of a home or business."

"We all have!" someone cried.

The judge looked in the direction of the voice. Decision and sagacity once again limned his stern features. "Be that as it may, whatever decisions are made here tonight, I pray that they will be made with regard to the best interests of the people—all the people, which includes the Indians."

Gasps of undisguised disapproval greeted that suggestion.

The judge straightened, his eyes narrow. "What we—all of us—fail to remember is that the Indians *were* here first. This was their land and we have taken it from them without their permission. In other words, we have stolen it from them in the name of Manifest Destiny. We do a lot of talking about what the Apaches do to us, but let us not forget that hundreds of Apache men, women, and children have been killed by white men." His gaze slowly traveled over the crowd. "I will now open the discussion to you, the people of this great Territory."

The applause was sporadic and halfhearted. Ginny looked around the room and got a strong sense that the judge's comments hadn't won anyone's good opinion but possibly her own and her friends'. The good citizens of the Arizona Territory were scowling as if he'd betrayed them. Obviously, they didn't want to be reminded that they'd stolen the Indians' lands, or killed hundreds of Indian people. They wanted to hear that they were the victims, and as such they had a moral right to rid the Territory of the evil Apache menace.

With a blast of frigid air, the Court House doors burst open and Bonner Kincade stepped inside. Ginny caught her breath. He looked angry, forbidding, and his buckskin coat and knee-high moccasins screamed enemy.

Apache.

Everyone in the room turned to look at him.

"What's that damn half-breed doin' here?" The man sitting behind Ginny's father spoke in private to his neighbor, but not so private that Ginny couldn't hear him. "He thinks just 'cause his pappy's a big man in the Territory that he's different than other Injuns, but he's got another thing comin'. He ain't no better than any of them bloody butchers."

Not Bonner, Ginny's mind yelled at the man. She would have given anything to stand up in Bonner's defense and tell everyone how he'd saved her and Greeley from certain death, how he'd reasoned with her drunken father, and how gently he'd kissed her in the moonlight. But, of course, she couldn't. She couldn't say anything at all.

"I'd be careful he don't hear you," another man said. "I seen 'im knife a man once and it weren't a purty sight, let me tell ya."

Low comments and whispers drifted to Ginny's ears.

A man near the front of the room shot up off the bench. "I thought this here was a meetin' fer the citizens of Tucson."

Judge Anderson eyed the man. "It's a meeting for the people of the Arizona Territory, Sherod. What's your problem?"

"Kincade there, he's the problem. Indians and half-bloods ain't citizens. Everybody knows that."

"Sit down, Sherod. You're out of line. Bonner Kincade is a long-time resident of this Territory and a civilian post guide for the United States Army."

"Jesus hell, Judge," the man shouted. "How can we talk about what we aim to do 'bout the 'Paches with the likes of him in the room? Why, no sooner will we make plans than he'll hightail it off to Cochise and spill the beans."

"Sheriff Ott, will you please escort Sherod outside and point him toward the closest saloon where his complaints will have a more receptive audience than they do here?"

The sheriff responded, going down the center aisle and standing at the end of the row next to where

Sherod sat. "Come on, Sherod. The judge says you're outta here."

"I ain't aleavin'. I gotta right to speak my mind jes like everybody else." He crossed his arms and stubbornly refused to budge.

Ott reached down, grabbed him by the back of his shirt collar, and dragged him off the wooden bench. "One way or another, you're leavin', Sherod. It's up to you."

"All right. All right." The man gained his feet and walked toward the doors. "Half-breed, bastard!" He spat a tobacco wad at Bonner's face, but missed and hit the sheriff instead.

"That does it, Sherod. You're goin' to jail!"

"Oh, God," Ginny said beneath her breath, then closed her eyes. How could people be so cruel?

Indy reached across Ginny's lap and took her hand. "Don't let people like that get to you, Ginny. Bonner doesn't. And he wouldn't like it if he thought you were feeling sorry for him."

Ginny nodded.

Indy leaned close to Ginny's ear. "This is the kind of thing I was trying to warn you about the other night," she softly whispered. "People treat him like that all the time—calling him names, questioning his integrity, his loyalty. You name it and they blame him for it. Even Jim and I get criticized for our friendship with Bonner."

Ginny bit down on her lip and nodded. She glanced over Indy's shoulder and saw Bonner walk to the very back of the room and lean against the wall. He didn't look the least bit upset by what had just happened. Because she knew that he wasn't a cold, unfeeling man, that he was in fact warmhearted and compassionate, she couldn't imagine that he wasn't hurting inside.

She was. Deeply. Grievously.

John Wasson stood, distracting the crowd's attention. He held up a piece of paper. "I have received a

Washington dispatch which gives General Stoneman's report following his inspection of the whole Department of Arizona," he stated. "I plan to summarize and extract from this document in next Saturday's *Citizen* as I'm sure my competitors will do as well." He turned to smile at Sam and Ginny. "However, I think the information is important enough that it be divulged here, tonight, before this assembly."

"If you think it's information we need to have, John, then stop beating around the bush and tell us what it is." The judge's impatience was beginning to tell.

Ginny and Indy looked at each other and smiled. The judge's abrupt, no-nonsense manner made him the perfect man to deal with such an emotionally charged crowd.

"As everyone knows, General Stoneman assumed command of the Department of Arizona in May of last year, at which time there were eighteen posts. Three have since been discontinued. Now, he recommends there be a concentration of troops at eight posts, that all the quartermasters' depots, except Yuma, be broken up and the civil employees be let go." Wasson paused and looked around the room. "He *says* this will increase the efficiency of the command and aid the Department in the reduction of expenses. Camps Bowie and Grant are to remain, but Camp Lowell is on the list of those he wishes to abandon."

Shocked silence followed the announcement.

Then, an explosion of voices.

"Our own government is abandoning us!"

"Stoneman's a damn fool!"

"We'll be left without any protection at all!"

"I'm packin' up and leavin' this godforsaken Territory. With the 'Paches runnin' amuck, it won't be safe for man or beast."

Ginny thought of Bonner standing in the back of

the room listening to all this. She wondered how he had any heart left for the white man.

The furor swelled.

People stood up in front of their seats and shouted at each other, at Wasson, at the judge.

Indy clamped her hands over her ears.

Ginny wrote down everything she could.

Judge Anderson banged his hand against the podium. "All right everybody quiet down now," he urged. "People, I said quiet down," he repeated. No one seemed to pay him any mind. "This kind of outburst won't—"

"It's up to us!" someone yelled. "The army doesn't care about us."

"Quiet!" the judge bellowed.

Ginny's pencil lead broke.

Sam handed her another.

She turned to a new page, trying to keep up with the pandemonium. She lifted her eyes to gauge the judge's reaction, her heart pounding wildly as she watched him reach beneath his coat and pull out a deringer.

"I order this assembly to be silent!" He raised the deringer above his head and pulled the trigger. The little deringer spoke loud and clear.

Gasps, shrieks, curses, and a woman's scream answered the report.

Gun smoke swirled in the air above the judge and bits of adobe from the ceiling rained down. "Now that I have your undivided attention," he said, his voice soft and cold. "I'll advise you that if there's another outburst like that, I'll aim lower! Now behave yourselves or I'll call the meeting adjourned and you can find yourselves another chairman! From now on, if you wish to speak, you will raise your hand and wait until I call upon you."

Ginny was secretly enjoying the disgruntled faces dotting the crowd. She couldn't resist drawing one on her tablet and sharing it with Indy who discreetly giggled behind her hand.

"Edward Fish. Your hand is up."

"Yes, Mr. Chairman. I'd like to say that I think Stoneman is out to ruin every merchant in Tucson, maybe even the Territory. We depend on army supply contracts for our livelihood. Once Camp Lowell and the quartermaster's depot are abandoned, I'll be out of business within the year!"

"I'm not sure why you think that, Ed," the judge replied. "It's my understanding that the government is obliged to advertise its supply needs and let contracts go to the lowest bidders. If you continue just as you have been, then nothing should change."

Ed Fish tossed his head in disgust. "That's the way it's *supposed* to be, but that isn't necessarily the case. With the quartermaster in Yuma, my guess is that the Californians will get the bids. For one thing, they won't have the freighting expenses we do. Besides that, I do a lot of business with the troopers themselves. With them gone, so is that business."

"Anyone else like to comment?" the judge asked. "You there in the back row."

"What this Territory needs is for Stoneman to be relieved of his command!"

At the first hum of agreement, the judge put his hand out in front of him to stop it. "Thank you for your comment."

Clay Foster raised his hand and was recognized by the chair. "I agree with that gentleman. Stoneman is nothing but a paperwork soldier anyway. If he paid as much attention to our Indian problem as he does to building new army posts and sprucing up the old ones, we wouldn't be here tonight trying to decide what course of action to take. Where were our troopers when Lahte attacked the Fish and Company freight train? Out surveying for a new road, that's where. If they'd been patrolling the field like they should have been, we wouldn't have nine new graves in our cemetery!"

Ginny lifted her gaze from her paper and glanced back at Bonner. Pain and sorrow stamped his darkly handsome features now, telling the world that he was not the bloodthirsty savage they thought he was. But nobody was looking. Nobody except Ginny. She had to fight an overwhelming urge to get up off the bench and go back there to comfort him. Something must have alerted him that she was watching him. His eyes met hers and he changed his expression to show her how unconcerned he was.

"Major Garrity, you were in charge of that detachment. Would you care to respond?" the judge asked.

Ginny turned to see Jim stand up.

"Yes, sir. Thank you, sir. For the record, I'd like to state that me and my men were not surveying roads. We were patrolling the main wagon road. I suggest Mr. Foster check his facts before stating them and they are erroneously printed in some of our local newspapers." He looked around the room, meeting the stares with confidence. "Once we saw the smoke, we rode post haste to the scene."

"A heck of a lot of good you troopers are if you can't be there when our people need you," a woman shouted.

Jim looked the woman straight in the eyes. "We can't be everywhere at once, ma'am. I wish we could." Jim turned to Foster and glared at him. "Unfortunately, nine of the ten teamsters were dead or dying when we got there and several of the wagons were engulfed in flames." Jim sat down, then stood up again. "Excuse me, but there's something else I'd like to say while we're on the subject of Lahte's attack."

"You have the floor, Major Garrity."

"I had a *personal* communication from General Stoneman last week. In it, he relayed information that would be in his report, which I'm sure Mr. Wasson can verify should there be a discrepancy. For some time now, the general has alluded that supply contractors are taking advantage of our troops by demanding exorbitant prices for fuel, forage, and beef. His report will cite specific instances to back that up. He also has reason to believe that some of Tucson's merchants—called the Tucson Ring—are inducing Apaches into hostilities for their own gain." Jim paused as the roomful of people whispered to each other. At length he continued. "Evidence reported to me by Bonner Kincade indicates that the Fish wagons were sabotaged by a ring member—a fellow merchant, Judge."

Ginny had no grounds for her suspicions, but she'd bet that Clay Foster had something to do with it.

"I don't believe it!" Ed Fish shouted, his face in a red rage. "There is no such thing as the Tucson Ring. My God, don't you think *I* would know about it?"

The judge pointed to a man in the front row.

"It figures that the army would try to take the blame away from the Indians. And that Bonner Kincade would be involved. But to accuse our own merchants—there's no end to their audacity, I tell you. No end to it!"

"The chair recognizes Clay Foster."

"Major Garrity. Do you really expect the good citizens of Tucson to trust evidence reported by a no-good half-breed?"

The muscle in Jim's cheek ticked as he eyed Clay Foster. "I'd trust Bonner Kincade over you any day, Foster. But the fact is, this isn't a matter of trust. We have evidence and we are about to make formal charges."

The moment Jim sat down, Indy twined her arm around his, showing her support.

"Rupert Stinnett has his hand up."

Ginny craned her neck to see the father of the boy who'd brought her the ambiguous theft note. A bram-

ble bush of dark whiskers surrounded his thin face
and a mustache outlined his downturned mouth.

"Seems to me we oughtta make sure everyone
knows what's goin' on. Now, I got me a small ranch
south of town. Until a few days ago I had me a couple
of good work horses, but the Apaches come in the
middle of the night and run off with them. And this
ain't the first time they've done it, no siree. Since I
couldn't come into town myself, I done sent my boy
with a note to give to the newspapers so's other folks
in the area could be warned. My boy, he come back
from town and tells me that two of the newspapers
done took the information and thanked him for it, but
the third one gave him nothin' but trouble and refused
to print the information. I thought the newspapers
were here to help folks, not hurt 'em."

Ginny was seething. Without even knowing what
she was going to say, she raised her hand.

"The chair recognizes the pretty young woman on
my left."

She stood up. "Judge Anderson, my name is Ginny
Sinclair and I'd like to respond to Mr. Stinnett's com-
plaint, since it was me who turned his boy away without taking his information. Mr. Stinnett's note stated
the Apaches stole two horses from his corral while
everyone was sleeping. My question to his son was, if
everyone was sleeping, how did his father know it was
Apaches who stole the horses? The boy replied that
his father just *knew* and that they stole from him all
the time. We have a motto at the *Tucson Sun* that
isn't just words but a way of doing business. The *Sun*
is the voice of truth and reason. Because I couldn't
determine that the information I received was truthful,
I didn't consider it reasonable to print it. Thank you."

Ginny started to sit down when her father caught
her arm and stood up beside her. "As the owner and
editor of the *Sun,* I'd like to say that I am in complete
agreement with my daughter."

As they resumed their seats, Ginny gave her father a hug. "Thanks, Pop."

"My pleasure, honey."

The judge took a drink of water, then said, "I call upon Rolfe Brown."

"I'm from back east and if it wasn't for Clay Foster, I never would have come here. I've always thought that the Arizona Territory was nothing but a worthless desert, unfit for habitation. I couldn't understand why anyone in their right mind would want to live here." He looked around, then shrugged his shoulder. "The truth is, that's the way most Easterners think. If I may be so bold as to suggest that if you want the authorities in Washington to sit up and take notice of your plight, you need to make them aware of the vast resources that are unique to the Territory as reported by last year's legislature."

"Well said, Mr. Brown. Next?" The judge pointed to Clay Foster.

"It's bad enough that the federal government is failing to defend us against the Apaches, but now they want to put them on reservations where the government can protect them and feed them! The reservations are nothing but refuges from which the savages can base their raiding activities."

Ginny clenched her fists. The *savages* were the deceitful, lying merchants who were responsible for killing their own kind.

There was more talk about the pros and cons of the proposed reservation system, Grant's Peace Policy, and the temporary *feeding stations* where Indians were given food and blankets. Complaints were brought against Colonel Green at Fort Apache for giving shelter and protection to a number of Apaches who professed to want to live in peace, build homes, and establish farms. The main objection was that Green was paying the Apaches to cut wood and hay so that they could buy food, blankets, and clothing. The contractors in the room were against this because the Indians were undercutting their prices.

At length, the conversation turned to the immediate problem of what to do about the Apaches. Was a volunteer force the answer to their prayers? Or should they try one last time to get the government to listen to their grievances with the hope that they would see the problem and take immediate and strong action?

Ginny listened, alternately amazed by the depth of hatred for the Apaches and eager for details as she scribbled her notes.

Finally, the judge called for a vote. Ginny was heartened when a citizens' militia was unanimously voted down. The majority of the people felt that they hadn't given the government a fair chance, and that the army was still the best bet since they had the men, the supplies, and the money. If, after every effort was made, there was still no resolution in sight, a citizens' army would be reconsidered.

On motion, Judge Anderson called the meeting adjourned.

Ginny continued to take notes even as she followed her father, Jim, and Indy out of the Court House. *People enthusiastic and optimistic. Hope for Arizona's future if Washington will only listen. Apaches, no hope.*

She stuck her pencil over her ear and covered her tablet. Once they were outside, she looked for Bonner but he was nowhere around.

Sam turned to Jim. "This business about the Tucson Ring and sabotage— My, God, Jim. That's incredible! I'm not going to ask who you suspect because I assume you have to keep it quiet until you make formal charges, but I am going to ask if you'd let me have an exclusive for the *Sun.* I'll do the story justice."

Jim nodded. "I know you will, sir. And if it's all right with my superiors, it'll be all right with me. The only reason I said anything tonight was because I figured if the ring knew the army was onto them, they'd think twice before sabotaging any more of our citizens."

"But, Jim—" A worried look worked its way across Sam's face. "These are ruthless killers you're talking about here. Don't you feel you're putting yourself and Bonner in jeopardy?"

"Bonner, me, and Indy—we talked about it and all of us agreed that it was a risk we were going to have to take."

Sam looked at Ginny and smiled. "I guess we know a little something about taking risks too. Don't we, honey?"

Ginny smiled back at him. "Well, it's not quite the same thing, Pop. But I'd say moving here to the frontier and starting up the third newspaper in a town of just over three thousand people, most of whom don't speak English, was something of a risk. Yes."

Sam patted Ginny's arm. "But it will be worth it in the end."

"I hope so, Pop."

Jim put his arm around Indy. "That's the same way we feel. It'll be worth it. Nine men are dead because of the ring's greed, and Lahte has twenty-four more Sharps and God only knows how many rounds of ammunition to kill more Arizonans."

"Ginny, honey. I want to talk to that Rolfe Brown for a few minutes. He seems like somebody I'd like to know a little better. I won't be long."

"I'll wait for you here, Pop."

"No, it's cold. You go on home." He glanced up at Jim. "Since you and your wife are walking that way, you won't mind seeing my Ginny safely home, will you?"

"Of course not," Jim replied.

"But, Pop. You might need me to take notes."

"I'm not going to interview him. I just want to talk to the man. Now be a good girl and go on home."

"Pop, promise me—" She stopped herself. He was

a grown man. He would either keep his promise to her or he wouldn't. "Don't be too long. We have a lot to do tomorrow," she reminded him.

"I'll be home early." He kissed her on the cheek. "You did a great job tonight, honey. I'm proud of you."

"Thanks, Pop. I'm proud of you too. Please don't let me down." Her eyes beseeched him.

"I won't. I promise."

Chapter 12

The Old Pueblo lay cold and naked beneath the winter moon. The streets shivered with the excitement of the meeting-goers as they headed off to their favorite saloons.

Ginny walked in silence beside Jim and Indy, lost in the privacy of her thoughts. Tonight's meeting had been an eye-opener in more ways than one. Judge Anderson's opening comments had made her see that the people of Tucson—at least some of them—owned up to the fact that white men had robbed the Indian of his lands and deprived him of his liberty. Yet, in spite of knowing they had wronged them, they refused to see the Apaches as anything but savages, fighting and raiding for the pure joy of it.

The citizens' meeting had given her a good overview of how the people of the Arizona Territory felt about the Indians and the army. Except for what little she'd picked up from Bonner and Jim, she knew practically nothing about how the Indians felt.

She wondered if either of the two editors in town knew more than she did, or even cared to know.

The trio had gone less than a block when Indy suddenly stopped. "We forgot Bonner! He missed supper.

I thought he might want to come home with us to have a piece of pie."

"I think he's probably gone on without us," Jim said.

They turned the corner just as a whiskey barrel rolled out into the street. Jim stopped it with his foot, then rolled it back to the side of the road.

"You always did think you were something, Kincade," an angry voice declared from the shadows to Ginny's right. "But the truth is you're nothing but vermin!" Ginny squinted into the darkness. There was no mistaking Clay Foster's syrupy Southern drawl or the steely baritone that followed.

"What'll it be, Clay? Fists? Guns? Knives? You call it. This is your fight, not mine."

"Oh, no!" Ginny covered her mouth with her hands.

"Jim, you should stop them," Indy pleaded urgently.

Jim shook his head. "Foster has been egging him on for years. They need to have it out once and for all. Especially now after the things he said tonight."

"I'll take my chances against your fists any day of the week, half-breed." Foster moved out of the shadows into the moonlight.

Ginny crossed her arms beneath her breasts, holding her shawl tightly against her. She'd never watched a fight before and didn't want to see one now. It was frightening but exciting. Wasn't that the way everything was that had to do with Bonner Kincade?

While Clay Foster meticulously folded his coat and draped it over the hitching post behind him, Bonner shrugged out of his buckskin coat and tossed it behind him to Jim, followed by his gunbelt.

"Don't forget your knife, Indian boy," Foster gibed, smiling as he rolled his shirtsleeves up to his elbows.

Bonner pulled the knife from its sheath and slid it across the ground to Jim.

Ginny grabbed Jim's arm. "Jim, please. Do something!"

Jim nodded. "Hey, Bonner. You'd better take your shirt off. You don't want to mess it up. Indy wants you to come back and have some pie with us."

Indy elbowed her husband in the ribs. "Jim Garrity," she scolded in an outraged whisper. "How can you treat this so casually?"

"Would you two stop worrying? Bonner knows what he's doing."

Bonner pulled his shirt over his head and flung it behind him.

Ginny reached in front of Jim and caught it. "You have enough to hold," she told him. She breathed in Bonner's masculine scent as she draped the shirt neatly over her arm and smoothed it with trembling fingers. He'd worn this same shirt the night he'd kissed her.

"Anytime you're ready, Foster. You make the first move."

Bonner stood near the center of the street, his broad back facing Ginny. She caught her breath at the way the moonlight silvered his black hair and spilled down around his leather-brown torso. He stood with his legs slightly apart, his arms straight against his sides, and his hands close to his thighs. His stance created enough of a strain on his buckskin breeches so that they looked to be molded to his buttocks and thighs. She stared at the lean swell of his thigh muscles wondering if those rawhide cross-stitches were going to hold.

Ginny chastised herself for thinking about Bonner's muscular virility at a time like this, but she could no more control her wayward thoughts than she could take her eyes off his body.

Putting his fists up in front of him like a boxer, Foster thrust his left arm toward Bonner's head.

Bonner raised his right forearm and diverted the blow, then kicked Clay in the knee.

Foster moved back and eyed Bonner carefully. He looked to be rethinking his strategy. He was nearly as tall as Bonner but his arms weren't as long or sinewy. Suddenly he darted forward and threw a fast right punch aimed at Bonner's groin.

Bonner sidestepped the punch and whirled about, his forearm slamming against his opponent's head and knocking him to the ground.

Bonner stood over him, his wide chest like burnished copper in the low light. "We can stop now if you like."

Foster groaned and rolled to his side. "No thanks. I've been waiting a long time for this and I aim to see it through. You've got a few moves I haven't see before, but I go one or two you haven't seen. So we're even."

"Whatever you say." Bonner stepped back and waited.

Foster picked himself up and tried some fancy footwork, then a left punch and a stranglehold, but each time he ended up right back on the ground.

"All right, Kincade," Foster muttered. "I'll admit you're stronger and quicker than I am." He rolled to his side, then slowly got to his feet. "So you won't mind if I even things up a bit, will you?"

Ginny saw Foster whirl around and gasped when she saw the glint of a knife. Bonner twisted away from it just in time, the blade missing him by a scant inch.

Ginny was outraged. But even before she could react, Jim put an arm in front of her to hold her back. "He's cheating!" she protested, grabbing Jim's arm with both hands. As if to wall her in, Indy moved around to her other side and put her arm around Ginny's shoulders.

"Be quiet, Ginny," Indy whispered. "Don't distract Bonner."

"But Jim has his knife!"

"If Bonner wants it, he'll ask for it. Now, shhh."

Ginny looked away, unable to bear seeing what she feared would be a bloody slaughter. She didn't understand how Jim and Indy could stand there and do nothing. They acted as if fights like this were a common, everyday occurrence. At the first grunt of pain—she wasn't even sure whose—a shudder passed through her and she thought she was going to be sick.

For what seemed an interminable amount of time, Ginny listened to the sounds of violence. A small crowd of people from the meeting gathered around them. None made a sound. They merely stood and watched, just like Jim and Indy.

Slowly, Ginny turned her head back around. Bonner was facing her now, some twenty feet away, but even from that distance she could see the lightning in his black eyes. He crouched forward, moving ever so slightly back and forth, a few inches to the left, then to the right, but never standing still for more than a moment.

Raising the knife above his head, Foster let out a roar of pure rage and charged Bonner. Bonner parried the downward thrust with his right forearm held horizontally above his head, then took a step backward.

"I'm getting tired of this, Foster."

"Not as tired as I am of you, half-breed!"

Ginny noticed that Foster seemed winded while Bonner took normal, even breaths.

Suddenly Bonner sprang like a cat against Foster, a move that got its momentum from nowhere. Bonner grabbed Foster's knife hand and twisted it back until the bone cracked.

The blade fell harmlessly to the ground and Bonner kicked it toward Jim, who picked it up and stuck it in his belt along with Bonner's.

Foster twisted away and grabbed his coat, wrapping

it around his hand like a giant bandage, and staggered off toward the center of town.

It was over.

The crowd dispersed, one and two at a time. One man grumbled to his companion that the fight hadn't lasted long enough or been bloody enough. Another complained that he should have bet more on the Indian, because everybody knew an Indian could outfight a white man.

Jim walked over to Bonner and handed him his weapon. "You want Foster's for a souvenir?"

"Keep it for a steak knife. It's got a pretty good blade."

Jim handed him a large kerchief, which Bonner used to wipe the sweat off his face, chest, and arms.

For the first time, Ginny felt the tears rolling down her cheeks. She quickly wiped them away.

"I'm glad *that's* over," Indy said, moving away from Ginny and toward Bonner. "How about coming home with us? It looks to me like you could use a bath and a rest."

Bonner shook his head. "Not tonight, Indy. But thanks for the invitation." He leaned forward and kissed her on the cheek.

Jim handed him his coat and gunbelt. "Try to stay out of trouble, will you?"

"Always." Bonner walked the few feet to Ginny.

She held his shirt out to him, then bent her head and looked down at his moccasins. She didn't want him to see how upset she was. "I'm glad you're not hurt," she said, trying to keep her voice from shaking.

Through her lashes, she saw him tilt his head to the side. He lifted her chin with his knuckle. "You've been crying."

"I—I was afraid for you."

He made a low sound in his throat, then reached up to take the pencil over her ear.

Ginny stepped back out of his reach. She couldn't let him touch her. It would be her undoing.

"Good night." She turned and walked away.

"Thanks for seeing me home." Ginny stood at the door of the *Sun*'s office and waved Jim and Indy good night. She watched them walk hand in hand down the street and couldn't help but envy them their companionship, their love, and the precious baby that would soon make them a family.

Ginny slowly closed the door, then twisted around and leaned her back against it. She was almost glad her father had gone off on his own so she could have a couple of hours to herself.

All the way home, she'd tried to convince herself that walking away from Bonner had been the *right* thing to do. She knew it had been what everybody wanted her to do—the *sensible* thing for all concerned. But the *right* thing? It didn't feel right at all.

Still, after what she'd seen and heard tonight, she knew that what Indy and Bonner had warned her about was true. For her to have any kind of relationship with Bonner, even a simple friendship, would be putting herself, her father, and the *Sun* at risk.

She'd never experienced so much hate. It had hovered over the assembly like a ghost. Unseen, untouchable, but making its cold, deadly chill known all the same.

Ginny heard a noise and looked down to see Greeley standing in a shaft of moonlight. He had an old shoe in his mouth and was wagging his tail, obviously trying to get her attention. She'd given him the shoe yesterday with the hope he would play with it, but he hadn't shown any signs of interest until now.

"What a good boy you are, Greeley." She squatted down and nuzzled her face into his fur. He dropped the shoe and licked her hand. "Such a good boy," she whispered, wrapping her arms around him and holding

him tight. He was soft and cuddly like the big rag doll
she'd had as a child. The doll had comforted her
through her childhood trials with its silent, uncondi-
tional love. In the short time she'd had Greeley, she'd
come to realize he was a lot like that doll, always
there for her, predictable, consistent, and loving.

"I wonder how late Pop's going to be," she said,
looking into his big brown eyes. "I hope to God he
doesn't do anything foolish." Greeley cocked his head
to the side. Ginny smiled and patted the top of his
head. "It won't do any good to worry about it. Mother
always told me not to borrow trouble." She picked
the shoe up from the floor and teased Greeley with
it, then tossed it across the room. He bounded after
it and brought it back to her for another throw. Ginny
obliged over and over again until she saw he was
tiring.

"That's enough for tonight," she told him. "Let's
go outside, then we'll get ready for bed." She took
him out behind the kitchen and congratulated him
when he came back so quickly. Then she went into
the bedroom and changed into her nightgown. Greeley
sat next to her dressing table and watched her while
she unpinned her hair.

Not for the first time, Ginny thought about how
different her life might have turned out if Tom hadn't
been killed. She'd always imagined they would have
lived in a big house in Albany, had three or four children, and she would have whiled away her leisure
hours writing her stories.

But now, oddly, she wondered if that would have
been enough to satisfy her.

Something strange was happening to her. Changes.
She'd vaguely acknowledged it Saturday when she'd
confronted her reflection in the mirror and thought
she wasn't the same old logical, sensible Ginny.

Before coming to Tucson she wouldn't have stood
up in front of a group of people and defended herself

the way she'd done tonight. If she'd had only herself to think about, she wouldn't have walked away from Bonner after the fight. She pulled the last of the pins out of her hair and stared once more at her reflection. It was quite possible the life she and Tom had planned together might not have been such a perfect life after all.

Lost in thought, she brushed the tangles out of her hair, until she heard her father's voice outside.

"I don' wanna wake her up."

Ginny held her hairbrush in midair. She looked down at Greeley and saw him perk his ears.

The office doorknob rattled.

"Confound it! It's locked. But I gotta key. I got lots of keys."

Ginny's heart sank. Though she'd told herself and Greeley that she wouldn't worry about her father, somehow she'd known this was how the night would end. She looked in the mirror and saw a glazed look of despair spread across her face. What was wrong with her? Why did she keep kidding herself? Pretending that her father didn't have a drinking problem wasn't doing either of them any good.

She heard the doorknob rattle again. Either her father had lost his key or misplaced it. She was tempted to just sit there and ignore him, but it was cold outside.

Greeley stood up when Ginny did. Tail wagging, he went ahead of her to the door, picking up his shoe along the way to greet her father like he'd done earlier with her.

Grabbing her shawl and wrapping it around her shoulders, Ginny padded barefoot across the cold floor, through the sitting room and hall into the office where she turned the wick up on the kerosene lamp. What excuse would Pop have tonight? she wondered. Cold weather? *Just* being sociable? He always came up with a good one. He had enough imagination to be a novelist as well as a journalist.

She managed to control her anger and open the door with a smile on her face. "Hello, Pop. Did you lose your key?" Her smile faded when she saw Bonner's stern face. He had his arm around her father, holding him up.

"I brought a frien' h-h-home," Sam said. He was so drunk his mouth was working even when he wasn't talking. "Ya go' anythin' t'eat? We're pow'rful h-h-hungry, arn' we, Bonner?"

Looking madder than a March hare, Bonner Kincade half dragged, half carried her father inside. Sam looked like a big puppet with his limp arms waving and his head bobbing out of control. Ginny had never seen him this drunk.

She stared at him, her anger turning to anguish. It hurt to see him this way. But it hurt even more to face the reality that his promises meant nothing, that his apologies were nothing but meaningless words.

No more, Ginny vowed to herself, no more pretending that he was anything other than what he was.

A drunkard and a liar.

"Ginny?"

For a moment Bonner was taken aback by the sight of Ginny's hair. It was longer than he'd thought, almost waist-length, and wavy all over. In the lamplight, the brown color was enriched with golden highlights. He was so used to black-haired Mexican girls and Apache women that Ginny's hair was a treat to his eyes.

She didn't answer him. He could see by her blank stare that her mind was off in another world. "Ginny," he said again, louder, and this time he got her attention. "What do you want me to do with him?"

She shook her head and shrugged. She looked utterly and hopelessly defeated.

"I can take care of myself," Sam protested, trying to shake himself free of Bonner's hold.

Bonner hadn't known that Sam had a habitual drinking problem until tonight, but now everybody knew. For all Sam's winning ways when he was sober, he was a nasty drunk with a mouth to match. Tonight, he'd insulted more than his share of townspeople and had been close to getting himself shot by a couple of pistoleros that he'd offended.

Usually, Bonner made it a practice to stay out of other people's business, but he liked Sam Sinclair and he knew Ginny wouldn't want to see her father get hurt, so he'd intervened and brought him home.

Ginny's expression was bleak. "Take him into the sitting—"

Greeley's low growl stopped her from finishing. She turned to see the dog standing in front of the door to the hall. He dropped his shoe and bared his teeth.

"Greeley! What's the matter with you?" Ginny started toward the dog.

"Ginny, don't!" Bonner warned. "I think your father's got him riled."

Ginny looked over her shoulder at Bonner. "What should I do?"

"We'll go back outside. When he calms down, put him in your bedroom."

Ignoring Sam's drunken protest, Bonner turned him around and took him back outside.

The moment the door closed behind them, Greeley stopped growling. Ginny approached him with caution. "Come on, boy. Let's go to bed." The dog picked up his shoe and led the way, head up, tail wagging, as if nothing had happened.

When Greeley had found the whiskey bottle in the wood pile the other day, she'd wondered if he associated it with his former master. Now she knew that he did.

She closed the door on Greeley and returned to

the office. Bonner was just coming back inside with her father.

"Confound it, Ki'cade. Lemme go!"

Bonner clenched his jaw and struggled to keep his temper. "Shut up, Sam." He had no tolerance for a man who couldn't hold his liquor and no respect for a man who didn't know when he'd had enough.

"Doncha tell me t'shut up." Sam hiccuped so hard his head jerked back. "This is my house and no damn heathen bastard is gonna order me—"

Pushed to the limit, Bonner let go of Sam and stepped away from him.

Sam stumbled backward, then fell to the floor like a rock. As far as Bonner was concerned, Sam could either pick himself up or stay there. Bonner had acted as the newspaperman's bodyguard because he liked him, but he'd be damned if he'd lift a hand for a man who called him a bastard. He'd had about all of the name-calling he was going to take.

"Bonner!" Ginny rushed to her father's side and started fussing over him. "That was uncalled for," she charged. "He's drunk. He doesn't know what he's saying."

"Don't kid yourself, Ginny. He knows what he's saying all right. He's just got more guts drunk than sober." When she squatted down, her shawl fell onto the floor, revealing the fact that she was in her nightgown. Bonner couldn't believe he hadn't noticed until just this moment. The only explanation was that he hadn't looked beyond her hair and shawl, maybe because he'd been busy getting Sam into the house.

The fabric of her nightgown stretched taut over her bottom. A very prettily rounded bottom from what he could see. And he could see very well, due to the fact that the nightgown was thin and white, and there was a kerosene lamp on the table behind her.

He wanted to shake her for coming to the door dressed like that—and with her hair down on top of it. She was all woman. A very tempting woman. He'd been noble up until now, but he had his limits. He was only human, after all, not blind nor made of stone.

"Come on, Pop. Let's get you to bed." Ginny managed to pull her father into a sitting position, then stood behind him and leaned down, grabbing him under his arms. "Put your legs under yourself and help me." Her voice sounded strained.

For a fleeting second, Bonner was treated to an unobstructed view of her breasts. He remembered seeing her silhouette in the office window and thinking how perfectly proportioned her body was, but nothing in that memory had hinted at the beauty he'd just seen.

Christ Almighty, he thought, disgusted with himself. He could feel the muscles in his groin tighten. He looked away, then back when he heard Ginny groan. She was pulling Sam with all her might toward the bedroom, and Sam was resisting her with all of his power.

"Lemme 'lone, dammit. I don' wantchu helping me."

Bonner felt a twinge of guilt. Sam outweighed her by at least eighty pounds. But he could see she wasn't going to give up. Damn stubborn woman. She was more trouble than Martine and that required some doing.

"Confound it, Ginette! Get your hands—" Sam's arm shot out and grabbed a chair by the leg.

Bonner couldn't stand watching her another moment. "I'll take care of your father. You go turn down his bed," he ordered, trying to keep his mind focused. He could care less if the chair toppled over on Sam— the fool deserved a good knot on the head. But Ginny could hurt herself.

Ginny didn't budge. "I saw the way you took care of him a moment ago. You knew he'd fall down if you let him go, but you did it anyway," she snapped. "So thanks, but no thanks. I'll manage him by myself."

"Like hell you will." He edged her out of the way, bent down, and scooped Sam up in his arms like a baby.

"Earthquake!" Sam bellowed, his eyes wild with fear.

"No, Pop. It's not an earthquake," Ginny said, taking his hand and patting it reassuringly. He panicked and grabbed on to her nightgown, tearing the shoulder seam. She pried his fingers away and stepped out of his reach, working furiously to tie the shoulder together.

Bonner saved her from further embarrassment by moving past her and going into Sam's bedroom. Ginny followed him momentarily and hurried to the bed to pull down the covers. Once he'd laid Sam down, she set about removing her father's shoes and socks.

"Does he do this kind of thing often?" Bonner asked.

Ginny glanced up from untying her father's shoelace. "Often enough to be the reason why we're here. He's lost six editorial jobs in five years, depleted our savings, and caused us to move from New York to San Francisco to Tucson." She dropped his shoes on the floor beside the bed.

"Is there a reason why he drinks?"

Ginny shrugged. "He started drinking right after my mother died. At first, it was just a glass of brandy before bed to help him sleep. I honestly didn't see any harm in it. He was so lonely and miserable." She shook her head. "Then he started needing a whiskey in the morning to help him work. Later, he needed a whiskey in the afternoon to get him through the day. I should have done something to stop him, but by the time I realized what was going on, it was too late." She would always regret her lack of action.

She glanced at Bonner standing by the bed, hands on hips. "Will you help me take off his coat?" she asked. Bonner lifted Sam and Ginny pulled his arms out of his coat sleeves. She laid the heavy garment over the chair next to the bed. "I suppose I should take his trousers off so he'll sleep comfortably," she said, reaching toward his belt buckle.

"Leave this to me," Bonner offered, covering her hands with his.

His touch paralyzed her. She stared down at his large, capable hands and wondered how they would feel touching other parts of her body. They'd be rough and demanding, she thought at first, then negated that thought and told herself they'd be gentle and encouraging. It was a long moment before sanity returned and she pulled back.

"You don't have to," she said, lifting her gaze to his.

"I know that. But when Sam wakes up, he'll feel a lot better if you tell him I took his pants off and put him to bed."

Ginny blushed. "I see your point. He *would* be embarrassed." Silence fell between them. Ginny ran her hand nervously down her gown. "Thanks. I'll just wait out in the sitting room. Would you like a cup of coffee or something?" Bonner shook his head and Ginny started for the door. "I know Indy said you'd missed supper," she rambled on. "How about if I warm up some leftovers? You must be starving after—" She hesitated, thinking of the meeting, his fight with Clay Foster, and bringing her drunken father home. "After everything," she said instead.

"I ate at the Shoo Fly, but thanks anyway."

"You're welcome. I'll just— Never mind. Be sure to cover him up. I don't want him getting sick."

Bonner nodded, his fingers already loosening Sam's belt buckle.

She turned and headed for the door, wondering why it was that whenever she came in close contact with Bonner she acted like a blathering idiot.

Ginny couldn't get out of the bedroom fast enough.

She closed the door behind her and stood there a moment, taking deep breaths.

Ginny walked out into the sitting room and saw her shawl on the floor. She picked it up, wrapped it around her shoulders, and clutched the ends together in front of her to protect herself from Bonner's penetrating gaze. She realized it was a little late now for a show of modesty. She was sure she'd already revealed everything she had. But late was better than not at all.

A moment later Bonner came out of her father's bedroom into the sitting room. "He's going to have one helluva headache in the morning."

"Good," she said in a cold, flat voice.

"What?"

"I said, good. I hope it's the worst one ever. He deserves to suffer . . . for breaking his promise." She looked away, unable to meet Bonner's dark, questioning eyes.

"What promise?"

"That he'd stop drinking. It was what got me to agree to move here and help him start up the *Sun.* I wouldn't have come if I'd thought he would do this again. I guess that shows you just how foolish I really am, doesn't it?" The enormity of what her father had done by breaking his promise for the second time hit her like a wave at high tide. She could see the familiar pattern forming. It always started with the one-night drunken binges, like tonight. Then, half the next day to recuperate—to get his head together, he always said. Then would come the missed assignments. The missed interviews. She didn't go any further with her thoughts. It wasn't necessary.

She knew where it would all end up. She didn't need to look into a crystal ball to know that it was only a matter of time before the *Tucson Sun* was just a memory.

"You believed in him," Bonner stated. "That doesn't make you a fool. Most people would have given up on him long ago. Just like I gave up on Greeley."

She appreciated the kind words but they didn't make her feel any better. "Thanks for bringing Pop home. Where'd you find him?"

"Congress Hall Saloon. He came in with Rolfe Brown, but after a couple of drinks, Brown left. Your father's a different man when he's drunk, Ginny. He's a loudmouth and a troublemaker."

"Pop? A troublemaker? That's a lie. He may be a lot of things but he's definitely not a troublemaker," she said with confidence, turning away.

Lightning quick, Bonner caught her arm and spun her around, her shawl falling to the floor around her feet. Before she could gather her wits about her, he had her shoulders pinned to the sitting-room wall.

"Savage. Bastard. Heathen. Liar. Everybody's got a name for me tonight." He pressed close to her, his face—his mouth—less than an inch from hers. She tried to break free of his hold but found herself firmly held. "Think what you want. Call me what you want, Ginny, but your father damn near got himself killed tonight by a couple of pistoleros."

"Killed?" Her eyes widened in surprise.

"The undertaker would be bringing him home in a box if I hadn't dragged him out of there."

"Oh, Bonner." She clutched his arm. "I—I'm sorry. I didn't realize—"

Bonner ran his fingers into her hair and made a fist. "Seems to me, Miss Sinclair, there's a lot of things you don't realize until it's *too* late." His dark eyes looked down between them. Her shoulder tie had come loose and the entire side of her nightgown had slipped down her breast.

Bonner was through being noble and trying to protect her from himself. It was her fault that he was half-crazy with wanting her. She could have taken care to properly cover herself. Now, it was too late.

Ginny followed his gaze, then made a halfhearted attempt to pull the material back up.

He grabbed her hand and held it. "Uh-uh, Ginny. Not this time," he said between his teeth. Her schoolmarm clothes had hidden her secrets well. Now, he wanted to see more. "If you expect me to act like a gentleman and walk away from you now, you can forget it." Slowly, he pulled the left shoulder of her nightgown down her arm until both breasts were revealed.

Seeing the desire flare in his eyes heated Ginny's blood. She wanted him. God, she wanted him. More than that she *needed* him. Longed for him to touch her. But there was a niggling little voice that said, "Risk."

"Bonner," she choked out. "You're forgetting—" He cupped her left breast and circled the nipple with his thumb. She swallowed, trying to concentrate, then began again. "The other night, you and Indy, you both said— It's too risky." Shivers of delight followed his touch. "Tonight's meeting—it made me realize— Oooh," she moaned when he lowered his head and licked her nipple. With a will she didn't know she possessed, she continued. "That's why I walked away from you tonight." She turned her head sideways against the wall and tried to ignore the overpowering sensations that were twisting and turning her insides. "Bonner, you're not listening to me."

"I am listening. I'm just past the point of giving a damn." He moved his hand down between her breasts and across her stomach. "What about you?" he asked. "Do you really give a damn?" His hand moved lower. "If you do, I'll stop now. But if you don't, I'm going to make love to you." He pressed his hips against hers as if to confirm that what he was saying was true. "I'm not a patient man, Ginny, so you'd better hurry and make up your mind."

That she didn't say anything at all seemed answer enough. He kissed her before she could change her mind, kissed her so hard and so thoroughly that she couldn't think about anything except what he was doing to her.

Ginny's head spun dizzily as Bonner's mouth moved lower with exacting precision over hers. His lips were wet and hot and they were doing things to hers that she'd never imagined. She closed her eyes, then opened them wide when he parted her lips with his tongue and plunged deep inside.

A low, hoarse moan came from way down deep inside her and she felt an urgent need to hold him and to be held. She wrapped her arms around his neck and clung to him as tightly as she could.

She'd never dreamed a man could kiss a woman the way Bonner was kissing her. This wasn't like any kiss Tom had given her. She wasn't even sure this was a kiss. It felt more like the act of love itself with his tongue thrusting in and out.

She made a moue of protest when he broke the kiss. His hands framed her face. "I've wanted you from the moment I pulled that damn pencil out of your mouth," he said, his voice a husky whisper that sent shivers all the way to her toes. "And then *that* night, when I saw you in the window—you were taking the pins out of your hair, one by one, so slowly I thought I'd go crazy." He ran his fingers through her hair. "I just sat there on my horse and watched you, spellbound. You're a witch, Ginny. Do you know that?"

With the tip of her finger, she touched his lips to silence him. He was embarrassing her. She shook her head ever so slightly. What could she say? She didn't see herself as a seductive sorceress. She was Ginny. Just Ginny.

He nipped the fleshy pad of her finger and continued talking. "All of a sudden you stood up and stretched." He grasped her arms and rolled her shoulders back so that she had to arch her spine. "Then you hugged yourself, and you moved your hands down your body just like this." He traced the path her fingers had traveled, down her sides to her waist. "Jesus, Ginny, I wanted to come to you, to be the man you were dreaming of."

His words and his hands took her breath away. "Oh, Bonner," she breathed his name on a sigh. "Don't you know? You *were* the man I was dreaming of."

His throat clogged with an unexpected rush of emotion that had nothing to do with the blood pumping into his groin, making him so hard he hurt.

Bonner swallowed a groan as he ground his hips against hers. He wanted, desperately wanted, to just lift her nightgown and drive himself into her, but for the moment he took pleasure in the small satisfaction that came with her arching response.

Ginny sensed she was in unfamiliar territory. In spite of the fact that she and Tom had made love, Bonner was quickly making her realize just how naive she was. Tom had been patient and gentle with her, coaxing her responses. He'd practically revered her body. But Bonner—Bonner wasn't giving any indication of being patient or gentle. Every move he made demanded she make one too.

"You aren't afraid of me, are you, Ginny?"

Suddenly one of his hands was under her nightgown, skimming along her naked buttocks and thighs, growing ever bolder, moving ever closer to her most private part.

"Y-yes." Then, "No," she whispered frantically. She couldn't decide. One moment she was afraid of everything and the next she was afraid of nothing. It was crazy. "You're going too fast for me!"

"I can't help it, Ginny. You feel so good. And I want you so much."

"But it's been six years since I—" His hand moved her legs apart making her forget what she was going to say. He slipped his fingers inside her and stroked her tender flesh. She rocked against his hand, wanting more, but having no idea what more was. The sensation was new to her—new and exciting.

"Kiss me, Ginny," he demanded.

She opened her mouth and he filled it with his tongue, thrusting in and out, duplicating the movement of his fingers deep inside her until she was squirming with need and anticipation.

"Bonner, please—" She had no idea what she was asking him for, but she prayed he would know and do whatever he had to before she went out of her mind. She was on the brink, caught between tremulous fulfillment and a desperate craving for something more.

With the instinct of an animal, Bonner sensed the height of her passion and sought to bring Ginny to a shattering climax by lengthening his strokes, plunging deeper and faster, all the while speaking to her in Apache, encouraging her with love words, sex words.

Ginny gave herself over to him and strained against his hand, feeling sensations of hot and then cold, of burning, hunger, and a few others she couldn't even put a name to. A spasm racked her, then another and another causing her legs to quiver wildly.

She clung tightly to his shoulders, afraid her legs would give out from under her. "Oh, God. Bonner. I—" The breath pent up inside her came out in a long whoosh. She struggled to hold on to the moment of fulfillment, but his hand coaxed her to let it go. To let it all go. For long minutes afterward, he continued to caress her, extending her satisfaction, exciting her anew.

Bonner nearly came to climax himself when he felt her body's first telling tremors and then the wet warmth of her pleasure against his hand.

Regaining some of her senses, Ginny wanted Bonner to feel the same satisfaction and excitement he'd given her, but she had only a vague idea of what to do. "I want—I want to touch you," she whispered breathlessly. She slid her hand down his side to his hip, to the hard swell of his manhood. "I've never done—" Startled, she pulled back, reconsidering. He was a big, tall, strong man. She should have expected that he would be big all over.

"I'll teach you," he said. Catching her hand in his, he guided her back to his groin.

Anticipation churning inside him, he reached down his leg and untied the rawhide thong that held his holster tight to his thigh, then unbuckled his gunbelt and lowered it to the floor. He was growing impatient with himself for all the trappings of civilization that had to be dispensed with just to release himself.

In his haste, he practically tore off the button to get his pants undone. Then, finally, he reached inside and pulled himself free.

He shuddered convulsively when he felt Ginny's trembling fingers close over his engorged flesh and slide toward his hand. He instructed her in the motion of how to please him and buried his lips against her throat while she delighted him with her explorations of his male anatomy. She was amazingly bold and brazen—touching him in delightful little ways he hadn't even considered. At the edge of his release, he grabbed her hand and showed her how else she might pleasure him.

A soft exclamation broke from him. It pleased Ginny to know that she'd been able to give him the kind of deep satisfaction he'd given her.

Suddenly he slid one arm around her shoulders and the other under her knees and lifted her. She drew in a quick, startled breath.

"Where are you taking me?"

"I told you before—I'm going to make love to you."

"But my father—"

"It'll be worth the risk, Ginny."

It seemed to Ginny every time she turned around now, she was tempting fate. But this was one risk she didn't have to think about taking. She wanted him. All of him. Regardless of the consequences.

Chapter 13

"The difficulty is, they [Apaches] furnish the wood so fast [thirty cords per day] that in a few days we shall have enough for the winter. When they furnished hay, they brought in as high as fifteen tons in one day; and it must be remembered that the former is broken off by hand or cut with worn-out axes, and the latter cut by knives, and all is carried on their backs. It is wonderful with what alacrity they go to work. It is true, nearly all is done by women and children, but a few men also work."

—Major John Green, Camp Apache,
in the *Tucson Sun*

At last. At long, long last.

Every look, every word, every accidental touch—they'd all been leading up to this.

Ginny refused to listen to her conscience scolding her for lacking common sense. Nor would she listen to its dire predictions about the consequences of her actions.

Now was the time to listen to her heart. And her heart told her that this was right.

That the town of Tucson would denounce her as a scarlet woman for even fraternizing with Bonner Kincade somehow added to the excitement of the moment. So did the knowledge that her father could wake up at any second and catch them in the act of making love.

Her thoughts shattered like broken glass the moment Bonner put her down on the sofa. He positioned her so she was half sitting, half reclining, then stood beside her, tall and handsome, exciting and dangerous—ten times more man than she'd ever known.

That exact same thought came again when he peeled

his tunic-length shirt over his head, revealing not only his muscled chest and corded arms but his hardened manhood. It suddenly occurred to her that not only was he ten times more man than she was used to, but possibly more man than her body could accommodate.

Worried, she swallowed and glanced up. His eyes said he knew exactly what she was thinking.

"Don't say I didn't warn you." He leaned down over her, positioning a hand on either side of her shoulders, his right knee finding purchase on the sofa next to her leg.

In spite of her worry, her body tingled with anticipation. "Warned me about what?"

His expression was gravely serious. "That a woman like you could stir up a *lot* of trouble."

She pulled a startled breath, remembering when he'd said it and seeing how the words related to him now.

"I'm not a virgin," she confessed, praying he wouldn't be disappointed.

"I know. Thank God!"

His reaction surprised her, but before she had a chance to think about it, he startled her again when he reared back and yanked up the front of her nightgown. His intense study of her body affected her in countless ways, emotionally and physically.

"God, Ginny, you're beautiful," he said, his breath stalling in his throat. Fingers splayed, he framed her ribs, then glided his hands down the length of her. Her skin burned beneath his touch, his stomach clenched and liquid heat surged through her abdomen. His thumbs seared a path down to the triangle of dark hair, then he parted her legs and moved between them.

"Come to me, Ginny." There was an urgency in his voice that hadn't been there a moment ago. He moved his hands beneath her hips, slid her down the sofa toward him, then onto him, pulling and plunging at the same time.

The shock of him made her gasp, dig her nails into his bare shoulders. She might as well have been a virgin, as resistant as her body was to receive him. She felt herself stretch and open and stretch some more. "No. Stop," she pleaded, sure he was too much for her.

As before, she realized he knew her thoughts by the look in his eyes.

He withdrew slightly, but just long enough for her to catch her breath. "Don't ask me to stop, Ginny," he said. "Try to relax. I'll go slow and easy. Like this." He rocked back and forth, slow and easy just like he said, until her body finally opened and accepted him fully.

She was panting, excitement and fear making her pulse pound loudly in her ears. She closed her eyes. In spite of his caution, his first hard thrusts were pure agony. Or were they ecstasy? She didn't know. At some point—she couldn't say when—didn't really care—any pain she'd felt had become pleasure. Joyous pleasure. Intense pleasure.

She was lost in her own private world—a world Tom had never taken her to. A world of flash, fire, and wonderfully strange sensations. She opened her eyes to see Bonner gazing down at her, his expression one of deep concentration.

A plaintive cry from her father's bedroom brought Ginny back to reality. She pushed against Bonner's chest, I think I heard Pop."

"Ya lied t' her, dammit," Sam said in a slurred voice. "Ya tol her ya hadn't been called."

Ginny struggled to free herself, but Bonner held her down, still embedded inside her, waiting.

"He's just talking in his sleep. It'll be all right," he said, listening, praying. But in an instant he knew it wouldn't be. Ginny was afraid of being caught and he couldn't blame her. Groaning, he eased back, unsatisfied and unfulfilled.

He stood up, pulled up his buckskin pants, and shook his head. "Come on," he said, offering his hand to help her up. "Put yourself together." Her nightgown fell into place when she stood, covering all that beauty. As he buttoned his fly, he saw that Ginny was having a great deal of difficulty tying the torn shoulder together. Probably because her hands were shaking so badly. He retrieved her shawl off the floor and wrapped it around her.

"Thank you," she said, her voice shaking as badly as her hands.

Bonner thought she looked on the verge of something—tears, a fit of apoplexy, hysteria—he wasn't sure. All he knew was that her discomfort was his fault. He hadn't used his head. He should have known better than to make love to her when her father was in the next room.

"I'm sorry, Gin—"

"Ya have t' tell her, Tom," Sam's voice cut into Bonner's apology. "She's gotta right t' know."

Ginny twisted around and stared at her father's bedroom door. She'd heard of people talking in their sleep, but the way Pop was carrying on, she fully expected Tom to answer him.

"Who's Tom?" Bonner asked.

"My . . . fiancé," she said, still in the throes of confusion.

"Fiancé?"

She shook her head. "He died six years ago. In the war. I—I can't imagine what Pop's talking about."

Bonner looked toward the closed bedroom door. "He's probably hallucinating." He raked his fingers through his hair. "Damn!"

Ginny glanced up at him. She was suffering from the same frustration and regrets that appeared to be torturing Bonner. "I guess I'd better go check on him." She turned and headed for the bedroom. She stood there at the door a moment listening, then lightly knocked. "Pop? Are you all right?" No answer.

She opened the door a crack and peeked inside. "Pop?" He was lying flat on his back, staring up at the ceiling. She opened the door all the way and walked in. If he noticed her, he didn't give any indication.

"Pop?" Ginny leaned over him and searched his eyes for some sign of wakefulness. Nothing. He wasn't even blinking. "Pop, it's Ginny. Wake up. You're having a nightmare."

" 'Yer worse than a bounty jumper," Sam went on, his voice rising with anger. "What kinda man are ya that you'd hire a substitute to fight in your place? I don't care that the law allows it. Yer a coward and there's no two ways around it."

Ginny's mouth fell open. "Pop! You're talking crazy."

Her father continued to stare up at the ceiling with unseeing eyes.

"Ginny," Bonner called to her from the threshold.

Unable to take her eyes off her father, she backed toward the door. His words tolled inside her head like a church bell.

Coward. Hire a substitute.

Coward. Hire a substitute.

Stunned, sickened, Ginny pressed a trembling hand to her mouth. Why hadn't her father told her? Why had he kept the truth from her all these years? She'd had a right to know.

She felt a hand on her shoulder and turned around. Bonner took her arm and led her from the bedroom. He no sooner closed the door behind them than he opened the opposite bedroom door and walked her inside.

Greeley wagged his tail in greeting, then stood back and watched.

"Your father's hallucinating. Heavy drinkers do that. I see it all the time." He pulled aside the bedcovers and sat her down on the edge of the bed.

"He wasn't hallucinating," she said, refusing to be swayed by his commonsense statement. "He couldn't possibly have made that up."

He reached behind her and propped two pillows together, then gently pushed her backward, ignoring her resistance. "You'd be surprised. Talk to him when he's sober. Until then, you don't know what the truth is."

She grabbed his forearms, afraid to let him go. "I think I do. And I think I'm seeing the light for the first time in six years." She caught a glimpse of her reflection in his black eyes. She looked wild and wanton with her hair sticking out all over the place, her lips swollen, and her eyes brimming with tears. "Looking back—I can see everything so clearly now—all the excuses, the little cover-ups. Lies. All lies."

He sat on the side of the bed. "If he did lie to you, maybe it was because he couldn't face telling you that he was afraid of going to war. A lot of men were afraid."

"It goes beyond lying. There's a matter of honor. You heard what Pop said—that Tom hired a substitute to go to war for him. I know about the conscription law, and I know what kind of men took advantage of it—greedy men, dishonest men. Cowards." A sob tore from her throat. "I believed in Tom. I trusted him. I *loved* him. I thought I knew him. How could I have been so wrong about him?" Tears filled her eyes and ran down her cheeks. "Oh, God. When I got the letter saying he'd been killed—I died too."

Bonner pushed her hair back away from her face. "Stop it, Ginny. It's in the past. Tom's dead. Whatever lies he told, he's answered for them."

Her eyes locked on his. "Not to me." She stared at Bonner's shirt, memories of Tom crowding her mind.

"All these years I've thought he was something he wasn't. I've held him in such high esteem that no one else could compare." Ginny felt a cold, wet nose nuzzle her right arm. Greeley had jumped up on the bed and was lying next to her. Out of habit, she stroked his fur. "I've been such a fool. With Pop too. I've been kidding myself. He'll never stop drinking. It's just a matter of time—" She couldn't get the rest of the words out past the knot in her throat.

"Don't do this to yourself, Ginny," Bonner said, grabbing her shoulders and pulling her toward him. "You're not a fool."

He held her. Just held her. And let her cry. He stroked her hair, her back, kissed her temple, her forehead, her tear-wet cheeks.

He knew what it was like to be lied to, to believe in someone and find out later they weren't who he thought they were. He also knew what it was like to stop trusting his own instincts.

Finally, she fell asleep. After laying her down, he gave Greeley a pat. "Take care of her, boy." Then he turned and strode toward the door.

Ginny woke herself out of a sound sleep, the words on her lips that she hadn't been able to say before. "There's nothing at risk—" Her eyes blinked open just as the door closed.

She threw the covers aside and jumped out of bed. "Ouch!" Pain shot through her left foot. She fell back, bouncing hard on the edge of the bed. Over the jangle of bedsprings, she heard the office door close.

He was gone.

She took a deep breath, leaned forward, and looked at the floor. Greeley's shoe. She'd stepped on the heel.

She crawled back under the covers, cursing herself for falling asleep, cursing Greeley for leaving his shoe where she could step on it, cursing Bonner for being so damn noble, and last, cursing her father for breaking his promise.

*   *   *

A winter storm was coming. He could feel it, smell it in the night air.

Bonner rode out of town, to the camp he'd made in the stand of cottonwoods beside the river. The density of the trees formed a natural and protective shelter in spite of their leafless branches.

After unsaddling his horse and sending it off to feed on the desert grasses, Bonner went in search of wood to build a fire. He brought it back by the armful, and when he had enough, he dug a firepit, using his hands to scoop out the sandy soil.

Building the fire helped to remind him of who he was. Watching those first tiny yellow flames grow into hungry tongues helped renew his spirit.

Once the blaze no longer needed his care, he stepped back into the shadows, stripped down to nothing but his moccasins, then pulled off the rawhide strip binding his hair.

He waited there in the darkness, wondering if he still had *diyi*. It had been a long time since he'd spoken to his power. He regretted having waited so long. His power was strong—it would help him see things more clearly.

He filled his lungs with air, then strode into the firelight and began to chant. "Hee-ay-hay-ee-ee! Hee-ay-hay-ee-ee!"

From out of the north, a biting breeze stirred the fire, making it hotter.

He chanted until his throat ached with the strain.

The wood crackled and spit.

Firebrands shot up into the sky.

The call of the hoot owl trembled the night air.

"Hee-ay-hay-ee-ee! Hee-ay-hay-ee-ee!"

In the distance the wind whistled, then grew to a thunderous roar as it approached the river.

"S . . . e . . . e . . . k . . . e . . . r!"

The ominous funnel danced across the desert floor, whirling, turning, disrupting everything in its path.

"Hee-ay-hay-ee-ee! Hee-ay-hay-ee-ee!"

"S . . . e . . . e . . . k . . . e . . . r!"

"I wait for you, Wind."

Wind circled the camp like a child at play. As before the head emerged from the mouth of the funnel and looked at Bonner, its eyes black as coal. "What is it you want, Seeker? More knowledge? I have given you much already."

"I want to know about the woman."

"She has great *diyi.*"

"But she is interfering with my plans."

"Because you are destined to protect her."

"She makes me lose sight of the things I must do."

Wind tossed its magnificent head. "It is she who will help you achieve your goals."

"A woman? A *white* woman?"

"The woman's power is strong. You need her."

"How can she—"

"Patience, Seeker. P . . . a . . . t . . . i . . . e . . . n . . . c . . . e," Wind whispered, its icy breath stealing around Bonner's body, whipping his hair into his eyes and his mouth. Bonner stood in defiance of the wind spirit's dizzying swirl, his feet apart, fists clenched at his sides.

Then it was gone.

Chapter 14

Most every fruit will (someday) grow in Arizona as well as in California, but every enterprise of a permanent nature hinges on the eternal Indian Question.
—*Arizona Citizen*

Bonner rode out to Camp Lowell early Tuesday morning and reported to Colonel Dunn about the citizens' meeting.

"Did they have a good turnout?" the colonel asked as he sat down in his chair behind his desk.

Bonner took the camp chair facing him and stretched his long legs in front of him. "Seventy or eighty in all."

"So what was the outcome?"

"Divided," Bonner said, his tone dry. "At first, half wanted a civilian militia. The other half wanted to appeal to Congress and other high-ranking government bodies. The conservative group convinced the others to temporarily hold off on the militia."

"Good."

"Meantime they're going to ask the territorial legislature to gather information and take testimonies of Indian depredations."

"For what purpose?"

Bonner shrugged. "They're convinced they have a better chance of being heard in Washington if an official body like the territorial legislature presents their case."

Dunn's striker entered the tent with a coffeepot. The colonel offered Bonner a mug, which he accepted.

"Maybe they do. I don't know. At least that gives us some more time here," Dunn said. "Things are far too tense right now to have a bunch of hotheads running around the Territory shooting every Indian they see." He sipped his coffee thoughtfully.

"If they're unsuccessful, they *will* go ahead with the citizen army," Bonner reminded him.

"Hopefully though the situation will soon change for the better and they won't feel the need—which brings me to your new assignment." Dunn cleared his throat and looked down into his coffee mug.

Bonner stared at the military man, curious as to why he was suddenly avoiding his gaze. "What is it?"

Dunn looked up. "I'm sending you to Camp Grant. You'll leave tomorrow at first light. It'll be up to Lieutenant Whitman, the commanding officer there, as to how long you stay." The colonel stood up and glanced down at some papers on his desk. "He's had several small groups of Apaches come into camp lately, and he'd like to have an interpreter on hand to determine exactly what they want."

The colonel walked to the tent opening and looked outside. "While you're in the area, I want you to go to your grandfather's rancheria and talk to him. Convince him the time has come for him to move his people to a reservation." Dunn sounded very matter-of-fact, as if making an ordinary, everyday request.

It was anything but.

Bonner narrowed his gaze. "I'm sure I don't have to remind you that Gianatah and his people are at peace. They haven't caused trouble for years. There's no reason to move him and his band."

"In fact, Kincade, there are a number of reasons," the colonel replied, a note of exasperation in his voice, "not the least of which is that your grandfather and his people will be safe on a reservation."

"Safe? They have nothing to fear as long as you hold to your promise to keep your troops away from—"

"That's my point, Kincade. I can't keep that promise anymore. I have orders!"

"Orders." Bonner spit the word back at Dunn as if it were a curse.

"Yes, orders. You know as well as I do that everybody's up in arms—saying the army isn't taking care of the Apache situation. Word has come down that I need to take stronger military action in subduing the Apaches."

Dunn let the tent flap fall back into place. He walked back to his desk and paused as if to gear up for the next round. "The powers that be believe the only way to accomplish peace is to get the Apaches onto reservations and keep them there." He picked up the rock he used as a paperweight and clutched it. "Your grandfather is a very influential man. Even as a subchief, he has the ear of all the Arivaipa Apaches. His cooperation will induce others to follow."

"Cooperation?" Bonner laughed. "Come on, Colonel. He'll be anything but cooperative about going to a reservation."

"I don't care how he goes, Kincade. Just so he goes." Dunn slammed the rock down on the desk. "Talk to him. Reason with him." Dunn planted both hands on the desk and leaned forward. "Consider it an order."

Bonner stood, moved to the tent opening, and tossed his remaining coffee outside. "Sorry, Colonel," he said, setting his mug on the chair he'd just vacated. "I'm a *civilian* post guide, remember? I don't have to take orders." He turned to leave.

"Kincade, you impertinent son of a—"

Bonner raised his hand, stopping him short. "Lately, I've developed a real aversion to people calling me names . . . sir."

The colonel sucked in a breath. "Kincade—I ought to have you thrown in the guardhouse."

"Sorry, Colonel. You can't do that. Like I said, I'm a—"

Dunn threw up his hands in a gesture of helplessness. "I know. I know. You're a *civilian*. But there's nothing that says I have to continue to give you assignments—which means you could find yourself out of a job." Dunn straightened, looking smugly confident. "I don't like the idea of sending someone else to talk to your grandfather, but I will if I have to. I doubt they'll be as patient and considerate—if you know what I mean."

Bonner's expression turned into an angry scowl.

Dunn ran his fingers through his hair. "This has gone beyond you and me and what we think and feel. By the end of next month, I have to send my troops on scouts into those mountains where your grandfather's rancheria is. They'll have orders to ferret out every Apache they can find and deliver them to a reservation. If they resist—well—I don't have to tell you the possible consequences."

"No, you don't," Bonner agreed, his tone sarcastic.

"Look here, Kincade. You know as well as I do that reservations are the only peaceful solution. We've talked about it at length. I don't know why you're fighting me on this."

"My grandfather is old. It will kill him to leave the rancheria."

Dunn looked him straight in the eye. "It'll kill him if he doesn't."

Bonner admitted to himself later, on his way back to town, that he'd known the day would come when he'd have to use his influence on his own family. He knew he should be thankful he was in the position of being able to give his grandfather advance warning of the army's intentions. No other Apache leader had that advantage.

Bonner reminded himself that one of the reasons he'd volunteered his services to the army in the first place was to help Gianatah and his band. There were other reasons too, but none so important as safeguarding those he loved. So if relocating his grandfather's people to a reservation was the only way to save their lives, why did he feel like such a traitor?

Bonner's jaw tightened. He resolved not to think about it until tomorrow during the ride to Camp Grant. He concentrated instead on completing his errands as quickly as possible. The first one took him to St. Joseph's Academy for Young Ladies. It was Sister Monica of the Sacred Heart who took him on a tour of the chapel, the classrooms, the sleeping rooms, and the dining room. She was a pious woman with a sense of humor that came across when she described the trials of convoying herself and six other nuns from their home convent in St. Louis by way of San Francisco to their new school in Tucson.

"I fear it was almost too much for us," she said, rolling her eyes. "We were seasick on the steamer from San Francisco to San Diego and our bones were nearly broken by the carriage that took us to Yuma. It seemed forever before we reached the Colorado River, at which point we almost drowned crossing it. Beyond that our only problem was fending off proposals of marriage—and the other kind—that we received from gentlemen we met along the way," she said, chuckling. "It was quite . . . exhilarating, if I do say so."

"I'm sure it was," Bonner replied, stifling a grin. Over all, he was impressed with St. Joseph's. The building had been fitted up to afford clean and comfortable accommodations, a rarity in Tucson.

"The educational course comprises every useful and ornamental branch suitable for young ladies," Sister Monica explained. "Our scholastic year is divided into two sessions, commencing on the first of September and ending the twenty-ninth of June. Pupils are received at any time and charged only from the date of entrance." When she finished the tour, she led him back toward the courtyard. A trio of older schoolgirls,

walking toward the chapel, started whispering and gig-
ling the moment they saw Bonner.

"Girls! Mind your manners," Sister Monica scolded.

In chorus, the three said, "Yes, Sister," then hurried
on past.

"Our girls lead very sheltered lives, Mr. Kincade.
Even our day pupils. When they're finished with their
studies here, we know that each girl will be ready to
take her place in society, find a suitable husband, and
raise a family."

"What if that isn't what she wants?"

"I'm afraid I don't understand."

"My sister, Martine—she isn't like those girls we
just passed. She wears buckskin breeches for one
thing. And she rides herd over cattle. She hunts and
skins and sews hides together for blankets and clothing. She's half Apache—"

Sister Monica raised her hand to silence him. "I
believe I understand, Mr. Kincade." She paused a moment. "As much as we'd like to enroll your sister, it
sounds to me like she wouldn't thrive in such a struc-
tured environment as St. Joseph's. Perhaps you would
do better to hire a tutor."

"Yes, Sister. I think you're right. Thank you for
showing me around." He reached his hand into his
coat pocket, pulled out a double eagle, and pressed it
to her palm. "For the poor box, Sister."

"Go with God, Mr. Kincade."

Bonner was glad he'd looked at the academy and
talked with Sister Monica. His father would trust his
word that St. Joseph's was not the place for Martine.

At the news depot, Bonner bought the latest newspapers from San Diego, San Francisco, Boston, and
New York. As he started to leave, he realized he
hadn't seen the *Tucson Sun.*

"Sold out within a few hours after we got them,"
the clerk said. "But I've got a used copy, if you don't
mind rumpled pages and coffee stains."

Bonner thanked the man, then tucked the papers under his arm. With so many papers to look through he was bound to find several female tutors advertising for positions.

While he was hunting up tutors, he could find out what was going on in the rest of the world. It had been a long time since he'd read any of the big city newspapers, and he was looking forward to whiling away a few hours reading. Since Camp Grant was such a quiet post, isolated from everything, he didn't think finding the time would be a problem.

Next on his list of things to do was talking to Doc Wilber about his father, but according to the house-keeper, Doc would be out of town until the end of the week. Moving onto the stage station, Bonner decided to consult with the post surgeon at Camp Grant.

Noontime found Bonner sitting outside the stage station, composing a telegraph message to Logan. He briefly outlined their father's condition and asked for Logan's medical opinion and advice. Then Bonner asked him to look around for a tutor. Bonner went into detail about her qualifications. Finally, he reminded his brother of his promise to come home for Martine's puberty ceremony.

He paid for the message to go out on the next stage, then sauntered over to Foster's Emporium where Clay Foster was busy at the back of the store giving instructions to one of his employees.

"I want to pick up an order for King Kincade," Bonner told the clerk at the counter. While the man looked for the order, Bonner busied himself selecting some high-quality tobacco for his grandfather. He put the tobacco pouches on the counter, then added some penny candy. Only last year had he discovered that his grandfather had a sweet tooth.

Out of the corner of his eye, Bonner saw the clerk talking to Foster, who pointed toward a shelf containing a brown paper-wrapped package. It wasn't the package that held Bonner's attention but the white bandage covering Foster's hand and wrist. Bonner cleared his throat and put his hand over the smile he tried to stifle.

The clerk returned momentarily. Bonner paid for his purchases and left. He packed up his saddlebags with the papers and his other goods, then mounted up and rode down the street toward the *Tucson Sun* to pay his advertising bill.

Ginny stood outside the *Sun*'s office on ground slightly higher than the street. Her arms were tightly folded over her shawl, her face pale as she waited for Greeley to pick a spot. She looked exhausted and disheartened, like a woman who had been made one too many false promises and deceived one too many times. Bonner knew her well enough now to know that she'd probably spent the entire night thinking about everything that had happened and worrying what tomorrow would bring.

Where Sam's drinking was concerned, Bonner was sure that Ginny hadn't realized the seriousness of her father's problem until just last night. From things she'd said, he knew she was berating herself for trusting in Sam, believing that he could stop drinking if he wanted to. She'd been naive, but only because she hadn't experienced the devastating effects of liquor before.

Bonner knew too well what it could do to a person. Liquor was to white men what *tulapai* was to the Apache. It took more than a strong will to break the habit.

Looking at Ginny, Bonner had a sense that there was more to her mood than her father's drinking. He imagined she was feeling the same sexual frustration he was, maybe even remorse for letting things go so far. And then there was the business of her dead fiancé's cowardice.

Bonner dismounted and walked over to her. The

moment she saw him, she straightened her shoulders. There was an unconquerable strength in her that seemed at odds with her delicate beauty.

Taking into account that they were in public and that people might be watching them, Bonner stopped an arm's length away from her. "You look tired. Are you all right?"

She tilted her head to look up at him. "I didn't sleep much. But other than that, I'm fine." Her beautiful blue eyes looked deep into his. "How about you?"

Her question kindled memories of the passion they'd shared and the fulfillment they'd been denied. "I survived."

She half nodded, half smiled. "Me too."

With an effort, Bonner reined in his thoughts. "Was your father telling the truth about your fiancé?"

Ginny glanced toward the office. "Yes. He apologized for keeping it from me all these years—said the time had never been right to tell me."

"He loves you, Ginny," Bonner said softly. "He probably didn't tell you because he didn't want to hurt you."

Ginny sighed. "I don't doubt that. I guess I'm more mad at myself than anything for idolizing Tom and ignoring the signs." She pulled her shawl tighter around her. "They were all there. I just didn't see them . . . or maybe I didn't want to see them."

An unfamiliar emotion welled up inside him as he looked at her. For a moment he didn't trust himself to speak. "I came by to pay my advertising bill . . . and to tell you I'm on my way out of town. I have to report for duty at Camp Grant. I don't know how long I'll be gone." He reached into his pocket and withdrew a handful of silver dollars. "How much was the ad?"

She thought a moment. "Four, no, three dollars."

When she reached out to accept the coins, he placed

them in her palm, then wrapped his fingers around her small, white hand and gave it a quick squeeze.

You are destined to protect her.

The words Wind had spoken flashed through his mind. He'd considered them at length along with everything else the wind spirit had said and had drawn his own conclusions. As far as he knew, he was the only person Ginny needed protection from. Last night, his desire for her had put her reputation and her future at risk. He couldn't let it happen again. He shifted his weight, uncomfortable with the words he knew he had to say, words that were bound to hurt her, words that conflicted with what was in his heart.

"Ginny, I wanted to say something—about last night. About what happened between us. It was my fault. I look advantage of you and I think it's best if I don't—"

"Took advantage?" she interrupted. "No, Bonner. That's not true. I wanted—"

"Listen to me, Ginny. There can't be anything between us. Not now. Not ever. There's too much at stake."

"Not anymore," she said. "I tried to tell you last night but you left so quickly I couldn't catch you."

"Tried to tell me what?"

"What Pop did last night—what he'll keep on doing—I know how it'll end up. Just the way it always does. Eventually, in two or three months, his drinking will destroy the paper." She shook her head. "So you see, there's really nothing at stake."

The woman's power is strong.

Bonner stared at Ginny, his mind clicking with the sudden realization of what Wind meant. Ginny's Power was the *Tucson Sun*.

It is she who will help you achieve your goals.

Bonner's goals were clear. He wanted to help the Apache people, wanted to teach them to live in the white man's world so they could survive. But how

Ginny and the *Tucson Sun* could help was unclear.
Bonner's mind raced to come up with a logical answer.
Then a mental picture came to him of Ginny standing
up at the citizens' meeting defending her reason for
refusing to print the Stinnett boy's report of Apaches
stealing his father's stock.

"You're wrong, Ginny. There's even more at stake
now than before," Bonner said, confident in his understanding of Wind's meaning. "You can't give up on
your father or the paper."

"There isn't anything I can do. I can't stop Pop
from drinking." Her voice throbbed with frustration.

"You have to keep the newspaper going in spite of
your father, Ginny. Tucson needs an honest newspaper that won't bend to the demands of the Tucson
Ring and won't conspire with them to print false stories of Indian attacks. You can help change people's
minds by making sure that the *Sun* reports the news
truthfully. *You* can be the voice of truth and reason,
Ginny."

"Me?" She put her hand to her heart, too startled
by his suggestion to offer a rebuttal. "People aren't
going to pay any attention to what I write. I'm a
woman! You know how these people are, Bonner.
They'd never support the efforts of a female editor.
Why, if they thought I was writing the editorials,
they'd—"

"Don't worry about what they think. Be strong,
Ginny. Don't give up on your father, the paper, or
the people of Tucson."

Ginny stood looking at him, tears beginning to fill
her eyes. A gust of wind caught her hair and whipped
it about her face.

"Thanks for stopping by to pay your bill," she said
suddenly, coldly. "Have a good trip." She pushed the
wisps of hair away from her face and turned toward
the door. "Greeley. Come here, boy."

Bonner stood looking after her a moment, then wheeled around and walked away.

Ginny leaned back against the closed door. Her father sat at his desk.

"Was that Kincade I heard out there?" Sam asked, his squinted eyes telling Ginny he had a bad headache.

"Yes, he's on his way to Camp Grant. He stopped by to pay his advertising bill." She set the coins down on his desk.

"Oh, I'm sorry I missed him. I wanted to apologize . . . and thank him," he said.

At least he remembered last night and was admitting the need to apologize. She supposed that was a good sign. Though a sign of what she didn't know. "You'll have to wait until he comes back to town," she said, hanging her shawl on the hook beside the door. "Although I don't know when that will be." She started toward the door into the hall. "If you have no objections, I'm going to take the afternoon off to catch up on a few personal things."

"No, I— Ginny, we haven't talked about last night and—"

She brushed past him. "There's nothing to talk about, Pop. Nothing you could say can take away last night—the things you said and did. So I'd just as soon you don't talk about it at all. If you want to be known around town as a drunkard, that's fine with me. Just don't expect me to stand by and watch you make a fool of yourself."

"Ginny, please, honey."

Closing the office door behind her, Ginny went into the sitting room, sat down on the sofa, and spent the next hour idly looking through her collection of laces. They'd been her joy and had always brought her peace and tranquility whenever she held them.

She kept them in her mother's bridebox. The hand-painted, oval box was one of the few sentimental items Ginny had managed to bring with her to Tucson.

She picked up a length of *point de gaz* needle lace. "So fragile and yet so strong," she said, smoothing her fingers over the fine white threads.

Bonner's insistence that she not give up on Pop or the paper told Ginny that she'd misinterpreted his want and need for love. Mortified, she closed her eyes and shook her head. She could imagine what he was thinking—that she was naive, foolish, maybe even a little desperate. She cringed at the way she'd opened herself to him, telling him that there wasn't anything at stake. She'd as much as thrown herself at his feet and begged him to take her.

"I love him," she said in a soft voice, for Greeley's ears alone. "But he doesn't love me." She put the laces back in the bridebox, then stretched out on the sofa and closed her eyes.

Chapter 15

INDIAN AFFAIRS

There was a large meeting of citizens on Thursday
evening. The committee appointed to take testimony
on Indian depredations had affidavits from approxi-
mately eighty well-informed citizens and army officers.
They show the loss of hundreds of lives and hundreds
of thousands of dollars in property during the last two
years . . . Additional testimony will be accumulated,
then published in book form.

—*Tucson Sun*

Bonner took the old wagon road north out of Tucson,
passing by Rillito Creek. Since his grandfather's
rancheria was closer than Camp Grant by several
miles, he decided to go there first, say what he needed
to and get it over with.

The road stretched out in a rough line before him.
He'd traveled it a thousand times coming and going
from Firehorse Ranch or his grandfather's rancheria.
He knew every wagon wheel rut, every pothole, and
every cactus.

The surrounding desert was utterly desolate yet
grand and sublime. It could be a harsh land, an unfor-
giving land if a man didn't understand it. Having been
born and raised in Arizona, Bonner supposed he understood it better than most. Unlike the White Eyes
who saw only the barren ugliness and incompatibility,
Bonner saw beauty and harmony.

There had been clashes between the peoples who
inhabited the Arizona desert dating as far back as the
cave dwellers. Bonner had grown up hearing how the
Apaches hated the Mexicans and how the government
of Sonora had put a bounty on Apache scalps. He
remembered when wagon trains filled with white set-

tlers started traveling through Apacheria. There had
been tolerance of a sort between the two peoples, but
it had ended immediately following the Bascom affair,
an incident in which Cochise had been wrongly accused of stealing a white boy. Tensions, mistrust, and
hate had escalated greatly after that.

Bonner didn't understand the White Eyes. He didn't
understand why they looked down upon the Apaches—
treated them like wild animals and thought of them
as nothing but obstacles to their civilization. He didn't
understand how they could think that the land of
Apaches had lived on, hunted on, and worked on for
centuries was theirs. By right of conquest, he told himself. Manifest Destiny.

In the last two years he'd seen a significant increase
in the piles of stones marking graves of travelers slain
by Indians. A cross fashioned out of mescal or Spanish
bayonet stalks identified the victim as a Mexican, a
son or daughter of Holy Mother Church. The graves
were a nagging reminder that things were getting
worse instead of better.

Near sunset, he stopped to water his horse in Arivaipa Creek, a shallow, pebble-bottomed stream lined
by huge cottonwoods and sycamores. Seeming to share
his eagerness to arrive at his grandfather's rancheria,
Bonner's horse quickly drank his fill, then picked up
his feet and moved along at a brisk pace, splashing in
and out of the water as the stream wound its way
through Arivaipa Canyon. The canyon walls grew increasingly higher the farther he rode, the towering
bluffs crowding closer and closer. The irreverent
screech of a hawk pierced the air, its shadow darting
across the highest promontories.

The hawk screeched again, only this time Bonner
detected a human quality in the sound and knew it
was the call of a *vidette,* an Apache sentry hidden
somewhere high in the bluffs above him. From this

point on, his progress would be carefully watched until the *videttes* could identify him.

As night fell, the rising moon helped him find his way through the canyon. His thoughts turned to Ginny. It occurred to him that she probably thought he didn't want her because he'd pushed her back toward her father and the paper. Interrupting his thoughts, a quartet of mounted warriors swooped down out of the boulders to greet him. Barking and yipping like dogs, they surrounded him, then heralded their approach as they escorted him to the village.

A couple of dozen wickiups, their doorways facing east, were clustered in family groups on the valley floor. The hide-covered domes resembled inverted melon halves. In front of each door a campfire burned.

Bonner reined his horse to a stop just outside the village circle. After dismounting, he searched through his saddlebags until he found the candy and tobacco he'd brought for his grandfather. He stuck the little packages into the pockets of his coat, then handed over his horse to a boy who would take it to graze in the pasture at the far end of the valley.

In the distance, Bonner saw the dark form of his grandfather standing alone before a large central fire. The old man was nearly as tall as Bonner and his back was straight as an arrow. His skin was the color of burnt leather. Though glad to see him, Bonner was respectful that a man should not show excitement. He released a breath, then cleared his face of all expression.

"I have waited long for you to come," Gianatah said in Apache.

"I have had much work to do," Bonner replied in the same language. He purposely refrained from mentioning that he worked for the army, since he knew the news would be met with hostility. Sooner or later, he'd have to mention it along with the reason why he'd come. Later would be better, after they'd had

time to visit but sooner would eliminate the strain
and worry.

Gianatah nodded. "It is good for a man to have
much work. Come. We will eat, then smoke."

"I have brought you gifts," Bonner said, patting his
coat pocket.

The old man's expression was wooden, yet Bonner
fancied that he saw his small black eyes brighten with
pleasure. Gianatah turned away and walked toward
the fire. Though well into his seventies, he moved with
the agility of a much younger man. In his youth, he
had been a fearless warrior. His daring raids into Mexico were legendary among the Apache people. Unlike
many Apache men of wealth, he had married only
once, to Kenitay. They'd had one child, Bonner's
mother, Ruey. Kenitay had died some years ago when
a smallpox epidemic swept the village.

Bonner enjoyed a meal of roasted venison, mescal,
and squash. The deer had been killed only that morning, while the squash had been taken from a pit where
it had been dried and stored after the fall harvest, the
season the Apaches called Thick with Fruit.

Unlike the Chiricahua, who were nomads, Gianatah's people were farmers. Their fields were located
along the banks of Arivaipa Creek, which made irriga-
tion easy. Corn was the main crop but they also har-
vested several kinds of beans and squash.

Finishing his meal, Gianatah broke the leg bone
he'd been eating and wiped the marrow on his forearms. Keeping with the traditions of his people,
Bonner wiped the grease from his hands onto his
lower legs.

Then they talked of small things—the harvest, the
weather, the increasing difficulty of finding game. Gianatah seemed satisfied with most things but missed the
freedom of going on expeditions beyond the
mountains.

He stared into the flames. "When I was young, I

rode with my warriors to the White Mountains, to Mexico, to the west where the great river runs, and to the lands of the Zuni and the Pueblo. Our people roamed like the deer. But no more. The White Eyes attack us when we leave our village. They make cages of our mountains and keep us here," he said, sorrow and bitterness weighting his words.

Bonner remembered the good times too. As boys, he and Logan had spent many days during the winter, the season known as Ghost Face, listening to Gianatah tell stories about the brave deeds of their people and of his own hunts and raids. They learned about the myths and legends of their people—wonderful tales of the sun and sky, the moon and stars, the clouds and storms. Gianatah had taught them to kneel and pray to Ussen for strength, health, wisdom, and protection.

In the spring, he taught them the skills they needed to become warriors. They learned marksmanship not only with bows and arrows but with rifles. Then they learned horsemanship and how to trap and break wild horses. There were lessons in discipline, tests to make them strong, to teach them survival. They learned to run great distances while holding water in their mouths. It taught them proper breathing habits. And they were taught to go for long periods of time without food or water. When each of them was old enough, Gianatah took them on their first raid into Mexico.

"What is this work that you do, my grandson?" Gianatah's voice interrupted Bonner's memories.

Bonner hesitated before answering. The time to speak of his job and why he was here had come. "I work for the army," he began, "but I do not wear the blue coat of a soldier and I do not wear the red headband of a scout. I am called a civilian post guide. My job is to help the *nantans* at the army camps and forts understand what our people say to them. Also to help my Apache brothers understand what the White Eyes say."

Gianatah's face wrinkled in thought as he stared at Bonner. At length he said, "*Enjuh*," which meant "it is well." "I have much hate in my heart for the bluecoats, but I think this thing you do is good."

Bonner smiled, relieved. "It is *very* good. It shows that many of the bluecoats want to understand our people."

"Do the bluecoats understand we wish them to take their wagons and their firewater and go back to the place where the sun rises?"

Bonner had to laugh. His grandfather was typical of all the older chiefs. They would hate the white man until their dying day. "Yes, they understand, but they want this land as much as the Apaches and they will not leave."

Gianatah gave a short, bitter laugh, then tossed a small stone into the fire. "Then you must speak to them again."

"It is you that I must speak to," Bonner said, his tone earning the old man's narrow-eyed look. "I have come from the *nantan* at Camp Lowell with words that he has asked me to say." Bonner looked away momentarily, hating that he had to be the one to do this, yet knowing he was the *only* one to do it. "These words—they are not words I wish to say but must."

Gianatah's eyes hooded over, his demeanor appearing as impenetrable as stone. "Last night I heard the hoot of an owl. It is the worst of all signs."

Bonner nodded. "My grandfather is wise like the owl." And thorny like a cactus and stubborn as a mule, Bonner thought to himself. "You remember that it was the *nantan* at Camp Lowell, Colonel Dunn, who came here last spring, during the season of Little Eagles. He said he would keep the bluecoats out of these mountains and away from the rancheria as long as he could."

"The *nantan* has kept his words," Gianatah admitted, "as I have kept mine and we live in peace."

"But the Pinal and the Chiricahua do not live in peace. And because they do not, they make trouble for all Apaches." Bonner watched his grandfather's eyes. They seemed to be looking right through him. "The great *nantan* in Washington—the place where the sun rises—wishes peace between White Eyes and *all* the Apaches. The great *nantan* is wise in all things. He says that only when all our people are living on reservations will there be peace."

"We have talked of this before," Gianatah pointed out.

"Yes, we have talked. And now you must make a decision. Many of our people are cold and starving because they make war instead of planting seeds, because they raid instead of hunt. They will not accept the new ways."

"The old ways are good," Gianatah argued.

"Some of them, yes. But not all of them. If our people are to survive, they will have to move onto the white man's reservations. They'll be fed and clothed and the bluecoats will protect them from their enemies—the Mexicans, the Papagos, and the Comanches."

"Our people are like the deer. They need to roam. This reservation—I have heard Cochise speak of it—it is like a corral for horses. The bluecoats wish to put the Apaches in corrals and tame them—like they have the Papagos who have no pride."

"Pride is a warrior's word, not the word of a great leader."

"We will smoke now and you will say no more." Gianatah fixed Bonner with fierce eyes.

"No. I will say what I came to say and my grandfather will listen," Bonner insisted. "Colonel Dunn can no longer keep his word to you. When the new moon appears in the sky, he will give orders to his horse soldiers to scout Arivaipa Canyon and take all the

Apaches they can find to the reservation in the White Mountains." Bonner sat forward. "Listen to me, Grandfather. You are old and your band is small. You have only a few braves to protect the women and children. You cannot hide from the bluecoats and you cannot fight them without great loss. You have always been a wise chief. Be wise now and hear my warning. If you refuse to go to the reservation, many of your people will die."

"*To-dah!* No! We will not go. This is our home."

"You can make another home in the White Mountains," Bonner argued.

"It is not our country. They are not our people."

"Do you speak for all your people or just for yourself?" Bonner asked, challenging him. No respected Apache leader would ever presume to have the authority to speak for his people without a discussion before the council. Bonner's eyes locked with those of his grandfather's in a battle of wills.

Gianatah's craggy face was tight with anger. "My grandson speaks with two tongues, my daughter's and my daughter's husband."

Bonner drew in a long breath. "I speak with the knowledge and power that the wind spirit has given me." Until now, he'd told no one of the results of his quest. He desperately hoped it would make his grandfather understand the seriousness of the situation.

Gianatah's eyes narrowed in suspicion. "You found Wind Cave?"

"Yes."

"The wind spirit gave you *diyi*?"

"Enemies-against *diyi*, the war power."

"The wind spirit has given you good *diyi*," Gianatah said, his tone filled with awe. The old man stared into the fire. "My mind will think on what you have said."

Bonner nodded, knowing there was nothing more to be said tonight. He removed the packages from his pockets and handed them to his grandfather. "I brought you tobacco and candy."

Gianatah accepted the gifts. Bonner was pleased to see him open the packages, smell the tobacco, and pop one of the hard candies into his mouth.

The four braves who had escorted Bonner through the canyon came to the fire and told Gianatah they wished to dance in celebration of their Apache brother's arrival. Gianatah approved their request with a single nod. Moments later two elders joined the group carrying drums made of hide drawn tightly over the tops of hollowed logs. The drummers took a position west of the fire and began a slow, insistent cadence.

Others came, by twos and threes. Those who wished to sing sat near the drummers, while the old people, the children, and the spectators sat on the fringes of the fire circle.

The beat of the drums filled Bonner's ears but not his thoughts. He wondered what he'd do if his grandfather refused to move to the reservation.

He watched the dancers from several yards away. They started out by dancing in place. Then they moved toward each other, changed sides, turned, and moved in a circle around the fire. As a guest, he would have to wait for someone to call him to the dance.

He glanced sideways and looked at his grandfather, who had rolled some of the tobacco he'd given him into an oak leaf. First, he blew smoke toward the east, then south, west, north, and finally up and down.

Bonner would give him until the middle of March to make up his mind about going to the reservation, then he'd come back. If the answer was no, he'd have only two options: go around Gianatah and talk directly to his people, which would make him lose face and humiliate him, or try getting a more tractable leader whom Gianatah respected to speak with him.

The chanters began to sing. One of them sang out

to Bonner. "You, Bonner Kincade, you are known to be a great warrior. We are calling you to dance."

Old habits never die, Bonner thought as he took off his coat and shirt and walked among the dancers. He moved in a clockwise circle around the fire with the other young men of the village. Soon, his skin was slick with sweat. He released the rawhide thong holding his hair and felt its blunt length brush his shoulders. One of the braves gave him a rattle—a short piece of wood embellished with rawhide thongs, bears' claws, bits of bone, and small stones.

"Hi yah, hi yah, hoo hoo," Bonner chanted in a high tone as he shook the rattle. "Hi yah, hi yah, hoo hoo."

The women added more wood to the fire until the flames grew as tall as the dancers. Firebrands shot up from the fire's heart and exploded into the night sky. Ashes rained down on the dancers.

"Hi yah, hi yah, hoo hoo. Hi yah, hi yah, hoo hoo." The voices of several dozen men, women, and children joined those of the dancers.

Bonner soon lost himself in the magic of the dance. His mind went back to another time, when he and Logan had watched the Crown Dancers perform a curing ceremony for their grandmother and a dozen or more others who had come down with the smallpox. Wearing magnificent headdresses and dark cloth masks, the Crown Dancers had danced and chanted until dawn. Still their grandmother and the others had died.

It was after that that Logan went into the mountains to talk to the Mountain Spirits. Three days later he came back and told their mother that he wished to go east to the white man's school and learn to be a great medicine man.

The dance lasted into the small hours of the morning. Bonner stopped occasionally to eat, visit, and drink *tulapai.* When the dance ended, one of the unmarried braves invited him to bed down in his wickiup.

A small fire, built in a shallow hole in the center of the earthen floor, threw shadows on the walls of the wickiup. Beds made of brush and grass and covered with skins looked good after a long day. But as tired as he was, he couldn't sleep. He spent the hours until dawn thinking about Ginny.

After what had happened between them, she had a right to expect some kind of pledge or commitment from him. Instead, he'd told her there was no hope for them. Worse yet, he'd completely ignored her reckoning that her father's drinking problem would destroy the *Sun* and thereby eliminate all risk. Then, on top of everything else, he'd berated her for giving up on her father and the newspaper.

Something told him he might have reacted differently—possibly taken her up on her implied offer—if the realization hadn't hit him that Ginny's power was the *Tucson Sun*. Because his goals for the Apache people were tied to Ginny and the *Sun*, he'd tried to convince her to keep the paper going.

His goals. Not Apache goals. Not the Tucson citizens' goals. Not even Ginny's goals.

Ginny's tear-filled eyes haunted him. He'd hurt her. He knew it. Yet he would do it again. He'd made a commitment to the Apache people—his people—and he would not shirk it—not even for the love of a woman.

The thought caught him off guard. He looked up at the smoke hole in the top of the wickiup. The last thing he needed was to fall in love. Especially with a white woman. He wasn't about to put himself or Ginny through the same kind of hell his parents had suffered.

Besides, he couldn't imagine Ginny being able to adapt to ranch life. She was a city woman, and while he might be willing to visit the big cities occasionally, his heart was in Apacheria and he had no intention of leaving it.

Bonner waited until the sun was high in the sky before saddling his horse and preparing to leave. He found his grandfather standing in front of his wickiup stringing a new bow.

"I must go now."

"May we live to see each other again," Gianatah said. He reached out his hand to embrace Bonner's forearm.

"I'll come back before the next new moon," Bonner replied. "Think about what I said."

Effortlessly Gianatah bent the bow into position.

Camp Grant lay fifty-five sagebrush-and-yucca-covered miles northeast of Tucson. It was a bleak military post made up of weathered adobes, mud-and-brush-covered jacals, and tents that should have been discarded long ago. Facing the parade ground was a row of two-room officers' quarters, the adjutant's office, guardhouse, post bakers, the hospital and quarters for enlisted men. The commissary and the quartermaster's storehouses were there too, each with corrals behind them.

The camp was situated on a plateau some fifty feet above the juncture of the San Pedro River and Arivaipa Creek. There was little to recommend the site or the camp itself other than it had good water, most of the year.

First Lieutenant Royal E. Whitman welcomed Bonner and quickly filled him in on what had been happening. Bonner liked Whitman right away, sensing in him a compassion and understanding for the Apache people that few army officers possessed—that few white men possessed. Adding to that, he found Whitman to be intelligent, conscientious, and dedicated to his job.

Bonner was assigned to a bachelor officer's quarters.

The last occupant had whitewashed the walls and covered the hard dirt floor with several brightly woven Navajo rugs. A row of insect-filled bottles lined the windowsill and a suit of armor, more than likely belonging to a sixteenth-century Spanish conquistador, had been polished and hung in the corner for decoration.

In the two weeks since Bonner's arrival, the only Apache he'd seen was Little Britches, a ten-year-old boy Whitman had taken under his wing.

Life at the post was monotonous. The center of social activity was the sutler's store where a man could drink warm or cold beer, depending on the weather.

Bonner liked beer. It didn't give him the spin that *tulapai* did, nor did it give him a headache. Unlike the soldiers, he didn't sit around the sutler's store gossiping or playing card games while he drank. To occupy his time he borrowed books and magazines from the few officers who had them, and he began composing a long, detailed letter to his brother.

Bonner's letter filled Logan in on the current status of the Territory, his recent run-in with Clay Foster, and his theory about Foster's involvement with the Tucson Ring. He told Logan about his conference with Colonel Dunn and his subsequent visit with their grandfather. He thought long and hard before telling Logan of his involvement with Ginny Sinclair. He struggled for the right words to describe how he felt, then gave it up, realizing words couldn't convey his feelings. He closed the letter describing his disappointment at not finding a potential tutor for Martine. None of the newspapers he'd brought with him even listed a schoolteacher looking for a new position. Admitting defeat, Bonner charged Logan with the task of finding someone.

To relieve the boredom of Camp Grant, Bonner volunteered to hunt and to lead half-day scouts, which took in a maximum twenty-mile radius. As they checked up on the surrounding ranches, Bonner learned the attitudes of the ranchmen toward the Apaches did not parallel those of the citizens of Tucson. In fact, the ranchmen were kind to them and treated them with respect.

Bonner had just returned from a scout east of Camp Grant when he saw five Apache women walk onto the post carrying a stick to which was tied a white flag of truce. The women walked slowly across the parade ground, their sudden presence bringing all activity to a halt.

Bonner finished unsaddling his horse, then turned him loose to roam free until he needed him again. Dusting himself off, he made his way toward the women. They were old and their clothing, what there was of it, was in tatters.

Whitman came running from his office, his saber clattering at his side. "Have you asked them what they want?"

"Not yet," Bonner answered.

Whitman nodded. "Introduce me and tell them they're welcome at Camp Grant."

Bonner conveyed the message. The women talked in mumbled whispers among themselves and nodded. Bonner could see that they were afraid. He could also see that they were cold and that they appeared half-starved. He told an orderly to get some jerked beef and some warm blankets for their visitors.

"Find out what brings them here," Whitman said.

Bonner talked with the women at length and learned they were Arivaipa Apaches in search of a boy who had been taken prisoner by an army patrol up north. The one who had carried the truce flag took a crumpled piece of paper from the pocket of her skirt and handed it to Bonner. He glanced at it, then gave it to Whitman.

"It's from Major Green at Camp Apache," Whitman reported. "He says these women are looking for a boy between ten and twelve years old who was captured back in October along the Salt River. He says if we have him, to give him to them."

"There's only one boy here who fits that description," Bonner said.

Whitman turned to the young private who had followed him across the parade ground. "Tell Little Britches to come here."

Minutes later the private returned with the boy. The women appeared to recognize him, but if they were glad to see him, they didn't show any emotion. The woman carrying the truce flag spoke directly to the child.

Bonner translated. "She's his aunt. She's telling him that her husband wishes him to return to their rancheria." Then the boy replied and Bonner said, "Little Britches doesn't want to go back with them. He says he likes it here."

"I can speak for myself," the ten-year-old said in English to Whitman. "I tell squaws I wish to stay here with *nantan* Whitman. Much food," he said, rubbing his belly. "Warm clothes," he added, tugging the sleeve of his woolen shirt. "Very happy. No go with squaws."

The boy's aunt looked crestfallen. "Our people are poor," she said to Bonner. "We have little food and our clothing is old and torn. We will not force the boy to come with us."

Bonner translated her words to Whitman, then added a few of his own. "I'd like to make a recommendation, sir." At Whitman's nod, he continued. "Invite the women to stay here a few days. That way they'll have time to talk to the boy. If he still refuses to go with them, at least they'll feel better about leaving him here."

"Good idea, Kincade. And while they're here, we'll show them just how hospitable the bluecoats can be."

Bonner made the offer. The women looked skeptical at first but then they talked among themselves and came to an agreement. "We will stay two suns. Then we go."

The women made camp just beyond the cavalry stable. Bonner stayed close to their camp so he could translate their questions and needs. Whitman gave orders that they be well fed, given old issue blankets, some tobacco, and a few yards of a coarse, white cloth called manta. Whitman sent his striker around to the officers' wives and laundresses to ask them to donate some of their old clothes. The squaws showed no outward sign of excitement or appreciation but within an hour after the items were delivered, they were wearing them.

On the morning of the third day, the women prepared to leave. As they headed out, their leader turned and asked Bonner if they could come back with a few others of their band. After conferring with Whitman, Bonner was pleased to translate that all would be welcome if they came in peace.

All the rest of the day and into the evening, the talk around camp was about Whitman inviting the Apaches back. Taps were being blown when Bonner answered a knock at his door.

"Lieutenant Whitman." Bonner was surprised by the unannounced visit. "Something I can do for you, sir?"

"You can invite me in, Kincade."

Bonner stepped aside to allow Whitman to enter, then pointed to a hide-covered chair. "What do you want to talk about?"

"Lieutenant Robinson seems to think I made a terrible mistake today."

"What sort of mistake?"

"He says I shouldn't have let those squaws on the post and that I was wrong to feed them and give them blankets." Whitman rubbed his chin. "He's even more concerned that I invited them back."

"They were old women. They came under a flag of truce. To turn your back on them in their condition would have been inhumane."

"That's what I thought, but Robinson feels that Apaches can't be trusted."

Bonner simply stared at the man. "I'm half Apache, sir. I don't know what to say."

"Just confirm my belief that I did the right thing."

"I don't see that any harm could come from it," Bonner said, crossing his arms in front of him. "In my opinion you did exactly the right thing. If I'm not mistaken, the army wants you to encourage the Apaches to make peace and that's what you did."

"That's the general idea—in theory anyway. The trouble is, I wasn't authorized to extend them the hospitality of the camp or to invite them back."

Bonner stood and looked out the window. Across the parade ground he watched lights go out one by one as the troops settled down for the night.

Whitman groaned as he stood up. "I guess we'll just have to wait and see if anything else happens."

"I guess so," Bonner agreed.

As Whitman shook Bonner's hand, a weary smile crossed his face. "Thanks, Kincade."

Eight days later the women were back. This time, they brought other women of their band along with some items they hoped to sell so they could purchase more manta.

Lieutenant Whitman treated them as before, and when they were ready to leave, they told Bonner their chief wanted to talk peace.

Bonner gladly translated Whitman's words. "I would be happy to talk peace with your chief."

Chapter 16

The driver of Thursday's eastern mail brought word that early this week a party of three men and one woman were attacked by Indians just this side of Apache Pass, resulting in the loss of their stock but no injury to their persons. From every direction that news can be received, Apache depredations are reported.

—*Arizona Citizen*

Thursday morning came and went quickly. When the clock struck twelve noon, Ginny looked at it in disbelief. She'd put herself on a self-imposed deadline and needed to get these last few sheets of newsprint run off before she could leave to do her interview with Marino Carrillo, the owner of the Gymnastic and Theatrical Company. His troupe would be playing in town Saturday and Sunday nights for the next three weeks.

A gust of cold wind caught Ginny's attention. She looked up from her work to see the office door opening and a woman coming in. She dropped a note onto the front desk, then left without a word. Another rush of wind ruffled the sheet of paper Ginny had been folding over the tympan.

"Crimeny," Ginny glanced at her father and swore beneath her breath. Wadding the now badly wrinkled sheet into a ball, she tossed it into the whiskey barrel she'd salvaged for their discards. At the rate she'd been making mistakes and ruining paper, the barrel would be full in no time.

You can't give up on your father or the paper. Bonner's words nagged at her whenever she became frustrated and started having second thoughts about the decisions she'd made.

She'd promised herself she wouldn't think about

what he'd said or what she wished he would have said. But every time she let her guard down, all the words and emotions came flooding back.

Tuesday, immediately after her quick conversation with Bonner, Ginny had felt hurt, embarrassed, and humiliated. She cringed to think of the things she'd said to him—that there wasn't anything at stake anymore. She'd intimated that now there *could* be something between them. How could she have been so bold? So brazen? She'd practically thrown herself at his feet and begged him to commit to her. He'd made love to her—or almost had—but he'd never said he *loved* her! Because of the passion they'd shared, she'd assumed he felt about her as she felt about him. She'd assumed wrong. His reply had been clear. He didn't want her, at least not in the way she wanted him.

She'd decided then that it would be best if she packed her trunk and took the next stage to California. From there she'd go east by railroad to Boston or Philadelphia and apply for a job at one of those suffrage newspapers or possibly with *Godey's Lady's Book,* since they were already familiar with her work. Once settled, she could begin sending money back to her father.

But the next morning, after a sleepless night, she swallowed her pride and changed her mind. Plain and simple, she couldn't abandon Pop or give up on his dream. She'd stay in Tucson and do the best she could. When Pop got to the point he couldn't function on a day-to-day basis, she'd run the newspaper on her own. She already had most of the skills and she could learn whatever else she needed to know over the next few weeks. It would be a great deal of work for one person, but she was willing to give it a try.

The biggest obstacle would be Tucson itself. With a little luck and a lot of effort and grit, she *might* be able to get the townspeople to accept a female editor. Not all of them certainly, but some of them. People like Mrs. Rolfe Brown, for instance. Of course, there was still the economic problem of the *Sun* being the third newspaper in a town that only needed one. If she could hang on until the *Arizonan* ceased operations, the *Sun*'s chances for success would greatly improve.

You can be the voice of truth and reason. Bonner had said that Tucson desperately needed a newspaper that had no political ties and no prejudices where the Apaches were concerned. He'd told her she could change people's minds simply by reporting the truth.

Ginny had come to Tucson with high hopes not only to see the *Sun* succeed but to become a journalist like her father—to inform and educate people with well-researched articles, and eventually, if the chance presented itself, with thought-provoking editorials. She'd wanted her writing to make a difference—to help make the world a better place. And she'd been happy to start with Tucson.

Could it be that what she wanted and what Bonner wanted for her were the same thing?

Ginny pulled the lever and the platen pressed the paper against the type to make an impression. When she checked the page, she frowned. The print was too light. Either more ink was needed or the lever hadn't been pulled hard enough. All she knew was if she didn't stop making mistakes, she'd never be the voice of anything.

The door opened again, this time admitting a man. He had a folder in his hand.

"I'll take care of it," Sam said, getting up from his desk and heading toward the front to wait on the man.

Ginny nodded, then went back to work. In the last four days, she'd spoken to her father only when circumstances demanded it. The strain of keeping her anger alive had begun to wear on her, but she wasn't about to give it up. Not this time. Once she did, he'd believe all was forgiven. Then he'd put the incident behind him and think everything was all right.

But everything wasn't all right. He'd broken his promise to quit drinking. From here on out, she'd never be able to count on him for anything, never be able to put her whole trust and faith in him. And every time she found a whiskey bottle in the wood pile or pushed to the back of the shelves or stuck under a piece of furniture, she'd feel the sting of that broken promise all over again.

As soon as the customer left, Sam returned to his desk and resumed his writing. He'd been working unusually hard these last few days, and he hadn't left the office other than on newspaper business. He'd been the exemplary businessman and journalist.

Glancing at him out of the corner of her eye, Ginny could hardly believe that the studious, bespectacled gentleman sitting at the desk was the same odious drunk Bonner had escorted home the other night, the man Bonner had said was a loudmouth and a troublemaker.

It seemed as if he were two people. One she loved. One she hated. Pop and Sam Sinclair. They were as different as night and day. Pop made the promises. Sam broke them.

Hearing her father's frustrated sigh, Ginny looked to see him mark a big black X through the top half of his editorial. When he did it again a few minutes later, Ginny knew he was having difficulty composing it. After all, he'd been working on it since early this morning. Now, time was getting short. It had to be finished by this afternoon or it couldn't be included in tomorrow's issue.

Greeley crawled out from under the printing press and barked. "Just a second, boy. I just have to lock up these forms." Knowing Greeley didn't interrupt her unless he was serious, she finished up as quickly as possible. She looked down at her ink-stained hands and the black smudges on her work apron and decided to take Greeley through the kitchen and out back where no one would see her. Newspaper printing could be a messy business and she'd managed to prove just how messy it could be.

After Greeley's break, she'd only have a half an hour to get the ink off her face and hands, change her clothes, and walk the four blocks to the Stevens House, where Senor Carrillo and his troupe had taken rooms. Afterward, it would be back to the office to write up the article, set the type, and start printing. Getting the paper out wouldn't be quite as difficult as it was last time, since two of the four pages had been printed yesterday. Still, it would be late tonight by the time they got the newspapers bundled and ready to go.

Ginny shook her head, hoping she'd have the energy to see it all through. Greeley did his part to help her by limiting himself to sprinkling the weeds closest to the kitchen door. Ginny thanked him with a pat and walked back inside to get ready.

A quarter of an hour later, scrubbed, brushed, and clothes changed, Ginny hurried back into the office. "Pop? I have to leave. I have an interview with—" She stopped abruptly. Her father wasn't at his desk. "Pop?" she called again, thinking he might be behind the privacy screen where they kept their extra printing supplies. But he didn't answer. It was then that she noticed he'd cleared his desk, as he always did when he'd finished for the day.

"He wouldn't leave without finishing his editorial," she said aloud. Greeley tilted his head and looked up at her. "He must have finished it while I was getting dressed." Ginny searched the worktable first, then looked through the mess on her desk, and finally rummaged through her father's desk drawers. She found it—what there was of it—in the top middle drawer. The banner line caught her attention.

WILL HATE DESTROY TUCSON?

A terrible disease is taking its toll on a great number of Tucson citizens: hate. From all appearances, it is spreading at an alarming rate and infecting not only individuals but whole families.

Several severe cases were seen Monday, January 23, at the Court House, during the citizens' meeting. One poor soul had to be dragged from the premises because his hatred had festered to the point that he was screaming out like a madman. Other people displayed varying symptoms: name calling, foul language, bigotry, extreme racial prejudice, uncontrollable outbursts of anger.

The disease is contracted through word of mouth and erroneous newspaper reports and it is expected to reach epidemic proportions—

Reading her father's words, Ginny understood why he'd been having difficulty. The message was a strong one. It was also poignant and would be thought-provoking if anyone took the time to read it. At the top of the page, he'd written some notes to himself: don't scold, try to give a solution, end on a positive note. Toward the bottom he'd scrawled out a familiar quote: *"The only good Indians I ever saw were dead."* General Philip Henry Sheridan, January 1869. And another one: use to illustrate point.

"The only good Indian is a dead Indian," Ginny whispered, reciting the more popular version of the now famous quote. Knowing how Pop worked, with notes here and there to remind himself of what he wanted to say, she could tell he'd been trying to link the public's attitude toward the Apaches with callous, insensitive, and irresponsible statements from leaders such as the one Sheridan had made. She'd often heard Pop say that men in power had a moral responsibility to the public they served to think before they speak— because eventually the whole country would hear them and be influenced by what they'd said.

She put the editorial back where she'd found it,

hoping Pop had merely stepped out to get his thoughts together.

Creaking and swaying, a long line of merchandise-laden wagons rolled down Main Street. The mules strained against their harnesses to pull the wagons through the rain-soaked streets.

Instead of dodging between them as many people were doing and taking the risk of getting splattered with mud, Ginny opted to wait until they'd passed. Once they were well down the road, she slowly made her way across the street, hopping over water-filled wagon ruts and walking around potholes as big as duck ponds.

The interview had gone extremely well, and as Ginny headed home, she thought how much she was looking forward to writing the story. The tantalizing smell of roasting pork coming from the Shoo Fly restaurant reminded her that she needed to stop and pick up a few groceries.

Ginny walked into the first mercantile she came to, squeezing through the door past a boy carrying a large wooden box of groceries. Composing a mental list of the items she needed, she turned left into the first aisle and headed for the shelves of canned food. "Let's see," she mumbled to herself. "I need canned peas, beans—" Across the store, she heard men talking but paid them no mind. Then she heard Clay Foster's distinctly Southern drawl rise above the others.

"Begging your pardon, gentlemen, but this isn't the time or the place to be discussing this."

Ginny glanced between the shelves to see a group of well-dressed men—probably local merchants from the cut of their clothes—standing in a semicircle around a potbelly stove. Other than Clay Foster, whose shining blond hair made him easy to spot, they were all standing with their backs to her.

"The meeting was a waste of time and energy as

far as I'm concerned," one of the men said. "It accomplished nothing. Absolutely nothing. I should have known better than to think something would come of it."

While she didn't want to be an eavesdropper, her journalistic instincts kept her frozen in place.

"I hold you responsible for this, Foster," the same man continued, his tone plainly annoyed. Ginny peeked through a space between the cans of peas. "You said we'd come out of that meeting with the go-ahead to form a militia. Instead, all we have is more talk."

"You can't blame me for the outcome, Mitch," Foster answered. "I didn't know there were that many Indian lovers in town. From all the talk, I assumed most people were as tired of the Apaches as we are. If you'd wanted a sure thing, you should have said so. I'd have taken care of it."

Taken care of it? Ginny's brow wrinkled in a frown. What did that mean exactly?

"Sure you would have," another man replied. "Just like you took care of Kincade. You really put him in his place, didn't you? Showed him who's who and what's what, didn't you?"

Ginny could almost feel the heat of Clay Foster's anger. "Kincade's a savage—trained from childhood in Apache warfare for God's sake. You try fighting him like a gentleman and see where it gets you."

Ginny scowled. A gentleman? No *gentleman* would pull a concealed knife on an unarmed opponent. It was everything she could do not to stomp out into the open and start regaling the group with the truth of Clay Foster's cowardice and dirty tricks. Instead, she snickered in disgust and headed for the door.

"I'll tell you what cinched it," said a new speaker whose voice Ginny had heard before but couldn't put a name or a face to. "It was that damn scribblin' woman gettin' up in front of everybody and spoutin'

off about how the *Tucson Sun* is the voice of truth
and reason." Like a professional speechmaker, the
man gave his words emphasis by raising his voice.

Ginny's mouth dropped open. She stopped in the
middle of the aisle, her feet frozen in place.

"I seen her kind before," someone else said. "A
regular drumbeater. Wouldn't surprise me none to
learn she was one of them temperance crusaders or
suffrage women."

"She's trouble," said another. "Nothing but pretty
poison."

"She *is* pretty," Clay Foster said, his tone indicating
a much deeper meaning than his words. "Very pretty
as a matter of fact. But she's *just* a woman, gentlemen.
And in the hands of the right man, a woman—even a
willful woman—can be easily managed."

Ginny clenched her teeth together. She was breathing so hard she could feel her nostrils flaring.

"And you think you're that man, huh, Foster?"

"I do indeed, my friend. I do indeed."

"I sure as hell hope so, because you can bet that
from now on she's going to scrutinize and question
every Indian report that comes across her desk. I don't
think I need to remind you that we've got a lot riding
on what happens in the next few months."

Ginny lifted an eyebrow. This whole conversation
was beginning to sound very suspicious.

"Sounds to me like somebody ought to have a little
talk with the Sinclairs and convince them that it's better to work with us than against us," said the man
Clay Foster had addressed as Mitch.

"Sam's no problem," Foster assured them. "Buy
him a drink and he'll do anything you want." Ginny's
stomach turned as the men chuckled. She hadn't realized that Pop's drinking problem was already a well-
known fact. She made a fist. Damn him anyway!
"Ginny, on the other hand," he continued, "will re-
quire more special handling."

"You can handle her, Foster. Show her some of that old-fashioned Southern charm you use on—"

Whatever else the man said was lost when two chattering women walked in, followed by the boy Ginny had passed on his way out a few minutes ago. A moment later the group of men broke into a round of laughter, which was followed by back-slapping good-byes and hand shaking.

With a supreme effort, Ginny remained where she was, peering out between the shelves, committing each face—one or two she recognized—to memory as they filed out of the mercantile. Once they'd gone, she collapsed on a step stool behind her and attempted to calm herself. She was so mad she was shaking.

A damn scribbling woman! Trouble! Pretty poison! Just a woman! Easily managed! Special handling! She didn't know which description of herself she resented more. They all made her boiling mad.

Just let Clay Foster try to *manage* her or *handle* her!

A half hour later, her outrage safely banked, she'd purchased her groceries and was making her way home down the soggy street when she saw her father coming out of a saloon. It wasn't even evening and he was already drunk. His eyes were glazed and his lips were moving as if someone were tickling them. When he'd left the office, she hadn't really believed he'd just stepped out to gather his thoughts since that was something he never did. She suffered the pain that twisted her heart and told herself that this was exactly what she'd expected.

Seeing that he was having difficulty navigating the potholes and wagon ruts, Ginny caught up with him and took his arm just as he was about to lose his balance.

"Ah, my little Ginette to the rescue!"

"Yes, Pop. Your little Ginette to the rescue. Now straighten up and hold on to me. I'm going to take you home and sober you up because you and I have got work to do. You hear me, Pop?"

His eyes met hers. "I hear you, honey. I promise I—"

"No more promises, Pop. Please. *No more promises.*"

After three cups of strong black coffee and a hot and hearty meal of fried chicken, mashed potatoes, and canned peas, Sam Sinclair began to sober up. While he finished his supper, Ginny read aloud the half-written editorial and made some notes of her own in the margins.

"It's too harsh," Sam said, wiping his mouth with his napkin. "Sounds too much like a sermon."

"No, it doesn't, Pop," she argued. "I think it's something that needs to be said. And it just might do some good."

Sam slowly folded his napkin, then put it next to his plate. "I doubt it. People can't see themselves as others see them. They'll read it and think I'm referring to everyone else *but* them."

"Maybe so, but at least you'll make people aware of the terrible hatred that exists here. That in itself might make a difference."

A world-weary expression crossed Sam's face. "I wish I had your optimism and enthusiasm," he said, setting his fork and knife on top of his plate. "I'm sorry, honey. I just don't know where to go with this editorial, and at the moment I don't have anything else in mind to replace it." He put his hands on the edge of the table and started to push backward.

Ginny put her hand on one of his, stopping him. "Let me help you," she said, leaning toward him. "Tell me what you want to say and I'll work it up."

He glanced down at her hand. "But that's just it. I don't know what I want to say, Ginny. I lost my focus."

"Well, let's start with your notes here." She looked

down at the page and read his own notes off to him. Sam shook his head and shrugged. "It looks to me like you meant to link things together—to illustrate how people tend to blindly follow leaders, never questioning the truth of their words or their motives."

"That's true, but I couldn't find the right bridge to link things together." His voice sounded dull, as if he'd lost hope, given up.

Ginny thought about Bonner, about the things he'd said to her outside the office the day he'd left. No matter how badly things had ended between them and no matter how determined she was to forget him, what he'd said made sense. She couldn't let her father give up.

"Listen, Pop. Think of all the leaders whose words have been taken as gospel. Think of all the people who have changed their beliefs because some leader with a talent for speechmaking inspired them. The public is always finding out too late—after all has been said and done—that they've been lied to or given false information."

Stubbornly, Sam shook his head. "Forget it, Ginny. Some things aren't worth the effort."

Ginny could feel her cheeks grow hot with anger. "That's right, Pop. Some things *aren't* worth the effort but *this* is. If your editorial touches even one person and helps them to see the hate that permeates this town, then it will have been worth the effort." She crossed her arms, sat with her spine straight against the chair, and glared at him. "Besides, we can't print a newspaper without an editorial and that's that!"

Sam stared at her a long time, as though trying to determine his chances of getting her to leave him alone. "All right," he said after a moment, his tone ringing defeat. He closed his eyes and rubbed his forehead. "What if I— What if I expound on how word of mouth has altered Sheridan's callous statement and turned it into a war cry for Indian haters? 'The only

good Indian is a dead Indian!' I could make the point
that it's become such a popular society phrase that it's
echoed in political meeting halls, ballrooms, and front
parlors across the country."

"That's good, Pop," she said, encouraging him.
"Keep going." Using her own abbreviations, she managed to write as fast as he talked. Before she knew it
the editorial was finished.

Ginny's heart swelled with pride. Even half-sober,
her father was a brilliant journalist. His words filled
her with exhilaration and deep satisfaction. And to
think that if not for Bonner, she might have given up
on him! She knew now that she could never give up
on her father no matter how impossible he became.

"I need to lie down and try to get rid of this headache," Sam said, rising. "I'd appreciate it if you'd put
the finishing touches on the editorial. I'll see you in
about an hour and we'll get that last page printed off
and those papers folded and bundled."

Three hours later, Sam still hadn't come out of his
bedroom and Ginny knew she was on her own. She
hadn't expected her responsibilities to increase so fast,
but they had, and now, tonight, it was entirely up to
her to put the paper to bed.

She stood at the end of the hall leading to their
living quarters and looked at her father's closed
bedroom door. Then she turned and looked back at
the printing press, her table full of galleys, and the
stack of blank newsprint. Finally, she looked at the
clock.

"Oh, Pop!" She pounded a fist against the door
frame, then went back into the office, put on her print-
er's apron, and got to work.

The following Friday, in spite of Ginny's pleas and
objections, Sam left the office just as he had the week
before. This time Ginny found no evidence that he'd

even begun an editorial, which didn't surprise her because she hadn't seen him working on it.

Disheartened, she sat down at her desk and rested her head in her hands. Every day she'd been confronted with something else that her father hadn't done and she would need to do. *No more than what I expected,* she reminded herself each and every time.

Now, the question was should she attempt to write an editorial in her father's journalistic style and let people think he'd written it? Or should she write it in her own style and alert readers of an editorial change?

She remembered the looks she'd gotten at the citizens' meeting when she'd stood in defense of the *Sun*. The good people of Tucson hadn't been too pleased that a woman had spoken up. With a sigh, she decided to hide the truth for as long as she could. Now certainly wasn't the time to risk the paper's position by announcing an editorial change.

February flew by so quickly Ginny hardly knew one day from the other. The talk around town focused on the book the citizens' committee was putting together, *Memorial and Affidavits Showing Outrages Perpetrated by Apache Indians, in the Territory of Arizona, During the Years 1869–1870.* With a title like that, no one would mistake it for anything other than what it was. Once completed, the book would be forwarded to all the leading newspapers, public libraries, and anyplace where lots of people would see it. Still more copies would be sent to makers of law and shapers of public sentiment.

Little mentions of the book, sprinkled throughout the pages of the *Arizona Citizen,* kept it in the news. "Arizona will be redeemed and prosperous. There was never more encouragement in this direction than now," claimed the *Citizen*'s editor.

After weeks of articles campaigning about the deplorable condition of Tucson's streets, Ginny ended her series with a story about a New York hotel owner who'd come to Tucson to see about opening up a twenty-room luxury hotel and restaurant. During his town tour, the man fell into a pothole of Main Street and broke his leg. Ginny wrote, *He left Tucson on Saturday's stage, angry, upset, and swearing to never return to this city. "Any town that doesn't care enough to keep its streets in decent repair isn't a town where I want to bring my business."*

The Tuesday after the paper came out, Ginny noticed a crew of men shoveling wagonloads of dirt into the potholes on Main Street. Ginny smiled. The power of the press coupled with the power of lost business revenue was getting the streets repaired.

Bonner was right. She *could* make a difference.

The smile faded from her lips. Every time she thought about Bonner, she felt a deeper pain than the one before.

By the first of March, she'd developed a work routine. Mornings, she sat at the front desk, doing her bookkeeping and waiting on customers who brought in advertising, news of weddings, deaths, births, and social activities. Anyone bringing in any kind of Indian report was thoroughly questioned and asked how they'd come by their information. If their answers were too vague, Ginny thanked them for the report but didn't put it in the paper. After what she'd overheard in the mercantile, she couldn't be too careful.

Afternoons, she wrote up everything she'd taken in during the morning and set type.

Her evenings were as full as her days, but quieter. She divided her time between reading out-of-area papers to gather national and foreign news for the *Sun* and comparing reports from the *Citizen* and the *Arizonan* to the reports she or her father had written on the same subject.

Nights, she went to bed with a book and read until the words blurred on the page. Then, she'd put out the light. Sometimes sleep would come right away. Most of the time it didn't.

For all the hard work she put in, day in, day out, she thought the least she deserved was a good night's sleep. But the battle she fought during the day to stay so busy she didn't have time to think about Bonner was lost to her at night.

In the weeks since Bonner had left Tucson, images of their night of lovemaking had haunted her mercilessly, firing her blood and keeping her restless and awake long into the night.

It was Ginny's turn to have an afternoon tea for her literary group. Indy Garrity was the first to arrive, followed by Mrs. Brown and two of her friends, Mrs. Christensen, a merchant's wife, and Mrs. Scott, the banker's spinster sister. The group discussed *A Beggar on Horseback,* of which they'd had only two copies to pass between them.

Before the meeting ended, Ginny unfolded her most recent issue of *Harper's Weekly* and opened it to the middle where the advertisements were located. "Let's order five copies of the same title from Harper and Brothers in New York so we'll each have our own. When we're finished, we can choose to keep it or we can donate it to the town library."

"You aren't calling that pitiful little space in the back of the Pioneer News Depot a library, are you?" Mrs. Brown looked positively stricken.

Ginny laughed. "No. I'm talking about Tucson's *future* library. We're bound to get one someday and they'll need donations. There are several interesting titles here," she said, looking over the advertisement. "Since we all liked *Beggar on Horseback,* let's try *Gwendoline's Harvest* or *Won—Not Wooed* by the same author. They sell for fifty cents. I realize this is a little expensive, but think of the good it'll do for our library."

Everyone agreed, then decided upon *Won—Not Wooed,* thinking it sounded like a romantic novel. After the meeting ended, Indy and Mrs. Brown stayed to help Ginny clean up.

Ginny's mind wandered as she began clearing away the plates and napkins. She remembered being surprised that Bonner was so well read. She also remembered being surprised that in spite of his savage good looks, he was a gentleman. Clay Foster, on the other hand, looked every inch a gentleman, but definitely was not.

"Considering it's only our second meeting, things are going quite well, don't you think?" Mrs. Brown asked as she stacked teacups and saucers.

Indy brushed crumbs from the snowy, lace-edged tablecloth. "Very well," Indy replied. "Don't you think so, Ginny?"

Her hands full of dirty dishes, Ginny walked past Indy to the kitchen without answering.

"I don't believe she heard you, dear," Mrs. Brown observed. "I daresay there were times this afternoon when she seemed a bit distracted."

"I'm sure she has a lot on her mind these days," Indy said. Indy repeated Mrs. Brown's question. And again, Ginny went about her cleanup and didn't answer. "Ginny! For heaven's sake." Indy reached out and touched her friend's arm. "I'm talking to you."

Ginny stopped midstride. "I'm sorry. My mind was a million miles away. What did you say?"

Indy laughed. "It isn't important. Just chitchat."

When Ginny came back, Mrs. Brown took her hand. "Ginny, dear, I never did get a chance to tell you how much I enjoyed your article on the women's rights convention. I've always been a supporter of women's suffrage and temperance, but of course there's rarely mention of it in the *Citizen* or the *Arizonan.* I was quite pleased to read it in the *Sun.* Might you be attending the convention this spring?"

Ginny shook her head. "No. I can't leave. I'm needed here."

"Indeed you are, dear. In just the short time you and your father have been in Tucson, my husband and I have become quite dependent on the *Sun*. In spite of all the bad news about Indians and war abroad, there's always something in the *Sun* that gives us hope." She squeezed Ginny's hand and smiled. "I really must be going home now. Mr. Brown will be expecting me. Try not to work too hard, Ginny dear. And give your father my best."

As soon as she was gone, Ginny sat down on the sofa to take a breather. "She reminds me of my mother."

"That's funny," Indy said as she finished her straightening. "She reminds me of my mother too."

The two women stared at each other across the room, then burst out laughing. Minutes later when their giggles had subsided, Indy sat down next to Ginny. "Why don't you tell me what's been bothering you."

"What makes you think something's bothering me?" Ginny stiffened and drew back.

"Ginny. You're not very good at hiding your feelings. Neither am I. Jim used to tell me that my eyes gave my thoughts away."

Ginny looked down at her hands. There were traces of ink embedded into the cuticles. "It's that awful Clay Foster," she admitted after a moment. She wrung her hands at the thought of him.

"I told Jim what you overheard," Indy said. "He wasn't surprised by anything Foster said."

Ginny gave herself a moment to gather her thoughts. "He frightens me, Indy." She took a deep breath. "He came by the office a few days after that incident in the mercantile, but of course I didn't let on that I'd eavesdropped. He wanted to talk to my father, but Pop wasn't there so he settled for me instead. He said he headed up a group of merchants whose only interest was in seeing Tucson prosper. But that the Apache situation was costing them dearly. Then he told me that the other two newspapers in town supported the merchants' efforts by publishing all reports of Indian depradations, no matter how small or seemingly insignificant." Greeley rested his head on Ginny's knee. She looked down at him and smiled. "He went on to say that Tucson needed the *Sun*'s support and that the merchants would show their gratitude by supporting the *Sun* with advertising." Ginny patted Greeley's head. "What's so frightening is that if I hadn't overheard him and didn't know what he was up to, I might have thought he was doing me a favor." She shook her head.

"How did it end?"

"I told him that Pop and I would only publish those reports that could be verified. Then, because I was so angry that he tried to bribe me, I told him that we'd been sold out of advertising space ever since we began and weren't really looking to gain more."

Indy's eyes widened. "Sold out of advertising space? That's wonderful, Ginny! I had no idea the *Sun* was doing—"

"It was a lie," Ginny interrupted. "A paper can never be sold out of advertising space."

"Oh. Oh, of course." Indy reddened with embarrassment. "I should have realized."

"He came by again a few days later and invited me to the Valentine's Day dance. I told him I don't dance—which I don't but it wouldn't have stopped me from going if I'd wanted to. Then yesterday, while I was out shopping, I ran into him at the Pioneer News Depot and he asked me to have supper with him any night of my choosing. I very politely thanked him but told him that I wasn't accepting any invitations."

"What did he say?" Indy asked.

"Nothing. He just glared at me. Then he walked away."

The women stared at each other in sudden tension-filled silence. Ginny switched her gaze to the window. "I think I've made an enemy of him. And if he's as evil as I think he is, there's no telling what he might do."

Chapter 17

LETTER FROM CAMP GRANT

A private letter from Camp Grant brings us news that
First Lieutenant Royal E. Whitman, 3rd U.S. Cavalry,
Commanding, has received at that post several parties
of hostile Apaches, the last of which included a war
chief who wanted to come in and talk peace. The chief
claimed to be the head of a small band of Arivaipa
Apaches. He wanted to put himself and his band
under the protection of the Government. On his own
authority, Whitman offered the chief and his band rations, blankets, and protection.

—*Tucson Sun*

The morning cold didn't stop Bonner from bathing in
the river. Anything was better than the slimy wooden
tubs the soldiers bathed in. Wearing only a
breechcloth, he waded into the icy water. Teeth
clenched, he wetted himself down, soaped and
scrubbed himself all over, then rose up out of the river
like a phoenix and shook off, beads of water flying in
every direction.

Bonner had visited the river so often in the last few
weeks that he knew almost every fish by size and
color. He'd even given a couple of them names. There
was Freckles, a pan-size rainbow trout, who peeked
out at him from behind a boulder in the shallow water
close to shore. And Wiley, who hid out in a deep-
water hole a few yards upriver. Bonner had accidentally stumbled upon Wiley's lair on his first visit and
ended up spitting and sputtering in water well over
his head.

Most of his visits had resulted because of thoughts
of Ginny.

Ginny.

Ginny standing in front of her window, hugging herself. Ginny's look of fear after he'd sliced off a piece of her hair. Ginny's eyes at the moment he'd plunged himself deep inside of her.

He headed for shore and dried off with an old shirt. His saddlebags were full of dirty laundry he planned to take to the laundresses as soon as he got back to the post. After that, he'd see if the mail detail had returned. No letter yet from Logan, but Bonner figured it would come any day now. The post surgeon hadn't been able to offer an explanation for the problem with his father's leg, but knowing Logan, his letter would have a dozen or more different medical possibilities and just as many treatments.

After he checked the mail, he would pick up copies of the Tucson newspapers. He'd made it a habit to read all three and compare the Indian-related reports. Week after week, he found the *Tucson Sun*'s reports to be fair, without the distortion of personal feelings, prejudices, and interpretation. And instead of challenging army actions, the *Sun* sustained them. *The voice of truth and reason.*

He'd seen an increase in the number of ads, which told him the paper was prospering. He took a small measure of pride and comfort in that, knowing that he hadn't underestimated Ginny's ability or the paper's potential.

He hadn't liked himself much after that last time they'd talked. He'd selfishly thought only of his goals and hadn't paid attention to her wants and needs. He'd left her thinking he didn't want her.

He should have told her about the power Wind had given him to help the Apaches and explained that he'd yet to exercise that power. He should have told her that she, too, had power—great power—and that it lay in the *Tucson Sun*. Instead of berating her for giving up on her father and the paper, he should have helped her see the need to keep doing what she was doing—to make the *Sun* the voice that spoke out against fear and hatred. And the guiding light toward peace.

Should haves. Could haves. Would haves. They all added up to one thing: regret.

Frowning, he got up on his horse and started back to Camp Grant. Halfway there, he looked up and saw white smoke puff skyward from two separate signal fires built on mountaintops.

Certain that Lieutenant Whitman would be anxious to know what they meant, Bonner tapped his heels into his horse's sides. "Come on, boy. Let's go." The animal broke into a full gallop.

Predictably, Whitman was pacing outside in front of his office when Bonner rode up. "What do they mean, Kincade?" Whitman halted and pointed toward the mountains. "The men are nervous and, frankly, so am I."

"It's nothing to be alarmed about," Bonner answered as he dismounted. "We're going to have visitors."

"Visitors? Apaches I assume. They're coming in peace, I hope."

"They're coming to talk."

"When?"

Bonner turned and studied the smoke signals. "Today. They'll probably be here this afternoon sometime."

"I sure as hell hope you're reading those things right."

Bonner smiled and nodded. "That makes two of us. I'd hate to find myself out of a job because I was wrong."

Whitman eyed Bonner narrowly. "If you're *wrong*, you won't have to worry about a job. You'll be dead. We'll all be dead."

Bonner kept a sharp eye on the smoke signals. He recommended Whitman post extra sentries as a precautionary measure just in case the messages were a trick to get the Apaches within rifle range of the post.

Whitman went a step further and ordered all officers and troopers to arm themselves and to be on the alert should any trouble arise.

Twenty-five Apache warriors showed up at the perimeter of Camp Grant an hour after the noon mess. One of the Indians, a short, stocky man in his early forties, carrying a lance decorated with eagle feathers and rawhide strips, stepped forward and raised his arm in greeting.

Lieutenant Whitman saluted in return.

The Apache then looked directly at Bonner, his small eyes seeming to take his measure. "You are Apache?" he asked in that language.

Bonner replied in the same tongue. "My mother is Apache. My father is White Eyes." He watched the chief's eyes for a negative reaction but there was none.

"You will speak *my* words to the bluecoat *nantan*?"

Bonner nodded.

"How do I know you will not change them?" It didn't surprise Bonner that the chief was worried about being misinterpreted. There had been a number of incidents—on both sides—where the translation had been deliberately altered for personal or political gain.

"I give you my word—as a brother that I will speak your words as you speak them to me." The chief's hard, unflinching scrutiny made Bonner feel as if he were twelve again and trying to keep a secret from his father.

At last the chief said, "I am Eskiminzin, chief of the Dark Rocks people, I want to make peace with the bluecoat *nantan.*"

Eskiminzin's reputation as a warrior chief among the Arivaipa Apache was well known. He was a son-in-law of Santos and had assumed the chieftainship after Santos had become too old to lead his people.

In spite of Eskiminzin's bedraggled clothing and that of his warriors, he exuded an aura of pride.

Bonner delivered the chief's words exactly as he had spoken them.

"Tell him I'll be happy to talk peace with him," Whitman replied. "Ask him to follow me to my office where we can sit and smoke."

Following Bonner's translation, Eskiminzin nodded, then followed Whitman across the parade ground with his warriors close behind him.

Walking off to the side, Bonner assessed the warriors. Only a few carried Sharps rifles and carbines. The rest were armed with bows and arrows, war clubs, and lances. Their clothing wasn't sufficient to keep them warm but not one of them gave any indication of being cold. Bonner wasn't surprised. Apaches were trained to hide their discomfort as well as their feelings. The warriors wore loincloths, long Mexican shirts, and buckskin moccasins that reached midthigh. Several of the party were barely old enough to have gone through their novice time, yet they carried themselves as though they were seasoned warriors.

Wary glances told Bonner they were nervous about being surrounded by so many soldiers, all of whom were armed to the teeth. He didn't blame them. They were taking a chance coming here.

Second Lieutenant Robinson was waiting next to Whitman's office door.

"I'd like you to join us, Lieutenant," Whitman said, his tone making it clear that he was not issuing an order but an invitation.

"Thank you, sir," Robinson replied, then stepped aside to allow his commanding officer to enter the office first. Eskiminzin hesitated on the threshold, then turned around and motioned for two of his warriors to accompany him. Bonner went in last, closing the door behind him. He carefully noted that the rest of

Eskiminzin's group had taken positions outside near the door.

Once inside, the chief's gaze roamed over every piece of furniture and accessory, including the ink well and pen on Whitman's desk and the pictures and maps on the walls. When the chief had completed his study of the office, he sat down in the chair Whitman indicated and pulled up to the table, his two warriors taking positions on either side of him. Whitman sat directly across from him, flanked by Robinson and Bonner.

Whitman's striker brought in a wooden box full of tobacco and cigarette papers and passed it around the table. Everyone rolled their tobacco and smoked their cigarettes in silence.

When the last man had stubbed out his cigarette, Eskiminzin began to speak, pausing between long sentences so that Bonner could translate his words.

"He says that there are one hundred fifty people in his band. More than half of them are women, children, and old people. Some are Pinal Apaches.

"Their home has always been along the banks of Arivaipa Creek but the soldiers attacked them and forced them to retreat deep into the mountains." Bonner saw Eskiminzin's facial expression change and knew that the chief understood more English than he'd let on. "Now they have no home. Wherever they go, they fear the cavalry will come," he continued. "They're tired of war. They want to return to their home, plant their crops, and live in peace."

"Suggest that he take his band north to the White Mountains where other Apaches are living in peace," Whitman said.

Giving himself a moment to think, Bonner smoothed his hair back from his forehead. Instead of translating Whitman's message, he leaned toward Whitman and said, "I know it's not my place, sir, but that particular suggestion won't be appreciated. The White Mountains is not their country and the White Mountain Apaches are not their people."

Whitman nodded. "I see." His face knotted in thought. "At least I think I do."

"I'll explain it to you later," Bonner assured him.

"Good. In the meantime . . . tell him I have no authority to make a peace treaty with him. Tell him I can't promise him that the *nantan* in the East will allow him to make a permanent home. But . . . he may bring his people here—in peace—and I'll give them food rations and blankets and report his wishes to the department commander."

Bonner knew how the army worked. Whitman's offer was considerably more than what he'd expected. At the very most, he'd thought the lieutenant would make a list of Eskiminzin's requests and tell him he'd present them to his commanding officer. Instead, he'd offered a temporary sanctuary and provisions.

Bonner looked at Robinson. The junior officer's face was marked with disapproval. Bonner optimistically extended the offer.

"No. We will not live in the shadow of the blue-coats," Eskiminzin said, a look of implacable determination on his face. "We want to return to our home."

Bonner studied the chief's expression. Eskiminzin was no fool. He had to know that a peace would be on Whitman's terms, not his. And he had to know that Whitman's offer was a good one.

Bonner translated Eskiminzin's words, then added a few of his own. "I suspect Eskiminzin is being obstinate because he feels he'd be letting his people down if he took your first offer, no matter how good it is. Negotiate with him, offer him something else, demand something else from him in return."

"There's nothing else I can offer."

"Look," Bonner said, leaning sideways toward the

officer. "The whole band is probably in desperate need of clothing, so—"

"I can't! Food, blankets—that's it!"

"Hear me out!" Bonner said, spreading his hands on the table. "Once his people are settled, and while you're waiting to hear back from Stoneman, you could put his people to work harvesting hay. Then you pay them—in vouchers, not money—that they can use to buy clothing or whatever else they need."

Whitman thought a long time before answering. "All right, but nothing else. And what I want in return is for him to understand that they will be counted every couple of days and that no rations will be issued to anyone who's missing from roll call."

Bonner turned to Eskiminzin and told him what Whitman had proposed. The chief repeated it to the two warriors flanking him. Sensing another rejection, Bonner spoke first. "I speak to you as a brother. You have come in peace and the *nantan* has offered to let you stay here—in peace—until he talks to *his* chief. There is nothing more he can do until he has spoken in council." Eskiminzin's expression was firm and unyielding. "If you lead your people back to Arivaipa Canyon, the *nantan* cannot promise that you will not be driven out or killed by the soldiers. And if you keep your people where they are, they will die of cold, starvation, or sickness." He saw a flicker of pain move swiftly across the chief's face. "But if you bring them here, they will be given food, blankets, and white men's medicine. In time, your people will grow strong again."

Eskiminzin glared at Bonner, his small eyes dark and cold. At last he spoke. "Tell the *nantan* I will accept his offer."

The meeting was over.

Later, after supper, when rank formalities were customarily dropped, Bonner sat in silence as Lieutenant

Robinson voiced his concerns to Lieutenant Whitman. "Eskiminzin is a troublemaker. I've heard his name before. You're kidding yourself, Royal, if you really think Eskiminzin is sincere in making a peace."

"Then why would he come here?" Whitman asked.

"He told you—he and his people are tired of being attacked by the cavalry. They want to rest, fill their bellies, get warm. As soon as they've gotten everything they need, they'll go right back on the warpath. That's the way they work."

"What's happened to you? You didn't used to be this pessimistic. You're beginning to sound like Oury and Foster and the rest of that Tucson bunch."

"Nothing's happened to me. I just don't trust them, that's all. They're Apaches," Robinson said as if that explained everything. "I can't believe you offered them what you did. I don't know what you were thinking."

"I was *thinking*—and I'm still *thinking* that this could be the first step toward a voluntary peace settlement, which is supposedly what Stoneman, Grant, everybody wants!"

"That's the key word—supposedly," Robinson countered.

Whitman let out a groan of frustration and pivoted on his boot heel to face the window. After a moment he turned and looked at Bonner sitting in a nearby chair. "You haven't said a word about this one way or another."

Bonner uncrossed his leg. "What do you want me to say?"

"I don't know. Something. Anything!"

"I want peace," Bonner said, rising to his feet. "That's why I became a post guide—to do what I could to help my people."

"*Your* people? Who are *your* people, Kincade?" Robinson asked.

Bonner didn't care much for Robinson's tone but

he decided to ignore it. He turned to Whitman. "For whatever it's worth, I think you did the right thing."

Whitman smiled and slapped Bonner's shoulder. "Thanks. I'll see you tomorrow."

For several days after Eskiminzin's departure, smoke signals continued to drift on the winds above the mountains. Over and over they signaled the same message: come, talk. Then the fires burned out and black smoke replaced white.

Two days later Bonner spotted Eskiminzin's band through his field glasses. They slowly made their way on foot down through the foothills. Half of the women plodded along under the weight of their family's belongings. The rest of them carried cradle boards on their backs or led small children. The very old and ill rode litters carried by the band's warriors.

Bonner sent for Whitman and waited at the perimeter of the camp, a deep, unaccustomed pain tearing at his heart as he watched the band move closer. Their clothing, what there was of it, was little more than rags. When they were close enough so that he no longer needed his field glasses, he saw that a number of them were barefoot. Their feet were bloodied and they were limping.

To see Apaches reduced to this state was something he hadn't been prepared for. In spite of what the White Eyes thought, there was nothing about these people to indicate that they regarded themselves as a superior race. Nothing to testify to their legendary strength and savagery.

Within minutes after they reached the edge of camp, Whitman had the band escorted to the parade ground. Through Bonner he told Eskiminzin that they would spend the night there and tomorrow they would be taken to a campsite near the post.

Officers and troopers alike pitched in to build a large central fire and erect small tents. They passed

out blankets and food. The army surgeon bound
bloodied feet and treated an assortment of illnesses.

Early the next morning, Whitman ordered up all
the wagons, horses, and mules on the post and led the
band a half mile east to a campsite beside the waters
of the Arivaipa. After unloading their belongings from
the wagons, they immediately set to work building
new wickiups, gathering stones for campfires, and cutting wood.

Eskiminzin walked over to where Bonner and Whitman were standing. "This is a good place," he said.

Bonner knew that was as close to a thank you as
the chief was going to get. Apaches were extremely
reserved in expressing gratitude. They believed it
should be understood rather than spoken.

"You will be safe here," Whitman promised.

Two days later, Bonner was reading his mail—a
long letter from Logan—when there was a knock at
his door. He reluctantly put the letter aside and got up
to answer it. "Robinson. Something I can do for you?"

"Lieutenant Whitman would like to see you. It
seems we have another band of Indians coming in."

Bonner grabbed his coat off the back of the chair
and joined Robinson outside. They cut across the center of the parade ground to the edge of the camp
where Whitman was waiting.

Looking through his field glasses, Whitman said,
"They look to be in a lot better shape than the others.
And they've got horses."

Bonner shielded his eyes against the sun's glare.
Squinting, he counted between forty and fifty men,
women, and children. It took him a minute or two to
pick out the leader.

Then he saw him.

Bonner's mouth went dry. Gianatah. He sat atop a
magnificent paint pony, his body straight, his head
high. In his left hand, he held a lance decorated with

black-tipped eagle feathers. He was dressed in fringed buckskins and wore a feathered medicine cap on his head. He looked every inch the Apache chief.

"Well, I'll be damned," Bonner said, thinking aloud.

"Who is he?" Whitman asked.

"Gianatah. My grandfather."

"Your grandfather?" Whitman stared at Bonner, his expression one of complete surprise.

Gianatah reined his horse to a halt in front of Bonner and Whitman. "I have come to make peace with the *nantan*," he said, looking straight at Bonner.

"Tell him I'll offer him the same terms I offered Eskiminzin," Whitman said, then went on to outline them in detail.

Bonner couldn't believe his grandfather was actually here, surrendering himself and his band. He wondered what had been the deciding factor—what he'd said to him, Gianatah's meeting with the council, or word of Eskiminzin's surrender. It didn't matter. He was here.

Unlike Eskiminzin, Gianatah didn't challenge the terms but accepted them without question.

"If you wouldn't mind, Lieutenant, I'd like to escort my grandfather and his people out to the campsite."

"Not at all," Whitman replied, his expression saying he understood. "Stay with them awhile if you like. Help them get settled. Rest assured, I'll send for you if I need you."

That night, the two Apache bands came together and danced in celebration of peace.

Bonner danced with them. Toward dawn he walked off by himself and climbed up into the rocks behind the campsite. Higher and higher he climbed, his heart pounding with the effort. At last he reached the top and found he had a view of the entire canyon.

He looked down upon the encampment, at the newly constructed wickiups, at the central fire, at the dancers, at the figures of his grandfather and Eskiminzin standing back away from the fire watching their people celebrate.

This was the way it used to be, Bonner thought, before the White Eyes came and the hatred began.

This was the look of peace.

For the first time, Bonner had a sense of his *diyi*. It wasn't the kind of power he'd thought it would be, but it was power all the same. Eskiminzin and Gianatah were testimony to that power—they'd both been swayed by his words, by his reason. It was the power of Apache called enemies-against. And the enemy had been mistrust.

"Speak to me, Wind," Bonner said into the night.

Not a bush stirred. Not a hair on his head blew.

For endless seconds he stared into the darkness, waiting, hoping. At length, he turned to leave, thinking himself foolish to believe that he—a mere man—could summon the wind.

"S . . . e . . . e . . . k . . . e . . . r!" a voice called from far away.

Bonner stopped and looked around. "I'm dreaming," he said when nothing more happened. "I just imagined I heard his voice." He had nearly convinced himself when he felt a billowy presence coming straight up out of the rocks beneath his feet.

"I am here, half-breed," Wind said, rising up from the center of the earth.

"Has the price of peace been met?" Bonner asked, then waited anxiously for the answer.

"Patience," Wind said.

"I have been patient. I want to know," Bonner angrily demanded.

Wind gathered himself into a slender funnel and swirled around Bonner. "It is not for you to know. I have given you much *diyi*. Use is where you can."

Anger and disappointment kept Bonner awake the rest of the night. Early the next morning he rode back to Camp Grant to finish reading Logan's letter. After seeing to his horse, he saw Whitman coming toward him across the parade ground. He had a newspaper in his hands and was shaking his head.

"Did you see this?"

"What?"

"This report. I can't believe it. This isn't anything like the letter I submitted."

"The *Sun*'s always been so fair in the way they've presented our letters. They never speculated or made conjectures. They reported the plain facts in an honest journalistic style. But this—I don't understand it." Whitman handed him the paper.

"What?" Bonner looked at the masthead on the front page. It was the *Sun*. He read the report. *"A private letter from Camp Grant brings us news that First Lieutenant Royal E. Whitman, 3rd U.S. Cavalry Commanding, has received at that post several parties of hostile Apaches . . ."*

Having read Whitman's letter, he was able to spot the differences—significant differences that changed the entire tone of the report. Word choices like *hostile* Apaches and *war* chief. And one particular phrase: *on his own authority*.

Bonner handed him back the paper. "With your permission, sir, I'd like to go to town and find out why this has happened. I know the publisher and—"

"Permission granted, Kincade. But don't be gone too long. I need you here."

Chapter 18

Letter from Camp Grant
PEACE AGREEMENT BY THE PINAL
DELIGHTFUL HOPES EXPRESSED

CAMP GRANT, A.T., March 7, 1871—The prospects that
your city will not be troubled by the Apaches for some
time, are very bright indeed. Lieut. Whitman 3d Cavl'y
and commanding officer of this post, has just concluded a peace with two of the petty chiefs of the
Pinal Tribe, who have sent runners out to all their
people, with the intent that they shall also come in on
a reservation. This peace was concluded under the
most auspicious circumstances . . . I feel confident in
asserting that no matter what other officer comes here,
if they are treated with the same kindness and fair
dealing as they are receiving at the hands of the now
Commandant and Commissary, the people of Arizona
need be under no further apprehension of any incur-
sions from this portion of the Apache tribe . . . I think
that these Indians being left San Pedro and Arivaipa
Valleys to cultivate, and receiving convincing encouragement by implements, seeds, etc., in fact everything
they would be requisite to start on their new career,
we will have no more of those Indian atrocities that
have so blurred the history of this Territory.
—A Soldier,
Arizona Citizen

Ginny sat at her desk, a newly sharpened pencil stuck
behind her ear and another in her hand, poised over
the banner line she'd just written for her fashion article.
THE CAMELS ARE COMING! THEIR HUMPS, THEY ARE
STUNNING.

She smiled as she read over what she had so far.
The factual information had come directly out of *The
Californian,* but she was reworking it into a light, hu-

morous fashion story that she thought would appeal
to both male and female readers.

> *A new fashion has made its appearance on the streets
> of San Francisco and is causing considerable amuse-
> ment. It is called the Grecian Bend. From all reports,
> only a few women have as yet dared incorporate it into
> their wardrobes as it is ridiculous in the extreme. Ladies
> who aspire to great fashion—to be* en règle—*suppose
> it is quite feminine and graceful. Its main feature is a
> depression of the bosom inward and an elevation of
> the posterior to an unrealistic position by way of an
> artificial composition of horse-hair, called a "pannier."
> Worn in conjunction with very high heels, the "bend"
> produces a completely new way of walking. The fash-
> ionable ladies are said to be suffering not only the
> taunting chants of small boys referring to them as cam-
> els and of grown-up scoffers who use phrases such as
> "Colic Stoops" and "lame kangaroos," but lower back
> pain as well.*

She made a couple of notes to herself to describe
the social scene in which the Grecian Bend was making its appearance and to end with a quote from one
fashion observer, *"If ever I do take a wife, I shall take
her as I take my brandy—straight!"*

She tucked the article into the desk drawer and
checked her list of things to do. Writing things down
helped keep her organized.

Pop had been gone all morning soliciting ads. It was
one of the few jobs he still did. Just last week he'd
turned over all the editorial duties to her, declaring
that he just didn't have the desire to write them anymore. Ginny had accepted but told her father that
now was not the time to make an official announcement. She'd explained that she wanted to get the
paper more established before announcing that a female had taken over the editorship of the *Sun.* Sam
had agreed and promised he wouldn't say anything,
but Ginny knew better than to trust his promises and

thought it was probably just a matter of time before word got out.

On a clean piece of paper, Ginny began experimenting with ideas on how to write the announcement. "Due to illness, Sam Sinclair has handed over the editorship of the *Sun* to—" She scratched out the word *illness*. Drunkenness was not an illness. Next she wrote, "While I will continue on as a consultant, my daughter will take over as editor—"

Ginny's thoughts were interrupted when someone opened the office door. Indy Garrity walked in, swathed in a heavy dove-gray cloak with a hood that hid her hair and most of her face.

"I hope I'm not interrupting." She closed the door behind her, then started across the room toward Ginny.

It wasn't until she pushed the hood back off her head that Ginny saw the dark circles under her eyes. "Indy! Are you all right? You look . . . exhausted." Terrible would have been a better word but she didn't want to hurt Indy's feelings on top of whatever else was troubling her.

"I haven't been getting much sleep," Indy admitted. "But I'll be fine as soon as Jim gets home."

"And when is that?"

"I don't know. Soon, I hope." Indy looked away but not before Ginny saw tears gathering in her eyes.

"Indy! For goodness' sake." Ginny got up from behind her desk and went to Indy's side. "Here, take my hankie," she said, pulling a lace-edged handkerchief out of her apron pocket.

Indy dabbed at her eyes.

"Where is Jim?"

"On a scout," Indy said between sniffles.

"How long has he been gone?"

"Five—six days—" She cleared the tremors from her voice. "What is today? March twelfth or thirteenth?"

"The thirteenth," Ginny confirmed. She'd never seen Indy so distraught.

"Jim left on the eighth."

Six days, Ginny thought, not overlong for a scout. In fact, not long at all. She remembered Jim saying that some scouts took only a day while others lasted a week or more. It depended on how far they had to ride and what their mission entailed. Ginny wondered if Indy's pregnancy wasn't causing her to worry unnecessarily. "I don't understand what you're so worried about," Ginny confessed.

Indy twisted the hankie until it looked like a piece of braided rope. "It's just that this time he's going— It's such a . . . dangerous assignment. I know he can take care of himself. He's practically an army within himself, but . . . he's not invincible."

Ginny sat Indy down in a chair and knelt next to her. "Where did he go?"

"He—" Indy's gaze swept the office, her eyes wide, cautious. "Is your father here?"

Ginny shook her head. "No. He's out soliciting advertising."

"Oh, Ginny," Indy said on a long sigh. "I've been on pins and needles worrying ever since Jim left. I've been wanting so badly to come and talk to you—to share my fears, but Jim made me promise not to tell anybody." She grabbed Ginny's hand and held it tight.

Ginny didn't know what to say. She didn't want to encourage Indy to break her promise to her husband, yet she couldn't imagine what could be so secretive.

"Indy, whatever it is, I'm sure everything will be just fine."

"Oh, I wish I could believe that but I can't. I know what Jim is up against," she said, beginning to sob. "I want to tell you, Ginny, but I need you to swear you won't tell anyone, not even your father."

"Indy, you made a promise—"

"And now I'm breaking it. I have to talk about it

to *someone* or I'll go mad. You're the only one I can trust." Indy's chest heaved as though she'd been keeping all her emotions pent up.

"All right. I swear," Ginny said reluctantly.

Indy untwisted the hankie and blew her nose. "Jim went after Lahte," Indy said, the words rushing out of her. "He plans to bring him back and question him about his involvement with Clay Foster."

"Lahte?" Ginny thought a moment, the name somehow familiar. But she couldn't remember why. Then it came to her. "Oh, of course! The Apache who attacked the Fish and Company wagon train."

"And killed nine men," Indy added. "He's a ruthless renegade. Not even Cochise will have anything to do with him because he rapes his female captives and scalps all his male victims."

"I thought all Apaches raped and scalped."

Indy shook her head. "It isn't their custom. They're a very superstitious people. Luck, power—they mean a lot to them. If a warrior rapes a woman, he risks losing his luck. And scalping—the Mexicans are the ones who started that."

Ginny shuddered, eager to turn the conversation away from those grisly crimes. "Jim didn't go alone, did he?"

"No. He took three men with him—men he trained last year at Camp Bowie. They're good men, don't misunderstand me. They know how to fight Apaches as well as Jim, but—"

"But you still can't help but be frightened and worried. I understand, Indy. I think that's a perfectly natural reaction, but you mustn't borrow trouble. You have to have faith in Jim."

"Once Lahte knows he's being chased, he'll go to any length to avoid capture. And Jim will go to any length to bring him in because it means exposing Clay Foster and the Tucson Ring."

"How does Jim know where to look for him?"

"Gianatah, Bonner's grandfather, told Bonner and Bonner sent a note to Colonel Dunn. Bonner would have gone after Lahte himself but what with all that's going on out at Camp Grant, he couldn't leave."

Ginny patted Indy's shoulder. "I think you're over-reacting, but in your condition it's expected."

"Not you too, Ginny! I'm so tired of hearing about my condition I could scream!" She let out a whoosh of air.

Feeling a little chagrined, Ginny softened her tone. "I know but—you *are* pregnant. It's a well-known fact that pregnant women tend to be more emotional."

Childishly, Indy put her palms over her ears. "All right. All right. I'm a bundle of emotions. I'm over-reacting. Making more of it than I need to." She leaned toward Ginny. "Which is why I needed to talk to *you*. I knew you could calm me down. Put my fears into perspective. After all, you *are* the voice of truth and reason."

Surprised by the comment, Ginny frowned. There was no mockery in it, but it made her a little uncomfortable nevertheless. First Bonner had said she *could* be the voice of truth and reason and now Indy was saying that she *was* the voice of truth and reason. Ginny was beginning to wish she'd come up with some other motto. Something like, "Truth is, and ever has been, and ever will be our highest aim," or "The Exponent of Truth, Justice, and Sound Morality." On second thought, those wouldn't have worked either.

Ginny smiled at Indy, pushing aside the pretentious-sounding creeds. "What you need is a nice cup of tea."

"Personally, I think what she needs is a kiss."

The unexpectedness of Jim Garrity's voice took the two women by surprise. Simultaneously, they turned their heads toward the door.

"Jim! Oh, Jim!" Indy jumped up out of her chair and flew across the room into her husband's waiting arms. "I've missed you so much. I've been so worried."

Jim laughed. "I've missed you too, Mrs. Garrity." The tenderness in Jim's expression warmed Ginny's heart. "But you should know better than to worry about me. As long as I know you're waiting for me, I'll always make it home."

Ginny stood up, walked back to her desk, and sat down. She couldn't help but feel a twinge of jealousy at the love Jim and Indy shared. It was the kind of love she'd always dreamed about.

Still clinging to her husband, Indy asked, "How did you know to look for me here?"

"Masculine intuition," he said, tapping his index finger against his right temple.

"Did you bring Lahte back?"

"Did you have any doubts, woman?"

She smiled and shook her head. "No. I knew you'd find him. That's what worried me."

Jim looked down at his wife. "I assume you told Ginny?"

Indy opened her mouth to speak but nothing came out.

Jim looked over his wife's head at Ginny.

Ginny tilted her head and knitted her eyebrows, doing her best to look confused, but she could see by Jim's expression that her efforts at artifice were in vain.

"Uh-huh," Jim surmised. "Well, I don't suppose it was fair of me to ask you to keep it from *everybody*."

"You aren't angry with me, are you?" Indy asked, looking less worried than her tone indicated.

Jim laughed. "No."

"It's just that I was so upset—I *had* to tell Ginny."

Ginny raised her hand as if giving an oath. "She made me swear I wouldn't tell a soul, not even my father."

"Good," he said, his tone earnest. "Because I don't

want Clay Foster finding out that Lahte is behind bars. If he gets wind of it, he'll run like a jackrabbit. Right now I've got enough on him to hang him three or four times."

Ginny's mind was in a whirl. She was seeing headlines: Tucson Merchant Ring Leader; Tucson Merchant Charged With Sabotaging Fellow Merchants; Merchants, Murder, and Mayhem. It was the kind of story that would be carried by all the Eastern newspapers, maybe even the foreign presses. She remembered then that her father had asked Jim for an exclusive. "I hope you're still willing to give the *Sun* an exclusive."

"I told your father I would, but it won't be for a while yet."

"Of course. I'll be looking forward— I mean, I know my father will be looking forward to getting the information. It should make for a fabulous story."

"Let's just hope it has a happy ending. And that the charges we bring against Foster rams home the fact that it's the white man's greed and avarice that's at the bottom of most of the Indian problems." He looked down at Indy and brushed a lock of hair away from her face.

"I'll make a note of that," Ginny said. "I'm sure it could be incorporated into the article."

"I have just one request, Ginny. I'd appreciate it if you'd give Gianatah credit for revealing Lahte's whereabouts. I think it might do some good toward creating goodwill."

"Of course," Ginny answered, then automatically realized she'd replied as though the decisions were hers. "I—I'm sure my father would be more than willing to give Gianatah credit."

Jim nodded, seeming satisfied. "Speaking of Gianatah, has Bonner come back yet? I want to congratulate him for his peace negotiations with Eskiminzin. The private who delivered the news to Camp Lowell said if it wasn't for Bonner, Eskiminzin would have walked out. Apparently Bonner convinced him that the only way to save his people was to surrender."

"Peace? Surrender? When did all this happen?"

"About a week ago. Just before I took out after Lahte. In fact, Whitman's announcement came with the same courier that brought Bonner's note on where to find Gianatah."

Indy looked bewildered. "I can't believe you haven't heard, Ginny. Why, it's all over town. Everybody's actually quite optimistic. Everybody except John Wasson, that is. He devoted his editorial to denouncing the military's judgment and to saying that even if the Apaches have offered peace, that they deserve more punishment."

Peace. Surrender. The words repeated over in Ginny's head, giving her an all over good feeling. She turned to look out the window and thought that the sky seemed bluer and the clouds seemed whiter. She smiled, thinking that Bonner must be feeling very pleased with himself right now. Very pleased indeed. She was glad for him.

"How did he manage it?" she asked, returning her attention to Jim.

The sound of galloping hooves pulled Jim's gaze to the window. "Looks like you can ask him yourself. He's just riding in now."

Ginny popped up out of her chair. Her first instinct was to run across the room and bolt the door. But in spite of the joy she felt for his accomplishment, she didn't want to see Bonner now, not today. She hadn't taken time this morning to properly groom her hair and there were ink smudges all over her apron and her hands. Even if she didn't look so awful, she still wouldn't want to see him because she'd yet to resolve her feelings from the last time they'd talked, just before he'd left for Camp Grant.

Ginny considered her options and realized she had

none. She could see Bonner's horse sliding to a stop in front of the hitching post outside the window. Then came the jingle of harness, the creaking of saddle leather, and the horse's winded snorts.

She held her breath and waited. Within seconds, the office door flung open and Bonner stormed inside. His dark, angry gaze found where she stood behind her desk and pinned her to the floor.

"Is this the kind of journalism that speaks of truth and reason?" he shouted, his words sharp as a pistol shot. Brandishing a folded newspaper, he moved toward her, completely ignoring Jim and Indy. The lightning in his raging black eyes made her take a step back.

"What are you talking about?" She shook her head, utterly confused.

"Your father's rewrite of the Camp Grant letter, that's what I'm talking about. Nothing like a few well-placed adjectives and editorial cuts to change the whole tone of Eskiminzin's surrender."

"Camp Grant letter?" She lowered her gaze, her mind frantic to recall what the letter said.

He gave her a cold look. "Don't pretend you don't know what it says," he warned.

She had no intention of pretending. She *didn't* know. So many army letters had come in, one from Camp Apache, one from Camp Bowie, one or two from Camp Lowell. She remembered them all as one big blur.

Bonner didn't give her time to respond. He took another step toward her and demanded, "Where's your father? I want to talk to him."

Ginny back away one more step, but there was no place left to go. Her hands pressed the wall as she looked up at Bonner. "He's not here," she said as calmly as she could manage. Which to her own ears didn't sound calm at all.

"When will he be back?"

"Soon, I'd think, but I don't know for sure. He's— he's somewhat *unpredictable* these days," she said, assuming he'd know what she meant.

Bonner threw the newspaper down on the desktop. "I thought the *Sun* was going to be different than the others. I thought *you* were going to make it different, Ginny."

Ginny felt the sharp stab of his disappointment and wanted desperately to assure him that she hadn't let him down. But how could she assure him when she hadn't read the letter? And how could he accuse her without proof she'd done something wrong? Fighting anger, Ginny picked up the newspaper, found the Camp Grant letter, and began reading. Halfway through, she knew she'd never seen it before. This was the letter that talked about Eskiminzin's surrender.

She stared at the letter a long time, then said, "Bonner, I—I'm not sure what happened here but I've never seen this letter before."

His onyx eyes flashed with undisguised anger. "What are you telling me, Ginny? That you don't read the letters you publish?"

"No!" she cried. "Of course I do! But—" She shook her head. "I read everything that comes across my desk. Everything! And I don't print anything I can't verify. You know that."

"You're not making any sense. On one hand you say you read and verify everything and yet here's a letter in a newspaper that *you* printed and you say you've never read it. What am I supposed to think?" He threw up his hands in question.

Jim walked across the room toward Bonner. "Mind if I take a look?" he asked. Ginny handed him the newspaper. At length, Jim turned to Ginny. "As I said before, Ginny, I was there when the Camp Grant letter came in. This isn't the letter I read."

"You're damn right it isn't," Bonner concurred. "It's not even remotely close." He pulled a badly wrinkled piece of paper out of his inside coat pocket. "*This* is the letter Whitman had his clerk copy and distribute to the newspapers." He handed Jim the letter.

Jim read it quickly and handed it to Ginny. "This is it, Ginny. The letter I read."

"Go ahead," Bonner snapped. "Read it, Ginny. Read it and tell me that this letter and your letter are the same."

Heart pounding, Ginny compared Whitman's letter to the one she'd printed. There was no comparison. For one thing, the *Sun's* letter was half the length of Whitman's. Most of the good news had been completely deleted. And she saw what Bonner meant by well-placed adjectives—*hostile* Apaches, *war* chief. Worse yet, was the last line, which didn't appear anywhere in Whitman's letter: *On his own authority, Whitman offered the chief and his band rations, blankets, and protection.*

"Well?" Bonner asked, interrupting her jumbled thoughts.

"I don't know what to say. I agree they aren't even close to being the same." She closed her eyes and prayed for an answer—some kind of explanation.

Outside and across the street, Sam Sinclair's voice rang out in song. *"Weep no more, my lady. Oh, weep no more . . ."*

In an instant, she knew her prayer had been answered. She *hadn't* printed this. Someone else had. "Pop!" she cried, and ran for the door.

Chapter 19

Our Camp Grant letter speaks confidently of the value of peace made with the Pinals. We hope it may be lasting, but no one should trust their person or property where they would not have done so before . . . Even if they have offered peace in good faith, they deserve more punishment, and a most terrible scourging would have made their peaceful professions more worthy of reliance . . . The Indian must most powerfully feel the government's superiority, ability, and determination to crush him, before his professions of peace are worth listening to by our officers or people.

—*Arizona Citizen*

Ginny stood at the door watching her father stagger toward her.

"We will sing one song for our old Kentucky home," he warbled, hiccuped, then continued, *"For our old Kentucky home, far away."*

Indy touched Ginny's shoulder. "Jim and I think it best if we leave now. This is between you, Bonner, and your father. Let me know if there's anything I can do."

"Thanks, I will."

On her way out the door, Indy leaned toward Ginny and whispered, "Don't be too hard on him."

Ginny gave a pinched smile. "I won't."

As Jim and Indy headed toward home, Sam waved good-bye. "Nice t'see ya 'gin, Major, Mrs. . . . Major." He made to salute but instead hit himself in the eye.

Ginny might have laughed if it had been anybody else making a fool of himself. But because it was her father, she didn't find his behavior the least bit humorous. She found it disgusting and him pathetic. She hated feeling that way. She knew she should be more understanding, but it made her sick to see him throw his life away. Sam Sinclair was a brilliant journalist and a good businessman. He could have made the *Tucson Sun* the informational organ of the entire Arizona Territory were it not for his drinking problem. Ginny frowned. His drinking *problem* was a problem of his own choosing. Simply, he chose to drink. Which meant he chose to ruin his life.

Which meant there was nothing Ginny could do about it.

Once Sam came inside, Ginny shut and locked the door, then put the CLOSED sign in the window and pulled down the shade. She glanced at Bonner hunkered down with Greeley a few feet away.

"We want to talk to you, Pop," she said as Sam headed for the hallway into the sitting room. There was a knowing, maybe even a worried look in his eyes as he turned back to her. "It has to do with the Camp Grant letter we printed in the last issue. You rewrote it and I want to know why." She made the statement with certainty.

He frowned at her, as if he wondered how she knew. "It was—bad writing. So I fixed it."

"Yes, you did, Pop," she agreed. "You pared it down to practically nothing, added a few descriptive adjectives, and expressed your own opinion—all in spite of the fact that it's against our policy to edit letters, especially military letters. You fixed it so that it doesn't even resemble the original letter." She moved directly in front of him, her face close to his. His breath smelled like the inside of a whiskey barrel, the alcohol fumes so strong she was sure that if anyone struck a match, the whole building would go up in flames. "I've never known you to do anything like that before," she said, trying to sound reasonable. "It's unethical, Pop. And you're not an unethical man." She put her hand on his shoulder and spoke low. "Why don't you tell me the real reason you changed that letter."

"I tol' you."

"I know what you told me, but I don't believe you."

He stumbled away from her and sullenly stood with his back to her. "Leave me alone. I got nothin' t'say."

"Clay Foster threatened you, didn't he?" After what she'd overheard that day in the mercantile, it seemed the most likely explanation.

"Leave it be, Ginny." Sam sat down, leaned his elbows on the desktop, and covered his face with his hands.

Ginny looked at Bonner. Her gaze fell on his mouth, set now in a grim, forbidding line, though she saw it in her mind as it had looked the last time he'd kissed her. Her pulse leaped in sensual alarm. Resolutely, she pushed the sweet memory of that kiss from her mind and turned back to her father.

"I'm not going to leave it be, Pop. I'm going to keep you right here, sitting at that desk, until you tell me what Clay Foster said to make you change that letter."

Sam didn't look up. "I did it for you, Ginny," he said, his voice pleading for her understanding. "I made you a promise. I brought you here to this awful place, spent all our money— And then—I failed you."

Ginny breathed in shakily, words of denial springing to her lips. But she didn't say them. They wouldn't have been true. He *had* done all those things. He *had* failed her. But more than that, he had failed himself.

"Pop," she persisted. "Tell me what Foster said."

Sam looked up and mumbled, "He said we'd be better off workin' *with* the merchant ring than again' it."

"Anything else?" she prompted.

Fear, stark fear, glittered in Sam's eyes. "He said—" He dropped his gaze again and clamped his mouth shut.

"Tell me, Pop. Tell me what he said."

"He said if I didn't do as he asked, one of us might meet with an accident," Sam ground out without slurring a single word.

An accident? Ginny stared at her father. "What kind of accident?" she asked. But her mind seemed to answer for her. A shot from an unknown assailant could accidentally strike one of them while they were in town. A horse could spook and run away from its owner and strike them down in the street. There were any number of ways Foster could create an accident.

Sam merely shrugged.

Ginny began to shake as the fearful images flashed through her mind. Suddenly Bonner was behind her, his big hands gripped around her shoulders, steadying her, reassuring her, soothing her fears.

Still looking down, Pop mumbled, "I knew as soon as I changed that letter I'd be sorry." His confession seemed to have sobered him considerably. "I shoulda stood up t'him. Shoulda told 'im t'go t'hell!"

"Yes, you should have, Pop."

"I'm sorry, Ginny. So sorry. I failed you again." Without a glance in her direction, he stood up and walked toward the hall. "I'll make it right," he said, his voice fading with each step. "I promise."

"No, Pop. No promises!" She gave a choked, desperate laugh, then twisted around and buried her face against Bonner's shoulder. She was overcome with terrible feelings of bitterness. What did her father say? That he'd done it for her? Had the whiskey so addled his brain that he'd thought she would approve of him giving in to a threat and compromising his integrity? Ginny closed her eyes. She felt drained, hollow, lifeless.

Bonner's first thought was that he was seven times a fool. Ginny had every right to be angry at him. He'd been wrong to storm into her office and accuse her the way he had. He'd acted no differently than the

White Eyes who automatically accused the Apaches of every stage robbery, every killing, every theft, without even knowing if they'd done it. And yet, after all he'd done, here she was, reaching out to him for comfort instead of berating him for not believing in her.

"Ginny." He bent his head toward hers and brushed his lips against her temple. "I'm sorry, Ginny. I should never have doubted you. I don't know what happened. Or maybe I do. I'd just come back from getting my grandfather settled in a temporary camp next to Eskiminzin's band when Whitman handed me the *Sun* and pointed out the Camp Grant letter. All I could think about was that just when everything seemed to be going right—Eskiminzin had surrendered—Gianatah surrendered—peace was a real possibility—the *Sun* takes a good, positive letter and . . ."

"I know, Bonner, but I'm the one who should apologize. I said I would verify every report that came across my desk."

"Obviously the Camp Grant letter didn't come across your desk, Ginny," he pointed out.

She pulled back and looked up at him. "But I had to have set the type for it. I *had* to. But I don't remember doing it."

"Are you sure your father couldn't have set the type for it?"

"Well, I suppose he could have—when I was in the other room or something." She sighed heavily. "I'm just so sorry it happened. Pop's never done anything like this before."

Bonner pulled her back into his embrace, his hand gently pressing her head down to his chest. It had been so long since he'd held her, he'd almost forgotten what it was like. Almost, but not quite. He doubted he could ever completely forget anything about Ginny. She was like no other woman he'd ever known.

She slid her arms around his waist and snuggled into him. Her little, wiggly movements caused his manhood to swell and harden. Within seconds he was straight as an arrow and hard as flint. She *had* to feel it.

"Dammit, Ginny, I—"

"What?"

He was both physically excited and mentally aggravated. "I'm sure you can probably feel *what.*" He imagined dunking himself in the icy cold waters of the San Pedro River. He thought about that time he'd fallen in old Wiley's hole. But nothing helped. There were some things a man couldn't control and this was one of them.

With something like amusement in her voice, she said, "It's all right, Bonner. I understand."

"I'm not sure this is the right time to tell you, but I don't know if or when a better time will come." Putting a finger beneath her chin, he tilted her head back so he could see her face. "I love you, Ginny. I love you. I want to be sure you know that."

Ginny couldn't talk past the lump in her throat. He loved her. After that last talk, weeks ago, she'd been certain he would never say those words to her, certain that whatever had been between them had ended when he'd ridden off to Camp Grant. But now, suddenly, everything was changed. He was here. He was holding her. And the warmth of his love was flowing through her.

"I have so little to offer you, Ginny. It's damn selfish of me to want you to be a part of my life—selfish because I know marrying you is going to bring you nothing but anguish. You'll be a half-breed's wife, an outcast, a traitor to your own kind. Except for Indy, no woman—not even the *putas*—in Tucson will have anything to do with you. They'll treat you with contempt—"

"Bonner," she said, pressing her index finger across his lips to silence him. "As long as you love me, they can't hurt me. I know it's not going to be easy, but neither is having a drunkard for a father, or running a newspaper by myself. I'm strong. I'm resilient. I'm—"

"Crazy," he said in place of whatever she'd been going to say. Then, before she could dispute him, he kissed her. *He* knew then that he was the crazy one— crazy with loving her, crazy with needing her. His nerves vibrated. In a roundabout way he'd asked Ginny Sinclair to marry him and she'd accepted. And this kiss—it was a seal.

He turned her around so that her back was against the wall and he could use his hands in more creative ways than just holding her. Use them for touching her breasts, for taking off her apron, for unbuttoning the front of her dress.

"Ginny. God, Ginny. I want you," he murmured as he smothered her neck with hot, wet kisses. No sooner had he spoken than his attention was diverted by a sound behind him.

"Well, what have we here? A little love tryst?"

Bonner silently cursed himself. How many times had Gianatah told him to never let his guard down, not even for an instant?

"What do you want, Foster?" Bonner turned, reaching an arm behind him to keep Ginny where she was, safely out of Foster's sight. But he felt her pull away from his grasp and knew that short of tying her up, he couldn't keep her from doing whatever she wanted to do.

"I came to talk to Ginny," Clay said, his gaze following her disheveled form across the room. "I was hoping to persuade her to have supper with me, but now I can see it would have been a waste of time." He looked back at Bonner, icy contempt flashing in his eyes. "And now I know why she turned down all my other invitations, though for the life of me I don't see what she sees in a filthy half-breed like you."

In three strides, Bonner was across the room and

had Foster within his grasp, choking the breath from his body.

Ginny screamed. "Bonner, no! He isn't worth it. Let him go."

She could scream all she wanted, but Bonner wasn't about to let him go. Not this time. He should have taken care of him long ago instead of toying with him all these years like a cat toys with a mouse. With his arm securely locked around Foster's head, Bonner reached for his knife. He was good with a six-shooter but he was a master with a knife. No one could match him. A little slice here, a well-placed prick there, and Clay would never again consider asking a woman to supper.

Anticipation coursed through his veins like warm *tiswin*. Then Ginny was there, pleading for him to release Foster. "Bonner, listen to me. Listen carefully. Jim has gone to a lot of trouble. He has everything all wrapped up. He wouldn't appreciate it if you spoiled things for him . . ."

Bonner refused to be swayed. This was the moment he'd waited for. Knife poised, he said, "Better that she loves a filthy half-breed like me than a mur—" A warning bell inside his head rang out, cautioning him to hold off. What was it that Ginny had said? Jim had gone to a lot of trouble? He glanced over at her and saw her wide-eyed look. She'd been trying to tell him something and he hadn't been listening.

She caught his look and gave a half smile. "Believe me, Bonner, after the way he threatened my father, there's nothing I'd like better than to see you lift his . . . hair, but it's not for us to decide . . ." Even if she hadn't put an imploring hand on his arm, her words would have stopped him. He looked down at her, his eyes asking if she really meant what he thought she meant.

She bit her lower lip and gave him a little nod.

Bonner released Foster with a suddenness that

made the man lose his balance and fall to his knees. "Forget it, Foster. Nothing is going to help you. Not even getting on your knees. You're a dead man."

"You bas—" Foster's words died in his throat when Bonner's knife flashed in front of his eyes. "Ah, Christ!" he yelled. In one fell swoop, Bonner cut off a large hank of Foster's shiny blond hair, then nicked the palm of his own hand so that drops of blood mingled with the hair. He held his trophy up for Foster to see, then burst out laughing when Foster started to scream. "You scalped me! My God. Oh, my God." Bonner stepped away from Foster and opened the office door.

"Get out before I decide to take one of your ears to hang on my lodgepole."

Foster struggled to his feet, then took off at a run.

When he was out of sight, Bonner closed the door and said to Ginny, "Come here you wicked, wicked woman."

At Bonner's request, Ginny closed up the newspaper office, then walked beside him down the middle of Main Street to Jim and Indy's adobe where they spent the afternoon eating and talking.

Bonner told the Garritys about Clay Foster coming into the office and the altercation that followed. He admitted that if not for Ginny's powers of persuasion, he would have killed Foster then and there.

Jim leaned back in his chair. "I guess I owe you a debt of gratitude, Ginny, for talking some sense into my *savage* friend here. You can bet that if he had killed Foster, the good people of Tucson would have charged him with murder and strung him up on the nearest tree."

Ginny grimaced at the image that flashed through her mind. "I'm just thankful you came by after Indy, or I wouldn't have known that Clay's fate was already sealed."

Bonner looked at Ginny and smiled. "I have yet to properly thank you, Miss Sinclair."

An unwelcome blush crept into Ginny's cheeks. She had no doubt as to how he intended to thank her. And in all likelihood, Jim and Indy didn't either. Bonner's innuendo had been about as discreet as a scream.

While Ginny and Indy were preparing supper in the kitchen, Jim told Bonner the details of Lahte's capture. "We got into a little contest of skills," Jim said, lowering his voice. But it wasn't so low that the women couldn't still hear every word. Indy clutched the edge of the worktable when she heard her husband describe the knife fight that had taken place between him and Lahte.

"He was fast on his feet, I'll say that for him. Faster than me," Jim admitted. "There were a couple of times when I thought for sure he had me."

"It isn't a man's speed with a knife that counts," Bonner offered in explanation. "It's his nerve. You've got to take chances. Do the unexpected. But you know that."

"Yeah, I guess I must, or I wouldn't be here talking about it."

Indy started to shiver and Ginny wrapped a comforting arm around her shoulders. "Don't think about it," she whispered. "He's here and he's all right."

Indy clutched Ginny's hand. "Sometimes I wish I'd fallen in love with a nice staid banker instead of a daredevil cavalry officer."

Out in the dining room, the topic of conversation turned to Eskiminzin's surrender. After putting the pot roast in the oven, Indy and Ginny returned to the table.

"But I never thought I'd see the day," Bonner was saying when the women took their seats, "when Gianatah would surrender."

"I remember him as being particularly ornery, with a virulent dislike for the White Eyes."

"You remember him correctly," Bonner concurred.

"What really surprises me is that Whitman acted without authority. He took a hell of a chance, you know."

Bonner thoughtfully rubbed his chin. "I know that. So does he. But you have to understand that he wasn't thinking about his career, he was thinking about peace. He told me he felt like he had the answer to the entire Indian problem in *his* hands."

"So, how were things when you left?"

"Peaceful," Bonner said, laughing lightly. "Right after Eskiminzin surrendered, Whitman sent a detailed report to Stoneman about what went on, but he hasn't heard back yet. Meanwhile, he's being guided by government general policy in similar situations. When I rode out this morning, there were nearly three hundred Apaches living and working together a mile upstream from the post. Eskiminzin was about to send out runners to other bands, encouraging them to come in as well. No telling how many will be there when I go back."

Jim sat forward, an intense expression on his face, as if he'd just discovered some deep, dark secret. "If more bands do come in, it could be the beginning— Jesus, Bonner! Do you realize what you could have here?" Jim ignored Bonner's nod and continued. "It's not entirely inconceivable that you could have the whole Apache Nation awaiting you when you get back."

"Now, that would be something, wouldn't it?"

Jim chuckled. "Yeah. That would be something."

After supper Ginny and Indy went outside to feed Paco. The little burro had become a beggar as well as a pest. Now, every evening about eight o'clock, he brayed at the front door until Indy came out and gave him something to eat. Because he was so loudly insistent, Indy told Ginny that she always kept a supply of carrots on hand.

Tonight, Ginny gave Paco his carrots. She was careful to keep her fingers well away from his teeth. As easily as he snapped the carrot, if her finger got in the way . . .

"I think it's time I asked Bonner to take me home," Ginny said. "It's been one of those days."

The words were barely out of her mouth when Jim and Bonner stepped outside. "I'll sure be glad when spring comes," Jim said, to no one in particular. "I've had enough of this cold weather."

"Me too," Bonner agreed, specifically thinking about all the nights he'd plunged himself into the freezing waters of the San Pedro River. But no more. Tonight would end his frustration. Tonight, he would plunge himself into Ginny, into her warm, willing body. The mere thought of finally possessing her made him grow hard.

"Are you ready?" he asked, a double meaning to his words.

"Uh-huh." Ginny hurried up and fed Paco her last carrot, quickly scrubbed at the bristly mane between his gigantic ears, then headed over to where Bonner was waiting for her. "I'm ready." A look—he wasn't sure what to call it—eagerness maybe, or anticipation—came into her eyes and told him she had caught his secondary meaning.

"I think we'll ride instead of walk this time," he said, checking his horse's cinch strap.

"B-but I've never ridden. I—"

"Well, then. It's about time you learned." Before she could think of a way to get out of it, Bonner lifted her up into the saddle, then quickly vaulted up behind her.

"Ginny, I'm going to work on getting you that exclusive as soon as possible," Jim said as he scratched Paco's ears. "I have a feeling now that we've got

Lahte, Colonel Dunn will be asking the sheriff to arrest Foster in short order. He's too big a fish to let get away."

Bonner took up the reins in his left hand and wrapped his right arm around Ginny's waist. "Thanks for supper."

"Yes, thank you, both of you," Ginny said, her voice a little shaky.

"By the way, Bonner. There's something I forgot to tell you." Jim walked over to the horse. "Congratulations on negotiating peace terms with Eskiminzin and Gianatah. In years to come, history may not give you proper credit, but I will. I'll make sure it's well documented in my journal. And I'll do my damnedest to let as many people as I can know what you did."

As the two men shook hands, Ginny added, "So will I. The next issue of the *Tucson Sun* will carry the detailed story. That is if Mr. Kincade here will give me an exclusive." Ginny leaned sideways to look at him.

Bonner laughed, then reined his horse around and headed up Main Street.

The office of the *Tucson Sun* was pitch-dark. Not even a light in the living quarters. As they approached, Ginny's pulse became erratic. She prepared herself for the awkward moments right after they dismounted, when they would go inside together. She decided to suggest they go into her bedroom. She wished there were someplace else, someplace where they didn't have to worry that they'd be overheard. But she could think of nothing.

"I'm not taking you home. Not yet," Bonner said, as though he meant to grant her wish. As though he'd read her mind.

"I—I don't understand. Where are you taking me?"

"I have a camp—a little ways out of town."

Ginny felt a shiver chase itself down her spine at the prospect of being completely alone with him. She shivered again—this time with pleasure—when his hand moved across her midriff and cupped her left breast. A faint mewling sound escaped her. She leaned into him and nuzzled her head beneath his chin.

"I love you," he whispered. Then he said the words in Apache, as well as other words whose meanings on his tongue were sensually clear.

Confident in Bonner's ability to control his horse, Ginny released her grip on the saddle. She drew her hands back across the tops of her thighs, to the top of his thighs. She felt him tense. He adjusted his position and sat a little taller. Ginny shivered. That she could have such an effect on him with nothing but a touch gave her a thrilling sense of power and emboldened her to experiment with other ways to arouse his senses.

She slowly spread her fingers until they came in contact with the rawhide cross-stitching that ran the length of his breeches. She hesitated a moment, then slid her second and third fingers in between the thongs and drew little circles on his flesh.

"Don't do that, Ginny," he warned in a dark, husky voice. "Or we'll never make it to camp."

Unconcerned, she ignored his warning. By the time they'd reached the outskirts of town, she'd become even bolder and was massaging the backs of his thighs, slipping her hands down between his buttocks and the McClellan saddle.

For every move she made, he made one too, fondling her breast, flicking his thumb across her hardened nipple. He placed hot, wet kisses on the side of her neck, then swept her hair aside and kissed her nape.

Ginny closed her eyes, savoring each and every tingle, each and every twinge. Within Bonner's arms, she felt safe and warm and loved. Except for the creaking of saddle leather and an occasional nicker, she could almost forget they were riding a horse.

With an effort that for a moment Bonner thought

might be beyond him, he pulled his thoughts together
and guided his horse into the sheltering stand of cottonwoods. The sound of rushing water greeted his
ears. Gaining the clearing, he reined to a stop.

"We're here, Ginny," he murmured, leaning around
her left side. He pressed his lips against the sensitive
area just below her ear and smiled when she let her
head fall back against his shoulder.

"Where?" Her voice sounded almost rusty.

"My home away from home." He set her up
straight, made sure she had a good hold on the saddle,
then dismounted. "Come on," he said, reaching up to
her. She had a sleepy, dreamy look on her face that
pleased him because he knew he'd put it there. He
grabbed her around the waist and slowly dragged her
toward him.

For weeks, he'd been thinking of all the things he
should have said and done the last time they'd been
together. He'd promised himself that if he ever got a
second chance, he'd make it up to her, say all the
right words and love her in ways she'd never dreamed
of being loved. No more regrets.

With a smile, she wound her arms around his neck
and kissed him. He gathered her close, his hands lifting and cradling her buttocks so she could feel just
how much he wanted her. He knew she felt him when
she groaned into his mouth and began grinding her
hips against his.

He pulled back slightly. "I'm going to build us a
fire, then spread out my bedroll." He saw her shiver.
"Are you cold?"

"No, I'm just—" She shrugged helplessly.

He took off his buckskin coat and draped it over
her shoulders even though he knew it wasn't the cool
March air making her shiver. She looked up at him
as she pulled it about her.

"I love you," she whispered, raising her hands to
his face. Ever so lightly she brushed her fingertips

across his mouth. "I think I fell in love with you that first day—when you came riding into Tucson with the Fish and Company wagons. There was just something about you . . . I couldn't take my eyes off you. Just like now," she whispered, staring at his mouth.

Without giving her any warning, Bonner scooped her up in his arms and carried her to a small outcropping of boulders next to the river. He set her down gently, then left her with a firm "Wait here" while he built the fire.

Within a few minutes he had a good blaze going, and moments after that he'd spread his bedroll next to it. Still hunkered down beside the bedroll, he looked up at Ginny and crooked his finger. "Come here."

Ginny took one step toward him, then another. She rushed over to him and fell to her knees on the bedroll in front of him. For a moment neither of them did anything but look at each other, then Ginny inched her body into the V between his heavily muscled legs.

"Ginny, I think you'd be more comfortable if you lie down," he said, but when her hands slid up the insides of his thighs, all thought of moving flew from his mind.

"Not just yet," she said on a shaky breath. "First, I want—I want to touch you," she whispered at the same time her hands came together in the center of the V.

Bonner groaned low in his throat. He didn't know how much longer he could stay crouched down the way he was, but the thought of getting up and missing what her hands were doing to him was worse that any cramp he might get.

Not wanting to waste even one second of precious time, he peeled his coat off her shoulders, halfheartedly rolled it up, and tossed it to the top of the bedroll. With slow hands, he pushed back her shawl and started undoing the tiny buttons at the front of her dress. He hoped to God she wasn't one of those women who wore layer upon layer of underclothing. When the last button was unfastened and the last ribbon untied, he pushed the garments out of his way and gently stroked her bare shoulders. Her flesh quivered beneath his hands as he traced the fine ridges of her collarbones, then slid down to surround her breasts. The thought came to him that someday those beautiful breasts would provide nourishment for a baby—*his* baby if he had his way. And he would.

His baby.

He bolted to his feet and stripped off his buckskins and moccasins. As he bent to set his clothing aside, he felt Ginny grab his ankle. He looked down and saw her crook her index finger in a now familiar gesture.

She'd removed the rest of her clothing and was stretched out naked in front of him, her head resting on his coat. Firelight bathed her naked body in a golden glow. An overwhelming emotion settled in the region of her heart. He never would have thought that loving a woman could be such a profound feeling. It was almost painful. But a good kind of pain.

Ginny stared up at him. She'd never imagined that a man's body could be so beautiful, but Bonner's was. He was perfect in every way. Not an ounce of spare flesh anywhere on his body, all sinew and muscle and sun-bronzed flesh. When he didn't make a move toward her, she crooked her finger again. "Come here," she whispered, issuing a gentle command, which she knew he wouldn't obey unless he wanted to. Momentarily he dropped to his knees beside her.

As though she had no will of her own, she reached for that part of him that she desired most and heard him suck in his breath when her hand circled him. Boldly she explored the length of him, the heaviness, the shape, and the texture. She left no part of him untouched.

"God, Ginny. I—" He covered her hand with his, tightening her hold on him.

Ginny's mouth went dry as she watched him move back and forth within the circle of her hand, seeming to grow bigger and harder with each thrust. She lifted up on her elbow, following an unexplicicable urge to kiss that most intimate part of him. Before she could think twice about what she was doing, his hand was behind her head, pulling her toward him, relieving her of making the decision. She heard a low moan but whether it came from him or her she wasn't sure.

With gentleness and patience, he tutored her in the seductive art of pleasuring a man, but the truth was the pleasure was all hers—a pleasure that moments later came back to her a thousandfold when he nuzzled his head between her thighs and kissed her as intimately as she had kissed him.

This was a part of lovemaking that was all new to her—new and wonderful and even a little frightening because of the powerful sensations that vibrated through her body. "Bonner," she cried out, not sure what it was that she wanted. "Please—"

She sounded like she was begging, and she was. Begging for him to stop. Begging for more. Then, finally, begging him to put out the fire he'd ignited inside her.

Seeming to understand what it was she needed, he caressed her in that special place one more time, bringing her so close to the edge she cried out for him, pleading.

Rising above her, Bonner watched her in fascination. He'd wanted to make sure she felt everything she deserved to feel, everything that circumstances hadn't let him make her feel before. But seeing the rapture light her face nearly undid him.

Like a sculptor, he moved his hands over her body, from shoulder to ankle, touching every inch of her. He kneaded her breasts as she writhed beneath him, molding them, groaning at the feel, like silk under his hands. Unable to help himself, he ran his tongue over her quivering flesh. The taste of her, the feel of her against his tongue, was heady stuff, more potent than peyote.

"Bonner," Ginny moaned, her seeking hands framing his chest. "Please, now—"

A slow smile curved his mouth as he took her by the shoulders. With one powerful thrust he pushed into her wet heat and Ginny gasped, her eyes wide. Then she smiled too, pleasure rippling her beautiful features as her body shuddered beneath him.

Bonner moved over her, reveling in the excitement and kissed her deeply, mimicking the movement of his lower body. Three months of wanting this woman, dreaming about her, imagining how he would feel once he was inside her, had full possession of her, drove him deeper, faster, and harder into her until he could hold on no longer. He tightened and gave one final thrust that bound them forever, one to the other.

Ginny snuggled her back up against Bonner's big body. She was exhausted, utterly and wonderfully exhausted. Their lovemaking had been incredible, an experience she'd never forget. A few feet away, the fire snapped and crackled. Red-hot firebrands jumped out of the flames into the night sky.

A gust of wind whistled through the trees. Ginny pulled the edge of the blanket up to her chin. She'd never slept outside before and imagined that she would have been afraid if Bonner hadn't been with her. All around her there were sounds. Bird calls. Water rushing over rocks. The hoot of an owl. A coyote's serenade. Night sounds.

"S . . . e . . . e . . . k . . . e . . . r?"

Ginny rose up on her elbow and peered into the night. "Who's there?" she asked. But there was only a chill, black silence. She strained her ears and heard . . .

something. A footstep? A low whistle? A long, windy sigh? Then it came again, clearly a man's voice.

"S . . . e . . . e . . . k . . . e . . . r!"

"Bonner. Bonner, wake up," she cried in a small frightened voice. "There's someone here."

He bolted to a sitting position, the blanket falling to his waist. "Who?"

"I don't know! He whispered something."

Fully awake now, Bonner looked around. "What did he say?"

"It sounded like . . . seeker. Only it was drawn out."

"Seeker?" Bonner wrapped an arm around Ginny and held her to him. "It's all right, Ginny. No matter what you see or hear, you have to believe me when I tell you that's there's nothing to be afraid of."

"I don't understand. What—"

"Shh," Bonner whispered in her ear. Then, over her head he spoke into the night. "I am here, Wind. I am here."

Ginny couldn't believe her eyes. A dust devil appeared at the edge of camp and from the top of its funnel, a head emerged. It spoke to Bonner.

"You have done well, half-breed. You have used your power wisely. But there is still a price to be paid for the peace you seek. You will have much need of your power in the days to come."

"What about Ginny? What about her power?"

"Now that you and your woman are one, your power will be one." As if wanting to get an up-close look at Ginny, Wind stretched closer to where she sat. His long gray hair swirled about his face. Then he looked at Bonner. "We will meet again, half-breed. I will come to you from nowhere." Unexpectedly, Wind began to move in a circle around them, closer and closer until his billowy presence embraced them in a cocoon of warmth and love.

Chapter 20

SENSIBLE AT LAST

A provision has been incorporated into the Indian appropriation bill passed by Congress a few weeks ago that hereafter no Indian nation or tribe within the United States shall be acknowledged or recognized as an independent nation, tribe, or power with which the United States can contract by treaty.

—*Arizona Citizen*

A gentle breeze touching her face forced Ginny awake. For a moment she wasn't sure where she was and started to panic. Then she felt Bonner's arm tighten around her waist and it all came back.

She snuggled into the curve of his body and watched the morning sky blush. At the back of her mind a dreamlike image hovered in the semidarkness between now and never. It swayed to and fro, its form so distorted she couldn't tell if it was man or beast. She squeezed her eyes shut, thinking she might be able to recapture the dream. The image stayed with her, but was no clearer than before. Then came a voice—a soft whisper, "We will meet again. I will come to you from nowhere."

"Bonner!" She turned toward him, her heart racing.

"What's the matter?" he asked in a sleepy voice.

"I saw something—heard something—I don't know what it was."

"It's just the wind," he said, gathering her to him. "It's always windy here."

"No—I think—" she started to protest but he cut her off with a kiss.

"You think too much, Ginny," he murmured, drawing her close.

Long minutes later she wasn't thinking about anything except what he was doing to her, the way he was making her feel. And when he'd finished making love to her, the image and the memory of it were gone.

Tucson was just waking up when Bonner and Ginny returned to the *Sun*'s office. He led his horse around the back by the kitchen door.

As soon as they were inside, Ginny turned to him and put her arms around his neck. "I wish you didn't have to go."

"I wish I didn't either, but orders are orders," he said, kissing her lightly on the mouth.

"How long do you think you'll be gone?" She dreaded the thought of him leaving.

He shook his head. "I don't know. A few weeks. Maybe longer. It depends on how things are going at the reservation. They've only got one other interpreter." He took her by the shoulders and forced her to look at him. "While I'm gone, I want you to think long and hard about what you'll be getting into if you marry me. And don't let what happened last night and this morning influence you."

"I don't have to think about it, Bonner. I love you. I want to spend the rest of my life with you." She looked down at the floor and said, "I want to be your wife, have your children, little boys with black hair and black eyes, just like you." It occurred to her there was a possibility that she'd already conceived, but she didn't think this was the time to say anything. She didn't want him to worry about her while he was gone.

He pulled her into his arms. "I want that too," he said. "But what I want even more is for you to have no regrets. No would'ves, should'ves, or could'ves." When she started to shake her head, he placed his hands on either side of her face to stop her. "Listen to me, Ginny. From here on out nothing is going to be the same. I know Clay Foster. He'll tell everybody what he saw yesterday. Once word gets around, people will start treating you differently and business will drop off. You can buy yourself some time by denying his accusations. Tell people that you spurned him and he's trying to get even."

"But that would be a lie."

"Not entirely. You did spurn him. I heard him say so. It just might save you, Ginny, and the *Sun*."

Bonner had been gone four weeks, one day, eight hours, and two minutes, not that Ginny was keeping track. His prediction that Clay Foster would talk about what he'd seen proved to be correct. At first, she'd been too busy to notice anything amiss. Then the merchants' wives were too busy to chat when she came to shop. Soon people she usually waved to turned the other way. Finally, advertising contracts that had run out weren't being renewed.

It all came to a head the day of the literary society meeting. Indy and Mrs. Brown were the only ones who showed up at Indy's house.

"I don't think we'll be seeing the others," Mrs. Brown said after waiting a half hour for anyone else to arrive. She put down her cup of tea. "I expect they've heard rumors, dear, about you and Mr. Kincade."

"Rumors?" She should have been prepared for this but she wasn't.

"Frankly, I think he's a perfectly charming man," Mrs. Brown said in her usual sophisticated manner, which Ginny had come to love. Smiling, the matron added, "He reminds me of my dear Rolfe in the days before the war. He was such a dashing figure in his uniform. I suppose it's Mr. Kincade's mixed blood that's the concern. We Easterners are a bit more open-minded. Why, look at the President's man, Ely Parker. He's a full-blooded Seneca Indian, and he's invited to all the best parties by all the most influential hostesses."

Ginny glanced at Indy, who looked suddenly very pale. "I'm afraid I've made an enemy of Clay Foster," she said, saying the first thing that came to mind. "He's repeatedly asked me to supper and to the theater but I keep turning him down. I remember that over a month ago, he came by the office and found Bonner here and . . . well, I guess—"

Indy sat forward. "I remember. That's the day Jim came home from his scout and couldn't find me so he came looking for me at your office. He'd only been there a few minutes when Bonner came in. He was upset as I remember—about a letter you'd printed on the Indian situation at Camp Grant."

"That's right. Then Clay came by—right after you and Jim went home," Ginny added, silently thanking Indy for her help. "The second Clay saw Bonner, he started making terrible accusations about the two of us. Bonner threatened him and he left. I was so upset that Bonner insisted I close up the office and that he take me to your house."

"It sounds to me like Clay's jealous," Mrs. Brown offered in explanation. "I understand that he and Mr. Kincade have been at odds for years, which would give him another reason for spreading vicious rumors."

Ginny bowed her head. She hoped God would forgive her this half lie but she didn't know what else she could have done. If she didn't stop the rumors, the *Sun* would be out of business in a couple of months and she and her father would be out in the street.

Later, Indy turned to Ginny after Mrs. Brown left. "I think she believed you. And if she didn't, I think she likes you enough to pretend that she did. Either way, she'll stop the talk just as efficiently as Clay Foster started it."

"I'm sorry to involve you in this, Indy," Ginny said, taking her friend's hand.

"I recall warning you what would happen and—" Indy shook her head. "I'm sorry, Ginny. I have no business lecturing you. You couldn't help falling in love with Bonner any more than I could help falling in love with Jim. I just hope it works out that you and he can be together."

"So do I."

On her way home from Indy's, Ginny made a detour and stopped by the news depot to pick up the out-of-area newspapers and to see if she had any mail. There was a letter from Bonner. She recognized the handwriting—a thick, bold scrawl.

She hurried home, eager to read it. This was the third letter Bonner had written her since he'd left. She loved reading them, not only for the personal message that bolstered her spirits and gave her renewed hope, but for the firsthand information he gave her, information that he asked her to include in her articles and editorials.

More than five hundred Apaches are here now. With each passing day, more arrive. They file in front of Lieutenant Whitman and give their names, which are then entered onto rolls.

You remember I told you Whitman had no authority to set up a reservation—that he'd gone out on a limb thinking he had in his hands the opportunity to bring peace to the Territory. You remember, too, that he immediately sent a letter to General George Stoneman at Department Headquarters apprising him of the situation and asking for instructions. Today, Whitman's letter was returned unopened, with an attached note explaining that it lacked the proper cover note specifying the contents. According to the clerk who returned it, Whitman had violated military protocol. So we continue to wait to find out that what we're doing is acceptable to the government.

Ginny sighed in frustration. Protocol. Peace was in the balance thanks to a self-important clerk deciding to exercise his power over the mail he received. What should have taken a couple of weeks at the most would now take a couple of months. It was at times like this that Ginny questioned her loyalty to the United States government.

She read on, her heart heavy as she was sure Bonner's was.

The water at the junction of the Arivaipa Creek and the San Pedro River dried up as it does every spring. Whitman gave instructions to move the Apaches five miles upstream, to the mouth of the canyon, where the water runs all year. My grandfather seems pleased with this place. The palo verde trees are green and lacy and covered with little yellow blossoms. Many of the people have begun to cultivate the rich bottomlands beside the waters of the San Pedro. Whitman has issued them corn and squash seed for planting.

I've escorted several groups into the mountains to gather mescal and to hunt wild game. Whitman is reluctant to let them go without a post guide because if anything happens, the blame will be on his shoulders.

We've devised a way for the Apaches to earn money so that they can buy clothing and other necessities. They've gone into the business of planting and harvesting hay, which Whitman buys from them. But instead of coin, he gives them vouchers that they can use to purchase goods from the trader's store.

Ginny kept Bonner's letters next to her bed and reread them often. Through his letters, she gained a better understanding of him, of the man and his goals. Bonner Kincade lived and worked with one purpose in mind—to help bring peace to a Territory gone mad with hate.

*   *   *

The peaceful interlude following the Apache surrenders at Camp Grant ended all too soon. Every day new reports of Indian depredations came into the *Sun*'s office.

News that Bonner had already written Ginny now reached the other newspapers. The fact that Whitman was paying the Apaches one cent per pound for hay caused a flurry of grumbles and complaints from Tucson contractors. They complained that the Apaches were undercutting their prices and stealing their business.

In the middle of March, Ginny got a report that President Grant's Indian policy was to be extended to Arizona and that a new Indian Agency would be formed by a member of the Dutch Reformed Church. A military order was issued by the department commander, General George Stoneman, to inaugurate and prosecute a vigorous, persistent, and relentless winter campaign against the Apaches. Scouting would cover a radius of thirty miles around the infantry camp.

The *Arizona Citizen* elaborated on an order from Department Headquarters that forbade the sale of intoxicating liquors to all military posts. Ginny was horrified when the *Citizen* suggested that the issuing of rations to Indians at several posts should also be forbidden. The writer—either Wasson or his assistant editor—made reference to post commanders feeding and fattening idle Indians at government expense. Ginny didn't even want to imagine what kind of comment Bonner would say to that.

Reports of murders by Indians tripled and Ginny wondered how many of them were true and how many were fabricated. With the help of the *Citizen*, the people's fears were heightened. Protest meetings were held and the speakers shouted their outrage.

Ginny got notification that a Committee of Public Safety had been formed. She wondered if this wasn't just another name for a citizens' militia. They'd named

William Oury, a former Texas Ranger and veteran Indian fighter, to lead them. Ginny had seen Oury once or twice but never been introduced to him. She knew he'd fought in the Texas revolution, narrowly missing the Alamo.

In the last two weeks there had been reports of a number of raids and killings in the Santa Cruz and San Pedro valleys. Through Indy, Ginny learned that people were beginning to suspect that Lieutenant Whitman was harboring a hive of thieves and murderers—that his so-called peaceful reservation Apaches were leaving the rancheria on the pretense of hunting or gathering mescal, when in fact they were raiding and killing.

"It's not true, Indy," Ginny cried, tears of frustration glistening in her eyes. "Bonner wrote me that he escorts the groups out to collect mescal and hunt wild game, that Whitman is careful not to let them go alone."

"I know it's not true," Indy replied. "Jim has evidence to prove it's the Chiricahuas doing the raiding and killing. But they won't listen. They hear only what they want to hear. They're just itching for an opportunity—any opportunity—to destroy the 'feeding station' as they call it out at Camp Grant." She paced the floor, her hand on the top of her stomach. "I'd give anything to leave this place. I don't want to bring up a child here. There's too much hate. It's like your father said—it's a disease."

Side by side Bonner Kincade and Lieutenant Royal Whitman sat astride their horses, looking down over the peaceful Apache encampment.

Whitman chuckled softly, a satisfied smile curving his lips. "I never thought I'd see the day when I'd be this close to an Apache camp and have no fear." He raised his arm and motioned with a gauntleted hand. "Look at them, Kincade. God, what an awesome sight they are. How many is it now— Four bands? Five? I've lost track."

"Five bands," Bonner confirmed. "Five hundred and ten men, women, and children." His words tasted like gall and he wasn't sure why. His life's purpose was bringing peace to the Apache people. Talking them into surrendering was the goal he'd committed himself to, the objective he'd forsaken all his own wants and needs for. And now his goal was becoming a reality. Yet there was no sense of satisfaction. Would it come only when all the Apaches had surrendered? he asked himself. Deep down inside he knew the answer. No. There was no joy in bringing the great Apache Nation to its knees. No reason to celebrate. They were surrendering for one reason and one reason only, so that they might survive. Satisfaction he would never feel, but accomplishment, yes.

It would have to do.

"Five hundred and ten," Whitman repeated, shaking his head as if he couldn't believe it. "I'd say they're living proof that the critics are wrong. Apaches *can* live together in peace and harmony. Hell, I've had fewer problems with them in the last month than with my own men!" He settled into his saddle and watched in silence. After a moment, he said, "This is all happening because of you, Kincade, because the Apaches respect you, trust you. No one but you could have accomplished this."

Bonner cleared his throat. He had never been comfortable with flattery. "I told them what they already knew—that their only hope for survival was to surrender."

"I don't envy you that, my friend. They're a proud people. They deserve far better than what they're getting. In the last few weeks, I've come to feel a deep respect for them. Some of them came here almost completely naked, yet they were unashamed. And the women—my God, the women—every day they go out into the hay fields and cheerfully work like slaves to earn money to clothe themselves and their children."

For an army man, Bonner found Whitman to be surprisingly in accord with him on many things, the most important being his way of dealing with the Apache people. The lieutenant was a do-it-yourself man. Instead of sending one of his junior officers to inspect the rancheria, he saddled up each morning and rode out there himself. He made it his policy to answer the people's questions, address their concerns, and tell them in plain, direct language whatever they wished to know. His warmth and sympathy won him Eskiminzin's respect and trust.

Bonner saw a uniformed soldier riding hell-bent for leather toward the rancheria, his horse kicking up a cloud of dust. Bonner and Whitman rode down the side of the hill to meet him.

"Begging your pardon, sir," the young private shouted as he saluted. "Captain Stanwood has arrived at the post to relieve you of your command. He requests a meeting with you as soon as possible to discuss the Apache situation. He says he has orders from General Stoneman."

Whitman gave Bonner a worried look, then turned back to the messenger. "Thank you, Hensley. Go on back and tell him I'll be there directly."

"Yes, sir." The private wheeled his horse around and rode off at a fast gallop.

"I'm not exactly sure what this means, Kincade, but I know Stanwood. He's a fair man. My guess is he won't make any drastic changes." He gathered up his reins. "I'll see you tonight at supper. My quarters. Seven o'clock."

Bonner sat staring after him long after he'd ridden away, until there was nothing but dust to mark his trail. He hoped to God Stanwood was bringing orders for Whitman to carry on exactly as he was.

Seven o'clock was a long way off.

Bonner spent the afternoon with his grandfather, teaching him how to use a six-shooter. Gianatah was a quick learner. Within a couple of hours, he could shoot a twig off a tree branch, but he refused to put on Bonner's gunbelt and learn to draw.

"I do not wish to wear one of these," he said, flicking his finger at the tooled leather gunbelt hanging low on Bonner's hips. Gianatah looked at the revolver in his hand, then at Bonner's holster. He shoved the revolver's barrel down into the waist of his buckskin breeches. "This good place to carry fire stick," he said, patting the revolver.

Bonner knew better than to argue with him. Once Gianatah had his mind made up, there was no changing it. "When everything is settled here, I thought I might go home and bring my mother and sister back here for a visit. Would you like that?"

Gianatah started walking toward his wickiup. "They stay long time?"

"No, probably only a few days."

"Then I like them to visit."

Bonner abruptly stopped, not sure he'd heard his grandfather correctly. He thought about what he'd heard, then started to laugh.

Bonner followed his grandfather inside the wickiup and sat down on a pile of animal skins. "Logan's coming home in a couple of months. He's a medicine man now, you know."

Gianatah picked up the arrow he'd been working on earlier. Bonner watched his hands—still flexible and steady—work the sinew tightly around the stem. He smiled at the memory of his grandfather taking him and Logan on their first hunting expedition. They'd each started out with a full quiver of arrows that they'd made themselves. By the end of the day, they'd hit everything but their quarry and returned to the rancheria with less than half the arrows they'd started with and nothing to contribute to the stew pot.

"I have heard this from your sister. He makes medicine to White Eyes."

"Yes," Bonner replied, trying to read his grandfather's expression. "Once he comes home, I'm going to try to talk him into staying here and making medicine for the Apaches too." Bonner lowered his head. "Seems like I've been doing a lot of talking lately. I just wish I knew if anybody was listening."

Gianatah looked up from his work. "I listen. And now I am here."

Bonner was momentarily speechless with surprise. His grandfather had never mentioned his reasons for surrendering, though Bonner had assumed it was because of Eskiminzin. Now he knew differently. Gianatah was here because he'd trusted in *him*—trusted *his* power. "I hope I have spoken wisely."

"The Mountain Spirits are strong in you. Do not question their wisdom."

Chapter 21

Interview with General Stoneman
REPORT OF VISITING COMMITTEE
APPOINTED BY THE CITIZENS

That your committee met General Stoneman on the evening of the 25th March . . . A "memorial" was presented to him, purporting to have been gotten up and signed by the people of Tubac, and those living in the Santa Cruz Valley . . . He concluded that a community representing 500 men could take care of itself . . . That the people of Tucson and vicinity could not expect anything more than had been done already; that he had only sufficient horses in his command to mount one cavalry man in five. He regretted that he was so circumscribed as to his means to do the work expected of him.

—*Arizona Citizen*

Tempers in Tucson were short. Spirits were low. The United States government wasn't going to help with the Indian situation. The people understood that now. General Stoneman had said it was up to citizens to protect themselves.

Every day, every place she went, Ginny heard people complaining and lamenting. They were angry, hurt, disillusioned. Some seemed to have abandoned all hope, caught up in a futile effort to live their lives in peace. They were fed up with the army and the Indians. And they were sick and tired of meetings that accomplished nothing and talk that went nowhere.

News of Captain Stanwood's arrival at Camp Grant was reported in the *Citizen*. Commenting editorially, Wasson wrote:

We have heard nothing but favorable remarks of Captain Stanwood as a thorough officer, and we believe, unless prevented by absolute order, he will Christianize the savages on the plan recommended by Henry Ward Beecher, for the border ruffians in Kansas about 15 years ago, i.e., by bullets from Sharp's rifles first, and doses of Bible afterward.

Ginny gave a detailed report on the captain's arrival but steered away from editorializing it:

En route to Camp Grant, Captain Stanwood met with General George Stoneman, whereupon the captain received verbal orders that he was to continue to offer provisions to the Apaches encamped there and that they were to be considered prisoners of war. Additionally, the captain was instructed to keep a party of troops in the field on scout.

After making an extensive investigation of the reservation and the distribution of provisions and employment, Stanwood has satisfied himself that the Apaches are sincere in their desire for peace and finds no reason to change any of Lieutenant Whitman's policies or procedures.

This wasn't the first time Ginny's report had been significantly different from the *Citizen*'s but it was the first time people stopped her on the street to ask her why. She replied with caution, telling people that all the papers received the same official reports—it was simply a matter of what the editor chose to use or not to use that made the difference.

She got the surprise of her life when, a week later, the San Diego paper reprinted her article and commented on how the *Tucson Sun* was reporting with favorable optimism while all the other territorial papers were reporting nothing but negativity.

Ginny's heart swelled with pride. She longed to share the good news with her father but he'd already gone for the day and there was no telling when he'd be back. She knew Bonner would be pleased, but she'd have to wait until he came back to Tucson before she could tell him.

Thanks to Mrs. Brown, the talk about her and Bonner had all but stopped. But all it would take to start it up again would be one person seeing her mail a letter to Bonner. She couldn't risk it.

Besides, hers was the only good news. She didn't want to tell him how tense things were in Tucson or how frequently the alarm drum was calling people to the Court House.

The drum sounded so often that Ginny felt she was spending more time at these impromptu meetings than at the office. The news was always the same. Reports of men being attacked while laying a road, the entire party killed and their bodies shockingly mutilated. Wagon trains attacked. Goods stolen. Men wounded. Stock run off.

Toward the middle of April, a Papago courier rode into Tucson with a report that Apaches in the area of the Mission San Xavier had run off with a dozen head of cattle and seven horses. By noon that day, a group of Tucson citizens had saddled up and gone after them. They killed only one Apache but recovered all the stock and returned to Tucson victorious.

A few days later, four Apaches attacked the San Pedro settlement. One man was killed and the Indians took off with a yoke of oxen and a horse. Several men from the settlement followed the trail only to find themselves under attack when the raiders joined up with a much larger group of about one hundred Indian braves.

The alarm drum sounded as Ginny and Indy were walking home from having supper at the Shoo Fly. Jim was on a scout and they'd decided to treat themselves.

"I wonder what it is this time," Ginny said as they passed the drummers.

Indy took Ginny's arm and turned toward the Court

House. "The only way we're going to find out is to sit in on the meeting."

As had become her habit, Ginny took a seat at the back of the room, where her presence wouldn't be obtrusive and where her facial expressions and reactions wouldn't be seen.

In all the weeks she'd been coming alone, not a single person had asked her where her father was. Obviously, they knew. It would be difficult not to know, she realized. Sam didn't try to hide his drunkenness. At times, he seemed to almost flaunt it. He spent most of his afternoons and every evening in one saloon or another. He'd become one of the *regulars,* one of the town drunks.

She also had to assume that people knew she'd taken over complete control of the *Tucson Sun,* that she now wrote all the articles and the editorials. She'd been going about the business of soliciting advertising to the locals—alone. She'd taken reports from the sheriff and from Camp Lowell—alone. She'd worked the office, taken in news reports, fielded questions, put the paper together—all alone. The townsfolk would have had to be blind not to have noticed. Surprisingly, she'd lost only a few local advertisers but had quickly replaced them with the out-of-town, mail-order vendors.

The lack of reaction to her editorship made Ginny realize she'd misjudged people. And this was one time she was glad to have been wrong.

She looked around the Court House hall, searching for familiar faces. This meeting was not as well attended as previous meetings had been but the main topic of conversation was the same. The Apaches.

"There can be no doubt that the Camp Grant-fed Indians are the ones who raided San Xavier last Monday," one man pointed out. "Because they were followed and deprived of their plunder, they returned to their sanctuary, rested up, got up a stronger force, and then attacked the San Pedro settlement."

Ezra Hurt, one of the few men left in town who still believed in the army, stood up and voiced his opinion. "When Lieutenant Whitman came here last year, we all thought he was a good and honest man. As far as I'm concerned nothing's changed that. If he says none of his Indians left the rancheria in large numbers, then I believe him."

"You're a fool," the first speaker replied. "The rancheria is five miles up the canyon from the post and there's more than five hundred of them red devils camped there. Are you going to tell me that you honestly believe Whitman can keep track of all of them—all the time? He might have been able to in the beginning when there was just a few of them, but not now, by God."

As more people came into the Court House, the more anxious the atmosphere got. The men seemed ready and willing to take up arms for the cause, provided they could obtain the animals they needed. The talk grew heated and the prominent orators built their case for getting up a militia right now, tonight.

A man sitting directly in front of Ginny spoke up. "Well, I for one ain't riskin' my hide with no guarantee of support from the army."

"You're a coward, then!" a voice rang out. Ginny couldn't see the speaker but she could hear him. "This is *our* land we're fighting for! *Our* womenfolk and *our* children!"

"Don't be wavin' no flag at me, Seth. I fought that war already. Lost damn near everything I had. Not again."

"He's right!" another man called from the front of the room. "Why should we take all the risk?"

A roar went up as the debate ensued, the call for the militia was vehemently fought with the argument that it was Stoneman's job. Like all the meetings before it, this one seemed to hit the same brick wall, angry shouts crescendoing into mayhem.

"Gentlemen! Gentlemen!" Clay Foster's voice rose above the crowd, rich with authority. Silence filtered through the room.

Ginny and Indy exchanged glances.

"Nothing will be settled in this manner," Foster continued and now all eyes turned to where he stood, near a window, off to the right. In Ginny's opinion, he looked very self-important.

William Oury stood up beside him. "Friends. Listen to me, please. I'll be brief. You're running out of time. The government has made its position clear. Tucson must protect its own."

"Tucson ain't under attack and neither is it gonna be!" Ezra Hurt argued. "I say we wait and see. Let Whitman and them other soldier boys do their jobs. As I hear it, 'Paches are pouring into other posts as well. There ain't *that* many of them. A couple thousand at the most. If things keep going the way they're going, it won't be long before they're all wanting to make peace. I'd rather have that than war!"

"It'll never be peaceful, man. The longer we wait to take action, the worse things are going to get, I say," Oury contradicted. "Soon there won't be any white men left in the Territory."

The roar went up again, but this time the dissenters were far outnumbered. Tears blurred Ginny's vision as she stared at the pencil in her hand and silently shook her head. She felt Indy touch her arm and took some comfort in knowing her friend was beside her.

Ignorance and fear were powerful weapons, and as Ginny listened to the call for the election of officers, she knew she had no way to stop them. Her helplessness made her furious. What could she say—what could she write that would make them see how wrong they were, to think only spilled blood could bring peace?

Ginny clutched her pencil as the ballots were read, scribbling "no surprise" on her pad as William Oury was voted to command the citizen soldiers.

A hat was passed to collect money for the needed horses, but the donations were small—only fifty dollars. Not enough.

When it got to Ginny, she tossed in a stub of a pencil for her contribution. Indy then took the hat from Ginny and carried up to the front and set it down in front of Foster.

"Kind of slim pickings, if you ask me," she said, then returned to her seat.

The meeting was adjourned.

Ginny and Indy were halfway home when Clay Foster stepped out into the street in front of them.

"Good evening, ladies. Did you enjoy your night's entertainment?"

Ginny took Indy's arm and attempted to walk around him.

"Not so fast, Miss Sinclair. I have something to say and I think you'd better listen."

"Get out of our way, Clay," Ginny said firmly.

"I warned your father, now I'm warning you. Certain people hereabouts don't like the tone of your articles and editorials. I suggest you change them to coincide with popular public opinion."

Ginny stiffened, hearing the threat in his voice. "And if I don't?"

Clay Foster smiled, a sinister, mocking smile. "Then you'd better watch your back. From what I can see, your half-breed isn't around to protect you."

Careful not to take his bait, Ginny jerked up her chin. "Thanks for the warning, but I'm not my father. You can't intimidate me, Mr. Foster." Ginny squared her shoulders. "And if you don't get out of our way this instant, we're going to scream our lungs out. Do you hear me?" She pushed past him and he caught her dress sleeve in a merciless grip. Ginny jerked free, feeling the sleeve tear. "Help!" she screamed. "Help!"

Indy threw her shawl on the ground. "Help!" she cried in unison. "Please, help!"

Clay ran like the coward he was. As soon as he did, Ginny and Indy stopped screaming. Within seconds, doors opened and people came out to see what all the ruckus was about.

"It's all right," Ginny told those who came rushing to their aid. "Thank you. We're fine. It was just a drunk. Our screams scared him off."

Later, back at Indy's house, they agreed they'd done the right thing by not accusing Clay Foster. There were bigger and better things in store for him and they didn't want to take the chance of interfering with Jim's plans.

The next day, Ginny purchased a pearl-handled derringer and hired the clerk who sold it to her to take her to the edge of town and teach her how to use it. Something told her Clay Foster wasn't going to stop at verbal threats and she wanted to be prepared.

Ginny was the first in line at the E. N. Fish and Co. store to buy a copy of the memorial and affidavits pamphlet that the legislative committee had published. She took it back to the office and compared it to the copious notes she'd taken earlier in the year. Not surprisingly, there were vast differences. Not lies exactly, but long elaborations that distorted the truth. As the pamphlets made their way into the hands of the citizenry, the sense of outrage increased.

Ginny likened Tucson to a teapot sitting on an unattended stove. The water was boiling and if someone didn't take the pot off soon, it would bubble over and boil dry.

The end of April rolled around and Bonner still hadn't returned from Camp Grant. In his last letter, he wrote that he thought it would be soon but just how soon he didn't know. He asked Ginny to be patient, told her that all was going well, better than he could have hoped for.

Bonner was fulfilling his purpose as a peacemaker. He was seeing his goals come to pass and that made Ginny's heart glad.

She prayed that the volunteer militia wouldn't interfere with Bonner and his efforts, but unless something happened to prove that the Camp Grant Indians weren't the ones who had struck San Xavier and the San Pedro settlement, it seemed likely that they would do more than interfere.

Eighty-two men had pledged themselves to the cause and signed their names to the rolls of the Committee of Public Safety. They'd drawn up a paper that said if one more outrage was committed, they would exterminate every Apache in the Arizona Territory. "Americans all," Oury had said proudly. "Valiant and doughty knights resolved to do or die."

Ginny knew that Jim Garrity kept Bonner informed of what was going on in Tucson. She also knew that Bonner got all the newspapers and read them religiously.

Just thinking of him that way made her ache. She missed him terribly. With each passing day, she became a little more dispirited. When her menses had come in early March, she'd almost gone into mourning. She hadn't realized until then how much she'd been looking forward to carrying Bonner's child.

Ginny sighed and tried to focus on what the reverend was saying. She and Indy had been attending church together for the last six weeks. The pews were full of women and children this morning but few men, a fact Ginny hadn't noticed until just that moment. The reverend preached on about how the devil used people to do his own bidding. How sometimes people didn't even know they were being used.

Sitting next to an open window, Ginny felt a warm

breeze stir her hair. She turned to look outside. The newly seeded grass around the church was growing and promised to be a bright spot of color in the mud-brown town.

The breeze played with the tendrils of hair that had escaped her chignon. As she pushed them back into place, she recalled the night she and Bonner had ridden to his camp beside the river. While sitting astride behind her, he'd swept her hair away from her neck and passionately kissed her nape. Ginny gave herself mentally and physically to the memory and tilted her head to the side. Her imagination was so strong, she could almost feel his mouth touching her, caressing her. Warm. Tender. Oh, so—

Indy's elbow poked her in her side and disrupted her daydream.

"What?" Ginny asked, a little annoyed.

"People are looking at you," Indy whispered, her mouth barely moving.

"Looking at me?" Only then did Ginny realize that she must have gotten a little carried away with her imaginings. "Oh. Sorry. I was thinking about—"

"Bonner. I know. With that dreamy look on your face, it's sort of obvious. But this is church. Try to concentrate on the sermon."

"I'll try," Ginny said, but by now she knew she wouldn't be able to. It was a boring sermon anyway and didn't apply to her. Clay Foster was the only devil she knew and she'd refused to let him use her. She sighed and stared at the pulpit and the man standing behind it, all dressed in black.

She gave listening to the sermon another valiant effort but after a while, her gaze drifted back out the window. At night at least, she could think about Bonner all she wanted, without interruption. She looked forward to going to bed just so she could dream about him.

Lately, however, another dream had been coming

to her. She lay in Bonner's arms, snuggled up to his naked body, when suddenly she heard a voice, like the wind whistling through the trees. "S . . . e . . . e . . . k . . . e . . . r."

The breeze outside picked up and blew in the window, snatching the untied ribbons dangling from her hat and whipping them about her face. With the breeze came an image—a funnel-like creature, made of dust and wind. His face—it was old, weathered. Indian.

"The devil is in Tucson today!" the preacher shouted from the pulpit.

Ginny snapped to attention. She'd never heard him raise his voice before.

"He walks our streets and talks to our friends and neighbors. I beg you, do not be swayed by his evil tongue. Tell him to leave you alone. Tell him that you follow in the Lord's footsteps." He bowed his head. "In Jesus' name we pray. Amen."

"Amen," Ginny said. She wondered what she'd missed that had brought the sermon to such a fiery conclusion. She'd have to remember to ask Indy.

On the way home, Ginny noticed there seemed to be more people about than usual. Maybe it was the warm weather bringing them outside. The livery fairly buzzed with men wanting their saddles repaired and horses shod. The blacksmith's anvil pounded out a steady tattoo as he turned out horseshoes and nails. Passing the gunsmith's shop, Ginny heard two men bargaining to buy rifles on account.

Something's going on, she told herself. She didn't know exactly what, but there was an uneasiness in the air. People were acting differently. Their nerves were up.

She spent the remainder of Sunday afternoon with Indy, going through the baby things her friend had sewn and bought. The only thing Indy didn't have was a christening gown. A particularly delicate piece of lace stored in her mother's bride box came to Ginny's mind. It would look exquisite sewn onto a plain white christening gown. Ginny decided that the next time she went shopping, she would look for one to buy.

Over the next few days, Ginny paid close attention to what was going on around her. Tucson was still buzzing with unusual activity and folks—only the men as far as she could tell—continued to act strangely. Ginny knew it wasn't just her imagination.

Something was definitely going on.

From her office window, Ginny could see much of the town. More than once, she'd seen suspicious looks pass between friends as they met on the street. Late Wednesday afternoon, Clay Foster approached the baker outside his shop, directly across from the newspaper office. Clay stood so close to the poor man that Ginny thought he would crawl inside him. It made her nervous just watching. All the while Clay talked, he kept looking around, as if he feared someone might be listening in on his conversation. The baker's facial expression told Ginny he didn't like what he was hearing. Nevertheless, they shook hands before they went their separate ways.

Thursday night, Ginny was busy setting type for Saturday's paper when Greeley got up and went to the door, letting her know he had to go outside. She put her work aside and took him out through the kitchen, not bothering to take a lamp along with her. Greeley never took long, and he didn't need a light to find his favorite spot.

It had been an unseasonably warm day but with nightfall there was a refreshing coolness in the air. After the stuffiness of the office and the constant odor of ink, Ginny found the fresh air invigorating. She'd spent the entire afternoon and evening standing at the worktable, placing letters on type sticks. She took a few deep breaths.

Dark clouds scudded across the sky, hiding the

moon. Except for Greeley's sniffing noises, the night was still. Two adobes away, the flare of a match caught Ginny's eye. She took a step in that direction, then thought better of it. This was Tucson, not San Francisco. Here, one didn't go wandering around alone between buildings in the dark of night.

"You're either with us or not, Mulligan," a hushed voice demanded in the stillness. It was the name—Mulligan—that drew Ginny's attention and kept her listening where normally good manners would have made her turn away and ignore it. She hadn't seen Mulligan since that day in front of the Congress Hall Saloon, when he tried to kill Greeley, then her. She'd hoped to never see or hear from him again.

"What makes you think you can trust the Papagos?" Mulligan queried. "They're Injuns. And Injuns is Injuns in my book. Not a one of 'em is any damn good."

" 'Cause they hate the Apaches even more than we do," the other man replied. Ginny didn't recognize his voice. "They said they'd join our expedition and I believe them. But in case you're worried, there's a bunch of Mexes coming too. And you know how they hate the Apaches!"

"I thought the volunteer militia was gonna take care of the 'Paches." Mulligan cleared his throat and spat.

"Yeah. That's what we thought. But it seems all most of them wanted to do was talk. There's only a few of them—Oury, Foster, Elias—that's got the nerve to take action. And they're the ones behind this expedition."

"I'll think on it," Mulligan said.

"Well, you'd better think fast because we're heading out tomorrow afternoon."

"Tomorrow? Christ! Doesn't give me much time. Where are you meeting up?"

"Like I told you earlier—we're trying to keep this under our hats until it's over. We don't want anyone stopping us. So we're leaving by ones and twos, taking different roads out of town. The Papagos will be waiting for us at the head of the Rillito, about eight miles north. If you decide to come with us, you'll need to pack enough food and water for a couple of days. Each man is supplying his own weapons. But the Papagos are supplying the war clubs."

"War clubs? What for?"

"Use your imagination, Mulligan."

There was a long silence, then, "Sounds good."

"You bet it sounds good." Ginny heard a chuckle, then a noise that sounded like a slap on the back. "We'll surprise those Camp Grant Indians. They'll never even know what hit them."

"Go ahead and count me in," Mulligan said in a resigned voice.

"I'll tell Oury. Meantime, I want you to swear you won't talk to anybody about this. Especially no gossipy women or soldiers."

"Yeah. Yeah. I swear."

"Tomorrow then."

"See you at the Rillito."

A terrible fear clamped Ginny's heart, making her weak and dizzy. She stayed where she was, afraid she'd be heard if she moved. Finally, the jingle of spurs told her they were gone. She quickly rounded up Greeley and went into the house.

Dazed, Ginny walked through the kitchen, the sitting room, then into the office and sat down at her desk. Now she knew what the strange tension in Tucson was about.

The citizens were making secret plans to attack the Camp Grant Apaches.

Chapter 22

Tucson has not in many years witnessed a stagnation in business so complete as that now exists. The resources of the whole country are being gradually cut off by Indian hostility, and scores who have here-to-fore found lucrative employment at cultivating land in the surrounding valleys have either found their graves there, or abandoned the Territory. To the few who remain, we would say; cling to your homes and watch well, a little while longer; the millennium is nearly at hand.

—*The Arizonan*, Final Edition

Ginny stared down at the half-written editorial on her desktop. Using information from Bonner's letters, she'd put together a sort of progress report on the Camp Grant Indians.

Tears slid silently down her cheeks and fell on the paper, making the ink run. She balled her hands into fists, then a moment later she swept the entire desktop clean. Papers, pens, pencils, ink, everything flew across the room.

Greeley ran for cover under Sam's desk.

She sat staring at the empty desktop, her thoughts racing in a dozen different directions. Then one thought popped out at her.

"Bonner!" she shouted his name. "Oh, my God!" She jumped to her feet. Panic bolted through her like lightning, stealing her breath. From his letters, she knew he spent more time at the rancheria with his grandfather than he did at the post. That meant he'd probably be there when the militia attacked. Panting, she stood there, staring at nothing, shocked and shaking.

A pulse began to pound in Ginny's ears—like the pendulum of a clock, ticking away the seconds.

She ran out from behind the desk to the front door but stopped just short of it. "What am I doing?" she asked in a breathless voice. She twisted around and leaned her back against the door. She needed to calm down, think rationally. There was nothing to be accomplished by dashing out into the street in the middle of the night screaming that there was going to be an attack.

"Calm down," she said aloud. "They're not heading out until tomorrow afternoon." That's what the man had said. Tomorrow. Tomorrow afternoon. There was time.

Time for what? Time to stop them! her mind cried, answering her own question. But how?

"Jimmy crack corn and I don't care. Jimmy crack corn and I don't—"

"Pop!" Ginny breathed a sigh of relief. Her father would know what to do. She turned and opened the door. "Pop! Oh, Pop. I'm so glad you're home. I need—" He stumbled over the threshold and fell face-down on the floor. "Pop!" Ginny knelt down and rolled him over. His eyes were closed and there was a nasty bruise on his forehead. "Oh, no. Pop." She shook him but he didn't respond.

Ginny stood up and before she could stop herself, broke into a fit of hysterical sobbing. Finally, choking back the sobs, she pulled her father all the way inside, then kicked the door closed. For long minutes she stood looking down at him, wondering what she could do to revive him. Then she realized that even if she was successful, he wouldn't be in any condition to give advice. Help would have to come from someone— somewhere else.

She took a deep breath and wiped the tears from her eyes. She had to get hold of herself. Now.

"Think. I have to think." She clenched her fists and walked around her father's unconscious body to her desk, trying to concentrate on what she'd overheard so she could get it clear in her mind. Oury, Foster, and Elias were leading the expedition, she reminded herself as she sat down. She remembered that the man talking to Mulligan had denounced the citizens' committee as a whole and said there were only a few of them that had the nerve to take action. So it was a small group, she concluded. No, she corrected herself. Not small. They were being joined by some Mexicans and Papagos at the head of the Rillito. A river, she thought. And the Papagos were supplying war clubs to do God only knew what with.

She forced herself to sit awhile longer. She needed a plan. But all she could think about was that Bonner might be killed. And his grandfather, and dozens—maybe even hundreds of others, innocent men, women, and children.

She leaned forward, placed her elbows on the desktop, and rested her head in her hands. "I have to find help," she said, out loud again. "I need to talk to . . ." She mentally ticked off a list of people she could trust. The list was short. Indy. Mrs. Brown. Jim—"

Jim Garrity! Jim would know what to do. Ginny glanced at the clock. Midnight. Should she wait until morning? No. The sooner she told Jim the better. The hour wouldn't matter. Lives were at stake.

Calmer now that she knew how to proceed, she took a few minutes to see to her father. She'd never be able to get him to his room. He was too big and heavy. But she could at least cover him up and put a pillow under his head.

Once that was done, she quickly cleaned the desk items off the floor and put them away. She didn't want Pop waking up and thinking the office had been vandalized. She thought about leaving him a note, but there was no time. Besides, he'd be out for hours.

She hurried to the door, opened it, and stood there a moment, then ran back over to the desk, retrieved the little derringer and its bag of ammunition, and tucked it into her pocket. "Greeley. Come, boy." She grabbed his leash and her shawl off the hook beside the door. "We're going for a little walk," she said, hooking his leash to his collar. "Let's just hope we don't run into anybody."

Ginny half walked, half ran down the middle of Main Street, keeping away from the shadowy recesses between buildings. There was only one saloon to pass before reaching Indy's adobe and it was ablaze with light. She veered to the opposite side of the street and made a dash through the yellow swath pouring out of the open door.

"Hey, you! Pretty missy. Come on over here," a man yelled.

Ginny picked up her skirt and ran.

Breathless, Ginny reached Indy Garrity's adobe. She pounded on the door.

Long moments later Indy came to the door. "Who is it?" she asked from inside.

"It's me. Ginny."

A sleepy-eyed Indy cautiously opened the door. "Ginny! What are you doing out at this time of night?"

"I need—I have to talk to Jim. It's urgent!"

Indy opened the door and pulled her friend inside. "He isn't here. He's on a scout down near the Mexican—"

Ginny grabbed Indy's arm. "When—" She choked back a breathless sob. "When will he be back?"

Indy's eyes widened in alarm. "A few days, a week. I never know for sure." She took Ginny's hand from her arm and clutched it. "What's wrong?"

Ginny's chest heaved with exertion and fear. "It's Bonner . . . the Apaches . . . and . . . the militia." Realizing she wasn't making sense, she put her hand to her throat, signaling her need to catch her breath.

Moments later she was able to tell Indy what she'd overheard.

"Dear God," Indy breathed out, sinking into the closest chair.

Ginny stood above her, wringing her hands helplessly. "I was counting on Jim to know what to—" Her voice broke and she gave into the tears.

Indy steepled her hands as if praying for strength. She stared blankly at the door. "Just because Jim's not here doesn't mean there isn't help," she said over the tips of her fingers. "Let me think a moment. If Jim were here, he would—Oh, God. What would he do? He'd—" She put her hands on either side of her forehead and rubbed her temples. "He'd go to Colonel Dunn," she blurted, grabbing Ginny. Then, with more conviction, she confirmed her answer. "Yes. That's what he'd do. I'm sure of it."

With an effort, Ginny pulled herself together. She squeezed Indy's hands, then let them go. "Then that's what I have to do," she said, taking a step toward the door.

"Ginny, wait!" Indy struggled against her bulk to get out of her chair. "Listen to me. There's time. You said their expedition wasn't leaving Tucson until tomorrow afternoon."

"Yes, but if I go now . . ."

Indy shook her head. "You can't go now. I know this town. You took a big risk coming here alone at this time of night. There's nothing but trouble on the streets between here and Camp Lowell." Indy put her arm around Ginny and walked her over to the dining table. "Let's have a cup of tea, calm down, and talk things over. Then, first thing in the morning, we'll go together to see Colonel Dunn. He'll still have plenty of time to do what he has to do."

"Are you sure?"

"I'm as sure as I can be," she answered.

"You're right," Ginny reluctantly agreed. Though

how she was going to get through the next six hours was beyond her. This was going to be the longest night of her life. She felt Greeley pull on his leash. She'd all but forgotten him. Bending, she put her arms around him and hugged him. "Good boy, Greeley." She looked up at Indy. "I brought him with me for protection. I hope you don't mind him being here."

Indy leaned over him and unhooked his leash. "Of course I don't mind. I love animals. You know that." She scratched his ears.

"If Colonel Dunn won't help us, I don't know what I'll do. I don't think there's anybody else we can ask."

Indy looked puzzled. "He'll help us, but why don't you think anyone else would help? Believe it or not there *are* people in Tucson who don't hate the Apaches. People who think as we do."

"Maybe a few," Ginny mumbled beneath her breath. "But not the majority. Haven't you noticed the odd way people have been acting the last few days? I think it started last Sunday. I noticed it on the way home from church." Ginny went on to tell Indy what she'd observed.

"I do recall thinking that there were a lot of people milling about, but then I got busy and didn't give it another thought."

Ginny waved a hand. "I think half the town—the male half, that is—knows what's going on. And not a one of them intends to do anything about it. How can people just stand by and let something like this happen?"

"I don't know, Ginny. I just don't know."

After two cups of tea, Indy talked Ginny into lying down and resting until sunup. Neither woman slept a wink. Instead, they talked and wept into the small hours. Then at sunrise, they were out the door and on their way to see Colonel Dunn.

*   *   *

"He isn't here," a young, fresh-faced private told them outside of the colonel's tent. "He's taken quarters in town. Got tired of tentin' it, I guess."

"Where in town?" Ginny asked, trying to keep her voice steady.

"Don't rightly know, ma'am. The colonel, he don't see fit to confide in the likes of me."

"Thank you, Private," Indy said. "Should he return here, will you please tell him that Major Garrity's wife needs to see him on urgent business?"

"Yes, ma'am. I surely will."

With Greeley in tow, Ginny and Indy walked back to town. "We should probably check the Stevens House first," Indy suggested. "Then if he isn't there—well, we'll just keep looking until we find him."

He wasn't at the Stevens House or the Shoo Fly or the Pioneer News Depot or any of the other dozen places they went to. Ginny became concerned for Indy. She was holding her stomach, obviously uncomfortable, but she refused to give up until they found the colonel.

The morning wore on. Outside the Congress Hall Saloon, Ginny recognized three men from the citizens' meeting. They were getting ready to mount up. She nudged Indy. "Those three—they're part of it. I've seen them at the meetings. They must have decided to leave early," she whispered, fear permeating her voice. They moved on. On the south side of the church square, Mulligan was saddling his horse. Ginny alerted Indy and they moved into an alley and waited until he'd gone. He might not remember her, but chances were good that he would have remembered Greeley. They continued on and a few minutes later ran into William Oury walking to the corral behind his house. He had a rifle under one arm and a bedroll under the other.

"Morning, ladies," he said, respectfully touching the brim of his Stetson. "Fine day, isn't it?"

Ginny turned her face away, unable to look at the man for fear of giving her feelings away.

"Have you by any chance seen Colonel Dunn?" Indy ventured.

It was all Ginny could do not to rush up to him and tell him that she knew where he was going and what he planned to do. But she was afraid. He had a mission to preserve. Men counting on him. He might see the two of them as a threat to his plans and take measures to keep them from telling others. They would have to be drastic measures to keep them subdued. Ginny didn't even want to entertain that thought. Heart racing, she gritted her teeth, kept her mouth shut, and let Indy do the talking.

"As a matter of fact," Oury said, "I saw him about an hour ago, heading toward Lord and Williams Corral. Something about his horse throwing a shoe."

"Thank goodness, we've been looking all over town for him. I need to get a message to my husband. We'll look for him at the corral, then. Thank you." As soon as they passed Oury's house, Indy let out a long sigh. "I don't know what possessed me to speak to him. It just came out."

"Nerves," Ginny said. "Probably just nerves." Her nerves were up so bad that she could hardly talk.

Both Ginny and Indy gave excited exclamations when they saw Colonel Dunn's blue uniform. He stood out against the brown corral and the brown building behind it.

"Mrs. Garrity. What a pleasant surprise. How nice to see you," the officer said as they approached.

"We need to speak to you, Colonel. In private," Indy said in a calm voice that didn't even get the notice of the farrier or his helper.

"Why, of course. Shall we talk over there in the shade?"

The three of them walked to where the overhang of the corral provided a large patch of shade. Indy didn't waste any time repeating what Ginny had told her.

The colonel received the news without noticeable excitement. "So that's what's been going on," he said, nodding his head. "I thought it might be something like that but I couldn't be sure. How did you come by this information, if I may ask?"

"I told her," Ginny said, stepping up next to Indy. "I took my dog outside late last night and overheard two men talking about it." She looked him straight in the eye. "Please, Colonel, you have to do something. And you have to do it *now*. We've spent precious hours looking for you all over town. On our way here, we saw Mulligan and Oury and several others preparing to leave town."

He rubbed his chin and stared down at her. "I'm sorry, I don't know your name."

"Ginny. Ginny Sinclair."

"Do you have some sort of personal interest in this or—"

"Yes. You could say that. I intend to marry Bonner Kincade." She boldly met his eyes. "But if you don't do something to stop those men from attacking the rancheria, not only will a lot of innocent Apaches be killed but Bonner might be killed too." The mere thought of what might happen was almost too much to bear. She covered her face with trembling hands and closed her eyes.

"Ira!" the colonel shouted over the women's heads. "Are you through shoeing that horse yet?"

"Yes, sir," the farrier called back.

The colonel returned his attention to Ginny. "I promise you, Miss Sinclair, nothing will happen to Bonner or any of those Apaches. I'll get on it right away. I'll send two of my best men out to Camp Grant to warn Captain Stanwood or whoever's in charge. Then they'll handle it."

Indy sighed with relief. "Thank you, Colonel. I

knew we could count on you." She took hold of Indy's hand and squeezed it hard.

"Believe me, Mrs. Garrity, I don't want to see those Apaches harmed any more than you do."

Ginny bolstered her courage and said, "I want to go with them."

His look told her he thought she'd lost her mind. "Miss Sinclair, I don't think—"

"Please! I insist," she cut him short. "I want to go with them I won't get in their way. I promise."

He shook his head. "It's absolutely out of the question. I'm sorry."

"Please." She grabbed his arm.

"No. Impossible." He gently removed her hand from his sleeve and walked away. Without a backward glance, he went to his horse, untied its reins from the hitching post, and mounted up. He lightly tapped his boot heels against the horse's sides and rode over to where Indy and Ginny were standing.

"I assure you, Miss Sinclair," he said, while putting on his gauntlets. "I *will* take care of this. Bonner Kincade is my best post guide and besides that, I happen to like him and consider him a friend. He wouldn't appreciate it if I let you accompany my men on such a dangerous mission. Surely you know that."

All Ginny knew was that it was useless to try to convince Colonel Dunn to let her go with his men.

She'd have to follow them on her own.

"I'm sorry, Colonel," she said with feigned remorse. "It's just that I've been so worried. Of course, you're right. I'd only be in the way. But this has been very upsetting as you can imagine."

"I'm sure it has. But you've done the right thing bringing the matter to my attention. Now let me handle it." He touched his forefinger to the edge of his campaign hat, then kneed his horse and rode off toward Camp Lowell.

Ginny stood staring after him in silence. "I need a horse," she stated flatly as he rode out of sight.

"A horse? Why?" No sooner did Indy ask the question than she gasped. "No. Ginny. Don't even think it."

"Too late. I've made up my mind. I'm going to get a horse and follow his men out to Camp Grant."

"It's too dangerous!"

Ginny took Indy's elbow and led her away from the corral. "I don't care about the danger. I'm going to do this and there's nothing anybody can do to stop me. If it was Jim out there, about to be attacked, you'd do the same thing. Don't try to tell me you wouldn't."

Indy rolled her head, then groaned in resignation. "Of course, I would. I'd do anything to save him. Anything!" A smile trembled over her lips and tears glistened in her eyes. "What can I do to help?"

Ginny gave Indy a hug. "Thank you for being my friend." Ginny leaned her forehead against Indy's. "It's going to be all right, isn't it, Indy? The soldiers will get there in time to warn the rancheria?"

"It's got to be all right," Indy said. "It's just got to be." She pulled away and started down the street. "Come on, let's get you that horse and the other things you're going to need." Looking over her shoulder she said, "Good grief, Ginny—do you even know how to ride?"

Two long, fast strides and Ginny was at her side. "No. But I'll learn. I'm not afraid. I rode with Bonner all the way out to the river so I sort of know what to do."

"You'll do fine," Indy assured her.

"I thought I'd take Greeley with me. For protection. What do you think?"

"I think you should take your derringer instead. One bark and Greeley will give you away. Leave him with me. I'll take care of him while you're gone. Now, walk faster. We're running out of time."

Less than a half hour later they'd rented a horse complete with saddle and tack. Ginny watched closely as the stable boy saddled and bridled it. Holding on to the saddle horn, she put her foot in the stirrup and climbed up. All the way back to Indy's adobe, Ginny listened to Indy telling her the ins and outs of good horsemanship.

"How long do you think it'll be before the soldiers leave town?"

"They're going to have to be briefed, then they'll get their gear together—forty-five minutes to an hour, I'd guess. When they leave, they'll take the main wagon road, which means they'll have to pass right by us." Indy waved her hand toward the window. "Quickly now, you'll need to change clothes," she said as she headed into the bedroom. Once there, she rummaged through a trunk and pulled out a pair of small-sized trousers and a plaid shirt. "Put these on. It's easier to ride in trousers than in a skirt and they'll protect your legs from brush."

Unquestioningly, Ginny did as she was told in spite of the fact that she hated the idea of wearing trousers. Next came a slouch hat and a warm, wool-lined coat.

"It's still chilly on the desert at night. We'll tie the coat up with your bedroll so it'll be handy if you need it." She handed Ginny the coat, then went about gathering up two canteens, some jerked beef, and an assortment of other supplies. Finally, all was in readiness. They'd no sooner packed up the horse than they saw the soldiers passing by.

Ginny mounted up and took hold of the reins. "Indy, I—"

"Don't say anything or I'll start crying," Indy warned. "Just, please . . . be careful."

Ginny took a steadying breath, then nodded her head. "Take care of Greeley for me and—" She bit off her words, gave Indy a hard look, then wheeled the horse around and started down the street.

* * *

At the edge of town, Ginny slowed her horse to a walk so the soldiers could get well ahead of her. Their horses left such a distinguishable trail of dust, she knew following them wouldn't be any trouble. But she was concerned about what to say if they discovered her. Unless the colonel had warned them about her, which she doubted, they had no reason to suspect she was following them. She'd simply say she was on her way to interview one of the local ranchers.

If, on the other hand, they knew who she was and were determined to stop her, Indy had given her money to bribe them to take her along. "The only people as poor as Indians are soldiers," Indy had told her. "For good or bad, they're easily bribed."

Riding a horse was not as difficult as Ginny had anticipated. Either that, or the horse was exceptionally well trained and obedient. Toward the end of the first hour, she had enough confidence in herself to start "finding her seat" as Indy had called it.

The heat of the day made Ginny glad for the hat Indy had insisted she wear. Its wide brim shaded her face and neck from the sun's harsh glare. Ugly as they were, she was glad, too, for the trousers. She could see how a skirt would have hampered her comfort and her mobility.

Bonner. His name echoed through her mind along with the names of Gianatah and Eskiminzin. Bonner had described them so often in his letter that Ginny felt she almost knew them. They weren't just Apaches—they were people. People that she'd grown to care about.

She felt the tears gather behind her eyes and knew she had to rid herself of those thoughts or they'd be her undoing. She turned her attention to the landscape and forced herself to have good thoughts. Positive thoughts.

It had been the dead of winter when she and her

father had set out for Tucson. She remembering thinking that the desert was one ugly stretch of nothingness.
Now, looking at the desert lands surrounding her, she
was surprised to see that it wasn't ugly at all. The
ground was awash with vivid color. There were clumps
of desert grasses and clusters of prickly pears with
large gold flowers emerging from waxy paddles. But
most impressive of all was the occasional saguaro that
stood tall and straight, its arms reaching out as if waving at her, encouraging her to go on to do what she
had to do.

Ginny wasn't sure how many miles she'd traveled
when suddenly she noticed that the dust trail up ahead
had thickened and was forming a large cloud. She
thought a moment, then came to the conclusion that
more dust meant more horses, more people. Perhaps
a wagon train. Or a detail of soldiers returning to
Camp Lowell.

Whatever the cause, she couldn't risk being seen.
With that thought, she reined her horse off the road,
angling northeast toward an outcropping of boulders.

The dust cloud billowed high into the air as though
a number of horses had come together in one place,
then slowly started to disburse. As the air cleared,
Ginny peered into the distance and saw a number of
dark figures moving about. Men and horses, at least a
dozen, choked the road.

She waited, impatient, watching for the soldiers to
leave, looking for their telltale trail of dust continuing
north. Ginny waited in the shadow of the boulders for
what seemed forever, anxious to continue. But nothing
moved, not even toward Tucson.

Ginny frowned, curious to know what was going on.
But she had no intention of getting closer to find out.
She couldn't take the risk.

She continued to wait awhile longer, then finally
decided she could wait no more. She had to go on,
with or without the soldiers. "If you lose them," she

remembered Indy telling her, "Just follow the wagon ruts. Camp Grant is less than fifty miles from the edge of town."

She guided the horse away from the boulders and eventually returned to the road. When she looked back over her shoulder, she saw a curl of smoke rising into the air and realized that now there was a campfire where the dust cloud had been.

She didn't understand what had happened to the soldiers, and though the idea of being out here alone was frightening, she knew there was no help for it. Ginny shook her head and continued on, careful to check behind her every so often just in case the soldiers had moved on.

But as the hours wore on and there was still no sign of them, Ginny started to feel uncertain and afraid. What made her think that she, Ginny Sinclair, a born and bred city woman, could save the day? She had no experience in such things. She was a newspaperwoman. A writer. Not an adventuress. The only adventures she'd ever had were when she vicariously lived through her characters, through Joaquin Murietta and others like him.

She realized she hadn't planned on being in this position. It had just happened. She had done all the sensible things, the practical things to get help. But in the end, nothing had worked.

Now, it was up to her. Not by choice, but by necessity. Maybe someday she'd look back at this as an adventure but right now all could think about was what would happen if she didn't make it through.

She forced her fears aside and kneed her horse into a slow canter. The sun had started going down and she needed to make a few more miles before nightfall.

At twilight she made a brief stop near a stream and watered her horse. She was careful not to let go of its reins in case it decided to wander off and leave her. The horse drank its fill, then shook itself off. Ginny tied the reins to a sturdy bush and rummaged around in her saddlebags until she found the fresh fruit Indy had packed for her.

After eating a large apple and drinking some brackish water from the canteen, she walked around and stretched her muscles. She was impatient to get going again but had to think of her horse.

Darkness had set in by the time Ginny mounted up. Without help, it was no easy task for a woman as short as she was.

A bright half-moon rode in the sky, giving off enough light to see the road. She walked her horse now, letting it pick its way along between the wagon rugs and potholes.

The silence of the night was broken by the clip-clop of hooves against hard-packed earth and the cry of an occasional unseen desert creature.

Ginny rolled her head to work the kinks out of her neck. She was tiring but she had to go on. If she reached Camp Grant by tomorrow morning, there would be plenty of time for whoever was in charge to send a warning to the rancheria. That is, if the vigilante group kept to its schedule.

She'd wondered how far ahead of her they were. A few hours? More? She'd have to keep a close watch. Surely, if they'd stopped for the night, they would build a campfire. She couldn't imagine not being able to see it from a distance.

"Rider comin' this way!" The lookout rode back into camp and delivered his warning. "He's all alone far as I can tell."

Clay Foster rose to his feet. "It must be somebody from the blockade."

William Oury tossed the coffee out of his tin cup onto a cactus. "Must be. Let's go see who it is."

Oury spotted the moonlit lone rider first. "He's riding real slow, like he doesn't know for sure where he's going."

"Either that or he's looking for us," Foster said. "Hey! You, there!"

Ginny gasped. She'd been seen. And the voice— Clay Foster! Where had he come from? She'd been so careful to keep an eye out. Fear clutched her heart.

She jabbed her boot heels into the sorrel's sides. The horse shot forward, then exploded into a ground-eating run. The wagon ruts wavered before her in lines that seemed to move from one side of the road to the other.

She quickly glanced over her shoulder. There were two of them. Foster and another man. She saw them whip up their horses and take out after her.

"Hold up there!"

"I'll shoot!"

Ginny ducked low over the gelding's neck. She kicked him to an even faster pace and felt him strain to do her bidding. She knew that as long as she stayed on the road, her pursuers wouldn't have any difficulty following her. But if she rode into the desert, she might be able to lose them.

The wide expanse of black yawned in front of her, beckoning freedom—closer, and closer still as the horse charged forward. Elation filled her as the pounding of hooves behind her faded away—or had they matched her pace?

Ginny turned, a quick glance over her shoulder revealing nothing but the black and choking dust. She exhaled a relieved breath, then cried out in despair as an arm snaked from the darkness, grabbed her waist, and dragged her from the saddle.

The vigilante camp was hidden from the road by a thicket of mesquite. It held a sizable group—a hundred and fifty or more, mostly Papagos and Mexicans. Ginny counted only six Americans, men she knew from town, men she'd sold advertising to. Some of Tucson's leading citizens.

They had themselves quite a laugh at her expense. Especially Clay Foster. Once he'd discovered who he'd captured, he'd practically laughed himself into hysterics.

"You continue to surprise me, Miss Sinclair," he drawled, smiling broadly. "You're an amazing woman."

"Unfortunately, I don't have the same opinion of you, Mr. Foster. You're nothing but a coward and a mur—"

He slapped her face, stopping her short.

Ginny reeled backward and stumbled to the ground. She lay on her side in the dirt, her face stinging. Never in her life had she felt such loathing for a person, such hate. She wished now that she hadn't put her derringer in her coat pocket, but Indy had thought it too dangerous to keep in her trousers pocket. She could easily shoot Clay Foster and not have a single regret.

He grabbed her arm and yanked her to a sitting position, then took her by the hair and jerked her head back so she was forced to look up at him. A sadistic leer crossed his face. "You've created quite a problem, Ginny. What exactly am I supposed to do with you?"

"Let me go," she suggested, brushing her hair from her eyes.

"Amazing and amusing," Clay observed. "The perfect woman." He met her gaze. "Too bad you prefer half-breed scum."

Rage coursed through Ginny. "Bonner Kincade is twice the man you are," she bit out. "When he finds out what you've—"

"I doubt that by the time you see him again, he'll care. Because he'll be dead along with Lahte."

Ginny didn't rise to his bait. When she tried to look away, he gave her hair another tug, then smiled. "You know, it'll do my heart good to kill that half-breed good-for-nothing right in front of you. I do hope you're not one of the namby-pamby females who faints at the sight of blood."

"No! Clay, please. Listen to me." The cold, emotionless glaze in his eyes frightened her to her very core, but she continued, hoping to reach the others. She struggled to get to her feet. "All of you! Please, listen to me. You can't do this. It's murder. No one will thank you for it. You'll be killing innocent people—people who want nothing but to live their lives in peace."

When Foster loosened his grip on her hair, she looked around the circle. No one seemed moved by her appeal. The Papagos sat together, their faces impassive. Each of them carried a bow and a quiver full of arrows. She turned to the Mexicans, but instead her gaze was drawn down to a pile of wicked-looking mesquite clubs.

War clubs.

Her stomach roiled and she thought she was going to be sick.

Foster made a growling noise and jerked her toward him. "Nice speech, Ginny. Was that for Bonner alone or the whole nasty mess of them?"

"You bastard!"

"Ginny. Ginny. Don't you see? No one really cares much what you have to say."

She fought him, fought him with everything she had, but it was a futile effort. He was too strong.

"Let me go, damn you! Let me go!"

Ginny wouldn't give up. She curled her fists and swung up, managing to free herself from Foster's hold. He grabbed her again and she kicked fiercely, screaming as loud as she could.

Oury hurried over to help, caught her flailing arms, and twisted them around behind her back. "I sure wish you hadn't followed us out here, ma'am." He tied a rope around her wrists and pulled it taut, then looked at Foster. "This isn't supposed to be personal, Foster. It's business. Why don't you back off and take her back to Tucson. By the time you get there, we'll have done our work."

"Hell, no! I've worked too hard for this to miss it. She got herself into this, now she can suffer the consequences. Besides, it'll give her something worthwhile to write about. I was getting real sick of all those women's rights articles and those serial stories."

"Then you take care of her and see to it that she doesn't get in anyone's way," Oury said, obviously annoyed. He walked away.

"My pleasure," Foster called after him. He turned and boldly looked her over. A moment later he walked away and joined the others around the campfire. Unsure as to what was expected of her, Ginny looked around for a place to sit down. She found a boulder and sat down in front of it. She leaned back and glared at the men around her.

There was Sidney DeLong, a freighter and merchant. He'd always impressed her as being a well-educated man, a gentle man. Obviously, she'd misjudged him. Next to DeLong sat the town blacksmith, Charlie Etchells. When he saw her looking at him, he lowered his gaze. Of all of them, Ginny was most surprised to see Mr. Bennett, the kindhearted manager of the Stevens House, Tucson's best hotel. Last Sunday, he'd sat in the pew behind her in church. And now here he was, a vigilante, a man intent upon committing murder.

In spite of her efforts to keep control of her emotions and not cry, Ginny's throat began to constrict and burn. She'd heard them talking and knew their plan—to attack at dawn, to club the Apaches to death in their sleep before they could give the alarm. Once the alarm went off, they'd use their other weapons.

Ginny hung her head and let go, crying until there were no more tears.

And then she prayed. For Bonner. For his grandfather. For all the Apaches.

Someone, she didn't know who because of the tears blinding her eyes, got her coat, lifted her forward, and put it around her shoulders. She would have shrugged it off if she'd had the energy.

The sun had been up a long time when Ginny awakened. Foster stood before her staring down at her.

"Have a nice rest, Ginny?"

She refused to answer.

"Time to go," Clay said, reaching down and grabbing her arm. She cried out in pain when he brutally yanked her to her feet. He ignored her cry, slung her coat over his arm, and pushed her toward the horses. She wondered how he expected her to ride with her hands bound behind her back, but her question was quickly answered when he started to untie the rope.

Ginny immediately began rubbing her wrists. They were red and raw where the fibrous strands had bitten into her tender flesh. Her hands were cold and nearly numb.

"Mount up," he said, giving orders like a general. Because of so many hours of poor circulation into her hands, she couldn't get the hold she needed on the saddle horn to pull herself up. After two failed attempts, Foster gave her a hand up, then held on to her leg, probably so she couldn't kick him.

Oury sat astride his horse in front of hers, holding on to the bridle. Evidently he was anticipating that she'd try to escape and was making every effort to see that she didn't. As soon as she had her seat, Foster grabbed for her hands, bound them in front of her, and tied the rope to the saddle horn.

"No, please. They're so sore."

"Shut up, Ginny, or I'll gag you too."

She didn't want to be gagged so she kept quiet and suffered in silence. She glanced around behind her when he tied her coat back to her bedroll. The derringer! It was in her coat pocket. Why hadn't she thought about it last night? Because she'd been too tired to think, she told herself. And even if she had thought about it, it wouldn't have done any good. With her hands tied behind her back, she couldn't have done anything with it even if she'd managed to smuggle it out.

Nevertheless, the thought of the little pistol so close gave her a small measure of comfort.

They headed out, veering away from the road, moving slowly because most of the Papapos were on foot. Ginny noticed a tension between the Americans. They snapped at each other like dogs over a bone. The higher they climbed, the cooler the temperature got, but the men were no less irritable.

By midmorning, the vigilante leader, Elias, found a better trail that continued northward under cover of growth from the river. It was just before noon when he came upon a large, well-concealed clearing. He held up his hand to signal the troop to halt.

"We'll rest here until nightfall," he announced, his voice carrying all the way to Ginny at the back of the column. The men on horseback started to dismount.

With her wrist rope tied to the saddle horn, Ginny was forced to wait until Foster decided to untie her and help her down. She cringed when he put his hands around her waist. It galled her to have to lean into him for support but she had no choice. He held on to her a few moments longer than necessary, his mouth close to hers.

"When this is all over," he said in a low voice, "I'm going to make love to you."

"I'd sooner make love to the devil!" Ginny spat contemptuously. He shoved her back, pushing her up against her horse, then stomped away. For long moments she stood there trying to catch her breath and gather her wits. She thought about the derringer and turned around feeling for it in the folds of her coat.

It was there. Hidden from the men. Loaded and ready to fire. Even with her hands tied, she knew she could get to it. But to take it out now just to shoot Clay Foster wouldn't help Bonner or the Apaches. She needed to wait—wait until the volunteers were within striking distance of the rancheria. Then a shot would warn the camp and the invaders would find themselves up against an army of warriors.

Meantime, she'd work on getting her hands free. For hours, when nobody was looking, Ginny bit and pulled at the rope with her teeth.

She listened carefully to the men talk. Elias has sent out an advance scout to determine the exact location of the encampment. He'd come back reporting that they still had a good ten miles to ride before reaching the rancheria.

As the evening wore on and the temperature dropped, Ginny asked Foster if he would get her coat. "You don't even have to untie me, just put it around my shoulders."

"Anything to accommodate a lady," he said in a heavily accented voice. Moments later he draped it around her shoulders.

"Button the top button, please, so it won't fall off."

He gave her a narrow look but did as she asked. "Anything else?" he asked sarcastically.

"No." She bit down on her lip and glared at him.

Before dawn, the order to mount up circulated through the camp. Foster put Ginny on her horse and tied her up to the saddle horn as before. "This is it, Ginny." He looked up at her, his eyes shining with fevered excitement. "In a few hours it will all be over and we'll ride back to Tucson as conquering heroes."

"There's nothing heroic in killing innocent men, women, and children," she said in a hissing voice.

"But then I really wouldn't expect a man who sabotages his fellow merchants to know what true heroism is."

"Sabotage? What the hell are you talking about?"

"Last January? The Fish and Company freight train? Nine men killed?" She clicked her tongue, scolding him. "How easily we forget."

He squinted up at her, his face a glowering mask of rage.

For a moment she thought he was going to strike her. But then he reached into his pocket and pulled out a kerchief. "It could be dangerous knowing so much about other people's business."

"I'm not afraid of you."

Mercilessly, he jammed the kerchief between her teeth, then tied it behind her head. "Either you're very foolish or very brave."

Just then, Elias rode up. "She's your responsibility, Foster. If she does anything to—"

"She won't," Foster cut him off. "I've got everything under control."

Elias gave Ginny a hard, cold look, then nodded. "You'd better hope so."

Moments later they rode out. Still determined to get her hands free, Ginny worked the underside of the rope over the sharp edge of the saddle horn where the stitching had come apart.

They were riding upstream now. The men divided into two wings. The Papagos followed Oury to the north, and the Mexicans and Americans went to the south.

Ginny knew it was only a matter of minutes before Elias signaled a halt. Then they would picket their horses and sneak up on the encampment on foot.

Panic rioted through her. She still hadn't gotten her hands free of the rope. And now, she was out of time. Keeping a close watch on Foster who rode ahead of her, leading her horse, Ginny leaned forward until she cold touch the right side of her coat. Gritting her teeth against the burning pain, she gathered the fabric toward her until she found the pocket.

Elias signaled the troop to halt. Then, in the first thin light of dawn, Ginny saw the wickiups. They stood like haystacks in a field. She worked feverishly to get hold of the derringer but her fingers were so numb she couldn't feel it.

Foster dismounted, picketed his horse, and came back to her. "If things go the way I think they will, I won't be long."

Ginny screamed at him behind her gag but the sound came out muffled. Laughing at her efforts to be heard, he picketed her horse next to his, then left to join the others.

Ginny watched in horror as the men readied their weapons. As soon as they started out, moving like snakes through the desert growth, she put all of her effort into getting the derringer.

At last her fingers curled round the barrel.

Chapter 23

BLOODY RETALIATION

The policy of feeding and supplying hostile Indians with arms and ammunition has brought its bloody fruits . . . the patient endurance of citizens was exhausted, and they resolved on retaliation, so with the aid of over a hundred Papagos, they started on the 28th April, reached Arivaipa last Sunday morning, killed 83, took 28 children prisoners and 7 escaped . . . The slaughter is justified on grounds of self-defense . . . To say this instance shows a spirit of barbarism in our people would be a gross slander.
—*Arizona Citizen*

Ginny shook all over as she finally pulled the derringer out of her coat pocket. She closed her numb hands around it, trying to hold on. Breathing in shallow, quick gasps, she eventually managed to curl her fingers around the grip. Carefully, she aimed over her horse's left shoulder into the darkness.

A woman's scream rent the air.

Too late, Ginny thought as she pulled the trigger. Her warning shot was too late! She started to fire a second shot but another scream—a child's scream—stopped her.

For a moment all her nerves hung by a thread. Then came the calming cold reality of what she had to do.

There were five shots left in the derringer. Five raiders killed meant five lives saved.

But first she had to get free of the gag and the wrist rope. Frantic, she scooted to the back of the saddle, pushing herself up the cantle. When she'd gone as far as she could, she bent forward and rubbed her right cheek over the saddle horn, trying to catch the kerchief on its frayed edge. After several unsuccessful tries, it caught and she was able to pull the gag out of her mouth and down off her face.

Ginny worked her jaw, then began biting and tugging at the rope around her wrists. Her jaw ached and she tasted blood in her mouth, on her teeth. Tears stung her eyes but she wouldn't give up. Then with one last fierce bite the rope gave way. Her hands were free.

Nightmarish screams echoed from the encampment. Ginny sobbed as she leaned over the horse and yanked up the reins. The picket pin popped up out of the ground. Ginny gathered the reins to her, picket pin and all, then dug her boot heels into the animal's sides. The horse bolted forward as if sensing her urgency. She reined it toward the encampment, giving the horse its head and letting it find its own way across the desert floor. Faster and faster it raced under the steady pressure of her knees.

A camp dog barked. Then another. Their barks turned to mournful howls. A wickiup went up in a fiery blaze. The stink of burning hides moved quickly through the air.

The predawn was full of sound. Screams. Everywhere the terrified screams and voices under the slump of war clubs.

Rifles spurted crimson flames. Men, women, and children ran, desperate to find cover, safety. Babies cried. Pistols spoke again and again, popping like Chinese fireworks.

At the edge of the encampment, Ginny slid out of the saddle and ran forward. Everywhere she looked bare-chested Papagos were pulling women and children out of the wickiups, raping them, clubbing them, mutilating them before her eyes.

"Bonner! Bonner!" Ginny cried, turning in a dizzying circle.

A frenzied scream behind her brought Ginny

around. She ran into the nearest wickiup and found a Papago warrior tearing the clothes off a young girl.

"Stop!" Ginny pleaded. He did, then he turned and came at her, his war club raised. Without a moment's hesitation, Ginny aimed the derringer at his chest and fired.

"Come on!" Ginny shouted to the terrified girl. "Now!" As the warrior fell dead, the near-naked girl flew into Ginny's arms. Together they fled the wickiup.

Desert dust and black, choking smoke swirled around them in stifling clouds. Ginny put her arm around the girl and crouching together they ran crookedly to the northern edge of the encampment where she saw others fleeing for their lives.

"Run," she yelled, pushing the girl away from her. "Run!" The girl scurried up the embankment into the brush.

Ginny turned back toward the melee, clutching her pocket pistol in front of her, ready to shoot.

Oury dashed past her, his knife blade shining with the reflection of the burning wickiups. Ginny took aim and shot. She missed and moments later he felled the squaw.

Ginny ran after him, intent upon killing him. Then, before her, out of the red mass, an old man staggered from the flames. Ginny ran to help him instead. "Come with me," she insisted. He fought her but Ginny held fast. She knew he thought she was one of the raiders, but she didn't have time to explain. Using every ounce of strength she had, she pulled him to the edge of the camp. Like the girl, she meant to send him running to safety but he collapsed.

"Get up. You have to get up!" she cried, frantically looking over her shoulder to see if anyone had noticed them. She looked down and saw that his rawhide leggins were covered with blood. Ginny moved around behind him, put her hands under his arms, and dragged him. But he was big and heavy. Hard to move. She kept pulling, desperate sobs choking her throat.

"Need a hand?"

She jerked her chin up, terror clamping her chest.

Clay Foster stood before her, a pistol aimed at the old man.

"Clay," she whispered.

He smiled. "I don't know how you managed to get free, Ginny, but I'm impressed. You're quite a woman. But I already mentioned that, didn't I? Too bad you're an Indian lover."

"Clay, please," Ginny begged. "Spare him. He's an old man. And he's badly wounded besides. For God's sake, leave him be!"

"He's an Apache, Ginny. You've heard the saying," Clay told her, leveling his pistol at the old man's head. "The only good Indian is a—"

"No!" Ginny raised the derringer, the barrel even with Clay's chest. "I've got three shots. If you shoot him, I'll shoot you."

"Ginny. Ginny," Clay drawled, meeting her gaze. "You don't want to kill me." His face showed nothing but that supreme arrogance that she'd always hated in him.

Without warning, he kicked his foot up, the toe of his boot striking her wrist. The derringer flew out of her hand. Lightning hot pain streaked through Ginny's right hand and arm. She reeled back and fell against the old man.

"I really didn't want to hurt you, Ginny, but you gave me no—"

Screeching like an eagle, a savage cry split the dawn and a breech-clouted Apache dove at Clay Foster from behind, knocking him to the ground.

Foster's pistol went off and Ginny felt something whiz past her head.

The Apache rolled to his feet. "Get up you murderous bastard. I want to see your face when I kill you."

Ginny blinked. "Bonner! My God. Bonner," she cried, not believing her eyes. He was here! Alive!

"What makes you think you can kill me, Kincade? I've got a pistol. You've only got a knife."

Bonner smiled with confidence. He moved back and forth on the balls of his moccasined feet as if securing his position. Ginny saw his leg muscles ripple like fluid beneath his skin.

"Go ahead and shoot me then," Bonner taunted. His knife blade twinkled as he waved it before him like a small flag, moving it from side to side.

Dawn was breaking over the Galiuro Mountains, bringing its clear light. Ginny sat behind the old man, cradling her right hand. Her wrist was broken but she hardly felt the pain.

She looked between Bonner and Clay Foster, shaking with fear for the man she loved. She knew he was skilled with a knife, had beaten Foster before, but there was no honor in his enemy. It was impossible to guess what the man would do.

Foster tossed his pistol away from him, then opened his arms. "You wouldn't kill an unarmed man, would you?"

"How many of the old men, women, and children you just killed were armed?"

"But this is war!" Foster declared.

"No." Bonner shook his head. "War is when armies fight each other. What you did here is a massacre!" He advanced on Foster with the stealth of a mountain lion.

Foster turned and ran.

His face a stony mask of hate, Bonner slowly drew his right arm back, then pitched it forward, sending his knife soaring through the air. It met its target, plunging deep into the middle of Foster's back.

Ginny gasped and covered her mouth. Foster

stopped abruptly, seeming to freeze in place. Then he
fell forward and hit the ground. In the throes of death,
his body twisted and twitched. And then he was still.

"Ginny!" Bonner grabbed her good arm and pulled
her to her feet. "You have to get out of here."

She looked behind her. "The old man. I—I can't—
I won't leave him. He's wounded."

Bonner bent down and helped the old man up, then
wedged himself under his left arm and started walking
him toward safety. Ginny followed Bonner's example
and moved under the old man's other arm. Together
they got him up the incline and to a hiding place
among an outcropping of boulders.

As soon as they set the old man down, Bonner examined his leg. He turned to Ginny. "Give me that
kerchief around your neck." She pulled it over her
head and gave it to him. He untied it and wrapped it
around the old one's leg. "This will have to do for
now." He looked up at her. "Are you all right?"

"My wrist is broken but I'll be fine."

He gave her a long look. "Stay here and don't move
until I come back."

Ginny flung herself at him. "No, Bonner. Please.
Stay with us. There's too many of them down there.
You'll be killed."

His arms circled her. "I have to go, Ginny. I have
to." He gave her a quick kiss on the mouth. "I love
you."

The sun was up and the sounds of the dead and
dying could no longer be heard. After cautioning the
old man to stay where he was, Ginny slipped out from
behind the boulders and looked down upon the
Apache camp.

The vengeful raiders were gone and the encampment was silent. Charred wickiups dotted the clearing,
black smoke curling from their smoldering mass. Vul-
tures flew overhead, wheeling in circles, diving close

to the ground, then soaring back up into the sky. Ginny knew they were eager to feast on the bodies that lay strewn across the ground.

Ginny shook with sobs. Bonner was nowhere in sight, but she couldn't accept that he was dead. "Bonner!" she cried into the eerie stillness. "Bonner!"

Something moved behind her. Gooseflesh prickled her skin. Slowly she turned her head to see what or who it was.

"Ginny."

She gasped, her heart in her throat at the sight of him, covered with blood. "Bonner. Oh, Bonner. You're—"

He dropped to his knees. "I'll be all right," he said so softly she could hardly hear him. She ran to him, fell down beside him, took him into her arms. "All I need is—you, Ginny. All I need is you."

Ginny stood in front of the open bedroom window watching the sun rise over the rocky cliffs that ringed the northern half of Firehorse Ranch. She'd been here with Bonner just two weeks, but already she'd fallen in love with this place and his family. If only she didn't feel so lost and disjointed, it would feel like home.

Like Lieutenant Whitman had told her at Camp Grant, it would take time. She'd spent a week there with Bonner, almost afraid to leave his side while he recuperated from gunshot wounds to his right upper chest and arm. Once the post surgeon had declared him fit for travel, Whitman got up an escort to take them to the ranch. Now Bonner was nearly healed, and Ginny—

"What do you see out there, Ginny?" Bonner whispered, coming up behind her.

She closed her eyes as his arms curled around her waist. She wanted to make something up—something about how beautiful the sunrise was—how it made her think of new beginnings—but instead she told him the truth. "I see women and children running, crying, screaming . . ."

She took a deep breath and she could feel Bonner against her back. She thanked God that he was here with her, but how many others who had been at the encampment were sharing this morning with their loved ones?

"You have to put it behind you, Ginny. And you have to stop blaming yourself. You did everything you could to warn the encampment. And Foster and Oury—they did everything they could to stop you."

She shook her head. "I keep thinking that I could have done something differently, that I should have moved faster or—"

Bonner jerked her around to face him. His black eyes pierced her, deep and intense. "You wouldn't have gotten through no matter what you did. Do you understand? Not even Dunn's two best soldiers could get through, Ginny. You have to accept that. You did all you could."

She nodded, tears stinging her eyes as she rested her head against his chest. He was right. She knew it. She knew he had his own feelings to work through, about his grandfather and Eskiminzin's people, and she wanted to help him. She wanted to be strong. But her guilt paralyzed her.

"I wish I was more like you," she said, her cheek pressed hard to his chest. The whiteness of his bandages were in stark contrast to his bronzed skin. She listened to his heart beating steadily beneath her ear. Three weeks ago she'd thought it might never beat again. "I don't have your power, Bonner. I don't think I ever will."

He put a finger beneath her chin and tilted back her head. She met his gaze, warm with love. "Maybe if you wrote about what happened," he suggested. "An article or a story—"

"No!" Horrified, Ginny backed away. "Oh, God, I

couldn't. I could never write about it. Never! It was too awful." The images returned. The screams. The cries. A sob broke from her lips, then another.

Bonner went up to her, wrapped his arms around her body, and pulled her close. She seemed to melt against him, as if she couldn't stand alone and that broke his heart. He would help her. Love her. They would help each other.

"You have the power, Ginny," he said to her. "You just don't know it yet. Be patient. You will."

"How?" she pleaded against him. "Bonner, how do we go on after something like this? How do we forget?"

"We don't forget. We bear the burden and go forward. We acknowledge what we've done and accept what we can't control. I'm the one who talked Eskiminzin into bringing in his band. I assured him that he and his people would be safe. It was because of me that my grandfather came in. Because he *believed* in me, *trusted* me." He felt a fresh surge of guilt for his undeniable part in this, but a sense of resolve as well. The dead were gone. He could do nothing for them. But the living—

"Your grandfather?" Ginny whispered, her voice hoarse. "Did he—Was he—?"

He ran his hand through her hair. "Remember that old man you saved? That's Gianatah. My grandfather."

Ginny looked up at him. "Your grandfather? Why didn't you tell me? Oh, Bonner, I had no idea. He never acknowledged you. He acted like he didn't even know your name!"

Bonner laughed, low and throaty. "Oh, he knows my name, but it's not the Apache way to call a person by name. My grandfather finds other ways to get my attention."

The laughter in his throat touched Ginny's spirit. She hugged him close. "You worked so hard to achieve peace," she said. "And for the first time there was real hope."

Bonner took Ginny's hand and together they walked outside. "There's still hope. Gianatah and Eskiminzin know that it wasn't the soldiers who attacked them. They've told Lieutenant Whitman that they'll stand by the peace they made." His arms tightened around her. He nuzzled his lips against her hair.

Ginny smiled. Peace. That there was still hope seemed impossible. As impossible as turning what she'd experienced into an article. But Bonner believed she could do it. Maybe she could. If she tried.

"Bonner. I love you so." She wrapped her arms around him. "I'll never forget standing there, looking down over the charred and bloody ground and thinking you were out there somewhere—that you'd never come back."

"I'll always come back to you, Ginny. Always." He lowered his mouth to hers and kissed her long and hard.

"Greeley!" Martine's shrill cry split the air and interrupted their moment.

Ginny turned her head to see his sister charge across the yard, her long black braids swinging as she ran after Greeley.

"Greeley! Bad dog! You come back here. That's my shoe. Mine, do you hear?"

"Martine! What's all the racket?" King Kincade demanded, appearing in the open doorway of the ranch house without his walking stick. Ruey squeezed past him, wiping her hands on a rag.

"Martine!"

"That—that hound Jim and Indy brought out here when they visited last week has destroyed two pairs of my shoes!" the girl wailed.

Ginny hid her laugh against Bonner's chest. She saw her dog run to King and Ruey for protection. "At least your parents like him," she said.

"That's because he hasn't gotten any of their shoes yet. But then nobody in their right mind would take one of my pa's boots. And Ma wears the only pair she has."

Greeley scampered up to the porch and practically dove into King. The big man laughed and hunkered down, ruffling the dog's fur.

"Greeley never liked my father. I think he associated the smell of whiskey with Mulligan," she said, sighing.

"Your father's got a new start, Ginny. Another chance. The job he took in Boston is perfect for him."

"Until he starts drinking again and loses it," she replied, hating the pessimism. Five years of broken promises had made her look at him that way. "I don't know. Maybe he'll surprise me. I'm going to miss him. Perhaps we can visit him in a year or two."

"If things are easing up here. I like Boston. I wouldn't mind going back."

From out of the east, a dust devil danced across the desert floor, crossing the boundaries of Firehorse Ranch. The horses stirred restlessly in the corral, their nostrils flaring, their ears pinned back against their heads in fear.

Ginny heard a roar and jumped, her body suddenly rigid. "What's that?" she asked.

"Wind," Bonner said, his mouth close to her ear. "Sssh. It's coming."

"What do you mean, it's coming?"

"Patience, Ginny. You have to learn to be patient."

"S . . . e . . . e . . . k . . . e . . . r!" Wind called in a roar of sound.

"We're here, Wind," Bonner answered, ignoring Ginny's questioning look.

Wind circled the corral, gathering itself into a tall, sleek funnel. From inside the top of the funnel, a grizzled head popped out.

Ginny gasped but she wasn't afraid. She'd seen this

vortex in her dreams. Only now, in Bonner's arms, she knew she wasn't dreaming.

"You have much yet to do, half-breed," Wind roared. "The Apache people still need you."

"I know." There was pride in Bonner's voice. Resolve.

Wind cast its gaze at Ginny. "Woman!"

She straightened like a soldier at the command in his tone.

"Your power is strong. You must use it to help the half-breed."

Ginny swallowed. "How?" she asked. "What can I do?"

"You have words," Wind said, and in that moment Ginny knew. Words. Power. She could help people see the truth. Courage flowed through her.

Wind moved about restlessly. "We will meet again, Seeker. I will come to you from out of nowhere."

Wind eddied about their feet and legs, empowering them, making them one. Ginny turned in Bonner's arms and raised her mouth to his. One in body, she thought. One in spirit. One in hope.

Afterword

I've attempted to stick as close to the time line and actual historical events as possible. Using more than fifty texts, diaries, and newspapers of the times, I found only a few discrepancies. In most cases, I used the information in the newspapers of the day rather than later published works.

I have to admit it was an effort to stay objective. I sympathized with the citizens' plight—they truly did suffer. But I sympathized with the Apache people too. The Arizona Territory was their homeland until the white man learned what riches there were to be had. In 1870 the legislature reported that "Nearly every mountain is threaded with veins of gold, silver, copper, and lead. Large deposits of coal and salt of an excellent quality are found. Nearly every foot of the Territory is covered with nutritious grasses, and stock thrives the year round without shelter or prepared forage. Nearly every product that grows in the temperate or torrid zone can be grown here to perfection and in abundance. There are vast forests of excellent timber; the mountains and valleys are amply supplied with pure water; the climate is warm, genial, and healthful, equal to any on the American continent."

The exact number of Apaches murdered during the massacre was reported by Lieutenant Whitman to be one hundred twenty-five. William Oury's accounting of the number slain was slightly different "about one hundred forty-four of the most bloodthirsty devils that ever disgraced Mother Earth." He neglected to say, however, that of those "bloodthirsty devils" only *eight* were men.

Twenty-eight children were taken alive by the Papagos and sold into slavery in Sonora, Mexico. A few were eventually returned to their parents.

Eskiminzin kept his word to Lieutenant Whitman. But no sooner had the Apaches rebuilt their village than a cavalry patrol from Fort Apache accidentally blundered upon them and opened fire. No one was hurt or killed but the incident was enough to make Eskiminzin take his people back into the mountains and begin plotting his revenge against the Americans.

The press made Lieutenant Whitman out to be a drunkard and a moral degenerate, undoubtedly to discredit him. They succeeded. On June 3, 1871, the *Arizona Citizen* had the following article: "Just by what means Royal Whitman became an enthusiastic admirer of the Indians, we must invite the reader's attention. A Soldier [see chapter 18] who was not court-martialed for his correspondence, wrote us from Camp Grant, under date of March 7, about Whitman's peace, etc. He said, 'This peace was concluded under the most auspicious circumstances. A short time since, five Indian woman came to this Post under a flag of truce. Then again, a buck and his lass came in, etc.' Reader, think of these 'auspicious circumstances'—five dusky maidens voluntarily surrendering to Lt. Royal E. Whitman, and so genial and affectionate was the treatment received by these forward women, that the next 'lass' who came in, deemed it proper to bring her 'buck' along! This ravishing subject and these 'auspicious circumstances,' unnerve us, and our pen drops powerless to do the subject justice."

Responding to the news of the massacre, President Grant called the tragedy an "outrage" and "purely murder." He notified Governor Safford that unless actions were taken to bring the murderers to justice before a civilian court, he would put the entire Territory under martial law and everyone involved in the massacre would be arrested and tried before a military court.

On December 5, 1871, the trial began at Tucson Court House. U.S. District Judge John Titus heard testimony for five days, after which the jury deliberated for nineteen minutes and came back with a verdict of not guilty for all the defendants.

I can't help but wonder what would have happened if there hadn't been a massacre. Would the year 1871 have gone down in history as being the end of the Apache wars? I'll never know. But I do know that the Apache wars lasted another fifteen years, until Geronimo and his followers were captured and herded into railroad cars like cattle and shipped off to Florida.

I welcome all letters. For replies please send an SASE to Bookends, 20354 Valley Boulevard, Tehachapi, CA 93561

For further reading on the Apache Indian Wars of the 1870s, the Camp Grant Massacre, the evolution of Tucson, and frontier newspapers, I found the following books invaluable to the writing of this novel:

Elliott Arnold. *Blood Brother.* New York: Duell Sloan and Pearce, 1947.

Keith H. Basso, editor. *Western Apache Raiding and Warfare: Notes of Grenville Goodwin.* Tucson: University of Arizona Press, 1971.

Sherilyn Cox Bennion. *Equal to the Occasion: Women Editors of the Nineteenth-Century West.* Reno: University of Nevada Press, 1990.

John Gregory Bourke. *On the Border with Crook.* (First published 1891). Glorieta, N.M.: Rio Grande, 1962.

Barbara Cloud. *The Business of Newspapers on the*

Western Frontier. Reno: University of Nevada Press, 1992.

John C. Cremony. *Life Among the Apaches.* Tucson: Arizona Silhouettes, 1951.

Grenville Goodwin. *The Social Organization of the Western Apache.* Tucson: University of Arizona Press, 1969.

William H. Lyon. *Those Old Yellow Dog Days: Frontier Journalism in Arizona 1859–1912.* Phoenix: Arizona Historical Society, 1994.

Thomas E. Mails. *The People Called Apache.* Englewood Cliffs, N.J.: Prentice-Hall, 1974.

Morris Edward Opler. *An Apache Life-Way.* Lincoln: University of Nebraska Press, 1941.

Don Schellie. *Vast Domain of Blood: The Story of the Camp Grant Massacre.* Tucson: Westernlore, 1992.

C. L. Sonnichsen. *Tucson: The Life and Times of an American City.* Norman: University of Oklahoma Press, 1982.

Dan L. Thrapp. *The Conquest of Apacheria.* Norman: University of Oklahoma Press, 1967.